MICHAEL WALSH-ROSE

The Island of Palm Trees

To

Lisa Kelly

Huge thanks for being a part of the tour.

I really appreciate it.

Best Wishes

M Walsh Rose

For Mum and Dad.
For Katie.
For the Walsh's and the Rose's.
For all the lads who watch the football at my house.

1

Fireworks

Approximately one hundred and thirty-six guests were staying at the Scarlett Grove hotel and Spa on Friday the nineteenth of June. But as the skies grew dark, most of the hotel was empty. Now it's important that you take note of the word 'most' because while most of the hotel was empty, there were still guests occupying three separate rooms. It's important to remember that.

Most of the guests were out on the beach. Some had been there for almost thirty minutes, eagerly awaiting what was to come. Of course, the small stretch of private beach was not usually so crowded at this time of night. In fact, quite the opposite. Under normal circumstances, the beach closes to guests when the skies grow dark (no specific explanation is ever given for this, just mutterings about a vague health and safety regulation). The circumstances tonight, however, were anything but normal. Friday the nineteenth of June was a special evening in the history of the Scarlett Grove Hotel and Spa. Or at least people thought it would be.

1

The Suite Diamante had opened its doors to the hotel's guests an hour ago, with everyone encouraged to spend their night enjoying the Scarlett Grove's Grand Ball. Several guests, including a rather unpleasant man named Richard, sniggered at this pretentious title and the lavish outfits that would not have looked out of place in the home of Jay Gatsby. But most guests thought the name was rather fitting, indeed the Suite Diamante was a magical place. Overflowing with laughter and music and alcohol and even the occasional bad decision or two. The crowning feature though, and this was rather unanimous amongst the guests, was the rear wall of the room. It was made entirely of glass, allowing guests to gaze out towards the sandy shores of Roquetas De Mar and beyond. Some guests opted to remain in the Suite Diamante and watch the display through the spectacular window. The ones who did stay were nearly all men, and while they claimed they only stayed to avoid the biting sea air, they were all much more concerned about protecting their close proximity to the Suite's open bar.

The display in mention was a firework presentation. The largest instance of exploding colours in the sky that the small coastal town had ever seen, or at least that's how it had been described in the posters scattered throughout the hotel. These posters had been printed by a very rich man. A man so rich that he didn't flinch at the thought of spending forty thousand pounds on a firework display. A man so rich that he made no effort to check whether his firework display was actually the largest in the history of Roquetas De Mar. He believed it was and that was enough for him. He didn't have much experience of people disagreeing with him. Nor did he have much experience of people scalding him should he fail to arrive on time. This applied to everything from business meetings to underground poker tournaments. For this reason, nobody paid any attention to his absence from the beach just moments before forty thousand pounds worth of colourful gun powder shot into the sky. The man didn't venture out to the beach at all. It's important to remember that.

The first firework was scheduled to shoot to the sky at nine on the dot, with the final explosion scheduled to ring out exactly fifteen minutes later. The company in charge of the display had overseen hundreds of similar events. They were actually, according to *TripAdvisor* at least, the world's leading authority in firework displays. Now, while there are a lot of things to consider when founding a firework company, nothing is more important than your ability to eradicate mistakes. And, given that they were the world's leading authority in firework displays, the company responsible for tonight's festivities simply did not make mistakes.

And yet, on the private stretch of beach just outside the Scarlett Grove Hotel and Spa, the world's leading authority in firework displays appeared to do just that. Sixty seconds before the spectacle began, a sudden bang echoed across the beach. There were murmurs of disappointment and even a startled scream from one of the more tightly wound guests, but soon enough everyone came to the consensus that a dud firework had exploded slightly too early. No harm, no foul.

The guests forgot about the entire incident in mere seconds. The employees of the firework company didn't forget quite so quickly though, in fact, they spent an awful lot of time trying to work out what had caused the noise. It certainly wasn't one of their fireworks.

Only two people knew what had really happened. The married couple in room fifty-seven. Thirty minutes would pass before anyone stumbled upon the horrid truth that lay within the walls of their room. And though two guests had checked into room fifty-seven almost two weeks ago, only one would check out.

Now although it was a man, a very rich man, who organised the firework display, the same cannot be said for the rest of the Grand Ball. That responsibility landed on the shoulders of Gabriella Glover, the manager of the Scarlett Grove. To say that Gabriella had been reluctant to plan the event would be an understatement. Gabriella's reluctance did not come solely from the fact that she'd been promised she wouldn't have to organise a single thing, but mainly because Gabriella didn't feel much like celebrating. You see, Gabriella has just endured the most stressful week of her life, a week she was dragged through by a wolf with sharp claws and a wicked grin. And to top it all off, Gabriella Glover despises the man responsible for organising the ridiculous firework display that would soon illuminate the beach outside of her hotel.

While these two people were directly responsible for organising this night of fun and festivities, neither of them were present on the beach when the fireworks began. None of the guests noticed their absence. They were far too preoccupied with the loud bangs and luminous, dazzling flashes of light to take stock of the people standing beside them. And with the noise of the fireworks, not a single guest heard the bloodcurdling scream that echoed through the corridors of the hotel. A scream that originated in the manager's office.

Now what's most surprising about the events that unfolded in both room fifty-seven and the manager's office of the Scarlett Grove Hotel and Spa, is that neither feature the protagonist of our story. You see, as the fireworks began, the protagonist of our story was bleeding onto the alcohol-soaked floor of The Clover, a miserable excuse for an Irish bar situated directly opposite the Scarlett Grove.

Despite staggering out into the brisk night air, there was nothing he could do to force his burning muscles to continue. His eyelids were steel blocks and he was destined to resign to the sweet relief of nothingness, with no guarantee he'd ever return to the world of the living. But then he saw something. He saw the only thing capable of giving him the strength he needed to carry on. And carry on he did. With warm blood gushing down his face and a pounding in his temple that refused to abate, our protagonist stumbled across the street and into the Scarlett Grove.

2

Books and Alcohol

Prior to the black hole that had engulfed Tom Jennings' life almost three years ago, he had been ordinary. Painfully ordinary. He'd spent his childhood surrounded by a mother who taught him to cook (though she never quite succeeded), and a father who taught him to be the next Cristiano Ronaldo (though he definitely did not succeed).

When his first day at St Vincent's Primary School arrived, Tom had precious little experience socialising with other children. Yet somehow, despite his legs that were too long and his hair that was seemingly even longer, Tom managed to make friends. These friendships were based on nothing more than a mutual love of the *Horrid Henry* books, but what else matters at that age anyway?

Tom spent his childhood with his nose buried in books and his head in the clouds. He read books that made him laugh, books that made him wish he had superpowers and even the occasional book that made him cry. But he had to wait until his final year of primary school to find a book that truly scared him. A book written by the man who would become his favourite author. Tom had been poking around in his father's office as he often did when the house was empty when he spotted a dog-eared copy of *Cell* by Stephen King. A glance at the blurb told Tom he simply had to read this book. He'd just been given his first mobile phone in preparation for his journey to and from high school each day, and the notion of that phone turning him into a blood-crazed monster excited Tom far more than it should have. He hid the book under his bed and read it whenever he got the chance. He didn't understand the larger words and there were a lot of times he stopped reading purely because he was too afraid to continue. Despite this, it took Tom just ten days to finish the book. He felt something new when he read the final line, a feeling he couldn't shake even as he returned the contraband to his father's study. He had experienced the horrifying events of the novel alongside the characters. He had run with them, hand in hand, trying to uncover what had caused such devastation. With his heart and brain racing, seemingly against one another, Tom made it his mission to read at least one new book each week. And to his credit, it was years before his life began to get in the way of this mission.

Despite Tom's love of reading, he never imagined himself capable of writing a story that people would want to read. A story that would keep them up far into the night, just so they could learn the fate of their favourite characters. But everything changed when Tom's high school English teacher, Mr Johns, encouraged him to enter a local writing competition for students in Manchester. Tom spent weeks crafting his short story, a twenty-one-page thriller entitled 'The smallest Tree in the Woods'. Three weeks later Mr Johns proudly informed Tom that his story had been selected as the Fiona Metcalfe Prize Winner. Tom never did find out who Fiona Metcalfe was and to be honest he didn't care. The only thing that mattered was the fact that, from a sample of over one thousand entries, his story had been worthy of recognition.

Tom's story was published in a novel alongside the other winning entries from across the country. The pride he felt upon receiving his copy of the novel was impossible to explain. He felt like a balloon that had been overinflated and if he burst nothing but sheer delight would explode from within him. From that day forward he had a goal. He wanted to see his name on the front of a book once again. His own book. He was going to be an author, and nothing could stop him.

Inspired by his first taste of success, Tom soon took to spending all of his spare time in front of his laptop, attempting to craft the most terrifying characters imaginable. As the years passed, new experiences slowly began to hamper the momentum of his writing. There were parties and alcohol and girls and clothes and girls and alcohol and parties and girls. He never stopped writing, but he didn't prioritise it anymore. He drank more, liking the person he became after a couple of beers or a chug from a bottle of wine. He could speak to people, people who listened to him. That was all he'd ever wanted.

With alcohol to support him, it seemed there was nothing Tom couldn't do. He spoke to girls. He kissed girls. He even slept with a couple of girls from his college. They never stuck around though. Tom wasn't much fun to be around without the assistance of alcohol and he knew it. The time between drinks grew shorter and the rage of his hangovers grew larger. Tom's parents soon noticed their son's dependence on liquid confidence enhancers, and after a frank discussion, Tom promised them that he would only drink at parties.

Two short years later and armed with a portfolio of both long and short, good and bad stories, Tom enrolled on a creative writing course at the University of Liverpool. He thrived in his first few months at university. The days were good and the nights were better. Everything was looking up until he answered a late-night phone call and his sobbing mother informed him that his father had died in a car crash.

Everything changed when Tom returned to Liverpool after his father's burial, which turned out to be four long hours spent in a room full of people eager to tell him just how sorry they were. Tom didn't write. He didn't socialise. He didn't answer his grieving mother's phone calls. He continued to drink though. For the first time in his life, he broke the promise he had made to his parents and began drinking alone in the cramped bedroom of his even more cramped student house. His mother worried relentlessly. She asked him to take a year out and move back home with her but Tom refused. Truthfully, there was nothing he wanted to do less.

After Christmas a tutor pulled him to the side and explained, in no uncertain terms, that if Tom continued down the path he was on, he would almost certainly fail the year. Despite everything he'd been through Tom still wanted to be an author, especially so he could dedicate his first novel to his father, hoping he'd see it wherever he was. And so, halfway through his first year at university, Tom made himself a promise: he would stay sober for at least four days every week. He didn't tell anybody else about his promise. It was his and his alone. It mattered more that way.

Two and a half years later Tom proudly crossed a stage to receive a First-Class Honours degree and a surprisingly firm handshake from the Dean. His mother cried as she watched. Tom wondered what his father would have done if he'd been there sitting beside her. Hopefully, he would have smiled. Hopefully, he would have been proud.

* * *

Tom decided to view returning to Bury as an opportunity. He arrived home on the fifteenth of May intending to outline an entire novel before the end of the month. He didn't know what the plot would be or where his story would be set. He didn't even know who the characters were, but he had hope. Nothing else mattered.

Tom gave up on the novel ten days later. He didn't have the space to think. His mum was always there, and pictures of his father littered the walls. Despite all the stress he never broke his promise. He visited his local pub three nights a week and drank as much or as little as he liked. When his mother asked who he was drinking with Tom would reel off the name of an old school friend, but he always drank alone. He preferred it that way.

Given that he couldn't write a book, Tom applied for an entry-level position at a local publishing house. The wage wasn't great, and the hours were long, but at least his foot would be in the door. Plus, with all his experience it seemed impossible to think he wouldn't get the job.

Tom received his rejection letter seven days later. He spent a couple of days wallowing in self-pity and binge-watching old episodes of *The Crystal Maze* before suddenly being struck by an idea. Or more accurately, he had an idea about where he might find an idea. He needed inspiration and there was only one man he could turn to.

Tom retrieved a well-thumbed copy of Stephen King's *Revival* and began flicking through the pages. He wasn't reading it (he'd done that enough times over the years) so much as he was desperately searching for something that would captivate him. He knew it was in there. Maybe he'd find it halfway through Chapter six or at the bottom of page one hundred and seventy-two. His inspiration was in there somewhere. He just had to find it.

What Tom eventually found had not been halfway through Chapter six, nor was it hidden at the bottom of page one hundred and seventy-two. Instead, it was sat on one of the very first pages of the novel. Tom Jennings found his inspiration on the 'About the Author' page, which featured a short description of Stephen King's many successes beneath a black and white picture of the man himself. It was this picture, a brooding image of the king of horror, that propelled a thought into Tom's head with all the speed of a steam train. He had overlooked the golden rule: Write what you know.

The only problem was that Tom didn't really know any-thing. He hadn't experienced a great love that he could bring to the page (pages read predominantly by acne-ridden thirteen-year-olds), nor had he experienced a road trip with friends that he could adapt into a screenplay (and hope the studio casts Andrew Garfield in the lead role). He had experienced loss, great loss, but he certainly wasn't ready to explore that yet. Besides, he doubted there'd be much of an audience for a novel about a shy kid who loses his father and then remains just as uninteresting as ever.

Tom was suddenly jealous of the authors he loved. Stephen King had struggled with addiction. Tommy Wallach had lived a life in music and J K Rowling had suffered in an abusive relationship. They were tragic, insane things to be jealous of, but they were things all the same. Maybe it isn't the specific thing that happens to you that's important, but instead just having anything happen to you. Tom needed something to happen to him. Something he wouldn't find in Bury.

Tom's decision to move to Roquetas De Mar was anything but easy. He searched for over an hour without finding anything even slightly suitable and was close to accepting the reality of the mundane town he was forever trapped in, when he stumbled across a vacancy at a hotel in a small town called Roquetas De Mar.

Tom researched both the town and the hotel. Roquetas De Mar, as it turned out, was a small coastal town once known for its fishing efficiency but now known for a small litter of elegant hotels and restaurants. Despite boasting a population of less than one hundred thousand people, Roquetas De Mar was fast becoming a popular spot for holidaymakers, with many people under the impression that in just a few years it will be held in the same esteem as Ibiza and Alicante.

While the town impressed Tom, he was blown away by the hotel. The Scarlett Grove Hotel and Spa was a luxury, five-star boutique hotel that earlier this year had been awarded the Diamond Hotel award for excellence. The announcement for which was plastered across the hotel's website in a font so bold it almost filled the entire screen, Tom guessed it was important. He also found several articles explaining that the hotel was in the process of being purchased by the Wyatt Foundation, a large conglomerate founded by a man rich enough to rival Lord Sugar himself. This seemed a shame to Tom. The hotel was authentic and genuine, and it seemed highly unlikely that the Wyatt Foundation would strive to maintain such feats. Regardless, Tom was certain that he wanted to spend his summer at the Scarlett Grove Hotel and Spa.

The role being advertised was vague and unspecific but that didn't matter. Tom would happily work in the hotel, whether that was behind the bar or making people's beds or even scrubbing toilets. He needed to meet new people and try new things, and the Scarlett Grove seemed like the perfect place to achieve such goals. Even if he had to do so from inside the men's room.

Tom's mother cried when he told her the news. He hadn't even gotten the job yet and she was crying. She told him not to worry about her, that she was just being silly, and she wanted him to do what made him happy. Tom knew she meant what she said, but he also knew how much she'd loved having him back home with her. Tom had enjoyed it too. He'd missed her during his time at university, but he missed his father more and being in this house without him somehow felt wrong. A large part of Tom wanted to stay, to try and help his mother begin the slow and agonising process of sticking the pieces back together, but he couldn't. He knew that if he didn't leave now, he never would. His father wouldn't have wanted him to stay. Or at least that's what Tom convinced himself.

After a long conversation with his mother, Tom composed an Email that, in his opinion at least, presented himself as professional, polite and committed. He sent the Email just after nine, not expecting to hear anything back from the hotel for at least a couple of days.

Gabriella Glover replied seventeen minutes later.

3

The Most Eager Man in all of Britain

The last twelve months had not been kind to Gabriella Glover. A year ago, she had been living comfortably in a four-bedroom home just outside of London; a home she had shared with her then-husband, Callum. Gabriella adored London. She adored the pubs and the tube and the red double-decker buses and even the pigeons. After spending her teenage years fantasising about life in a big city, it was surreal to finally be engulfed by one. The hustle and bustle of the crowds, somewhere to go at all hours of the day, weird and wonderful people on every street corner. Gabriella had finally decided to take the plunge on her twenty-eighth birthday, swapping cloudless skies for overcast ones and leaving everything and everyone she'd ever known behind in the process.

Gabriella's move to London came as an exploration of who she was beyond the hotel she'd spent practically every waking second of her life in. She had taken her first breath in the Scarlett Grove. She had taken her first steps in the Scarlett Grove. And at the age of sixteen, she'd taken her first role as part of the staff, cleaning the floors for a handful of euros an hour. She loved her family passionately and wouldn't change a single detail of her childhood, but there was more to the world than the delicate shores of Roquetas De Mar and Gabriella was determined to find something new.

Gabriella worked odd jobs whilst in London. Nothing too time consuming or mentally straining. She hadn't journeyed across the Atlantic Ocean just to find another job; she was looking for new experiences, exciting experiences, and any money she earned simply helped extend her stay in this ridiculously over-priced city. She met the man who would become her husband on a bus of all places. Callum was witty and intellectual and committed and wealthy, and maybe Gabriella never loved him, but she had loved the idea of him. They tied the knot exactly a year and a day after they first met and the year that followed, spent in Callum's comfortable four-bedroom home, was everything Gabriella had ever wanted.

She became a housewife. She cooked and cleaned and took pride in all the little things she had never before had the time or energy to take pride in. It took less than six months for Gabriella to realise she hated life as a housewife. Cooking was uninteresting. Cleaning bored her to tears and it seemed that anytime Callum wasn't inside of her they fought. And yes, Gabriella initiated most of the arguments but in her defence screaming at Callum was far better than the awkward silences that engulfed them anytime they tried to talk about something pleasant.

Gabriella cheated three months later. It didn't mean anything. Neither did the next two men and if she hadn't been caught with the fourth, he wouldn't have meant anything either. But Callum returned from work early to surprise her with tickets to the theatre (although Gabriella had never once expressed any interest in a trip to the theatre) and found her naked with another man's arms wrapped around her. Gabriella's fourth indiscretion suddenly went from meaning nothing to meaning that her marriage ended. It meant she had to vacate her four-bedroom home and move into a dingy flat, during which time the last of her savings quickly dwindled. She was contemplating taking out a payday loan when she got a midnight phone call informing her that her father had passed away. He'd suffered a stroke in the middle of the night and, given that her mother had passed away when Gabriella was nine, there had been nobody there to help him. Three hours later Gabriella was on a flight to Almeria headed back to the hotel she had called home for so many years.

A week later, with her father resting in the ground beside her mother, Gabriella took up the reigns as the manager of the Scarlett Grove Hotel and Spa. Only then did she realise just how much trouble the hotel was really in. Only then did she realise just how desperately she needed help.

Given everything that was happening in Gabriella's life, it's safe to say the search for somebody to run the sun lounger hut on the small stretch of private beach behind the hotel was quite literally her smallest concern. Regardless, it was a concern all the same and in the ten days since she first posted the job advertisement, she was yet to receive a single application. The role was usually snapped up rapidly, mainly because the money on offer was staggering. Maybe things were different this year due to the uncertainty regarding the takeover of the hotel. But even still, nine euros an hour, free accommodation and the chance to spend all day on a beach seemed an offer far too good to be passed up on.

Needing to think about something else, Gabriella left the solitary confinement of her office and strode across the marble floor of the hotel's reception area, greeted by the familiar tapping of her heels. She slipped behind the bar, gave a knowing nod to the bar manager Nico, and slipped away again with a bottle of white wine stored safely beneath her arm. She heard Nico tut loudly as she left and knew that he would no doubt make sure all the bar staff heard about the bottle of wine their bitch of a manager swiped, but right now, she just didn't care enough to do anything about it. She couldn't make her staff like her, just as she couldn't make them understand why she was selling the hotel to a tyrant of a businessman.

Back in the confines of her office, Gabriella returned to her desk and removed the wine glass she'd stashed in the top drawer of her desk. Did Gabriella like that she was now the type of woman who stored wine glasses in her desk drawer? Certainly not. But she needed something to distract her from the million and one things she still had left to do. With a large gulp of the quite frankly piss poor wine warming her stomach and lifting her spirits, Gabriella refreshed her inbox and was surprised to find an unread Email with the header: Job Application.

He may have been the only applicant, but Tom Jennings' Email didn't read particularly well. Either he genuinely thought the opportunity to waste his days on a beach was an incredible career opportunity or he was about as desperate as they come. Regardless, it didn't matter to Gabriella. She was going to hire the most eager man in all of Britain. She glanced over the rest of the lengthy Email in which Tom waffled on with the finite details of the summer he'd spent working in a cinema and the eighteen months he'd spent working part-time in a pizza van in the heart of Liverpool.

Gabriella wasted no time in replying to the most eager man in all of Britain. She inquired about the earliest date Tom would be able to get his eager self over to Roquetas De Mar.

Tom lived up to his new nickname. The most eager man in all of Britain replied within minutes, informing Gabriella that he could arrive in Roquetas De Mar on the first of June and that he would book his tickets that night. He signed off by stating that he could not wait to meet Gabriella and begin his work at her fine hotel.

With only the entertainment of Tom Jennings' Emails and a third glass of piss poor wine settling in her stomach, Gabriella found herself laughing for the first time in months.

4

The Airport and the Window Seat

Waking up at three in the morning is not a pleasant experience. Neither is saying goodbye to your weeping mother or spending forty minutes in the queue for airport security. Tom's final morning in Manchester did not get off to a good start, and from there things only got stranger. He'd browsed idly through three shops without inspiration before heading towards Duty-Free, where he would find a sample bottle of Shamrock's Irish Whiskey and a girl with long auburn hair, a lilac backpack and a pair of eyes that made the whole room brighter.

'Excuse me.' She said politely as she squeezed past Tom who'd been busy staring at Raybans he'd never be able to afford.

Tom turned in time to catch a glimpse of her and a glimpse was all he needed. Her cheeks were defined and her jawline bold. Her hair reminded him of autumn although he'd never be able to explain why. She wore a short-sleeve white T-shirt, blue cuffed jeans and white trainers that appeared to have been scribbled on. Tom wanted to know more about her, he didn't know why, but he needed to know more. Without logic or reason, Tom allowed his feet to take tentative uncontrolled steps, heading after the girl whose hair reminded him of autumn.

The walk allowed Tom a better look at what turned out to be drawings on the girl's shoes. Amongst a colourful firework and a large black X, he saw *Patrick Star* waving back at him. While somebody else could have drawn on her shoes, Tom felt certain these were the girl's own handiwork. He knew nothing about her and yet he felt sure all the same.

The acne-ridden young lad responsible for handing out samples of Shamrock's Irish Whiskey visibly trembled as the girl arrived in front of him. His patchy beard twitched and he made no effort to meet her gaze, instead he stared at her chest although her top wasn't at all revealing.

'Do you want to try some?' He blurted out a little too loudly. 'It's free?'

Tom stopped at a stand filled with bottles of vodka that cost more than most of the clothes in his suitcase. He watched the young lad nod as if this girl had stolen his entire vocabulary.

'Go on then.'

The young lad poured out a tiny ration of Shamrock's into a tiny plastic shot glass and handed it to the girl.

Sensing that this was his only opportunity to speak to her, and to sample a whiskey he'd never before been willing to fork out for, Tom stepped towards the girl. The young lad, whose name tag read Kevin, made every attempt to ignore Tom. Tom turned to the girl who was now swilling the whiskey around her mouth. She hadn't even noticed him. Her lack of interest stung. But at least the close proximity allowed Tom a good look at her face. A face he would never forget. Her eyes captivated him the most. They were deep and brown, somehow both soft and vicious at the same time.

'How is it?' Tom asked, desperate for her attention.

The girl turned to Tom. Her face remained neutral as she saw him for the first time. Tom wasn't surprised, all girls faces remained neutral when they saw him for the first time.

'Better than the stuff in my local.'

Kevin finally relented and acknowledged Tom. 'Would you like to try some?'

'Please.'

Kevin poured Tom a considerably smaller portion than the one he had given to the girl and handed it over without a smile. Tom drank it quickly, and despite his best efforts, he couldn't resist the wince that forced its way up from his throat.

'That was cool.' The girl's sarcasm was so sharp Tom worried she might cut him.

With no idea how to reply and the knowledge that any attempt at humour would undoubtedly result in further embarrassment, Tom turned to Kevin and completely changed the subject.

'How much is this?'

'Erm.' Kevin leaned forward to read the sign on the display, a sign that Tom could have (and probably should have) read himself. '£25.99.'

Tom was about to guess whether or not that was a fair price when his eyes were once again drawn to the girl by his side. She had unzipped her backpack and in doing so, spilt a handful of loose pieces of paper across the floor. Tom and Kevin were both on their knees retrieving pages within seconds, as if they were each in a battle to prove they were more chivalrous than the other. Tom risked a glance at one of the pages, finding a drawing similar to those inked onto her trainers. In his hands, he held a drawing of a crescent moon, partially obscured by clouds. It was haunting, an image Tom would never forget.

With all the papers gathered, Tom rose to his feet to return them to the girl who drew on her shoes. Only she wasn't there.

'What?' Kevin asked. Tom found it funny that some people were incapable of having a thought without pronouncing it to the world. Then again the girl had laughed at him, so there weren't any winners here.

Tom glanced up and spotted her autumn hair and lilac backpack heading for the exit. Without a word he snatched the papers Kevin had collected and headed after the girl, hoping that maybe he could salvage his pathetic introduction.

'Excuse me.' He said as he tapped her on the shoulder. 'You dropped these.'

The girl turned around and surprised Tom. There wasn't an expression of relief on her face. There wasn't surprise or anger or sadness. There was nothing. As she collected her scattered drawings her face was completely blank. Tom wondered if he'd done something wrong. If maybe he'd violated her privacy by looking at her drawings. He was about to apologise when the girl unzipped her backpack to return the paper and Tom realised he wasn't the guilty party. She was.

She made no effort to conceal the sampler bottle of Shamrock's now resting snugly amongst the paper. Instead, she looked up at Tom with a face that was no longer blank, smiled, winked and disappeared into the hustle and bustle of the crowded terminal.

Tom thought of nothing but the autumn haired thief as he killed time in the terminal. He thought of her smile, he thought of her wink, of her eyes that refused to be ignored. It was only as he boarded the plane and found his seat that he managed to think of anything else. Now he could only think of his disappointment that he was to spend the next few hours sitting beside the plane window. He wasn't scared of flying exactly, he just didn't like to be constantly reminded that he was seated in a metal tube soaring thousands of miles above the earth. Thankfully, Tom was a writer (or at least he wanted to be), and therefore inventing a plausible reason to swap seats with whoever should be sitting next to him shouldn't be too difficult. He was so lost in his own head, searching for the answer to his problem, that he failed to notice a familiar face as she boarded the plane and made her way towards him.

'Hello.'

Tom looked up to find a pair of eyes that refused to be ignored.

He didn't know if it was the beginning of a nightmare or one of his dreams had come true. The odds of her being here, in the seat beside him were astronomical. He wondered if she recognised him. The only witness to her crime. Should he mention it? Should he pretend not to recognise her? His heart was pounding against his ribs and beads of sweat rolled down his spine. Almost twenty seconds passed before Tom, out of sheer desperation, decided to ask a glaringly obvious question.

'Are you sitting here?'

'Well, I'm supposed to be, but I wanted to ask if you'd mind switching seats with me? I don't see the point in being so high up if I can't see the view.'

'Definitely. I was going to ask to swap anyway.'

'You're not afraid of flying, are you?' She asked with a hint of a smile.

Tom waited until he had finished awkwardly shuffling past her in the tiny space between seats before answering her question.

'No, I just like to get up and stretch my legs every now and then.'

The girl said nothing. Tom had a feeling she didn't believe his answer. He made himself comfortable in his new seat, expecting the conversation to be finished, only to be surprised almost immediately.

'I was worried I was gonna have to bribe you.'

'With what?'

Without replying, the girl opened her backpack and proudly displayed the bottle Tom knew to be stolen. His stomach dropped as if the plane had hit turbulence.

Tom smiled awkwardly before blurting his name out rather loudly. 'I'm Tom, by the way.'

'Nice to meet you, I'm Joy.'

It's funny, how deceptive a name can be.

The conversation between the passengers in 8A and 8B fizzled out rather quickly after that. Joy buried her head in her phone and left Tom with only the in-flight magazine. He'd barely made it past the contents page when a stewardess with all the warmth of a British winter arrived at his side.

25

'Excuse me, Sir.' She began with a smile so fake Tom wondered if she was capable of genuine warmth. 'I'm going to have to ask you to slide your bag further under the seat in front of you. Otherwise, you'll have to place it into the overhead lockers.'

Tom looked down at the bag that was almost completely hidden under the seat in front of him and then back to the stewardess.

'Yeah, OK.' He nudged the bag with his foot. It moved forward an inch at most.

'Thank you very much.'

The stewardess transferred her attention to Joy, who was listening to music with her eyes closed. 'Excuse me, Miss.'

Joy didn't move. The stewardess abandoned attempting to communicate verbally and instead stretched across Tom to tap Joy on the shoulder, prompting her to finally remove her earphones.

'I'm going to have to ask you to switch your device to Airplane mode. You should have seen these instructions in your safety card.'

Joy held up her hands in apology and flicked her phone to Airplane mode. The stewardess nodded in satisfaction before moving down the aisle to scold somebody else.

'She was nice.'

'Really nice.' Tom replied, wishing he'd thought of something funnier.

'I don't get it though. Look at the size of this plane. Flying is statistically the safest way to travel and what? If I don't have my phone on Airplane mode, the plane will explode?'

Tom hoped Joy hadn't noticed him squirm at the mention of the plane exploding. He found himself gripping the armrest tighter than before and he tapped his feet nervously.

'It's like the brace position.' Joy continued.

Tom didn't know what Joy meant by this, nor did he want to know, but he couldn't help himself. 'The brace position?'

The plane began to move. Through the window, Tom saw the terminal building grow smaller.

'Yeah, you know. Heads between your knees, hands on either side of your head and elbows out in front of you.'

Unsure of what to say, Tom just nodded.

Joy shifted closer to Tom, ensuring he couldn't miss a word. 'So, they make out like the brace position is here to increase our chances of survival and all that. But it's not. It's the opposite. It's so if the plane does hit anything, we'll all break our necks. That's how the airline companies want it. No survivors to pay and nobody to point the finger at them.'

Tom felt the colour leave his face.

'Anyway, I suppose there's only one way to test my theory.'

With that, Joy flicked her phone out of Airplane mode and smiled at Tom once more. Tom didn't return her smile. He simply couldn't.

Much to Tom's relief, the plane reached its cruising altitude without a hint of turbulence. Once the seatbelt sign had been switched off, Tom rummaged in his backpack looking for the copy of Tommy Wallach's *We All Looked Up* that he'd stashed away.

'Excuse me, Sir.' A familiar voice interrupted. 'Anything to eat or drink?'

'Sorry, I haven't had a chance to look yet.' Tom explained as he began rifling through the in-flight magazine. He heard the stewardess sigh and was about to give up and order nothing when he was interrupted by the girl in the seat that should have been his.

'We'll have four cans of coke, please. Full Fat. I don't see the point in diet.'

'Four?' The stewardess asked, her thin-lipped smile replaced by a grimace.

'Yes please.'

Tom had no idea what was going on. He felt as though at least one of those drinks had to be for him, although he didn't know why.

The stewardess scowled as she poured the drinks. 'I don't suppose you want anything else?'

'I think that's everything, thank you.'

The stewardess handed the four cans to Tom whilst Joy plucked a ten-pound note from her purse and handed it to the stewardess, before uttering three simple words that ruined her day completely.

'Keep the change.'

The stewardess didn't thank Joy. In fact, she didn't say another word.

'There you go.' Tom said as he moved the drinks from his tray table to Joy's.

'What do you mean? Those two are yours.' Joy said, returning the cans to Tom.

'Oh, thank you. How much do I owe you?'

'Nothing. If it wasn't for you, I'd be drinking on my own and there's no fun in that.'

Before Tom could reply, Joy took a large sip from one of her cans before removing the stolen bottle of Shamrock's from her backpack and discreetly topping up the can.

'Hurry up then.' Joy urged.

Tom had no idea why, but he suddenly found himself taking large sips from each of his cans so she could make him complicit in her crime.

'Are you sure about this?' He asked as he returned the cans of whiskey and coke to his tray table.

Joy let out a sigh of mock frustration. 'Jesus, yes. But if you don't have a sip in the next ten seconds, I will change my mind.'

Tom, accepting that the damage was already done, did as she asked without hesitation. The burn of the whiskey surprised him once again, and for the second time that day, he found embarrassed himself in front of Joy.

Joy laughed. 'Twice. Wow'

Tom couldn't think of a suitably witty reply, and so he instead manoeuvred the conversation back towards Joy.

'So, are you going on holiday then?' Tom cringed internally as the question escaped him. 'That's a daft question, isn't it?'

Joy laughed, but much to Tom's relief it was without malice. 'It's not that daft. I erm… I don't know really.'

Now it was Tom's turn to laugh. 'You don't know if you're going on holiday or not?'

'Well, I'm going to Spain. I suppose it just depends on what you mean by holiday?'

'I suppose it's going somewhere with a pool and the sea and I dunno, a place to get a tan.'

'So, Prague in January isn't a holiday then?'

'Yeah, you've got me there. I suppose I just always thought of a holiday as a week in summer with my Mum and Dad, you know, going to Crete or Lanzarote or somewhere like that.'

'Pretending to enjoy overcooked chicken from the all-inclusive buffet?'

'That's the one.' Tom laughed, momentarily unconcerned about the girl sitting beside him or the crime he knew she had committed. 'So, if it's not a holiday, what are your plans for Spain?' He asked, desperate to keep the conversation going.

'You're pretty nosy, aren't you?' Joy asked.

'Shit. You're right, I'm sorry. Just ignore me.' Tom's cheeks flushed red.

'I didn't say it was a bad thing. If anything, it helps to keep the conversation interesting.' Joy drank half of her first can in one long gulp. 'I just needed a bit of a break, you know. An escape from the mundane. And anywhere with a bit of sun seemed like a preferable place to escape too.'

'I get that.'

Tom waited for Joy to return the favour, to ask him why he was headed to Spain just as he'd asked her, but she never did. Tom took another sip to fill the silence. He managed to avoid wincing this time but he still couldn't enjoy the drink. Not knowing where it had come from. Not knowing that every rule he had been taught as a child had been broken by the girl sitting beside the window. A girl Tom was content to make pleasant conversation with.

'You might as well just ask me.' Joy said. Something in her tone had changed. She sounded almost impatient.

'Ask you what?'

'Honestly, just ask.'

Tom said nothing. His heart rate increased.

'You could ask me why I took it? You could ask how I knew I'd get away with it? You could ask if it's the first time I've done something like this?'

30

For what seemed like an eternity, Tom said nothing. Finally, he settled on a lie that he knew neither he nor Joy would believe.

'I honestly don't know what you're talking about.'

'So, it wasn't you who brought my paper back to me?' Joy's eyes burned with accusation.

Again, Tom said nothing. He could almost feel any respect that Joy had for him dissipate.

'Jesus. OK.' She said, in total disbelief.

'Well it doesn't matter, does it? It's none of my business anyway.'

'You're right. It isn't any of your business, but you won't stop staring at your cans like a guilty kid.'

'I'm not trying to. I don't know why I am.' Tom insisted, his tone now more than a little defensive.

'Probably because you feel guilty that you didn't do anything to stop me.' Joy finished her first can. 'Speaking of which, why didn't you?'

'Why didn't I what?' Tom took another sip too, hoping the alcohol would help him navigate his way out of the corner he'd been backed into.

'Why didn't you try and stop me? Or tell somebody what happened?'

'I don't know.'

'Of course, you do. You made the decision not to do anything. You must know why.'

Tom was growing angry. He wasn't the thief. What right did she have to put him on trial?

'Believe it or not, when I woke up this morning, I wasn't exactly hoping I'd get to report a petty crime to the security team at Manchester airport.'

'There's a lot of petty crime at Manchester airport.'

'Yeah, like what?'

'I think a lot of people would agree that whacking an extra thirty percent on the price of everything just because you're in an airport counts as petty theft. And airlines dropping down their baggage allowance so they can charge you an extra twenty quid when your bags a centimetre too wide, I'd say that is too.'

'So, because they overcharge you it makes it fine for you to steal from them?' Tom asked, his disbelief shining through.

'Yeah.' Joy answered with absolute certainty.

'That's not how things work!'

Tom was beyond frustrated now; he was angry. Angry that he was being lectured by a thief and angrier still that, although he wouldn't admit it, he found himself agreeing with her.

'Why not?' Joy asked.

Tom didn't answer. Joy waited a short while, before eventually losing all interest in the conversation and retreating to her earphones. But not before leaving Tom with three words that caused a knot in his stomach and formed a cloud of shame above his head.

'Enjoy your drinks.'

As the wheels bumped down onto the landing strip in Almeria, Tom felt nothing but relief. Partly because the journey had been smooth and without the interruption of turbulence, but mainly because he could finally escape the unbearably awkward silence echoing between seats 8A and 8B.

In one final act of chivalry, Tom stepped aside and allowed Joy to disembark first, a decision which meant Tom got stuck behind an elderly lady with a limp and ended up being one of the final passengers to disembark the plane. By the time he arrived at baggage claim, Tom was sweaty, frustrated and admittedly a little bit tipsy. From there, his day only got worse.

Tom knew the open suitcase was his almost immediately. His belongings were scattered across the carousel for all to see. He gathered his exposed belongings as quickly as possible, trying his best to ignore the accompanying giggles from the passengers who found amusement in his situation. With everything back in the suitcase, Tom used one of his socks to tie the handles of the case together and went off in search of assistance.

To credit the security staff, they genuinely did try to help. The problem was they couldn't quite understand exactly what Tom was asking from them. They told him it would take at least twelve hours to access the CCTV footage, but Tom doubted he'd even hear from them again. He thanked them for their help and left his mobile number and email address should they find anything, although he knew they wouldn't.

With nothing achieved, Tom took his overflowing suitcase in both arms and flagged down a taxi. As the car began to move and the turquoise sea came into view, Tom began to feel hopeful. At least from here, things could only get better.

5

The Scarlett Grove Hotel and Spa

Gabriella Glover had never been a patient woman. She hated being kept waiting almost as much as she'd hated the look on Callum's face when he'd found her naked beneath another man. Despite her best efforts, somehow that image pries its way into her dreams most nights. Dreams that soon become nightmares.

Despite her lack of patience, over the last six weeks, Gabriella has found herself waiting for Roger Wyatt almost every time they meet. Each time more infuriating than the last. When it comes to Roger, she has no choice but to bite her tongue and smile. But when it comes to the most eager man in all of Britain, she has no intention of being so understanding. He was forty-five minutes late now, and with each minute that passed, Gabriella grew increasingly frustrated.

Still, a chance to escape the rigorous and unrelenting demands of the hotel wasn't all bad. And though she certainly wouldn't admit it to Tom, she felt grateful for the chance to take the weight off her feet, even if it was just for a short while. Her grandfather, a man wiser than anybody Gabriella had met, had taught her the importance of reserving a small portion of the day for herself. He said that to really appreciate something, be that a room or a place or a person, you needed to find three things: breath, life and light. He explained that the breath was found within yourself. He said a good, deep breath could help a whole host of things, but most importantly it slowed time, allowing you to take stock of what really matters. The life, he explained, is found all around us, in the people we see, the stories we read, even the memories we hold dear. No matter where we are, we are always surrounded by life. And finally, there was the light. The light could be anything from a glistening sunrise to a beaming smile and everything in between. Recently, Gabriella had struggled to find the light. She wasn't sure if this was a result of her busy schedule or just because her world had seemed pretty dark recently, but now, in the reception area of the Scarlett Grove Hotel and Spa, Gabriella found her light in the leather chair she sat in. She had the time to breathe deeply and slowly, and right now, that was everything she needed.

Gabriella was enjoying the light for the first time in weeks, when she was interrupted by a voice she would soon become familiar with.

'Excuse me, are you Gabriella?'

After a long journey in a dilapidated taxi driven by a man who refused to adhere to the speed limit or switch on the air conditioning, Tom couldn't describe his relief to finally arrive at the Scarlett Grove Hotel and Spa. The building itself was spectacular, standing an impressive five stories high with walls made entirely of white limestone. The door frames were sunken and the windows large, allowing the building to absorb as much of the Spanish sun as possible. There was one aspect of the building however, that seemed strange to Tom. The centre of the roof was topped by a spire that had to be at least six or seven feet tall. Tom didn't know a whole lot about Spanish architecture, but he hadn't seen many other spires on the buildings he'd just driven past. Not that he had the time to question it. He was late and he had no intention of making his first impression any worse than it already was.

Gabriella opened her eyes to find a young man with a thin frame, dirty blonde hair and a sweaty brow. Either he'd walked here from the airport or he'd taken to the heat like a dog to chocolate. While Gabriella knew that the most eager man in all of Britain didn't yet speak a word of Spanish, she hadn't been aware that he was also unable to speak to members of the opposite sex. His eyes were so fixated on the floor that Gabriella began to wonder if he was even speaking to her.

She'd been more than ready to give Tom the lecture she'd prepared whilst waiting, and Jesus it was a good one, but something inside her suddenly changed. Maybe her short-lived sit down had changed her perspective on things, because Gabriella had no urge to make things worse for the young man still staring at the ground.

'I am. How can I help you?' She asked, although she already knew the answer.

'My name's Tom Jennings. I was supposed to be here about an hour ago but there was a problem with my suitcase at the airport.' Tom's voice trembled.

Gabriella looked down and saw that Tom's suitcase had

been shoddily tied together with a sock.

'Come on. You can tell me about it in my office.' She gestured towards a corridor at the far end of the reception area.

Finally, Tom looked up.

Although Tom had never before stepped foot inside the manager of a five-star hotel's office, he had a clear idea of what he expected to find. A desk made of dark wood, a window looking out towards the beach and walls filled with framed awards and pictures of family and friends. As it turned out Tom was half right. Gabriella's desk was indeed made of wood, but it was light in colour. The office boasted a window that looked out towards the staff car park as opposed to the beach. And while there were an array of awards displayed proudly on the far wall, there was not a single picture of a loved one.

Gabriella perched herself down behind her desk and gestured for Tom to sit on the leather chair opposite. As Tom sat down his eyes were drawn to an award displayed boldly in the centre of Gabriella's desk. The plaque read 'Diamond Hotel Award for Excellence - 2021'. The award had been designed to replicate the Scarlett Grove in its entirety, from the floral garden beside the east wall to the unusual spire at the very top of the building. The award was made entirely of glass. Tom quite liked it.

'Is that the award the hotel won recently?' Tom asked, gesturing to the replica.

'Look, I don't mean to be rude, but I don't have time for pleasantries. What happened today?' Gabriella's tone was stern.

'I don't know to be honest.' Tom hoped his nerves didn't make it sound like he was lying. 'I was one of the last people off the plane and when I got to baggage reclaim my case was open and all my clothes had, kind of, scattered across the carousel.'

Gabriella took a pack of cigarettes from her pocket, removed one and balanced it between her teeth. As she lit the cigarette, she offered the pack to Tom who politely declined with a shake of his head.

'I don't want you to get the wrong impression or anything, I know you're telling the truth.' Gabriella said through a cloud of smoke.

Tom breathed an audible sigh of relief.

'And I don't want this to sound rude.' She continued, 'Although it probably will and I'm sorry, but I have to be blunt. I don't have the time to worry about you or your role here because neither matter to me.'

'Oh.' Tom felt his heart sink, suddenly realising that this opportunity, the opportunity he believed would be the making of him, was looked down upon as if he were cleaning toilets or shovelling shit.

'I'm not saying it isn't a job that needs doing well. It does. And I'm not saying that the experience won't be rewarding for you, because I hope it will be. It's just there's a lot going on right now and there's only so many hours in the day, you know?'

Tom nodded, though he was hardly listening anymore.

'Have you heard that we're in the process of being acquired by the Wyatt Foundation?'

'I saw something about it when I was looking into the hotel.'

'Good. Well, we're coming to the back end of all that now.

Everything's set in stone but there are an awful lot of T's that need to be crossed and I's that need to be dotted and it falls to me to do pretty much all of that.'

'OK.'

'And because of that, I can't afford to worry about any of the more trivial aspects of the hotel over the coming weeks. Unfortunately, the beach hut falls into that category.' Gabriella exhaled more smoke. She waited for a reply, but Tom only stared at her blankly. 'This is just my way of explaining why I won't be able to spend any more time waiting for you or worrying about you like I did today.'

Tom's heart dropped. He sensed the direction in which this conversation was headed and despised the destination at which they would arrive.

'Wait, are you sacking me?'

Gabriella laughed, just as she had whilst reading his emails. 'No. No, I'm not sacking you.' She stubbed out her cigarette. It was her first in over a week, which by her standards was quite the success. 'You're still starting tomorrow, bright and early. I just wanted to make it clear that something like this can't happen again.'

Tom felt a strange mix of both anger and relief swell within him. More than anything he was relieved that he still had a job and a place to live for the next few weeks, but he still felt hard done by finding himself on his last chance before he'd even spent an hour at the hotel.

'It won't happen again.' Tom said, though he wanted to say a lot more.

'Good, well before I show you to your room, I need to take a quick picture of you if you don't mind.' Gabriella fished out a flashy camera from the top drawer of her desk.

Tom stared at Gabriella apprehensively.

'It's for the website. We put up pictures of every member of staff.'

'Oh OK.' Tom replied, wondering how terribly his sweaty brow and ruffled hair would look when captured on film.

'We'll do it in the corridor if that's OK. It's better to have a plain background. Oh, and to answer your question, yes. That is the award we won recently. It's the first time we've ever won it actually.'

'That's good.'

'My Dad was always desperate to win it.'

'He must be chuffed.'

'I dunno. He's probably just gutted he didn't live to see it. Anyway, follow me.'

While the rest of the Scarlett Grove was undoubtedly a five-star establishment, the same could not be said for the room designated for Tom. As they walked, Gabriella explained that the rooms on this block, a corridor stretching down the far east side of the hotel, were reserved for staff. It was easy to see why. Guests certainly wouldn't be willing to spend their hard-earned cash on a place like this.

The room was furnished at least. There was a double bed, a shower, a kitchenette, a couch, a TV and even Wi-Fi access, although it only seemed to work in certain places. But it wasn't a room that anybody would want to call home. The bedsheets were old and worn. The shower was erratic, spitting out cold water for five minutes before unleashing a surprise burst of scalding water. The kitchenette needed a good scrubbing down, so too did the couch. If Tom had arrived at the hotel on time, he might have asked for some fresh bed sheets and cleaning supplies, but he hadn't, so he sucked it up and thanked Gabriella for the wonderful room.

After a tour of the room that lasted all of thirty seconds, Gabriella provided Tom with a brief insight into the history of the hotel. She explained that the building process had begun in the summer of 1978 after her grandfather earned a staggering amount of money thanks to a workplace injury settlement. Gabriella avoided any details of the injury, but it must have been pretty severe if the pay-out was enough to construct an establishment as fine as this one. The Scarlett Grove Hotel and Spa, although the Spa aspect was limited to massages and facials Gabriella explained, finally opened its doors in the summer of 1979.

The locals had taken to the hotel quickly, mainly due to the Spanish architecture and her grandfather's promise that at least seventy percent of the staff would be Spanish locals, thus ensuring the hotel never lost its authenticity. Ironically, this was also the reason many locals had taken issue with the Wyatt Foundation's acquisition of the Scarlett Grove, knowing that with the Wyatt's in charge the hotel would lose its identity and become just like the sourly disliked Hilton Hotel that had opened two years ago. The Hilton was just a short walk up the beach and despite the outrage, it had stolen much of the Scarlett Grove's business.

With her history lesson complete and another reminder that Tom was to meet her at quarter to nine tomorrow morning, Gabriella handed Tom his keys and disappeared down the corridor, her heels clapping as she left.

Tom watched Gabriella disappear around the corner, waited for five seconds, and then set off in the same direction. Adventure awaited, and it certainly wouldn't be found in his disappointment of a hotel room.

6

The Lobby Bar

During their long, blunt conversation, Gabriella had made it explicitly clear to Tom that whilst his accommodation was free, food and drinks at the hotel were not. With his recent warning still fresh in his mind, Tom had entered the Dining Hall intending to pay for his meal, but the polite waitress at the entrance of the restaurant hadn't asked if he was a guest. In fact, she hadn't asked him anything at all, nor had she checked to see if Tom was wearing one of the yellow wristbands given out to guests lucky enough to enjoy the all-inclusive package. Instead, she led Tom to a table, explained the buffet system, and left with a smile.

With a heaped plate of food and a tall glass of red wine warming his stomach Tom no longer felt guilty about eating for free. In fact, he decided to stretch the night out a little further and headed to the Lobby Bar. Another drink couldn't hurt. Could it?

The Lobby Bar, which Tom thought to be a strangely American name for a hotel opened by two Brits, would not have looked out of place in central London or upstate New York. The bar was made of black marble, contrasting the white marble floor, which was so clear it could be used as a mirror. The wall behind the bar and the two almost aggressively friendly bar staff (an elderly, blonde woman named Ava and a plump man with thinning hair named Nico) was filled with large bottles of every spirit, liquor and gin ever distilled. There was even a Banana flavoured liquor called Juanita which, unsurprisingly, remained unopened. The booths, tables and chairs all faced out towards a huge window, offering immense views of the colossal swimming pool and the gentle sea beyond it. Tom had been enjoying the view for over an hour when he happened upon a pair of eyes that he'd last seen disembarking from seat 8A.

Joy sat down beside Tom without a word.

'Hi.' Tom said, attempting to sound nonchalant.

'I didn't expect to see you again.' Joy replied, sipping from what Tom assumed to be a Shamrock's Irish Whiskey and coke.

'Neither did I.' Maybe it was the alcohol or maybe it was those eyes that managed to make the whole world fade, but Tom decided to seize the moment. 'I'm happy about it though. I feel like I probably owe you a drink.'

'Oh, you do. But given the circumstances, it probably makes more sense for me to get this round.'

'What do you mean?'

Joy held up her right wrist, presenting a yellow wristband adorned with the Scarlett Grove Hotel and Spa logo.

'I can't argue with that, can I?'

'You'd be weird if you did.' Joy teased.

44

Tom relaxed. It felt good to finally have someone to share this magnificent view with.

'So, what are we drinking?' He asked.

Joy made a buzzer sound, similar to the noise played when a contestant answers a question incorrectly on a game show.

'That's wrong I'm afraid. The correct question is what are we drinking first?'

'So, here's my thinking. And don't worry, it's logical thinking.' Joy began as she returned to the table holding two drinks, neither of which appeared to be the vodka and lemonade Tom had politely requested. 'There are hundreds of different types of alcohol behind the bar there.'

'OK.'

'I don't mean different brands of the same alcohol though, because let's be honest if you've tasted one gin you've tasted them all.'

'Yeah. I get that.' Tom replied, trying to hide his apprehension. 'What do you mean then?'

'Different types of alcohol. Anything other than wine and vodka and gin.'

'So, basically the drinks nobody ever orders?'

'Well yeah, I suppose so.' Joy pushed one of the glasses towards Tom. 'But what if nobody ever orders them because, like us, they've never tried them. Your favourite drink could be sitting behind that bar, and you'll never try it because you've gotten used to drinking the stuff that was handed out at house parties.'

'Do I want to know what I'm about to drink?'

'Port.' Joy replied proudly.

'Like pirates drank?' Tom asked before immediately filling

with regret as he realised pirates drank rum.

'That's a weird question.' She teased. 'I think they drank rum. But weird questions aside, I'm assuming you've never tasted port before?'

'I haven't.' Tom replied quickly, keen to avoid further embarrassment.

'Good. So, we're going to drink these, and then we're going to order something else that we've never tried before.'

'When do we stop? When we've tried every type of alcohol?'

'Exactly.' Joy said with a grin.

Whilst the port was hard to stomach (it was easy to understand why even pirates avoided the stuff), the conversation was not. The awkwardness of the plane was never mentioned. Instead, Joy listened intently to everything Tom had to say. She seemed genuinely interested in stories that Tom knew to be rather uninteresting. She found the story of Tom's unwanted staff picture awfully funny, claiming she couldn't wait to see it once it was uploaded.

With their glasses empty and spirits high, Joy returned to the bar to fetch glasses of Campari, which tasted like a chocolate orange had been thrown into a blender along with the entire contents of a pensioner's spice rack. While the foul drink was poor to taste, it did at least provide Tom with some much-needed Dutch courage, allowing him to finally raise the subject he'd been avoiding since Joy arrived.

'I'm sorry about what I said on the plane, by the way.' Tom avoided Joy's gaze as he spoke.

'Don't be.' Joy dismissed the subject as suddenly as Tom had brought it up. 'I tell you what, the Campari gets better as you finish it.' She set the empty glass down proudly.

'So, does everything.' Tom joked, but he wasn't quite finished with his apology yet. 'But seriously, looking back I think I actually agree with what you said.'

'You don't have to say that.'

'What do you mean?'

'If you agreed with me you would have said so on the plane. You don't have to pretend that you do now. We can disagree and still talk.' Joy spoke calmly. She was clearly accustomed to people disagreeing with her.

'No, I know. But now that I've thought about it…'

'Honestly, you don't have to.' Joy interrupted.

An awkward silence engulfed the pair of them. Tom took another sip from his Campari and winced once again. He expected Joy to laugh, maybe even make another joke at his expense, but her attention lay elsewhere.

'Is everything OK? Tom asked, worried he'd ruined everything by reminding her of the plane.

'Yeah, it's just…' Tom followed Joy's eyes to the far end of the bar, where two middle-aged parents were sitting opposite their young children. Both parents were lost in the digital worlds of their phones and both children were lost in the Mushroom Kingdom. Tom had to admit that seeing a family together and yet so separated was tough.

'Twenty years ago, that family would have been talking about the day they've had or playing cards. At the very least they'd actually acknowledge each other. But right now, one of those kids could wander off and neither parent would notice.'

'It's sad.' Tom replied sombrely.

'It's just how things are now.' Joy took one final sorry look at the disengaged family and returned her attention to Tom.

'I reckon it's your turn to pick the drink. Don't let me down.'

With that, Joy produced another yellow wristband from her pocket and offered it out to Tom.

'Are you sure?' Tom asked gingerly.

'There isn't much point in me wearing two of them.'

Tom took the wristband from Joy. 'How come you've got two of them?'

'I don't like to drink alone.' Joy smirked.

'Won't be a minute.' Tom said and headed for the bar. He settled on two glasses of Creme De Violette, a liquor that Nico insisted tasted just like violets, and turned back around to find that Joy had disappeared. The table was empty.

Joy hadn't noticed Connor as he entered the hotel. She was too engrossed in her conversation with Tom, but eventually, she'd seen him lingering at the far side of the bar, staring at her seemingly without blinking. He hadn't changed, but then again men like Connor never do. His hair was short and sprayed into place, his arms were muscular and tattooed and even from across the room, she could see the cuts on his knuckles.

Once Tom's back was turned, she made her way across the bar, towards a man she hadn't seen in almost three years.

'What the fuck are you doing here?' Joy asked and Connor's smile faded.

'Business.'

Joy scoffed.

'It's true. I'd picked up what I needed and was about to leave when I saw a girl who looked an awful lot like you. I almost ignored it and left because it couldn't be you, you wouldn't come back here, especially without telling us. But then I decided to check, just to put my mind at ease. So, I turn around and come in here and low and behold, it is you. You're back. And I suppose I'd just like to know why the fuck that is?' He almost purred his words. When Connor asked a question, people answered him.

'I want to know why you think that's any of your business?'

'He's going to want to see you.'

'Don't tell him. Don't tell him I'm back Connor. Not yet.' Joy's demeanour changed. Her shoulders slumped and her lip trembled. She was no longer in control.

Connor ignored Joy's plea. 'Your friend's looking for you.' He pointed towards Tom, who was now glancing around the bar whilst still holding two glasses of Creme De Violette.

'Fuck.' Joy regained some of the composure Connor had knocked from her. 'Give me two minutes.'

'Who is he?' Connor asked, his eyes never leaving Tom.

'Wait here.'

Tom knew immediately that something had changed within Joy. The light in her eyes had fizzled out.

'Is everything OK?' He asked tentatively.

'Yeah, I um, I've gotta go.'

Joy was flustered. Tom didn't know what had caused such a strange reaction. He hoped it wasn't him.

'Oh, OK.'

'Do you like tapas?' She asked rather suddenly.

It took Tom a second to manage a reply. 'Tapas. The food?'

'I don't know what else tapas could possibly mean.' For a fleeting moment, the spark returned to Joy's eyes.

'I like tapas.'

'There's a nice place a couple of minutes from here. Platos

Y Bebidos. Do you want to meet me there tomorrow? At eight maybe?'

Tom couldn't quite believe it. In fact, he was so shocked that it took him an uncomfortably long time to formulate a rather simple reply. 'Yeah. That sounds great.'

'You'll be able to find it, won't you?'

Tom nodded, worried that if he opened his mouth he would somehow ruin everything.

'I'll see you tomorrow then.'

Joy left with a smile. Tom didn't think anything could break his mood until he saw Joy leave the hotel with a handsome, muscular man covered in tattoos. He quickly drank both glasses of Creme De Violette, thinking maybe the alcohol would help him decipher what had just happened. But with both glasses empty, Tom was still none the wiser.

7

First Day On The Job

That night Tom discovered, rather unsurprisingly, that drinking whiskey, red wine, port, Campari and Creme De Violette all within a twelve-hour period can only result in one thing: a night spent with your head in a toilet. The hours of vomit and migraines flew by until there was only an hour left before Tom was due to arrive at the beach. He pulled himself somewhat together and assessed the damage. His eyes were bloodshot, his hair was ruffled and the stubble on his cheeks had transitioned from rugged to haggard. Thankfully it seemed his nausea had emigrated back to Britain, allowing him to shower, shave and pull on an outfit that seemed suitable for both work and spending a day at the beach - a plain white T-shirt, a pair of denim shorts and a pair of beige loafers. Tom left his room with fifteen minutes to spare, ready to begin his new adventure.

The sun was overwhelming as Tom stepped out from the air-conditioned safety of the hotel. The air was thick with heat and after only a few steps sweat began to trickle down Tom's spine. The pool area was surprisingly crowded for such an early hour but Tom knew as well as anyone how competitive the fight for a good spot by the pool could be. Many guests were already enjoying a beer or two, and given Tom's experience at the Lobby Bar last night, he understood just how difficult it could be to resist the temptation of free alcohol. At the end of the pool stood a large wooden gate that could only be opened with a code given out at reception each week. Tom entered the magic four numbers (7142) and stepped forward into paradise. The waves were calm. The sand was white and soft. Tom couldn't believe this would be his life for the next few weeks.

'You're early. That's a nice change.'

Tom had been so preoccupied enjoying the magnificent view that he'd failed to notice Gabriella waiting against the brick wall separating the beach from the pathway. He was so startled by her unexpected input that he let out a high pitched and hugely embarrassing squeak.

'Are you OK?' Gabriella asked. She was dressed casually today, in a navy blue dress and designer flip flops.

'I think so.'

'Good. Let's get you to your office then.'

The office in question was a wooden hut located in the centre of the beach, positioned between row upon row of sun loungers. Inside the hut, which was roughly five by six meters, there was a cotton couch, a wooden desk with a chair to match and a battery-powered radio.

'So, this is going to be your home for the next couple of weeks, during the day at least.' Gabriella gestured to her surroundings. She seemed quite proud of it all. 'There's no power, unfortunately, so you'll have to charge your phone and whatever else overnight.'

Tom nodded in approval. The hut, despite its lack of power, was far more impressive than he'd imagined.

'What else is there?' Gabriella asked herself. 'Obviously, you know that the beach opens at nine each morning and closes at seven each evening. You get thirty minutes for your dinner, but I'd prefer it if you waited until later in the day before eating, just so you don't miss any latecomers. Believe me, you'll get a lot of latecomers.'

'Not a problem.'

'Once the afternoon rolls around you're free to do anything you like really, so long as you stay in the hut and you know, no alcohol or anything like that.' Gabriella wasn't sure exactly why she added that, but something told her it was necessary.

'Of course not.' Tom replied, hoping the stench of last night was no longer clinging to his breath.

'And I think that's everything. If there are any problems you know where I am. Oh, and once everybody's gone, I'd appreciate it if you could just give the beach a quick once over, get rid of any cans or cigarettes that have been left. People pay a lot of money to come to this beach but they never seem too fussed about keeping it clean.'

'That's how things always are, isn't it?' Tom replied whilst staring through the beach hut door, out towards the ocean and the infinite nothingness behind it.

'Sadly, you're right.' A pause descended. A pause Gabriella quickly swept aside. 'Well, I suppose I better leave you to it. Guests should start rolling up any minute now. Good luck.'

As Tom's fourteen pound Asos watch struck nine, he was greeted by a startling number of guests all looking for sun loungers as close to the sea as possible. He took their money (six euros per bed, three euros for an umbrella), smiled politely and pointed them in the direction of loungers they could call their own for the day. When there were no more free loungers, the latecomers were forced to settle for a towel on the sand. By midday, the beach was a bustling picture of life and laughter.

During his lunch break, Tom retrieved his laptop and returned to the hut ready to scour the depths of his brain, hoping to fish out the premise of a story and unleash it upon the page. While he was unsuccessful in his search for a premise, he did stumble upon the outline of a character. A female character with unwavering confidence and no aversion to breaking rules she didn't agree with. It wasn't exactly hard to decipher where the inspiration for this character had come from, but he finally had something to work with, and that was all that mattered.

When Tom finally checked the time, he was surprised to discover that the end of his shift was fast approaching. He would soon be forced to evict any remaining beach dwellers for the night. Thankfully, that wouldn't be a long job. The beach was almost empty. In fact, just one couple remained, sitting on loungers not far from the hut.

The man was tall, middle-aged and equipped with the beer belly so commonly associated with men of his age. His hair was untidy, and his eyes were glazed, which was undoubtedly a result of the nine beers he'd enjoyed. The woman beside him was of a similar age, her hair short and blonde and her figure petite. Unlike her husband, her eyes were not glazed. They were sad though.

Tom had only spent thirty seconds in the company of this

couple, but he felt he had a fairly good idea of how their relationship worked. The wife said nothing as her husband tossed an empty beer can onto the sand beside him, ignoring the bin just five feet away. Nor did she object as the man shouted the word cunt at the end of a foul story, even though children were playing in the sand beside him. Tom didn't blame her for staying quiet. He guessed she knew better than to object to his behaviour.

Tom left the hut, ready to tell them to pack up and move on, but stopped in his tracks almost immediately. He couldn't believe what he had just seen. His body was frozen and his heart was still. A chill ran through him despite the blistering heat. He wanted to run away, to make sure the husband didn't see him and inflict the same punishment, but he couldn't move. Instead, he replayed the incident again and again. The couple were arguing, arguing about something big. Whatever the topic was it mattered. It mattered to both of them. Things appeared to be dwindling when suddenly the woman leant towards the man and slapped him across the face. Hard. The man's cheek was stained red and he wasted no time in retaliating. He returned the favour in a flash, catching his wife just above her right eye. When he pulled his fist away, it was speckled with blood.

8

The Best Pizza in the World

For the past year, Sarah Tyler has hated the thought of going
on holiday. Although perhaps that's an oversimplification
because for the past year Sarah Tyler has hated the thought
of just about everything. She's hated the thought of shopping.
She's hated the thought of working. She's hated the thought
of sex. And the worst thing is that just a year ago Sarah had
loved these things. Just a year ago she had been happy. It's
funny how much can change in a year.

The reason Sarah Tyler has grown to hate all these things
she once loved is both simple and sad. It's because she has no
choice but to share these activities with Richard Tyler, and
there's nothing she hates more than her husband.

Sarah had dreaded their holiday to Spain ever since Richard
had announced he'd booked it without consulting her. He'd
insisted it would be good for them. That it would help distract
them from everything. More than anything it was what
they needed. Sarah disagreed. The last thing she needed
was to spend three weeks surrounded by happy couples and
children, but she couldn't tell Richard that. He'd been in a

good mood when he booked the holiday, and Sarah knew not to rock the boat when the waters were calm.

It hadn't always been like this. There had been a period, quite a long period actually, when Sarah had loved Richard with every fibre of her being. Richard had certainly felt the same way back then. Though whether he loved Sarah now was much less certain. Truthfully she felt confident he did not.

Sarah didn't want to love her husband anymore. She wanted to hate him and a part of her did. But only a small part, and that would never be enough. A much larger part of her still loved him, just as she had from the very first night they spent together. Although that feels like a very distant memory now.

Sarah first met Richard Tyler eleven years before their spontaneous trip to the Scarlett Grove. She was twenty-two at the time and spent her days working in a salon in a rough part of Wigan. Although 'Kath's Salon' was hidden away in a rather sketchy corner of town, the clientele was anything but. These elegant ladies travelled well outside of their comfort zones to have their hair, nails and eyebrows tended to by Kath and Sarah.

Sarah had taken to Richard almost immediately. He wasn't handsome in a conventional way (his large nose and bushy eyebrows put a stop to that), but he was stocky and rugged, and he reminded Sarah of the rugby players she'd grown up admiring. What truly set Richard apart from the men Sarah had dated previously, and what she in truth was most attracted to, was his startling lack of confidence. Given that Sarah was young and attractive (and back then she really had been young and attractive), she'd become accustomed to men of all shapes and sizes leering after her in nightclubs. Some were kind, some were frightening, but all were unwelcome.

Richard was different. He only looked at Sarah when her attention was elsewhere. And though Sarah never usually initiated conversation with men in clubs, she found herself wading through the dance floor to introduce herself to the man who would become her husband.

'Oh, hello.' Richard said awkwardly, sipping his beer to appear casual.

'That's it? Hello. That's all I get?' Sarah said playfully, although she saw Richard's unease increase immediately.

'What did you want me to say?'

'I don't know. Most blokes have a line prepared. One of the classic terrible ones like telling me that your shirts made from boyfriend material or asking how I like my eggs in the morning?'

'Do you actually want me to ask something like that?' Richard asked, clearly a little disappointed.

'I suppose I'd settle for anything better than hello.'

With nothing else to say, Richard decided to take a chance on something he was confident everybody loved. 'Do you like pizza?'

Sarah smiled. 'Yeah, I like pizza.'

'There's a takeaway round the corner that does the best pizza.'

'The best pizza in Wigan or the best pizza in the world?'

'The world.' Richard locked eyes with Sarah for the first time. For a brief moment, she lost herself in them.

'And I assume they've run some sort of test to verify what you're saying?'

'Come and try it. See what you think.'

'Lead the way.'

Richard led the way and when Sarah woke in his arms the next morning, she realised he had been right. It was the best pizza in the world.

* * *

Having a child is the best thing that can happen to anyone.

The next couple of months blurred by in the way that only a new relationship can. There were kisses and long chats and nights spent exploring every aspect of one another. Sarah quickly found herself falling for a man who no longer had any trouble meeting her gaze. Richard's promising career as a journalist was just the cherry on the cake, and the substantial amount of money stored safely away in his savings account didn't hurt either. He even talked about eventually opening a salon for Sarah to run, an idea that excited Sarah more than she could ever explain. Everything was beginning to fall into place.

Sarah was happy. Truly happy.

Having a child is the best thing that can happen to anyone.

They were married two years later. A Hollywood ending to their Wigan-based romance. They tied the knot in The Kinmel, a small country house in Wales. The Kinmel boasted a ballroom so exceptional that once Sarah and Richard saw it, they simply couldn't imagine getting married anywhere else. A huge window looked out over the Welsh countryside showcasing a magnificent array of luscious greens. The only downside of the Kinmel country home was that it was in no way prepared to host such festivities, which made the planning process a great deal more difficult. They rented a bar-on-wheels to supply the alcohol. They hired an entire catering team to supply the food and a small construction team to build a stage for the band. Despite all of this, the night was perfect, and as Richard's hand wrapped around her own, Sarah couldn't quite believe how perfect her life had become.

Sarah's Salon opened three months later, and bookings were solid from the off. This was it. All of her dreams had come true. Things could only get better.

Having a child is the best thing that can happen to anyone.

Sarah and Richard had been married for two years when Richard was made redundant. With money scarce and the bills mounting up, Sarah's Salon closed its doors for the final time twelve months later. At around the same time, Richard began to find solace at the bottom of a whiskey bottle.

Having a child is the best thing that can happen to anyone.

Sarah and Richard had been married for four years when he first hit his wife. Admittedly, Sarah had been provoking him, hoping for a reaction from the man who'd become such a disappointment to her, but she'd never believed he was capable of something like this.

Sarah remembered looking up from the floor, blood streaming from her nose, and seeing nothing but shock on Richard's face. The expression didn't last for long. It was soon replaced with disinterest. Richard left Sarah alone on the floor, bleeding and crying and wondering how everything had gone so wrong so quickly.

Having a child is the best thing that can happen to anyone.

Sarah and Richard had been married for five years when Sarah discovered she was pregnant. She cried and cried, sobbing because now she was trapped. She'd wanted to leave Richard for months, she'd maybe even convinced herself to finally bite the bullet and pack her bags, but now she knew she never would. She couldn't put her child through that.

Having a child is the best thing that can happen to anyone.

On the final day of August Sarah cradled her baby boy in her arms for the first time. Marcus Richard Tyler weighed seven pounds and seven ounces. His eyes were tiny little emeralds. Richard, who had insisted the baby's middle name mirrored his own, had become kinder during the pregnancy. His drinking had faded and so too had his temper. He even managed to get a job working in the kitchen of The Brown Cow, a local pub in which Sarah had spent the last three years waiting tables. Sarah had reservations about Richard working in an environment surrounded by the one thing she wanted absent from his life, but right now the money was all that mattered.

The nine months had flown by and now here she was, cradling the only thing she would ever love more than words could explain. Once again, she allowed herself to believe that nothing could go wrong. She and Richard had toiled through a rough couple of years but that was all in the past. Their future was bright.

Having a child is the best thing that can happen to anyone.

A little over three years passed between the magical day that Sarah was first introduced to Marcus and the day she stood at the edge of a hole dressed in black, ready to say goodbye to him forever. She was empty and she always would be. She cried as the tiny coffin was lowered into a black hole, similar to the black hole that would forever engulf her heart.

Richard blamed Sarah for Marcus' death. Not that anybody besides God or Buddha or whoever the fuck you believe in can be blamed for cancer, but that didn't matter. He made it clear how he felt, but Richard's disappointment would never compare to the all-consuming sorrow eating away at Sarah from the inside.

Losing a child is the worst thing that can happen to anyone.

How Richard had managed to afford three weeks in the Spanish sun was a mystery to Sarah. He'd been sacked from the pub about two months after Marcus' death and hadn't worked a day since. His days hadn't been empty though. He'd tried everything to fill the void growing inside him. Booze, pills, sex (both with and without Sarah). Nothing worked. A part of him knew nothing ever would. But maybe life would hurt a fraction less on a beach beneath the Spanish sun.

Losing a child is the worst thing that can happen to anyone.

Sarah didn't want to go to Spain with Richard, but she'd been numb for the past year. Numb to the lewd comments made towards her at work. Numb to Richard's drinking and affairs. Numb to the impending anniversary of Marcus' death. Numb to her own life.

Losing a child is the worst thing that can happen to anyone.

With their bags packed ready for their trip to the Scarlett Grove, Sarah cried. She had no idea what she was doing anymore. She couldn't think of a single reason to continue torturing herself with the life that had ruined her.

Losing a child is the worst thing that can happen to anyone.

* * *

The Tyler's first day in Spain unfolded much as Sarah had expected. They sat by the pool without speaking. Richard drank and at some point, Sarah joined him, because why not? They ate in the Dining Hall before wandering over to The Clover, the brash Irish bar opposite the hotel. The decor inside The Clover was tacky. So too were the men behind the bar. Richard didn't notice. He insisted they remain in the loud, murky bar until the lights came on and the music stopped. Once they were finally back in their room, Richard kissed Sarah for the first time in eleven days. His breath tasted of whiskey but that was nothing new. He thrust himself inside of her before she was ready but that was nothing new. He finished before Sarah even got close but that was nothing new. And once it was over, he rolled away without so much as a word, but again this was nothing new.

She didn't consider it rape. No matter what Richard had become, Sarah still liked to believe that he would respect her wishes if she asked him to stop. Not that she ever would. She didn't feel anything anymore. She didn't want to.

Their second day in Spain had been largely the same except Richard decided to swap drinking by the pool for drinking by the beach. He bought himself a crate of local beer and a bottle of red wine for Sarah although she much preferred white. Richard was in a foul mood all day. For the most part, Sarah ignored him. But late in the afternoon, Richard crossed a line that Sarah never thought he would, and then, just for the briefest of moments, she was alive again.

'Do you ever think about where he is now?' Richard asked suddenly.

'What's that, sorry?'

'Marcus. Do you ever wonder where he is?' There was no emotion in Richard's voice as he mentioned his dead son.

'Heaven. He's in heaven Richard.' Sarah had never been religious. In fact, before the birth of her son she had thought the notion of a man living in the sky was ludicrous. But now she clung to the hope. She couldn't bring herself to admit that her son was just gone.

'Do you really believe that?'

'Yes. I believe that one hundred percent.'

'But you've never been to Church or anything? We didn't even have a Catholic wedding.' Richard chuckled which only infuriated Sarah further.

'Why does that matter?'

'Because if you believed in heaven and all that, you wouldn't have had a non-religious wedding because you'd be worried about offending the big man up there.' Richard used his right hand, which was clutching a warm beer, to gesture towards the sky.

'That's not how religion works.'

'You wouldn't know.' Richard laughed. 'You don't know the first thing about it.'

Not for the first time that day, Sarah bit her tongue.

'Although maybe that's what happened.' Richard added.

'What?'

'Maybe God was pissed off with us and that's why it happened.'

'Why what happened?' Sarah felt every muscle in her body tighten.

Richard only shrugged but it was all the confirmation Sarah needed. Once again, her husband was suggesting that she had been responsible for Marcus' death. She was no longer numb. Without thinking, Sarah threw her right hand out and slapped Richard across the face. Hard. Richard's expression was momentarily blank, as if he couldn't make sense of what had happened. But quickly his jaw clenched and his shoulders locked and Sarah knew what was coming next. Richard returned the favour with lightning speed, twice the force and a clenched fist. Sarah began to cry and Richard left without a word. Neither noticed the young lad from the beach hut watching on in horror.

9

Small Plates and Big Drinks

Tom stayed on the beach for quite some time after his shift finished. He stood alone and deep in thought, trying to make sense of what he'd seen. When he finally broke free from his trance, he had less than an hour to prepare for his date with Joy. Knowing he couldn't afford to waste a single second, Tom decided against reporting what he'd just witnessed to Gabriella. After all, what happened on the beach seemed like the sort of incident she'd have cause to worry about, and Tom, as selfish as it may sound, just couldn't give her any reason to reconsider his employment. With a dark grey cloud of liquid guilt floating above him, Tom made his way through the reception area, never once looking towards the corridor that led to the manager's office. He promised himself he'd tell Gabriella eventually. And for today that seemed to be enough.

Tom showered, shaved and dressed quickly, opting for a pair of black denim shorts, his best white shirt and a pair of fake designer glasses he'd purchased from a sketchy looking man at the beach. It took just ten minutes to walk from the hotel to Platos Y Bebidos. During the walk, Tom convinced himself that Joy wouldn't be there. That she'd be spending her time with the muscular, tattooed man she'd left with. Tom wouldn't blame her. Most girls would rather spend time with the other lad. Why should Joy be any different?

Tom stepped onto the ruby red patio of Platos Y Bebidos and all his worries ceased. Not only was Joy here but she was all he could see, wearing a light blue denim skirt and a loose white cotton T-shirt that, like her trainers at the airport, boasted a selection of doodles. She smiled at Tom. Her eyes smiled too.

As Tom took his seat opposite Joy a plump waiter arrived at the table. The waiter, Xabi, was armed with two strawberry daiquiris and an infectious smile.

'I put a little extra kick in there, just for you.' He exclaimed proudly whilst throwing a playful wink Joy's way. 'So, are you ready to order or you need longer?'

Xabi's heavy accent made it difficult for Tom to decipher what he was saying, but his English was by no means bad. His hair was blonde and his skin was pale, which was most unusual for people born in these parts, but in terms of charisma, he was more than adept.

Tom was about to politely ask for another minute to browse when he was interrupted by the girl sitting beside him.

'We're about as ready as can be, Xabi. And don't worry, we're going to make it easy for you.' Joy seemed keen to equal Xabi's charm.

'Easy peasy.' Xabi replied in his thick accent.

'I think we'll just try one of everything please.'

'No, no, no.' Xabi's face was full of panic as if Joy had asked

67

for uncooked chicken or a pint of bleach. 'Too much. Too much food.'

'It's tapas. You're supposed to try a bit of everything.'

'Yes, but it's too much.' Xabi's charm momentarily abandoned him.

'I think we're up to the challenge. Don't you Tom?'

Joy's attention swiftly transferred to Tom, who was grateful for the chance to get involved in the conversation.

'I reckon we can give it a good go.'

From the look on Joy's face, Tom knew he'd answered correctly.

'Trust me, trust me.' Xabi begged. 'Too much.'

'There's no point in only serving tiny plates of food if the customers can't try everything. Trust us, we'll manage.' Joy spoke with such unwavering confidence that Xabi was forced to accept defeat.

'You do like strawberry daiquiris, don't you?' Joy asked once Xabi was out of sight and earshot. 'Xabi told me he makes the best strawberry daiquiris in Spain and you can't say no to that.'

Tom had never tried a strawberry daiquiri, or any daiquiri for that matter, but it didn't prevent him from saying 'I completely agree.'

Thankfully the extravagant red cocktail was delicious. Maybe Xabi was right. Maybe it was the best strawberry daiquiri in Spain.

Preparing twenty-four tapas dishes was by no means a quick process, which left Tom and Joy with a lot of time to talk. Thankfully, the conversation never ran stale. Joy told tom about the books she'd read, films she'd seen and music she listened to. Tom was overjoyed to learn that Joy shared his love of horror novels, and they both liked the American show about the people who work in a terrible Irish bar. They talked about the show for a while, but Tom began to worry that the conversation was becoming generic and uninteresting. He wanted tonight to stand out amongst other dates Joy had been on, assuming this was a date anyway, and more than anything he wanted to know her, the real her. Suddenly, he knew just what to ask. He finished the last of his second strawberry daiquiri, knowing that drinking again put him at serious risk of breaking his three-day rule (although right then he didn't care at all), and dived in.

'So, I wanted to ask about the drawings.' Tom gestured to the bottom of Joy's T-shirt.

'Oh.' Joy looked down at her top. Tom couldn't decide if it was a flash of amusement or embarrassment he saw in her eyes. 'I dunno. I just get bored sometimes.'

'They were on your shoes too, weren't they? Yesterday, I mean.'

'I suppose I get bored a lot.' Joy laughed and retreated to the safety of her cocktail.

'Can I see them?'

'Yeah, I suppose so.' Joy shuffled her chair back to allow Tom a better look at the drawings that littered the bottom of her T-shirt.

Tom learnt more about Joy from the doodles scattered across her white top than he had from anything she'd told him. There was a drawing of the *Ghostbusters* logo, beneath which there was a sketch of the sea. She'd also drawn the night sky, the biggest of all the doodles, complete with dark storm clouds and an incredibly detailed crescent moon.

69

From everything he'd seen, Tom decided there were two sides to Joy. There was the pop culture side, the side that drew *Patrick Star* and the *Ghostbusters* logo. Then there was the side that Joy chose to hide, the side of her that drew calm seas and dark, stormy nights.

'See anything you like?' Joy asked, having grown uncomfortable with Tom's long pause.

'I like it all.'

'I think this one's my favourite.' Joy said as she tucked into a tender piece of beef coated in a delicious red wine jus.

'It's in my top three. But I don't think anything beats the chicken.' Tom took a large gulp from his fifth cocktail of the evening.

'To be honest I'm still most impressed by these daiquiris.'

'I'd have to agree with that.'

'So, all this delicious food aside, what are you really doing out here then?' Joy asked with genuine interest.

'I thought I told you yesterday. I'm working at the hotel over the summer. I rent out the…'

'You rent out the sun loungers on the beach.' Joy interrupted. 'You've told me that. But you haven't told me why you came all the way to Spain for a summer job. There's definitely a story there.'

'I erm, I dunno really.' Tom tried to find the right words. 'I want to be a writer.'

'But you came to work on a beach in Spain. Why's that?'

'It's probably going to sound stupid when I say it out loud but I um, I just couldn't think of anything to write at home. Everything was dull and unexciting.

'You don't think there's a market for dull and unexciting

novels?' Joy asked with a wry smile.

'If there was, I wouldn't be spending my summer in a wooden hut on a beach.'

Joy smiled. She seemed to like it when Tom made jokes.

'So, you're on the hunt for inspiration then?'

'I suppose so. It was just that everything seemed too easy at home, you know. Everything was simple and I didn't want my writing to be simple.'

'Have you found any yet?'

'I hope so.' Tom couldn't believe how open he'd become. Clearly, cocktails were his romantic kryptonite.

'I'll help you find it.'

Suddenly time stood still. Joy was leaning towards him. Nothing else mattered. Nothing else even existed. Tom was about to lean forwards when Joy suddenly veered away from his lips and instead arrived at his ear.

'Let's leave.' She whispered.

'What?'

'Let's leave.'

'But we haven't finished. We haven't even paid yet.' Tom argued, wondering if the cocktails were responsible for his confusion.

'Exactly. I thought you were looking for something new.'

'I was thinking more along the lines of meeting new people and trying new food.'

'You've met me, and you've eaten tapas, so let's go.' Joy's eyes were alight, convincing Tom to bend to her will.

'This is mental.'

'It'll make a good story.'

'I really don't think it's a good idea.'

Without warning, Joy leaned forward and kissed Tom

gently. Tom, after recovering from the initial shock and euphoria, made sure not to miss a single second of it. When Joy slowly eased away, he found himself mesmerised by a pair of eyes that he barely even knew yet.

'Trust me.' She whispered.

He did.

* * *

Xabi had been in and out of the kitchen all night. He delivered drinks, checked on his customers, removed empty plates and even peeled the veg for the kitchen staff. But tonight Xabi had only one goal. He wanted his new favourite customers to be happy, and he wanted to earn as generous a tip as possible.

He was pouring two shots to accompany his new favourite customers' monumental bill when he was startled by a flurry of movement behind him. Before he'd even turned around, he knew what had happened. It wasn't an entirely new experience, but this was the first time he hadn't seen it coming. Or maybe he had. The girl at that table had eyes that could start wars. Xabi didn't bother chasing them. Her eyes could start wars and Xabi was not a soldier.

* * *

Tom didn't know what had possessed him to agree to this insane idea. He didn't know how his legs were supporting him when all the strength appeared to have drained from them. But most of all he just couldn't understand how a single kiss had convinced him to do something so outrageous. Not that he cared. In fact, with Joy's hand coiled around his own, he knew that he'd do it again if she asked him to.

When the bright lights of the Scarlett Grove finally came into view, sweat was pouring from Tom's forehead. He checked back over his shoulder and was filled with relief to find there was no sign of Xabi wheezing after them with his fists raised. Not yet at least.

'Come on.' Tom gasped, checking over his shoulder once again. 'I know where to go.'

The beach was almost empty. There were only a handful of guests who'd come out to stargaze or wander down to one of the popular beach-side cocktail bars, but none of them seemed to notice Tom or Joy as they sprinted onto the beach.

The beach itself had only the blanket of stars and the shine of the moon for illumination. As they stepped onto the cold sand, Tom began to wonder if he'd made the right decision. Would Joy see this moonlit destination as a romantic gesture or as a strange attempt to separate her from potential witnesses? It seemed that right now the two could be easily confused. Thankfully, Joy once again seemed to read his mind.

'So, your master plan was to hide at the beach?'

'Yes and no.' Tom's voice trembled. Joy didn't seem nervous at all. Had she done this before?

'He didn't even chase us.'

'Why not?'

'I honestly don't know.' Joy thought about it deeply. 'I thought he would have done.'

'Have you done that before?'

Joy said nothing, instead, she just stared out to sea. Tom decided not to press her, grateful for the opportunity to catch his breath. Finally, she turned towards him.

'Why'd you bring me to the beach?'

'Me first.' Tom insisted. 'Have you done that before?'

'I'll answer honestly if you do.'

'Deal.'

'I've done it before.' Joy replied, completely void of emotion.

'Really? Why? Why risk it?' Tom tried and failed to keep the judgement from his voice.

'Nope. I'm owed an answer first.'

'I dunno. I just thought it would be a good place to hide.'

'Be honest.'

Tom wanted to be honest, but he didn't want to scare her.

'We made a deal.' Joy pressed.

'I thought it would be nice to be here with you.' Tom stared down at his feet and tried not to think about the burning in his cheeks.

'I don't do it a lot.' Joy replied as if Tom had said nothing at all.

'Why do it at all?'

'Because I might die tomorrow. I might get struck by lightning or hit by a car or shot in the street.'

'What about the people that work there? What about the money they lost?'

'Do you know who owns the place?' Joy asked, staring out towards the lapping waves.

'No.'

'It's owned by the Wyatt Foundation. Bill Wyatt is worth more than everybody in this town put together. His staff earn minimum wage.'

'So, that's why you do it? Because he underpays his staff.' Tom asked, wishing Joy would turn back to face him. Then again, maybe she shouldn't see the look of judgement on his face.

'No. I do it because I can. But you asked me about the staff and the money they lose out on and they won't be losing out on anything. The only person who loses out is Wyatt, and I don't think he'll miss it too much.'

'Aren't you scared of getting arrested? Imagine if he'd chased us. What would you have done if he'd caught us? He could have killed us.' Tom persisted.

Joy looked at Tom for a long time. Her caramel eyes seemingly staring straight through him.

'If you could do anything right now, what would you do?' She finally asked.

'What do you mean?'

'You just said we could have been killed tonight. Let's say you're right. You've just survived a near-death experience. You can do anything you want, what would you do?'

Tom didn't have to think about his answer. He stepped towards Joy and kissed her more passionately than he'd kissed anybody before. When the kiss was over, Joy took his hand.

'Show me the hut.' She said with a smile.

Tom did as she asked without hesitation.

10

The Suite Diamante

Tom awoke with a hangover that would force Charlie Sheen to rethink things. Sand clung to his damp forehead and it took him a long moment of panic and confusion to finally remember why he had slept in the beach hut. He remembered flashes of last night. Flashes of Joy's eyes, of her gentle lips pressed against his, of losing himself in her. And then Tom remembered the moment the night had turned. Suddenly it wasn't just his Spanish hangover that filled him with regret.

His hands had been lost in Joy's hair, but when he tried to slide one down her neck Joy had leapt back as if she'd been slapped. Tom apologised profusely, although truthfully he had no clue what he'd done wrong, but Joy insisted it wasn't his fault. She told him it was just the alcohol, and though Tom knew she was lying, he didn't press the subject any further. Instead, Joy nestled her head onto his shoulder and they fell asleep together on a small cotton couch in a small wooden hut.

To say that he'd fallen asleep in a picture of togetherness, he'd awoken in a world of loneliness. At some point in the night, Joy had slipped away without a word, without even saying goodbye.

Tom stumbled out of the hut accompanied by the aches and pains that anybody who enjoys a drink or twelve will be all-too-familiar with. Thankfully, the beach was empty. Though Tom had no idea of the time because his phone was long dead. Deciding he needed a shower before welcoming the sun-cream wielding guests, Tom rushed through the reception area and back to his room, taking care to steer well clear of the corridor that led to the manager's office. He doubted Gabriella would take kindly to the fact that he had spent the night in the beach hut, especially if she knew he hadn't been alone.

It turned out Tom had exactly forty-three minutes before his shift, more than enough time to make himself presentable. He showered and changed, opting for a pair of grey denim shorts and a navy T-shirt. With ten minutes to spare, Tom checked his now-charged phone to find nothing. No message from Joy. He didn't even have her number. Tom collected his laptop and left his room feeling deflated. Unable to shake the feeling that he'd never see Joy again.

That day something happened to Tom that he hadn't experienced in years. In fact, he hadn't experienced such a rush of inspiration since he'd written *The Smallest Tree in The Woods*. Back then he'd written thirteen pages of his story in the space of a single day and his arrogant teenage self had assumed it would always be that easy. Over the following years, Tom had begun to question whether the writing rush would return. That is until, on a beach in Spain, he rediscovered the spark that had been absent from his life since his teenage years.

Tom spent his entire working day, after a brief prelude showing guests to their loungers, churning out words without forethought or planning. Writing as if he were telling a story he'd known his whole life. By the day's end, he had outlined the first chapter of his novel. A chapter in which his female character, Rose Evans, made the tough decision to turn her back on her family and everything she'd ever known.

Rose had spent the first twenty-two years of her life being treated like a second-class citizen in her own home. Neither of her parents worked but they happily collected the wages Rose earned at her part-time job. Despite Roses' many pleas to attend college, her parents made it abundantly clear it was not an option. Instead, she had been sent off to find full-time work, and when she found a job in a nearby *Asda* her parents happily collected the money that they believed belonged to them.

Five years passed before Rose finally decided to take matters into her own hands and squirrel away some of her wages for herself. Things got a little better after that. Rose began to feel like an individual for the first time in her life. But everything imploded when her parents found the money she'd hidden. They threatened to make their only daughter homeless. Rose apologised and handed over the money, spending the next few days in a pit of sorrow and pain until suddenly she saw her parents for what they really were. Creatures incapable of love. Her life would never change with them holding her back.

Rose took every single penny of her next wage and spent almost all of it on a plane ticket to Barcelona. The chapter will end with Rose at the airport, where she will throw away her mobile phone before boarding the plane and leaving her old life behind forever.

* * *

Though tourists flock to the beach upon the appearance of the first rays of the sun, they also retreat to the safety of their rooms upon the appearance of a cloud. Unfortunately for Tom, any such retreat means he must dig out the rubber gloves and bin liners and clean the beach. Today's sand-covered litter included empty plastic cups, a half-eaten hot dog and a crusty clump of tissues. After twenty minutes of disgusting work, Tom was just about nudging the last tissue into the bin-liner when Gabriella paid him an unexpected visit.

'It's good to see that you actually clean the place.'

To say that Gabriella had startled Tom would be an under-statement. A more accurate description would be that she scared the living shit out of him. Tom jumped so fiercely that he thumped his head against the sun lounger he'd been crouching beneath.

'Bloody hell.' He exclaimed, much louder than intended.

Gabriella tried and failed to remain professional. She keeled over and laughed from the depths of her belly.

'I'm sorry.' She said as she finally stopped laughing. 'I didn't realise I was so terrifying.'

'No, no. I was just in a world of my own.' Tom pulled himself to his feet.

'That's a relief. How are you getting on so far?'

'I'm really enjoying it. This beach is something else.'

'It's not too bad, is it.' Gabriella briefly lost herself in the view. 'I actually came here to tell you to close up for the day.'

'Really?'

'Yeah. I was hoping you'd help me out with something.'

'Of course. What is it?' Tom asked, eager to make amends for his terrible first impression.

'Some people from the Wyatt Foundation are coming down for a fancy little dinner. Business talk and good food, you know?'

Tom, who had never talked business or eaten delicious food, only nodded.

'Anyway, one of our waiters called in sick and it's not the first time he's done it, so I told him not to bother coming back. I wondered if you'd be able to fill in, just for tonight of course?'

Tom liked the idea of Gabriella owing him a favour. Maybe the next time he woke up with a Spanish hangover, he'd be able to spend the day in bed.

'I can, but I don't have any experience.'

'Can you carry plates?' Gabriella asked.

'Yes.'

'What about glasses?'

'Yes.' Tom replied with a smile, understanding where this conversation was headed.

'Could you carry both at the same time?'

'Probably.'

'Then you're qualified.' Gabriella laughed, then her expression soured as if she'd bitten down on a lemon. 'A bit of warning though. It's a boy's club, the Wyatt Foundation.'

'I don't know if I'm the type of person you want chatting to them then.' Tom murmured, now considerably less enthused for the night of work ahead.

'No, you're probably not.' Gabriella replied honestly. 'But I need help and you're basically my only option.'

* * *

Tom didn't have long to prepare. He pulled on the unwashed shirt he'd worn last night and paired it with a black tie, black trousers and black suede shoes. He then left his room ready for a night with the Wyatt Foundation. Ready to listen to their stories, laugh at their jokes and no matter what happened, resist the urge to spit in their food.

Tom was so lost in his thoughts (thoughts of tapas and strawberry daiquiris) that he completely forgot he was waiting outside Gabriella's office. As a result, Gabriella startled him for the second time that day merely by leaving her office. The door swung open and Tom jumped back as if he'd spotted a tarantula crawling across his shoe. Gabriella smiled, but she was far too preoccupied to laugh.

'Again, really?' Gabriella smiled. 'I'm starting to worry you might croak it before the end of the summer.'

'Hopefully not.'

'You look smart. There's a stain on that sleeve though.' Gabriella said without judgement or disapproval. Tom had no idea how she'd so quickly spotted a stain that he hadn't seen at all.

'Shit. I'm really sorry.' He made a feeble attempt to remove the stain. It wouldn't budge.

'It's fine. Just get some soap on it before dinner service. Can we walk?' Gabriella didn't wait for an answer.

'Where is the dinner tonight?' Tom asked, struggling to

match Gabriella's pace, which was particularly impressive considering she was wearing high heels and a tight black dress.

'The Suite Diamante.'

Tom had no idea where or what the Suite Diamante was, but he kept his questions to himself. He followed Gabriella into the reception area and past the Lobby Bar, travelling down a corridor that he'd never seen before. Gabriella eventually came to a halt outside a pair of large oak doors. A polished gold plaque stood above the door. The words 'Suite Diamante' were printed on it in elegant letters.

The Suite Diamante was the most accurately named room that Tom had ever stepped foot in, narrowly beating the bathroom in his uni house that was literally just a room with a bath. The Suite was a breath-taking achievement in architecture. A magnificent crystal chandelier dangled from the centre of the arched roof. There was an angelic marble sculpture displayed proudly in front of a wall made entirely of glass, allowing Tom to gaze through it towards the choppy sea. Strings of fairy lights streamed from the chandelier, making it seem as though the roof itself was twinkling. Gabriella's heels echoed throughout the Suite as she led Tom to a mammoth table adorned with a white satin sheet and solid silver cutlery waited. Tom understood now more than ever why the Wyatt Foundation were willing to pump so much money into acquiring the hotel.

'What do you think?'

'I think it's the nicest room I've ever been in.' Tom answered honestly.

'Me too. I'll take you down to the kitchen now and the staff will give you some more information but here are the basics. Don't use a plate unless it's spotless. If you see a half-empty glass, fill it up. More than anything, make sure to mention how great both myself and the hotel are whenever you get chance.'

'That sounds easy enough.'

'What do you think of the hotel?' Gabriella asked in a mock cockney accent.

'It's great.'

'And the manager of the hotel? What's she like?' Gabriella continued with the terrible accent.

'She's also great.'

'Very creative. Test passed. Let's show you the kitchen.'

* * *

Ten minutes until dinner service.

Enjoying what would likely be her only spare minute all night, Gabriella nipped behind the Lobby Bar and poured herself a particularly strong Jack Daniels and coke. Nico was busy serving customers, but he sighed loudly enough to ensure Gabriella heard it. Tonight was most certainly not the night to test her, and Gabriella decided there would be no better time to stoop to Nico's level.

'Tuck your shirt in!' She barked.

Nico did as he was told with a scowl. It was just a tiny victory for Gabriella, but it was a victory all the same. The bigger victories, she was sure, would be much harder to come by.

Seven minutes until dinner service.

In the stifling kitchen, bowls of soup were being prepared at an incredible speed. Tom watched on in awe as head-chef Juan and his team paraded around the kitchen, increasing the heat on a stove here and adding seasoning to a dish there. It was the culinary equivalent of a ballet performance.

Two minutes until dinner service.

Armed with two bowls of soup and stood shoulder to shoulder with waiters both older and vastly more experienced in the soup carrying game, Tom headed back towards the large oak doors of the Suite Diamante.

Dinner is served.

11

Magic Powder

Roger Wyatt cares as little about the Scarlett Grove as he does the Wyatt Foundation, which is to say he doesn't care about either of them. In fact, there's very little that Roger Wyatt does care about. He enjoys the time he spends with women, in the right capacity of course, and he enjoys the financial security granted by his surname. But he'd always found it amusing how so many people seemed to think he'd won the lottery just because he originated in the bollocks of a man with more money than he could ever spend. They were right to some degree, but Roger's life had never been as easy as people assumed. Yes, he could have been born in a slum without running water or electricity. He could have died after suffering from some God-awful disease and, of course, that would have been an immeasurably worse life. But money doesn't solve everything, and it certainly doesn't make people better than they are. Roger's father Bill was living proof of that.

Bill had never been overtly cruel or abusive. Actually, Roger didn't really know what his father was like. His mother,

June, who was ironically born in January, had raised him as a single parent. Bill had shown his face at most of the big events, he'd come home for Christmas and birthdays, but Bill much preferred to spend his time in one of the seven Wyatt buildings scattered across all the major cities in the world. Roger preferred it that way too. His father was cold and often made it clear just how disappointed he was in his only son. Roger didn't mind though. He wasn't all that fond of his father either.

The limo drove slowly, but Roger felt queasy all the same. His head throbbed and the thin remains of last night's baggie certainly wouldn't do anything to ease the pain. He had such little magic powder that he didn't know how he'd possibly get through the night.

Cocaine had been Roger's best friend ever since he'd first tried it on his fifteenth birthday. Like every great friendship, it had begun slowly. They would only see each other once a fortnight and on special occasions. But as the months passed they became increasingly close, to the point where Roger could no longer remember the last day he'd spent without his best friend. One of the lads Roger hung around with back in his double-denim filled teenage years had offered him a bump and referred to the white powder resting on his key as 'magic powder'. Roger had laughed at the time, insisting nothing could make coke less cool than such a cartoonish name, but eventually it stuck. Now he was nothing without his best friend. Nothing without his magic powder.

The Wyatt money tap supported Roger's addiction and ensured that nobody asked too many questions, just as it had swept his drink-driving charge under the rug. The Wyatt money tap couldn't cure cancer though. Pancreatic cancer to be precise. Bill Wyatt had been diagnosed a little over four months ago and, despite medical advice from the finest doctors, it seemed nothing could be done. He had some time left. A year at most seemed to be the most common estimate but nobody could be sure. Something about being faced with his mortality brought about a change in Roger's father. Bill didn't become kinder or make more effort to spend time with his son. Instead, he decided he simply couldn't face the possibility of dying without a successful heir to carry his legacy forward.

A month later the Wyatt money tap turned off, with clear instructions to remain off until Roger could prove himself worthy. It was his father's final insult. A final fuck you to the son he despised. But Roger wouldn't give his father the satisfaction. He'd take this shitty Spanish hotel and make a success of it. The old man could spend eternity thinking about how wrong he'd been. Roger couldn't think of a more fitting end.

Roger emptied the contents of last night's baggie onto his gums. The thrill was sharp but short. He'd need to top up at some point but he'd figure that out later. He'd taken enough to hit a familiar euphoria. The euphoria that made normal life so mundane and absent of colour. His father would never understand. Running a successful business was the only high Bill Wyatt would ever experience. To that extent at least, it seemed they were both addicts.

Though Roger hated the two months he'd spent in this shitty town dealing with this shitty hotel, he had found one unexpected perk. Gabriella. He'd wanted her from the first moment he saw her, and his desire had only grown since. She wanted him too. That much was obvious. She made an effort whenever he visited. Dagger high heels, pencil skirts, sometimes even a tight dress with a low drop exposing her cleavage. Those memories were Roger's favourite. They were the ones he thought of when he was alone in his hotel room with nothing but his magic powder and his right hand for company.

One day he'd have her. Just thinking about it made him hard. She'd treat him right. She wouldn't say no to him because she'd know that his needs come first. Not like the girl from last night. Roxy had looked nice enough. Dark hair, darker eyeshadow and even darker lingerie. Roger's instructions had been clear. He wanted a girl with no inhibitions. A girl who would do anything he asked without protest or complaint. The prick on the phone had told him Roxy was exactly the girl he needed. She ticked all the boxes. Or at least that was the lie he told.

Roxy hadn't been willing to submit. She protested against the gag and she tried to wriggle free when Roger wrapped his hands around her throat and began to squeeze. She stopped wriggling after Roger threw the first punch. After that, the room fell silent. At some point, she'd started to cry but Roger hadn't noticed. He finished inside of her and collapsed onto the bed, asleep the moment his head hit the pillow.

The crimson bloodstain on the pillow beside him was the only indication that Roxy had been in his room when Roger awoke the next morning. His Rolex was gone too. Roger didn't care enough to do anything about it, but if he ever saw Roxy again he'd make sure she knew what he really thought of her. Roger pulled himself out of bed and massaged his swollen knuckles. He'd never punched a woman before. He was afraid of how much he'd enjoyed it.

Roger's car arrived outside the Scarlett Grove just as Gabriella demanded that Nico tuck in his shirt. Roger stepped out of the car with magic powder on his gums, hoping Gabriella would be wearing something tight and short.

* * *

The late Spanish sun glared down on Roger Wyatt as he entered the hotel. Gabriella watched on with a sense of dread. She felt like a child of divorce waiting on the pavement outside her mother's house as her father's car approached; a father she despised. Roger grinned and waved as he closed the gap between them. Gabriella gritted her teeth and mentally prepared herself for another evening spent listening to Roger drone on about the future of the Scarlett Grove and pretending not to notice as his eyes lingered on her chest.

Six months prior, Gabriella had returned to London to finalise her divorce and have one final, honest conversation with the man who had been her husband. Their conversation unfolded about as well as Gabriella had expected. Callum was still angry, which of course he had every right to be, and Gabriella quickly realised that he would spend the rest of his life hating her. The conversation didn't last very long after that.

Gabriella spent the bus journey back to the dingy Peckham hotel that would be her home for the next two nights wondering just how she'd pass the time in the city that had once been her home. Despite everything that had happened, she'd hoped Callum would be more forgiving. She'd even opted for a double bed just in case. A decision that merely emphasised her solitude later that night.

In an effort to distract herself from her all-encompassing loneliness, Gabriella glanced around the bus. A man was looking for gold up his nose, a woman was texting so furiously Gabriella worried her fingers might bleed, and an elderly woman was reading a newspaper. Gabriella's eyes lingered on the paper and a headline she would never forget.

Wyatt's wolves hunting for fresh blood.

Gabriella couldn't read the article (the pensioner was too far away for that), but she saw the accompanying picture clearly. Bill Wyatt was sitting proudly in a chair that cost more than Gabriella's car. Beside him stood Roger, grinning proudly in a suit that cost more than the chair and Gabriella's car combined. That was the first time she ever saw Roger's grin, although to Gabriella it was not a grin at all. To Gabriella, they were the bared teeth of a predator ready to pounce. Gabriella had never managed to rid that awful smile from her memory, and now here it was again, hundreds of miles from London. Only this time it was dedicated to her and her alone.

'Gabriella. It's great to see you again.' Roger purred as he took her hand in a vice-like grip and pumped it up and down three times. The Spanish heat suddenly became unbearable.

The three men and lone woman accompanying Roger all did the same, although none spoke, which was good because Gabriella didn't remember any of their names anyway.

'You too.' Gabriella lied.

'I tell you what, every time I come back here I'm more amazed by this place. It's something special, it really is.'

If Gabriella hadn't met Roger before she probably would

have believed the sincerity in his voice. She may even have admired his charm. After all, the tall gentleman with the shaved head and the designer suit was by no means hard on the eyes, but Gabriella had seen through to the real Roger Wyatt. To the predator that lay beneath.

'That means a lot.' Gabriella lied again. 'I hope you're still enjoying everything Roquetas De Mar has to offer.'

'I might never leave.' Roger laughed heartily at his own joke. Gabriella struggled to match his enthusiasm.

'Well, I suppose I should show you to your table.'

'Sounds wonderful.' There were those teeth again. Those awful, awful teeth.

If you asked Tom Jennings his opinion on the matter, which nobody did, he would have told you that the dinner service went remarkably well. He served the first three courses without a hiccup and even received a compliment from one of the friendlier guests. He was relieved of his duties after the main course, a paella that smelt exquisite, and given the responsibility of topping up wine glasses.

Tom first spoke to Roger Wyatt when the man in the designer suit called him over to order a bottle of red wine for himself and Gabriella to share. Gabriella didn't seem particularly keen on the idea, but she didn't object as Roger poured her a glass. About thirty minutes after Tom's first interaction with Roger, he was summoned again. Only this time Roger asked for something that couldn't be found on the hotel's menu.

'Roger Wyatt.' Roger plunged a clammy hand towards Tom, who was helpless but to shake it.

'I'm Tom.' He replied awkwardly.

Gabriella had excused herself to use the bathroom and Tom quickly found himself wishing she'd made the effort to hold it in.

'You fancy a chat?' Roger asked with the confidence of a man who knows everybody wants to chat to him.

Moments later Tom was standing outside the hotel's entrance watching Roger light a cigarette next to him. He used one of those old flip-up lighters that were popular in the sixties. Roger was about to speak when a *TUI* bus crammed full of tourists arrived and people began to disembark, eager to top up their tan and their blood-alcohol level. Roger smoked silently for a long time, waiting for the area to clear before finally turning to face Tom and diving in with his request.

'So anyway, I have a little problem I was hoping you might be able to help me with it.'

'Um, sure.' Tom replied unenthusiastically. 'How can I help?'

'Well, you know, I'm kind of needed back in there.' Roger gestured towards the hotel with his cigarette. 'So, I don't want to be outside any longer than I have to. But I've got a friend who's on his way over here. He should be here in the next sort of,' Roger checked his phone. Tom wondered how a man as rich as Roger Wyatt could function without a Rolex. 'Twenty minutes or so. He's coming down to drop something off for me but, as I say, I don't want to have to excuse myself again. So, I was hoping you'd be able to meet him, hold on to what he owes me and then run it up to me. How's that sound?'

'Sounds fine.' Tom lied. Nothing about this sounded fine.

'I knew you were the man for the job.' Roger said with a

false smile, before removing a thick wad of notes from his pocket. He thumbed a fifty euro note and handed it to Tom. 'There's another of those when the job's done. OK?'

'OK.' Tom replied with a fake smile of his own. That was the moment Tom knew what a mistake he'd made by agreeing to help Roger Wyatt.

For the first time since he'd arrived in Roquetas De Mar, Tom found himself with the time to simply stand still and take in his surroundings. The clouds were thin and scattered and the air was warm. There was a reddish hue in the sky that to Tom seemed to be a visual representation of passion. Tom liked that thought so much that he decided to make a note of it on his phone. Making the note reminded him of an old writing method he'd used at university. The method was incredibly simple but particularly effective. It was called 'Writing the Six.'

The method consisted of the writer using a single word to capture, in a single moment, what you can taste, smell, hear, touch, see and, most importantly, feel. After using this method quite extensively throughout his three years at university, Tom often found himself amazed by just how well a single word could capture a feeling. With that in mind, Tom opened a fresh note on his phone and wrote the word TAPAS in bold. Underneath which he wrote the six.

Daiquiris
   Patatas Bravas
   Mischief
   Electricity
   Beauty

Alive

Once again Tom was amazed by just how well a single word could capture a feeling.

Tom didn't know how long he'd spent with his head buried in his phone when his concentration was suddenly broken by a yell that he assumed was aimed at him.

'Oi.'

Tom looked up to find a black *Mercedes* with tinted windows parked opposite him. The front window was lowered and Tom recognised the driver immediately. He was the muscular, tattooed man who had left with Joy the night they had decided to try every type of alcohol.

'You here for Roger?' He asked with no indication that he recognised Tom.

Tom nodded anxiously. This was a mistake. He shouldn't be here.

'It's him.' Connor said to whoever was waiting in the back seat.

The rear door of the car flew open and Tom's heart stopped. The man climbing out had long, light hair wrapped in a bun, a thin beard running the length of his jaw and an even thinner moustache. He was so gaunt you'd have thought he'd never eaten, either that or he had a serious addiction. Yet it was not the man's unusual appearance that caused Tom's heart to stop. The person responsible for momentarily stopping Tom's heart was sitting on the far side of the back seat. She didn't see him, she was too busy looking out of the window, but Tom saw her. He'd recognise those eyes anywhere.

The long-haired man slammed the door behind him, taking no notice of Tom's mouth hanging slack, and approached him with an outstretched hand.

'I'm Tom.' Tom shook the man's hand and felt a small plastic bag pressed against his palm. He now realised exactly why Roger hadn't wanted to meet this man himself. For a moment he forgot how to breathe.

'Nathan Piner.' The long-haired man said proudly as if his name meant something to people around here.

Tom nodded and said nothing. He had no intention of giving his name to Nathan Piner, the man-bunned drug dealer.

'And your name is?' Nathan pressed.

Tom panicked and decided to use the name of the actor he liked from all those action films. 'Tom.' Shit.

'Tell Mr Wyatt I'm sorry for the delay in finally meeting. I've been pretty busy these last couple of weeks.' Nathan paused as an elderly woman waddled past. 'Anyway, tell him this here is the finest product Spain has to offer.'

'I will.' Tom mumbled, keen to escape as quickly as possible.

'Oh, and here.' Nathan handed Tom a business card which he pocketed without reading. 'That's my personal number. Tell him if to get in touch if he needs anything, and I mean anything. You got it?'

'I do.'

'Good. I'll be off then.' Nathan winked and turned away.

As Nathan opened the car door Tom got another look at the back seat. It really was Joy. She'd spent the night with her head on Tom's shoulder and now she was twiddling her thumbs in the car of a drug dealer. Tom would have been confused if he wasn't so upset.

As if she could hear his thoughts, Joy looked towards Tom. She saw it was him and looked away quickly. There was shame in her eyes. There was shame in Tom's too.

If Tom were to write the six for this moment the final word would be heartache. Once again, he was amazed by just how well a single word could capture a feeling.

12

The Manager's Office

For Gabriella Glover, the evening had been anything but pleasant. Between worrying about what the hotel would become under the woeful reign of Roger Wyatt and her constant attempts to keep his hands off her body, she found the night to be even more stressful than she'd expected. Her anxiety had only grown when she returned from the bathroom to find that Roger had taken Tom outside for a private chat. And Roger's explanation, that Tom was simply greeting one of his friends, did nothing to set her mind at ease.

Ten minutes later Tom returned and Roger abruptly excused himself from the table with a half-chewed profiterole still lining the walls of his mouth. Gabriella nodded politely and quickly turned to Tom, who looked more sheepish than ever. Roger jogged over to him and gestured that Tom follow him outside. Tom returned to the suite moments later. He glanced uncomfortably towards Gabriella before taking orders from the diners whose glasses were bare.

Roger returned five minutes later with pupils so dilated it

appeared as though his eyes were completely black. If the last few hours had been bad, what was to come would surely be unbearable.

With the dessert plates cleared away and Roger's staff in homeward taxis, Roger insisted that Gabriella join him for a drink in the Lobby Bar. Gabriella politely refused three times before finally giving in. Roger ordered their drinks without so much as a glance toward Gabriella, opting for two double pink gin and tonics. Roger, like most children, assumed all women liked pink things. Gabriella did not.

Once they'd settled in a booth, Roger began to manipulate the conversation towards his chosen subject; Gabriella's failed marriage. Gabriella had only spoken about this with her ex-husband or her recently deceased father, but Roger was relentless. She eventually gave him a rough overview, avoiding any mention of her infidelity, and Roger replied by insisting that her ex-husband was probably a 'queer'. Gabriella chose to ignore him.

'The thing is Gabby (Gabriella hated being called Gabby); I just really think you could do a lot more.' Roger blurted out after a large mouthful of gin and tonic.

'In what sense?'

'With this place. I think there's a lot more to be done.'

'Like what?' Gabriella asked through gritted teeth.

'I think we need an expansion. A capacity of fewer than three hundred guests just doesn't cut it anymore. Not if you want to compete with the chains anyway. That Hilton up the beach holds at least a thousand and I won't lie to you, the penthouse I'm staying in really is spectacular. If we're not careful places like that will steal our business.'

Gabriella hated the fact that Roger used the word 'we' almost as much as she hated his assumption that he could run this hotel any better than she or her father had.

'We've always believed it's better to treat fewer guests perfectly than to treat more guests adequately. We're not willing to compromise our quality to increase our quantity.'

'There are other things too.' Roger continued undeterred. 'The Suite Diamante, for example.'

'What about it?'

'It's Spanish.'

'I'm sorry.' Gabriella was close to losing her temper. She prayed this was all some twisted nightmare. A nightmare from which she would soon wake up.

'Suite Diamante. That's Spanish.'

'It translates to Diamond Suite. It's simple enough.'

'No, I know.' Roger had clearly forgotten which drink was his because he took a large sip from Gabriella's untouched glass. 'But we attract mostly English guests and that's our target audience for the foreseeable future. Spaniards aren't holidaying in Spain, are they?'

Roger didn't wait for an answer.

'It just seems strange to me.' He continued. 'That we're not catering to the British guests in every way possible. Trust me. I do this for a living, you know?' Roger smiled, expecting a laugh that never came.

'We're a Spanish hotel with Spanish roots. English people don't come abroad to pretend they're in England.' Gabriella willed herself to stay calm.

'I suppose that's true. Maybe I'm wrong.' Roger spoke with the conviction of a man who knows he isn't wrong. 'I still think you need to branch out a little though.'

Gabriella said nothing but her silence said plenty.

'You strike me as the sort of person who puts work before everything, but I can help you with that. Come out with me tonight.'

Gabriella was saved from launching a vicious, verbal attack by a young receptionist named Clara.

'I'm sorry to interrupt Miss Glover, but there's been an issue with a member of the kitchen staff. She's waiting for you outside your office.'

'Jesus.' Snapped Roger. 'Isn't there anybody else who can handle it?'

'It's fine.' Gabriella interjected. 'I'll handle it. Wait for me by reception.'

Clara hurried back to the reception desk.

Gabriella returned her attention to Roger. 'Sorry.'

'Don't be. I understand.' Roger's voice made it clear he did not understand. 'Next time though?'

'Of course.' Gabriella lied.

'Did I do OK?' Clara asked as Gabriella arrived beside her at the reception desk.

'You did sensationally. Like a young Meryl Streep.'

'Who?'

'It doesn't matter.' Gabriella wished, just once, a member of staff would laugh at one of her jokes. 'I appreciate it. Really.'

Gabriella didn't sense Roger watching her as she walked away. He loved watching her in those tight dresses. He'd think of her later that night as he made a prostitute bleed for the second time in twenty-four hours. He'd even call Gabriella's name as he climaxed inside the trembling young girl.

Gabriella hadn't actually expected to find a member of the kitchen staff waiting for her outside her office, which meant she jumped backwards when Tom stepped towards her. He rushed to apologise as Gabriella attempted to settle her racing heart.

'Shit! I'm sorry. I thought you saw me.'

'Don't be.' Gabriella managed a laugh. 'I guess that makes us even.'

'I suppose so.'

'What are you doing here?' Gabriella opened the door to her office and gestured for Tom to follow her inside. He did.

'I thought I should tell you what happened with Roger.' Tom explained as he sat opposite Gabriella's desk. She resumed her usual position behind it.

'You don't have to. I know it wasn't your fault.' Gabriella spoke matter-of-factly.

'I'm sorry. I just really didn't know what to do.'

'I would have done the same thing.' Gabriella sighed. 'That's a sad thing to say out loud.' Gabriella visibly deflated.

'Tonight seemed to go well.' Was Tom's feeble attempt to change the subject.

'I appreciate you helping out. Next time you need a day off or a late start or I don't know, water-park tickets, just let me know.' Gabriella smiled but it was empty and joyless.

If Tom felt this bad after being roped in just once, he hated imagining how that man must have made Gabriella feel over these last few weeks. He wanted to help her. It seemed Gabriella could sense it too because she leaned back in her chair and offered him an ice-cold conversation starter.

'Do you want a beer?' She asked, removing two bottles from a mini-fridge hidden beneath her desk.

Tom took a second before answering. If he were to drink today that would make it four days in a row. He liked to think that if Gabriella didn't seem so defeated, he would have said no, but truthfully he wanted the ice-cold bottle of San Miguel more than he wanted to see her smile.

'I'd love one.'

Gabriella opened both bottles and handed one to Tom. Tom reached out to grab the bottle and in doing so exposed the yellow all-inclusive wristband that he'd tucked up his sleeve. Gabriella eyed it and then met Tom's gaze.

'I suppose I don't owe you a favour anymore.'

Tom waited for more, for the tongue-lashing that was bound to arrive, but it never did. Gabriella sipped at her beer nonchalantly. Tom quickly tucked the wristband back up his sleeve and drank a large mouthful of his beer.

'What do you think of the hotel, honestly?' Gabriella asked without looking at Tom.

'It's the nicest hotel I've ever been to. By far.' Tom resisted the urge to finish his beer in another long gulp.

'And if I asked you what the Suite Diamante translates to in English?'

'The Diamond Suite.' Tom answered slowly as if expecting the question to be a trick.

'Congratulations. You're officially more intelligent than Roger Wyatt gives the English credit for.'

'There's something for the CV.'

Gabriella held out her bottle for Tom to tap his own against.

They spent the next two hours talking about a lot of things. About Gabriella's time in London, her brief, ongoing stint as manager of the hotel and the early days of the Scarlett Grove.

They talked about Tom too. About his life, his family, and his ambitions. By the time Tom left Gabriella's office, he'd enjoyed five bottles of San Miguel. Gabriella herself had only managed three.

As Tom climbed into bed, his tipsy mind drifted to thoughts of Joy. Why had she been in that car? How was she involved with Nathan? Why had she left him alone on the beach? These thoughts rattled relentlessly around his head as he stared at the ceiling and willed sleep to consume him. Despite the alcohol, it took a long time for Tom to fall asleep. A very long time indeed.

13

The Island of Palm Trees

Five beers were not enough to produce a hangover quite as pungent as the morning before, but nevertheless, Tom awoke with a head that buzzed like a phone vibrating on its weakest setting. Thankfully though, his work at the beach was pleasant. What's more, it seemed his creative adrenaline had carried over from yesterday. Tom didn't feel as though he was hitting the keys but instead merely watching as the words typed themselves. He didn't worry about character arc or structure, he simply wrote the story as it formed in his head.

In the world of his novel, Rose quickly comes to realise that she hasn't thought her spontaneous trip through. She spends her first day grappling with the gut-wrenching burden of finding a job and despite her best efforts, she ends the day without employment. With nowhere else to go, Rose settles for a hostel. There she meets Zach. He's a thin man with clammy palms and a groomed beard that runs along the length of his jaw. Zach barely introduces himself to Rose before offering her cocaine. Rose politely declines, but soon regrets the decision. With that comes only shame.

Tom was in the process of allowing Rose to finally fall asleep when a familiar voice broke his concentration. Tom stood slowly and ambled to the door, doing anything he could to delay an unpleasant conversation with an unpleasant human.

'Hello. Anybody home?' Richard sounded cheery today. For that at least, Tom was grateful.

Richard was wearing a blue Hawaiian shirt with yellow flowers and yellow swimming shorts with blue flowers. Most people would consider this overkill but clearly not Richard. He carried a weighty backpack that Tom guessed was filled with nothing but alcohol.

'Thought you were sleeping on the job then mate.'

'Sorry, I was just finishing up some work.' Tom hated himself for apologising to this man.

'No bother mate. Any chance I could grab a bed?'

Tom wished he could say no, but of course, he couldn't. 'Yep. The only ones left are all far back from the sea though.'

'Doesn't matter to me mate. As long as I don't have to sit with sand in my shorts, I'm happy.' Richard laughed. 'Ten euros enough to cover it?'

'With change.'

'Don't worry about that. You keep it.'

Tom couldn't decide if Richard was being cheery in an attempt to mask what Tom had seen yesterday, or if he was just genuinely upbeat today.

'Thank you.' Tom replied without a hint of gratitude.

Richard retrieved his wallet from the pocket of his jeans and in doing so gave Tom a glimpse of his freshly swollen knuckles. Tom was suddenly filled with anger. He needed to do something.

'It's just you today then?'

'What's that?' Richard asked a little defensively.

'You were here with a woman the other day, weren't you?'

'Oh yeah. She's the missus. Sarah. I'm Richard, by the way.' He stumbled through the sentence as if desperate to reach its conclusion.

'I'm Tom.' Tom reluctantly shook Richard's hand, which allowed him a better look at those ugly, purple bruises. 'Isn't she here today?'

'What's that?'

'Sarah. She didn't fancy the beach today?'

'She's got a dodgy tummy.' Richard lied effortlessly. 'We ate out last night and I don't think it agreed with her. Asian food, you know how it is.'

Tom nodded without making any attempt to hide his disbelief.

'So which bed's mine mate?' Richard asked, keen to escape a conversation that had lasted much longer than he intended.

'Follow me. I'll show you.'

Tom led the way and Richard followed closely behind as they passed through sun loungers supporting sleeping guests and excited children before arriving at a sun lounger at the far corner of the back row. Richard set his bag down and opened it up eagerly. It was filled with cans of cheap beer.

'Thanks a lot, mate.' Richard said as he unfurled onto the lounger and cracked one of his beers open.

Tom knew he should leave. Leave without saying the words that were building within him. But he couldn't.

'Before I go, I do just have to make you aware of something.'

'What's that then?'

'There were some complaints about your behaviour last time you were here.'

'What?' Richard's entire body tensed.

'There were complaints regarding your language in front of children and another regarding an incident of violence. I just wanted to bring these to your attention because staff are currently investigating both incidents.' Tom was surprised at how flawlessly he'd lied, but he was proud of himself nonetheless.

Richard said nothing. He glared at Tom with an equal mix of fury and disbelief.

'Is that OK?' Tom asked nervously. Richard's fist was clenched awfully tightly around the can he was holding.

'If you wouldn't mind fucking off, I'd like to enjoy the beach now mate.'

Tom left without another word, smiling as he went.

* * *

The rest of Tom's week flew by in a moment. He worked, ate, slept and wrote, although his productivity slowed considerably. After breaking his three-day drinking rule in Gabriella's office, Tom decided there was no sense in seeking sobriety for the rest of the week. He didn't go overboard with his drinking, he just had enough. Enough to make the food in the Dining Hall taste better. Enough to help him sleep at night. Enough to stop him thinking about Joy and why she hadn't made any attempt to get back in touch with him yet.

Richard never returned to the beach and for that at least Tom was grateful. Gabriella asked Tom if he'd be willing to

107

work the weekend shift and he agreed. He'd barely written twenty pages since his run-in with Richard, but at least another two shifts would give him an excuse to try again.

Tom tried, really he did, but by the end of his shift on Sunday he'd only written an extra eight pages and he was beginning to lose track of where his novel was heading. It suddenly felt as though Rose was a stranger. A stranger he would never come to know. By the time the sun began its slow descent on Sunday evening, Tom was certain he'd never see Joy again. He didn't know how and he didn't know when, but at some point in the night they'd spent together, he'd ruined things and he doubted he'd ever get a chance to put it right again.

With these thoughts overwhelming him (and wanting to waste some time before his nightly visit to the Lobby Bar), Tom headed to the laundry room. With his dirty washing spinning, Tom sat down with a dog-eared copy of *Gerald's Game*, ready to search from cover to cover for hidden inspiration. Not that he had the time to do any searching. Before he'd even opened his book, he was interrupted by a voice he hadn't heard since she'd whispered goodnight in the beach hut.

'Well, this is awkward.'

Joy was right. It was awkward.

They didn't say much to one another as Joy loaded a handful of clothes (the majority of which had been drawn on) into an empty machine. They'd exchanged hello's but beyond that, the conversation had fallen flat. Joy was wearing a white dress that seemed to be just an oversized shirt. The doodling on this outfit seemed confined to the large wooden buttons that fastened the shirt/dress. Joy had transformed each button into a face, similar to those annoying little emojis used on texts. There were seven buttons and six of them bore sad expressions. Tom tried not to read into this, but it seemed important, almost as important as the lone smiling face beaming out at the world as if it were the only day of sunshine in a month of rain.

With her laundry loaded and the machine spinning, Joy took a seat beside Tom. She was careful to leave a considerable chunk of space between the two of them, as if Tom might leap over and attack her, demanding to know why she left that morning.

'Is that any good?' Joy asked, breaking the awkward silence that had engulfed the laundry room.

Tom was so relieved that the responsibility of breaking the silence hadn't fallen on his shoulders that he almost forgot to reply. 'What's that, sorry?'

Joy pointed to the book resting on Tom's lap. 'I watched the film first and loved it so I didn't want to risk reading the book, you know, just in case it didn't live up to the film and tainted it for me.'

'Oh. I did it the other way round. I read this and loved it and then very sceptically watched the film and it scared me so much that I ended up sleeping with the light on. Which I realise now is an incredibly embarrassing thing to admit.'

'I'll have to give it a read then.' Joy replied lightly.

The uncomfortable silence returned with a vengeance. Tom decided he needed to ask the question that had been rattling around his brain ever since he woke up alone on the beach.

'So um, how come you left the other day?' He asked, trying

and failing to sound casual.

Joy looked around the laundry room as if the answer to the question might be printed on one of the cream walls. 'I honestly don't know.'

'I thought maybe I'd done something wrong.'

'No. No, believe me, you didn't.' Joy's eyes, usually so full of life, dropped down to the floor. 'I just, I didn't feel great. I didn't wanna burden you with that.'

That was the first time Tom heard Joy tell a lie. It unsettled him.

'Are you OK?' He asked tentatively.

Joy managed to look up from the floor to nod.

'You sure?'

'How could anyone not be OK in a place like this?'

Tom looked around the dingy room in which they sat. 'The laundry room?'

'No, you muppet.' Joy laughed and Tom's spirits lifted immeasurably. 'I mean here. The Scarlett Grove. Roquetas De Mar. The beach. The sea. The palm trees. The whole shabang.'

'Are there palm trees here?'

'Oh, you haven't seen them?'

'I can't say I have.'

'Trust me. It's an island of palm trees.' Joy was smiling now.

The room fell silent again for a moment, but it was no longer awkward. Joy stared at Tom intently, as if she were trying to visually determine the type of person he was.

'I can't work you out.'

'Is that a good or a bad thing?' Tom asked nervously.

'That depends.'

'On what?'

'Who you turn out to be.'

Tom didn't want to say what he was about to say, but there was still a lot of time left on his washing machine and any conversation was better than sitting in silence.

'I suppose it'd probably help if I explained what happened outside the hotel the other day.'

Joy's eyes flashed with intrigue. 'I must admit I was surprised to see you there.'

'I reckon I could say the same thing about you.' Tom replied with a rare twinkle of confidence.

'Go on then. What happened?'

'Well, it sounds like a lie.'

'Never a great start to a sentence.' Joy teased.

'I guess it's safe to assume you've heard of Roger Wyatt, considering we spent the other night in a restaurant owned by his father?'

'Shaved head. Rich. Loves himself more than anybody else ever could.'

'That's him.' Tom chuckled at the accuracy of Joy's description. 'Well he was here for a fancy dinner and he called me over and…'

Joy listened intently as Tom explained the unfortunate chain of events that led to him accidentally becoming the middleman in Roger Wyatt's drug deal. When he was finished Joy took a couple of seconds to soak in the details.

'That makes sense.' She finally replied, her voice flat.

'What do you mean?'

'I didn't understand why Nathan spoke to you himself. He wouldn't normally do that.'

'Why did he?'

'He wasn't really speaking to you, was he? He was speaking

to Roger.'

Tom had never given Nathan's introduction a second thought, but the way Joy explained it made perfect sense. She suddenly seemed lost in her head once again.

'Do you know him then? Nathan?' Tom asked, dreading the answer.

'Not really. No.'

Tom shot Joy a look of pure disbelief.

'I knew him in school.' She added reluctantly.

'Is he the reason you came out here?'

'No.' Joy almost whispered before seeming to regain her voice. 'Definitely not.'

The silence returned. It wasn't awkward so much as it was sad. Or at least Joy was sad. She was staring down at her feet whilst fiddling with one of the buttons on her shirt (the only one with a happy face drawn on it).

'I'm sorry about leaving the other morning. I genuinely had a nice time.' Joy added, still twiddling with the button.

'So did I.'

'Do you have any plans for tomorrow?' She asked softly.

'Work. Another fun day at the beach hut.'

'Do you think you could get somebody to cover for you?'

'Probably.' Excitement swelled within Tom. 'How come?'

'I was hoping that maybe we could do something. But like a proper day of it this time instead of just a meal.'

'Definitely.' Tom took a second to compose himself. 'Yeah. I'd love that.'

They spent the rest of their time in the laundry room talking about general nonsense and nothingness, the way two young people first exploring feelings for each other often do. Tom showed Joy his staff photo and Joy laughed at the sheer awkwardness of it. They planned to meet by the pool at midday and take it from there. Tom was ecstatic at the prospect of spending an entire day with Joy but still, something was gnawing away at him. He couldn't shake the image of Joy picking at her clothing as they talked about Nathan. He'd never seen anybody look like that before. Sadness had never looked so beautiful.

Tom's visit to Gabriella's office was surprisingly short. She saw no problem in Tom taking tomorrow for himself, despite the fact he was giving her less than twelve hours' notice. They made polite conversation for a couple of minutes before Tom uttered his thanks and left Gabriella's office with a spring in his step and tomorrow on his mind.

* * *

Sarah Tyler had not left her room on the second floor of the Scarlett Grove in several days now. She'd been asleep when Richard first returned to their room after their altercation at the beach, sleeping rather soundly until she felt his hands tighten around her neck. She awoke with a gasp and Richard released his grip immediately. He quickly took three steps away from her, as if only distance could prevent him from laying his hands on her once more.

'What happened today?' He asked calmly, although Sarah could see through his facade to the fury that lay beneath.

'You were out of order.' She replied, matching Richard's intensity.

'Fuck me.' Richard shouted. Now the facade was gone. 'We

have to be able to talk about him, Sarah.'

'Not you.' Sarah whispered.

'What?'

Sarah said nothing.

'What did you say?' Richard's hands were balled into fists and the veins in his neck stood to attention.

'Not you. You can't talk about him.'

Rage exploded from Richard. He punched the door of the wardrobe with all his might. Wood shards flew everywhere as the bottom half of the wardrobe door exploded.

'Fuck.' He screamed. Sarah did not doubt that the people in the surrounding rooms had heard him. Whoever was working on the reception desk tonight was bound to start receiving some angry calls about the crazy people in room fifty-seven.

'He was my son too, Sarah.' Richard whispered.

'And that meant about as much to you as me being your wife.'

'You have no idea what he meant to me.'

'He was scared of you Richard.' Sarah spat the words as if they left a bad taste in her mouth.

'Shut the fuck up.' Richard commanded through gritted teeth.

Sarah said nothing.

'He wasn't.' Richard said, seemingly to himself.

Sarah said nothing. Richard somehow took her silence as an act of defiance. He stormed towards her with his fists clenched, stopping only an inch from her face. Sarah got to her feet too. Her husband had raised his fists to her enough times for her to know it was best to stand her ground. Richard snatched at Sarah's wrist and pulled her towards him. Sarah looked deep into Richard's eyes and saw nothing of the man she'd married. She saw only hatred.

'He was not scared of me!'

'He was. You know he was. And what's worse is you liked it.' Sarah shouted, although truthfully the liberation of finally speaking her truth filled her with a sick form of pleasure.

Sarah barely saw the punch coming. Even in his current state of intoxication Richard still possessed frightening speed. She may not have seen it, but she certainly felt it. A rocket of pain exploded against her temple and all the colour drained from her world. She didn't feel her knees collapse or her head strike the floor as her body betrayed her. As everything dissolved into blackness, she heard Richard utter five words, his voice choked with tears.

'He wasn't scared of me.'

By the time Sarah came around Richard was long gone. She had no idea how long she'd been unconscious or if there'd been any repercussions from their screaming match. She guessed not, because if anybody had come to check on them, she surely would have woken in a hospital bed as opposed to the cold, hard floor of her hotel room.

There were two packets on the bedside table. One of paracetamol and another of ibuprofen. Richard left these presents when he woke up sober and saw the damage he'd caused. Maybe it was his way of apologising. If it was, Sarah didn't accept.

She tried to distract herself from the pain by looking through the window. She'd always enjoyed watching people go about their daily lives, although she was usually in a better state of mind when she did so. She saw little of interest, although she did the young lad from the beach hut meet a rather sketchy looking man. She was shocked, the young lad didn't look the type. Then again, Richard hadn't looked like the type of man who'd one day leave her unconscious on the floor. Clearly, she wasn't the best judge of character.

When she finally accepted the pain wouldn't subside, Sarah took two pills from each packet and washed them down with as much water as she could manage. With nothing else to do and her head still throbbing, Sarah climbed back into bed and disappeared into oblivion once more. If she was lucky, maybe she wouldn't wake up at all.

Richard spent the week in a drunken blur. One drink became another and one bar became another and at some point, he'd managed to forget what he'd done to Sarah. He'd managed to forget what she'd said to him, the lie she'd told about Marcus. His son had loved him. He'd loved him like every son loves their father and that was all that mattered.

He and Sarah hadn't spoken. The truth is they'd barely seen each other. They shared a bed at night but there was a lot more than just distance between them. Days had passed but the spiteful, dirty bruise on Sarah's face was more pronounced than ever. Her hair covered a chunk of it but the purple and red stain on her forehead couldn't be hidden entirely. Every time Richard saw it, he was reminded of how much he despised himself. And as he sat at a beer-soaked table in The Clover on Sunday evening, he began to cry.

Nobody seemed to notice the man crying into his beer. If they did, they certainly didn't care.

* * *

Roger didn't remember what he'd said on the phone. He didn't even remember who he'd spoken to. But whoever it was had helped. They'd told him everything would be OK, and right then that was the only thing he needed to hear. Tears were rushing down his face and blood was gushing from his nose. Things like this weren't supposed to happen to men like him. It wasn't fair. It wasn't his fault.

He didn't remember her name. He'd given her a new name. The moment she stepped into his penthouse she had become Gabriella Glover. It wasn't his fault. None of it was. It was going to be OK. The person on the phone had told him it would. He just needed to remember that.

His magic powder seemed like the obvious solution. He lined it up, snorted it and collapsed onto the bed, entering a world without screaming whores, judgemental fathers and uptight hotel managers.

It wasn't his fault. Everything was going to be OK.

14

A Blue Biro and a Spot by the Pool

The pool area was swamped with guests when Tom arrived at just after ten in the morning. Laughing children lathered in thick layers of sun cream splashed each other in the children's pool whilst their parents read bestselling novels they'd purchased at the airport. The swimming pool was split into two huge semi-circles which were separated by a walkway on which the pool bar and snack house were built. The semi-circle closest to the hotel was reserved exclusively for adults, whereas the semi-circle closest to the beach was exclusively for families, boasting a pirate-themed waterslide that was constantly occupied by giggling children.

Tom wandered around awkwardly before miraculously spotting two vacant sun loungers on the adults-only side of the pool, just a short walk from the pool bar. Tom settled in and made himself comfortable, wondering all the while if Joy would even show up.

Tom's worrying ceased just two hours later. He spotted Joy the second she stepped out of the hotel. She was wearing a thin white sarong, through which Tom could see a navy-blue bikini. He wasn't the only person to notice her either. It seemed that wherever Joy went at least three pairs of eyes followed her. Tom wondered if she noticed the lingering eyes or if she was immune to it by now. She strolled between the loungers, glancing from left to right, trying to catch sight of him.

Finally, she did.

Tom thanked the gangly man working at the pool bar and headed back to Joy with a glass of red Mirto in each hand. Joy was eager to continue their quest to sample every obscure drink served at the hotel, and Tom certainly wasn't going to object. Today was their first official date, and Tom would taste every disgusting liquid concoction beneath the sun if it meant the date went well.

Joy smiled when he arrived back at her side. 'What are we starting with then?' She asked as Tom handed her a glass.

'Red Mirto.' Tom replied as he laid down on the lounger beside Joy. 'It's made from a magical berry or something.'

'Sounds exciting.' Joy took a sip and smiled. 'I tell you what, it's better than the port.'

She was right. It was better than the port.

They talked about everything and nothing. Tom told Joy about the food in the Dining Hall (Joy enjoyed reminding Tom that she'd given him the shiny yellow wristband that enabled his feasts), and some of the more amusing moments from his time working in the beach hut (Joy laughed heartily when she heard about the old man who, after being knocked down by a large wave, climbed back to his feet without realising his trunks had floated away). After that things went silent. It wasn't awkward, not at all. It was the familiar silence of two people enjoying their time together.

Time passed and the sun rose. They relaxed on their loungers, enjoyed the sun and sampled a glass of Suze each. Things had been quiet for a while when Joy asked Tom a question that piqued his excitement.

'If I ask you a question, do you promise to answer it honestly?' From the look on her face, Tom knew that whatever Joy wanted to ask was important.

'Go on then.'

'The other day when we left the tapas place and you thought the waiter was chasing us, how did that make you feel?'

'At first, I hated it. Honestly, I did. I felt terrible.'

'And then?' Joy asked although Tom felt sure she already knew the answer.

'Something changed. I dunno how to explain it without it sounding pathetic but I um, I felt free. Like if I could do that then what couldn't I do? And the day after was probably my most productive day of writing ever, so I suppose that's something.'

Joy smiled. Perhaps his honest answer had been exactly what she'd wanted to hear.

'Anyway, I suppose a more pressing question is when exactly I get to read the novel that I helped to inspire? She asked cheerfully.

'Wow, wow, wow. No chance.' Tom spoke with mock offence. 'It's my turn to ask a question now.'

'Unfortunately, that does seem fair.'

'When did you first do it? Leave a restaurant without paying or something like that?'

'Pretty young. Probably like seven or eight. It's just

something we've always done.'

'Who's we?' Tom pressed.

'Nope. It's my turn again. Let me think.' Joy took another sip of her Suze as she did so. 'I'll save my other novel-related questions for later. Who was your first kiss?'

'A random blonde girl at a party. I think she'd been sick because her breath was awful. All in all, it was a terrible experience.'

'That does sound terrible.' Joy replied with a giggle.

'So, who's we?' Tom asked tenderly.

Joy seemed to tighten up. The smile disappeared from her face and she looked up at the sky, taking care to avoid Tom's gaze. 'Me and my Dad... We've never been rich or anything and um, we just did what we had to do. We moved around a lot when I was younger. We'd stay in little run-down houses or on caravan parks.'

'Really?' Tom asked, attempting to keep his voice neutral.

'Yeah. I mean we weren't like Brad Pitt from Snatch or anything, we just couldn't afford a nice place and we never really found anywhere that felt like it could be a home.'

'You must have seen a lot of England then?' Tom asked, careful not to seem as though he was prying.

'Most of it.' Joy stared into her glass as if pictures of all the places she'd seen were hidden in there. 'Not a lot of it's worth seeing. I'm not sure anywhere is.'

'Not even the island of palm trees?'

'It's not bad, I'll give you that.' Joy cracked a smile, but it didn't fool Tom. 'Everywhere has cracks though.'

'Cracks?'

'The people usually.' Joy replied without a hint of emotion.

Tom wanted to respond. He wanted to ask who or what

had made her think like this. He wanted to know the truth of her past. But more than anything he wanted to see her smile again. Unfortunately, he couldn't think of a single thing to say. So he merely lay back and allowed silence to engulf them both.

Tom didn't pay much attention to his choice of drink at the bar. He was distracted by something resting on an empty table in the shaded area of the bar. It was a blue Biro pen, and suddenly Tom knew how to turn the day around.

'Should I be excited?' Joy asked as she took the glass from Tom.

'You certainly should. It's an amaretto and coke.'

'You cheat. We're supposed to be trying new things.'

'We are. It's just not the drink.' Tom made himself comfortable and took a sip, enjoying the only pleasant drink he'd tasted today.

'I'm intrigued.' Joy replied with a flicker of a smile.

Tom took the Biro from his pocket and held it up proudly.

'A pen?' Joy asked, spectacularly unimpressed.

Tom held out the bottom corner of his white T-shirt to Joy.

'You know what to do.'

She did.

Thirty minutes later Joy was no longer the only person sitting by the pool of the Scarlett Grove with doodles on her clothing. She had drawn a palm tree, a knife and a large glass of what Tom assumed to be Xabi's strawberry daiquiris. She then instructed Tom to draw three things of his own. Tom's drawings took significantly longer and were significantly worse, but he eventually produced a fairly-presentable pencil and bottle in addition to a horrifically lopsided sketch of the beach hut. Joy stared at the finished products with sheer delight.

'Very impressive.' The fire within her eyes was roaring once again. 'What do they mean?'

'Oh, I dunno. I did it without thinking.' This was the first lie Tom told Joy. He knew what each of the drawings meant to him and his life, they were all rather self-explanatory. The pencil represented his lifelong goal of becoming a successful author. The bottle represented his three-day alcohol rule, a rule that Joy was (thankfully) not yet aware of, and the beach hut represented the beach hut (obviously).

Joy smiled at Tom as if to say she knew he was lying, but she was happy not to press him further.

'What do yours mean?' Tom asked.

Joy flashed her eyes widely, implying she wouldn't be answering a question that he himself had ducked out of.

'I have to say, the drawing of the palm tree is quite spectacular.' Tom said, a hint of flattery in his voice.

'It's my pride and joy.'

Tom loved how effortless his conversations with Joy were becoming. The questions he asked and the answers she gave fit together like jigsaw pieces.

'What do you reckon his pride and joy is?' Joy gestured across the pool to a young boy with dyed blonde hair. He was lay on his lounger without a care in the world, wearing a pair of Armani swim shorts, Rayban sunglasses and Beats earphones. An Apple Watch was strapped to his wrist and a pair of Supreme flip flops rested beneath his sun lounger beside a Nintendo Switch with a cracked screen. 'He's got all that and we've got a pen.'

Tom looked at the young lad, once again astounded by how easy some people had it. He thought of Roger Wyatt, a man so privileged he hired others to collect his drugs. But then again, this young boy, who couldn't possibly be older than thirteen, was all alone. His parents were nowhere to be seen. Maybe his life wasn't that easy after all.

'It's crazy, isn't it?' Joy remarked.

'I bet we're having a better time though.'

'Well yeah, that's a given. But more the fact that I haven't seen his parents or whoever he's here with once since I got here. It's as if they think arming him with designer clothes and expensive shit is enough. Who needs parents when you have an Apple Watch?'

'It's sad.' Tom mused.

'It's inevitable.' Joy replied icily.

'Do you think he'd be happier without it all?'

'Maybe. I doubt he'd notice if half of it went missing.'

Tom couldn't decide what to say so he said nothing. He was about to change the subject, maybe ask if Joy wanted another drink or a quick dip in the pool when Joy snapped free of her trance.

'We should test it.'

'Test what?' Tom asked, suddenly anxious.

'Let's see if he notices or not.' She said excitedly.

'You want to take all his stuff?' Tom asked sceptically, fast realising that today was not going to be as peaceful as he'd hoped.

'Not all of it. Just one thing, just to see if he notices. If he does, we'll take it back and tell him we found it lying around somewhere.' Joy spoke with absolute certainty. She had this all planned out.

'What if somebody notices you take it?' Tom asked sheepishly.

'I'm not going to take it. You are.'

'No. No, I can't.' Tom found himself suddenly sweating.

'Why not?'

'It's stealing for one thing.'

'It won't even be the first time you've stolen something this week. Plus, if he notices we're going to take it back.' Joy's voice was firm and unwavering.

Maybe it was all the alcohol in Tom's bloodstream or maybe it was the high of spending an entire day in Joy's company, but he was beginning to think her plan made sense.

'What if somebody sees me?' He asked, putting up one last line of defence.

'Nobodies looking at you. They're all sleeping or reading. Trust me, you'll be fine.'

Tom was astounded by Joy's power of persuasion. He felt certain that, had she been born in the 1800s, she would have been accused of witchcraft and burnt at the stake.

'How do I do this then?' Tom asked, finally succumbing to the witch's powers.

The answer to Tom's question had been much simpler than he expected.

They waited for the blonde lad to leave his lounger. It didn't take long. He gathered up his phone, slipped his feet into his two-hundred-and-fifty-pound flip flops and headed to the beach. Maybe his parents had been down there all along, although it seemed an awfully long distance to be left between a parent and their child, especially for hours at a time. Tom waited for five minutes before beginning his rescue mission.

He passed a woman with her nose buried in a thick novel and a middle-aged man who'd fallen asleep with a beer in his hand, blissfully unaware that his stomach was turning an alarming shade of red. Tom's heartbeat steadily increased as he approached his destination. The Switch was there, hidden away like a pile of gold at the end of a rainbow, waiting to be collected. He waited until he was beside the lounger and intentionally flicked his flip flop beneath it. As he bent down to retrieve it, Tom grabbed the Switch and stashed it beneath his T-shirt. With a final look to make sure nobody was watching, Tom headed back. Joy kissed him upon his return, and for a reward like that, Tom would steal anything she asked him to.

The boy with the dyed blonde hair left his lounger for the final time almost three hours later. Tom's heart stopped as the lad crouched under the lounger, reaching out for his flip flops and the Switch console he'd left down there just hours earlier. He found both of his flip flops and stretched back to his feet, never once wondering about the missing games console. He didn't remember his Adidas towel either. He simply disappeared into the hotel without looking back. Joy was right again. Tom couldn't believe it.

With the latest Nintendo console in their possession, Tom and Joy decided to return to the safety of their rooms to see what all the fuss was about. Joy insisted her room was a mess and therefore it wasn't fit for the pleasures of Mario Kart. Tom argued that her room would almost certainly be nicer than the one he'd been given, but Joy persisted and Tom relented pretty quickly. It certainly wasn't a problem that Joy wanted to visit his room, in fact, he'd been hoping for it.

They laughed long into the night. A night spent drinking, chatting and throwing red shells at one another. They ordered room service and drank wine, both agreeing the food here was nothing compared to the twenty-four dishes they'd tasted at Platos Y Bebidos. When nightfall arrived they were both good and drunk. As it turned out, the fire in Joy's eyes was only amplified with alcohol.

They were well into their second bottle of wine, Joy's head resting on Tom's shoulder, when Tom suddenly blurted out the question he'd wanted to ask since Joy sat down beside him at the pool.

'Joy.' He whispered.

'Yes.' She replied in a similarly hushed tone.

'Can I kiss you?' Tom's heart thudded against his ribcage with the jarring speed of a jackhammer as he waited for a response.

'Just once.' Joy whispered as she turned to face him.

He kissed her quickly, pressing his lips against hers firmly and inviting her tongue to tease his top lip. He kept his hands to himself, keen to avoid a repeat of what happened at the beach hut.

When the moment was finished and their lips parted, Joy stared deep into Tom's eyes. Tom got the feeling she was torn, fighting an internal battle from deep within.

'Can I stay here tonight?' Joy asked quietly.

'Of course.'

'Just sleep though. Nothing else.'

'Yeah. That's fine Joy.' Tom said, and it was.

He didn't dream that night. He didn't need to.

15

A Midnight Phonecall

As Tom was sleeping soundly beside a girl who doodled on her clothes, Gabriella Glover was sat in her office with a dry martini, a lit cigarette and a pounding headache. She hadn't slept in the last twenty-four hours and it seemed impossible that she would fall asleep in the next twenty-four either. She'd tried to sleep. Willed it upon herself even, but there was just too much on her mind. Awful thoughts. Dark thoughts. Gabriella would give anything to escape them, to close her eyes and succumb to the blackness. Nothing could hurt her in there.

Gabriella had been alone in her office when her phone vibrated on the table. She'd just finished drafting an Email to send to every member of staff. It was an unpleasant Email, informing the staff that following the sale of the hotel she could no longer guarantee their job security. She signed off by thanking them all for their loyal service. It had taken her well over two hours to write just seventeen lines, during which time she concluded there was no good way to tell somebody they might be made redundant. It was almost three in the morning by the time she finished the draft and her bed beckoned her. She loaded up one quick game of solitaire before heading to her room (she liked to solve at least one game every day to keep herself sharp), and only managed three moves before her phone started vibrating.

She heard his cries first. Roger was sobbing with all the devastation of a man who has just endured the single most painful experience of his life. Gabriella said nothing. For what seemed an eternity she listened in silence, far too afraid to speak. After waiting as long as she could, Gabriella finally plucked up the courage to break the silence.

'Roger.' She whispered, the way a teacher might attempt to comfort a troubled child. 'Is everything OK?'

Roger's breathing tightened as if he'd been unaware anybody was sharing the line with him.

'Gabriella.' Roger continued to sob as he spoke. 'I didn't mean to do it. I could never.'

His voice trailed off. Gabriella assumed Roger was under the influence of whatever he'd made Tom fetch for him the other night. Maybe this was just a hallucination. Clearly, Roger was higher than the Eiffel Tower and his brain was melting because of the substance he'd abused it with. Everything happening to him was happening solely inside his mind. Gabriella could hang up and tomorrow he wouldn't remember a thing. But she couldn't. She couldn't end the call because she didn't believe it was a hallucination. She believed something truly terrible had happened and she believed Roger Wyatt was solely responsible for it.

'It's OK Roger. Tell me what happened. I'll help you fix it.'

'Can't.' Roger was slurring his words, his breathing rapid and wheezy. 'Can't fix it.'

'Why not? What's happened?' Gabriella asked, dreading the answer.

Nothing but tears.

'Roger?'

His tears began to slow. His breathing too.

'Roger, tell me what's happened?' Gabriella's voice was firmer now.

The crying finally stopped. Now there was only silence. Gabriella immediately missed the tears.

'Roger?' Gabriella pressed, ready to hang up if he didn't reply this time.

But Roger did reply, and in just three words he ruined Gabriella's life.

'She's dead anyway.'

Before Gabriella could reply, the line clicked dead.

Logic told Gabriella to push the awful conversation to the darkest corner of her mind, a corner so difficult to reach she would never again find it. It was possible, she knew that for sure. She'd done it often. The darkest corners of Gabriella's mind were overflowing with the most abhorrent moments from her life. Moments like the time she'd had her stomach pumped after her twenty-first birthday. Moments like the time her husband had caught her in the arms of another man. Moments she'd locked away forever. Her conversation with Roger was different though. This time somebody's life was at risk. Or if Roger's final remark was true, somebody's life had already been taken.

Having spent every second since the line clicked dead thinking of nothing but the call, Gabriella decided to take some positive steps to set her mind at ease. She opened

Google and began scouring through every local news outlet she could find. She didn't search for anything specifically; she still wasn't entirely sure what she should be searching for, but she felt sure she'd know it if she saw it. She found herself incapable of typing the words racing through her head. Words like assault. Words like rape. Words like murder. That would make it real and more than anything, Gabriella didn't want this to be real.

As Gabriella scrolled through the articles she was struck by a sudden twang of shame. Something truly abhorrent had likely happened last night, a person was hurt or even worse, but all she could think about was the devastating impact it would have on the Scarlett Grove if the man tasked with completing the Wyatt Foundation's acquisition of the hotel was discovered to be a murderer.

On that thought, Gabriella refreshed the site and continued to scroll.

In one of Gabriella's many hypothetical scenarios for the night of Roger's call, she guessed that he'd hit the town with a group of friends. She was wrong about this. Roger was alone. He had no friends in Roquetas De Mar. Like every night since he'd arrived here, he planned to make friends during the night. Single serving friends. Friends who wandered over after catching a glimpse of the flashy man at the bar ordering thousand-euro bottles of champagne.

Roger attracted six new friends that evening, all of whom were English and on holiday. There were three lads, all of whom were thin and intimidated by the successful man with a wallet worth more than their cars. Roger didn't bother learning their names. There were also three girls, all dressed flawlessly and desperate to impress the man who could give them the affluent lives they'd always dreamed of. Roger learned all of their names. There was Amber (who was, in Roger's opinion, the ugliest of the three and therefore his least favourite), Dani (who was, in Roger's opinion, fairly attractive and therefore his second favourite) and finally, there was Rosie (who was, in Roger's opinion, the best looking and therefore he showered her with attention and cocktails).

Roger, the three uncomfortable lads, Amber, Dani and Rosie spent the night exploring the most expensive and exclusive bars and clubs that Roquetas De Mar had to offer. At some point Roger managed to ditch the lingering army of cock-blockers, meaning he was free to enjoy the rest of the night as he wanted to, surrounded by women.

Much to Roger's relief, the girls shared his love of the magic white powder that made him feel invincible, and after a quick visit from Nathan, who had been all too pleased to finally meet Roger Wyatt in the flesh, Roger was able to scratch the itch that had been bothering him all night. He and the girls continued to drink excessively and dance ridiculously and snort discreetly and as midnight arrived, Roger was beginning to think all three ladies might return to his penthouse with him.

His spirits crashed and exploded in a ball of red-hot fire about twenty minutes later. He and the girls were sitting in a quiet corner of whichever club they happened to be in at that time, with Roger pretending to listen as they droned on about things he would never care about. He was about to suggest his spontaneous idea, carrying on the party back at his penthouse, when he heard Rosie mention her upcoming wedding. After further questioning, questioning so aggressive that the girls became visibly uncomfortable, it was revealed that all three girls were in serious, committed relationships. Even Amber, the ugly, long-nosed cunt.

Roger was flooded with rage. How could they lie to him? How could they betray him like this? After all the money he'd thrown at them, all the shitty jokes he'd laughed at. Rosie hadn't objected as he'd gently grazed his hand against her leg. Dani hadn't objected as he'd pressed his crotch against her on the dance floor. Amber hadn't objected as he'd spent the night ignoring her and her mayonnaise jar of a body.

At this point in the evening, Roger's memory became blurry. He remembered kicking the table and smashing the cocktails. He remembered one of the girls, probably the lard arse, screaming and calling him a psycho. He remembered smiling as a large man with a bald head asked him to leave the club. He remembered how the man swiftly changed his mind when Roger flashed a wad of euros in his direction. He remembered laughing so hard that his stomach ached as he watched the very same large, bald man swiftly escort Rosie, Amber and Dani out of the club.

He didn't remember much after that. He emptied the bag of magic powder he'd bought just three hours earlier in the taxi back to his hotel. He was angry and horny and frustrated. He wanted something, something he could treat the way he wanted to treat the girls who'd betrayed him. He remembered kissing somebody and wrapping his hands around her throat.

From that point on Roger saw only blackness.

Roger woke almost twenty hours later to find himself sharing the bed with a woman who'd been dead for hours. There was blood on the pillow and a little on the sleeve of his shirt. At the mere sight of the crimson stain, everything Roger had put into his body yesterday came flooding out. He barely made it to the toilet before a slew of purple liquid exploded from his mouth and nose.

Sanity slowly returned to Roger. He didn't check the time; he didn't need to. The world outside his window was still dark, dark and quiet, and that was good. If he was going to get himself out of this, he needed to act quickly. He needed to move, he needed to move her and then he thought of her face that was drained of colour and her eyes that were black and frozen and he vomited again.

He was still vomiting when he heard the first knock at the door. He had no idea who would visit him at this time. Maybe he'd ordered another girl, in which case he could just send her away. Maybe he'd ordered more drinks from room service. Maybe he'd ordered more coke. He hoped so. His magic powder was exactly what he needed right now. It would help him think straight. Just one bump would show him the way out of this hole.

There was a second knock at the door. Roger had been so lost in his head that he'd completely forgotten somebody was waiting for him. Moving slowly, careful to make as little noise as possible, he crept towards the door and peered through the peephole. Waiting outside was a man who Roger had first been introduced to just twenty hours earlier. A man keen to impress one of the richest men to ever visit Roquetas De Mar. A man who could give Roger the magic powder that he desperately needed. Roger just had to play his cards right. He took three deep breaths and opened the door a crack, taking care to keep his blood-stained sleeve well out of sight.

Nathan didn't wait for an invitation. He barged in, sending

Roger stumbling backwards.

'No, wait.' Roger cried desperately as Nathan paced into the room and quickly took in his surroundings. 'I… I can explain.' He whispered perilously.

'You rang me.' Nathan explained calmly. 'Shut the fucking door.'

Roger did as instructed. He vaguely remembered making a call, but he could have sworn it had been hours ago.

'What did I say?' Roger whispered.

'Everything. But that's OK. I'm going to fix it. Do you understand?'

Roger nodded. At that moment he began to believe that things might just turn out OK. Five miles away in the Scarlett Grove, Gabriella Glover was trying to convince herself of the very same thing.

16

A Busy Day in the Manager's Office

Gentle rays of sunlight tiptoed into Tom's room, illuminating Joy's face in such a way that Tom couldn't help but stare. If it were up to him, he'd spent the entire day lying here beside her. Unfortunately, staying in bed wasn't an option. Not if he wanted to continue living in Spain without paying for his accommodation anyway. His shift was due to start in half an hour and, even though his relationship with Gabriella had improved steadily after its disastrous start, he still wasn't brave enough to risk upsetting his manager. Ironically, had Tom decided to spend the day in bed with Joy, Gabriella wouldn't have cared. In fact, she wouldn't even have noticed. Right then Gabriella had more to worry about than ever before. The beach hut never once crossed her mind.

Tom pulled on a clean pair of shorts and a navy T-shirt and decided to wake Joy. It seemed the polite thing to do, he didn't want her to worry when she woke up alone. He knelt on the bed and nudged her gently.

'Joy. Are you awake?' He whispered.

'I am now.' She replied without opening her eyes.

'I'm off to work. Feel free to, I dunno, use the shower or borrow clothes or anything like that.'

'If you've woken me up just to tell me that you're leaving I'm going to be so pissed off.' Joy said lightly, but her eyes remained closed and Tom guessed there was probably some truth to her words.

'What sort of psychopath would do that?' He teased.

'Get to the beach. There's gonna be chaos if you're not there on time.' Joy's eyes remained closed, but she smiled all the same.

Tom's day at the beach was largely without incident. There was no sign of Richard or Sarah. Come to think of it he hadn't seen Sarah since his first shift. He hadn't thought of her much this week, not since his uncomfortable run-in with Richard anyway, but today he thought of her a lot. He felt guilty that he hadn't passed on what he'd seen to Gabriella or anybody with the power to make a real difference. He decided to give it one more day. If another day passed without a sighting of Sarah, he'd tell Gabriella what he'd seen and accept whatever punishment followed for his cowardice in not telling her earlier. He tried to convince himself that Sarah had been spending her days exploring the town or relaxing in the spa, but deep down he knew that wasn't true.

With yesterday fresh in his memory, Tom transported words from his head to the page in a blur. Rose was by far the most complex character he'd ever created. She was passionate and damaged and alone, yet desperate for somebody to share her life with. She was guarded and blunt but more than anything she wanted somebody to see through her facade. A facade constructed by parents who never loved her and friends who never understood her and a world that never showed her where she belonged. Now she found herself in a strange and unfamiliar place being courted by a strange and unfamiliar man, the type of man she'd been told her whole life to avoid. But maybe that was wrong. Maybe she needed to find out for herself what (and who) was best for her. It was finally her decision. She could live however she wanted to. Be whoever she wanted to be.

That night Rose agreed to Zach's offer. She tried cocaine for the first time and Zach gave her a tour of the town. Everything seemed wonderful. The colours were brighter. The music was louder. The people were happier.

Rose was happier.

With the beach empty and the discarded ice cream cones removed, Tom headed back to the hotel. More than anything he wanted to head straight to his room in the slim hope that Joy was waiting there for him, but he needed to make a quick pit-stop first. Gabriella had ensured him that his weekly wage would be transferred into his account on the first day of each week. Yet that day had come and gone, and Tom's bank account was just as depressing as ever, meaning a trip to the manager's office was unavoidable.

Tom knocked but there was no answer. He knocked again and again there was no answer. He thought about knocking a third time, under normal circumstances he probably would have done, but something unnerved him. Something was wrong. The lights were on in Gabriella's office, he could see them shining through the frosted glass. He could also see Gabriella's silhouette, sitting beside her desk and typing away furiously. She hadn't looked towards the door even once.

Something about Gabriella's silhouetted image felt ominous. Tom wanted to walk away and leave her to whatever she was dealing with, but he couldn't. Even if she didn't want anybody to talk to, at least she'd know somebody was willing to listen. Tom eased the door open, the problems with his wage suddenly forgotten.

Gabriella hadn't heard Tom knock, nor did she have any idea of the time. Sleep continued to elude her, and she was edging closer to delirium with each passing minute. The articles she'd read were beginning to blend into one. She was struggling to remember if Roger's midnight call had even been real.

Tom had arrived at her door as Gabriella stumbled upon an article from the early 2000s entitled:

Wicked Wyatt Expelled Again

She skimmed the article, unaware that Tom was studying her through the frosted glass. She was horrified, but not surprised, to learn that Roger had been expelled during his final year of high school for threatening to accuse a teacher of paedophilia unless he gave him the answers to Roger's forthcoming GCSE exam. Gabriella wondered how something like that could be swept under the rug, but there probably wasn't anything that couldn't be swept away with a handful of notes and the promise of more.

Tom appeared before Gabriella without warning or introduction. Gabriella was so shocked that for a second she thought he was a hallucination.

Tom couldn't quite believe the woman sitting behind the manager's desk was Gabriella. Her hair, normally straight and sleek, was thick with grease. The dark circles surrounding her eyes were so large that it appeared as if she had two black eyes. Her hands trembled softly, and her skin was so pale it was almost transparent. She was staring up at him with an equal mix of wonder and horror.

'Gabriella, are you OK?'

Gabriella jumped a little in her chair as if she hadn't known Tom was there even though she'd spent the last thirty seconds staring at him.

'Tom. What are you doing here?'

'I um, I knocked. Didn't you hear?'

'No.' Gabriella finally snapped into focus. 'No, I didn't hear you because if I had I would have told you to come in, wouldn't I?'

'You're right. I'm sorry. It's just I knocked a couple of times and you didn't respond and... I'm sorry. I'll just go.' Tom conceded, realising that now was certainly not the right time to ask Gabriella about anything as trivial as a payment error. He turned and headed to the door. Gabriella sighed loudly behind him.

'No. Don't leave, it's fine.' She lied. 'What are you doing here?'

Tom didn't reply. Gabriella noticed his eyes drifting towards her computer screen. He only saw the word 'Wyatt' before Gabriella swiftly rotated the screen away from him. Gabriella's sudden movement snapped Tom back to life. He suddenly remembered who he was, where he was and why he was here.

'I um, well it's just that I noticed I haven't been paid yet. And I um... well I remember you said I'd be getting paid directly into my bank but I um, I haven't had anything yet.'

In what had easily become the longest day of Gabriella's life, she'd forgotten her day-to-day duties still existed. How she was supposed to deal with something as mundane as payment troubles or stock deliveries anymore she didn't know. Maybe those things would never matter again.

'Do you need it right now?' She asked sternly.

'Um, no, not right now. It's just you said I'd get paid each Monday, and I just thought…'

'Look I get that it's annoying, it is.' Gabriella interrupted, speaking quickly, without compassion or understanding. 'But right now I've got a hundred and one things that I need to be getting on with and if you're not desperate for it, which you just said you're not, then can it please wait until tomorrow? If not, I'll open my purse right now and give you whatever it is that I owe you. Which do you want?'

Tom couldn't believe how small he felt. Nor could he believe that Gabriella was talking down to him like this. He thought they'd built up an understanding. After all, he'd helped Gabriella more than most of her staff in his week at the Scarlett Grove. Although he certainly regretted it now.

'Tomorrow's fine.' Tom mumbled, desperate to escape from the confines of this office and the witch who'd possessed his manager.

Gabriella felt herself soften, realising she was taking her frustrations out on the wrong person.

'I'll shoot off then.' Tom turned for the door.

Gabriella wanted to apologise. She wanted to admit to her mistake and ensure Tom knew he'd done nothing wrong, but she couldn't. She needed to carry on with her work, her new work, work that she'd assigned to herself. Work she couldn't turn her back on. Gabriella stayed silent and watched as Tom opened the door.

141

Tom paused. He was furious with Gabriella, there was no doubt about that, but mostly he was worried about her. Something, clearly something monumentally big, was weighing on her. Tom wondered how many people she had left to turn to. Not very many, he thought, if any at all. Tom took a deep breath and turned back into the lion's den.

'Gabriella, is everything OK?' He asked tentatively.

Gabriella looked at Tom with a softer expression. Her eyes were brighter, and her lips were no longer pursed. For a split second, Tom thought she would confide in him. Then everything reverted back. Her eyes were dark, her lips were pursed, and Tom knew he should have left.

'Tom I've got a lot of work to be getting on with. A fuck-load to be honest. Please can we just leave this for today? Surely there's somebody else you can speak to if you're just after a chat.'

Tom's cheeks stained dark red. He'd just received the verbal equivalent of a slap across the face. He left silently, without looking back at the woman he'd just lost all respect for.

* * *

Nathan talked quickly and clearly. He encouraged Roger to repeat each instruction back to him, ensuring he understood everything. He ushered order after order and demand after demand, before finally deciding Roger knew everything he needed to know. He ended his lecture by relaying one final piece of advice.

'When we next see each other, don't ask me any questions about today. Never. Do you understand?' He spoke with absolute certainty. This rule was not to be broken.

Roger was a lot of things, but he was by no means an idiot. The less he knew about the whole procedure, from the disposal of the body to the scrubbing of the room, the better. The only problem was that Roger did have questions, lots of questions.

Some things had been made abundantly clear. It was clear Nathan wasn't helping Roger simply out of the kindness of his own heart, he expected to receive a payment for his assistance. A generous payment at that. The two didn't arrive at an exact figure but Roger knew when the time came, he would have no sway on the negotiations. Never before had he been so powerless. Never before had he fucked up so spectacularly. He could picture the smile on his father's face when the story broke. He couldn't let that happen. He couldn't prove that cold bastard right.

Nathan accepted the fact that Roger couldn't leave the country immediately, at least not until his business with the Scarlett Grove was complete. But he made it perfectly clear that as soon as every last T had been crossed and every last I had been dotted, Roger was to book a seat on the first plane back to London. Roger didn't expect his business to last longer than a fortnight, maybe less if he could get a fire started beneath the many lawyers and solicitors overseeing the various contingencies and clauses in place. The problem, Roger thought, would arrive much later (if he was fortunate enough to escape without punishment). It seemed more than likely that his father would insist Roger continued to oversee the progress made at the Scarlett Grove, and that responsibility would bring with it regular visits to Roquetas De Mar. Regular visits to the scene of the crime.

The first thing Roger had been told (ordered) to do seemed quite simple on the face of things. He just had to go about his day as if nothing untoward had happened, which as far as everybody else knew, it hadn't. He started by visiting the gym. It was a small and exclusive gym that charged far too much for exactly the same equipment available at every other gym in town. He cut his usual session in half, much to the disdain of Marko, his trainer, and left the gym sweating profusely, though his tame workout was certainly not to blame.

Nathan had made it clear just how important it was for Roger to get himself seen in as many different locations around town as possible, which meant that after leaving the gym Roger headed to the small strip of shops on the beachfront. He spent twenty minutes browsing through various articles of clothing and accessories without any real interest. Upon finally deciding the employees had noticed him, Roger left the shops and walked down to the beach.

Whilst walking on the sand, trying to blend in with the crowd of merry tourists enjoying their well-earned relaxation, Roger was once again faced with the almighty storm of questions billowing throughout his mind. What was Nathan going to do with the body? How would he get it out of the hotel without being seen? And most importantly, who was the woman lying dead on his bed?

At first, Roger had been sure she was Roxy, the woman who'd refused to submit and stolen his watch. But looking back now, diving through the dirty memory of last night, he began to question himself. Roxy had been taller than the body growing stiff on his bed. Her hair had been darker too, and Roxy's skin had boasted the olive complexion of somebody lucky enough to have spent their entire life beneath the

Spanish sun. The corpse on his bed hadn't shared these traits. Her hair had been lighter at the roots, it had been dyed recently, and her tan was the result of a week spent by the pool, not a lifetime in this town. Roger felt a sudden twinge of relief. Whoever she was she hadn't come from Dream Girls, and that could only be a good thing. Businesses like that don't react well when their property isn't returned on time.

Roger's relief didn't last long. It was swiftly replaced by a ball of dread clanging down into the pit of his stomach. The girl may not have been a prostitute, but that meant Roger had no idea who she was, and somehow that was worse. Roger couldn't take any more of this. He could feel eyes burning into the back of his head. He began to worry that maybe his hands were still stained red, even though he'd spent an eternity scrubbing them, convinced they would never be clean again. His lungs seemed to have collapsed. His vision was blurred and no matter how hard he tried he couldn't catch his breath. He needed answers and he needed them now. He took his phone from his pocket and opened his call log. He was about to call Nathan and demand the answers he so desperately needed when he noticed something that caused his thudding heart to stop. It turned out that during his drunken panic, Roger had made not one call but two. It wasn't just Nathan to whom Roger had reached out for help, and he doubted Gabriella Glover would be quite so understanding.

* * *

Although Gabriella could have sworn at least two hours

had passed, there was only a twelve-minute gap between Tom leaving her office and Roger arriving at her door. Gabriella had spent those twelve minutes scouring through the Internet, unearthing any dirt she could find on Roger Wyatt and the man who'd raised him. In those twelve minutes, she'd found precious little, so little in fact that she was close to admitting defeat and retreating to her room.

She froze when she heard him knock, surprised that even a knock at the door can be sinister depending on who's waiting on the other side.

Roger didn't knock a second time. He allowed five seconds to pass before pushing the door open and entering the office, he was in no mood to be kept waiting.

Gabriella stared up at Roger, dumbfounded and scared beyond belief. He bared his canine grin and suddenly Gabriella knew what she had, after over twenty-four hours of Google searches, been unsure of. Roger Wyatt was capable of murder.

'Sorry, I didn't mean to barge in.' Roger spoke slowly, attempting to recapture some of the charm he was so synonymous with. 'I did knock but I don't think you heard me.'

For what seemed an age, Gabriella was unable to speak. She should have known Roger would come here. Of course, he was going to come. He'd want to gauge her reaction, work out if she was a threat or not. She should have been better prepared. She needed to play this perfectly. Her day of research would do little good if she misspoke and encouraged Roger to silence her once and for all.

'Gabriella, is everything OK?' Roger asked with all the sincerity of an abusive husband.

Finally, Gabriella's brain flicked into autopilot. She plastered her most genuine fake smile across her face and remembered how to speak. 'Sorry. Everything's fine. I'm just a bit snowed under is all.'

Roger's serpent-like eyes studied her every move. 'Sounds like you could use a drink.'

'I could use a thirty-hour nap. But I'll settle for a drink.'

Gabriella reached into the mini-fridge beneath her desk and produced two bottles of San Miguel. She offered one to Roger and watched his brain whir as he contemplated how best to conduct himself.

'Go on then.' Roger's mind was made up. He was going to allow this unexpected scenario to play out until he knew whether he had cause to worry about Gabriella. 'It's not like I've got anywhere to be tonight.'

Gabriella wondered how much alcohol it took to unleash the beast that lived within Roger. She had no intention of nearing that threshold tonight.

'Can I sit down?' Roger gestured to the empty chair opposite Gabriella.

'Be my guest.'

Roger settled in the chair and took a long sip from the bottle, studying Gabriella all the while. Gabriella thought of the last person she'd shared a drink with and felt a twang of guilt. She owed Tom an apology.

'Dare I ask why you keep bottles of San Miguel beneath your desk?' Roger asked, keen to keep the conversation light, initially at least.

Gabriella wondered if Roger had shown those haunting canine teeth to the poor girl he'd hurt. She wondered just how hard he'd tried to charm her; how relentless he'd been in his pursuit of her.

147

'Wait until you're running this place, then you'll understand.'

'I won't ever be running this place.' Roger said calmly, and, after noticing the shocked expression resting upon Gabriella's face, he added 'Well technically I'll own the hotel, of course. We're not pulling out of the deal or anything, don't worry. I just mean that I won't ever be running this place. You will.'

Gabriella tried and failed to hide the rush of delight that surged through her. For a brief moment, the horrors of Roger's midnight call were forgotten.

Roger saw Gabriella's glee and bared his sharp teeth once again. Suddenly Gabriella remembered why he was here, and now she saw Roger's reassurance for what it really was: blackmail. Her delight evaporated just as quickly as it had arrived. Her decency was being pitted against her greed and she didn't like how closely fought the contest was.

'I thought you were looking for Spanish managers?' She finally said. 'You wanted a more authentic experience.'

'That was my Dad's idea.' Roger laughed heartily at the lunacy of Gabriella's suggestion. 'And like most of his ideas, it wasn't a particularly good one. You'll still be managing this place. Trust me.'

Roger, clearly pleased with himself, took another long sip from his bottle.

'Well, that's great.' Gabriella allowed herself a sip from the bottle. Just a sip though. She needed to keep her wits about her, now more than ever. 'Is that what you came here to tell me?'

'More or less.' If Roger sensed that Gabriella was fishing for information, he didn't show it. 'I wanted to apologise too.'

'Apologise for what?' And here it was. The moment had arrived. Gabriella braced herself and prepared her story.

'I think I accidentally rang you the other night, didn't I?'

There it was, finally out in the open. Gabriella did her best to act as though she hadn't spent every moment since thinking of nothing else.

'Oh, I remember.' Gabriella began, her voice steady and unwavering. 'Well, I remember it happening, but I don't remember what was said quite so much.'

'Oh really?' Roger continued to study her with those reptilian eyes of his.

'Yeah, it's embarrassing but truth be told I had one too many of these that night.' She gestured to the largely untouched bottle of San Miguel in her hand. 'I don't remember much of anything after ten.'

Gabriella prayed she'd done enough to convince Roger. Surely the fact she had a mini-fridge stocked with beer beneath her desk would help. If alcohol hidden away in her office wouldn't make Roger question the reliability of her character, what would?

'Ten at night or ten bottles?' Roger asked lightly.

Gabriella laughed. Relief wrapped itself tightly around her like a blanket. 'Admittedly a bit of both.'

'It's funny you should say that.' Roger said after a long pause. 'I was a little worse for wear that night myself. I don't remember exactly what I said but I imagine it was a blur of drunken nonsense.'

Gabriella flashed Roger her best fake smile, the same smile she'd shown to Callum during the final few months of their marriage. 'Oh, well now I'm upset that I missed it.'

Roger laughed along with Gabriella before draining the

last of his beer. 'Well, if you're keen to hear some drunken nonsense, why don't we grab a drink one night this week?' It seemed the Roger that Gabriella knew and greatly disliked had returned. 'And I don't mean just in your office.'

Gabriella fought back the urge to vomit as she prepared to abandon her morals. Maybe the horrors were just beginning after all.

17

A Long Walk and a Long Talk

Sarah recovered steadily as the days ticked by. When Sunday arrived she was no longer reliant on aspirin and paracetamol to get her through her days. Her pain was manageable now and her appetite had returned. Richard brought her food, whatever he could sneak from the Dining Hall each day. If there wasn't enough she ordered room service, which she preferred because she didn't have to pretend to be grateful to Richard when the food arrived. Richard didn't apologise for what he'd done, but this was no surprise. She couldn't remember the last time he'd apologised to her.

Richard left early on Monday without telling his wife where he was going or when he would return. Sarah decided she wouldn't waste another day sitting in her room with the curtains drawn and the air conditioning blasting. Today she planned to explore this town that so many people raved about.

She left the hotel and wandered aimlessly, although she made sure to steer well clear of the beach and The Clover, knowing Richard would likely be there making his way through a bottle of something strong and cheap.

Sarah was taken aback by the beauty of the town. She wandered by parks, on which children played merrily whilst their parents watched on. She walked past restaurants in which waiters scrambled to ensure everything was ready for the impending dinner service. She walked past statues dedicated to people she would never know. She walked down the coast and let the tide tickle her bare feet. The sea was calm today. It seemed to Sarah that this was good an omen as she could have hoped for.

She had walked for at least an hour when she stumbled upon a quaint, secluded stretch of beach separated from the crowded sand by a wall of sharp, hazardous rocks. She eased herself slowly across the rocks, almost losing her balance once or twice, before jumping down onto the soft sand that waited for her. She laid out a towel and made herself comfortable, staring out into the infinite emptiness of the ocean.

She stayed there for hours, knowing Richard wouldn't return to their room until hunger forced him to. She thought about a lot of things with her head resting on the sand. She thought about her early days with Richard, how she'd fallen in love with him bit by bit until suddenly her love for him was the centre point of her entire existence. She thought about her days in the salon and how devastated she'd been to close the shutters for the final time. She thought about the first time Richard hit her, and how in the weeks that followed she'd convinced herself it was all her fault. She thought of the first time she noticed Richard sneaking vodka into one of his drinks and assuring herself it was nothing to worry about. She thought about Marcus. She thought about him a lot. She thought about how he'd learnt the alphabet a week before he turned three. She thought about how he watched *SpongeBob SquarePants* whilst he ate because he wouldn't touch his vegetables otherwise. She thought about his green eyes and his cheeky smile and the curls in his hair. She thought of the day they discovered the extent of his illness. She thought about the day they buried him, and how she'd heard her heart break as her son's final resting place disappeared beneath the earth.

She didn't let herself think of this for long. She couldn't, she wasn't strong enough. Instead, she thought of how he'd danced when he was excited. How he'd declared his love for her at least five times a day. She thought of his smile. As long as she had that memory, maybe that would be enough.

When the clock struck four Sarah packed up her belongings and headed back to the hotel with her spirits lifted. Today had been the best day she'd had since Marcus had passed. She allowed herself to smile for the first time in a long while. Knowing there were places like this made things a little more bearable.

Her joy dissipated when Richard returned and suggested they eat together. He said he wanted the chance to speak to her, to make up for the time they'd missed together. Sarah didn't point out that Richard was responsible for the missed time. She wanted to but she didn't. And she agreed to eat with him. She didn't want to but she did.

They talked of little whilst they ate, only pleasantries such as how they both enjoyed the food and how lovely the hotel had turned out to be. Sarah was all too relieved when it came time to return to the room, hoping that Richard would head out to a bar and leave her alone for the night. He did not.

153

The sex didn't last long. It never did. There was no foreplay and as usual, there was absolutely no consideration for Sarah's wants or needs. Although if Richard were to consider Sarah's feelings, they wouldn't be having sex at all. Like each time Richard decided to take claim of his 'marital rite', Sarah felt as though she left her body. She wasn't aware of Richard's frantic thrusting or his hands wrapping around her throat as he neared his climax. Sarah wasn't aware of anything in room fifty-seven because she was somewhere else, in an empty room with white walls and no windows.

Sarah enjoyed her time in this windowless room more than she enjoyed her time on earth. It was the only place where she felt free. Ever since she'd first contemplated taking her own life, which had been three days after Marcus' death, she'd hoped this room would be her afterlife. Just this room forever. This room where she could see her son.

Marcus was pleased to see her, same as always. He didn't speak. He never did. Sarah didn't know why. Maybe a part of her was worried that the voice wouldn't be right and hearing some shallow imitation of Marcus' voice would be worse than never hearing it again. He understood her though. He rushed over and wrapped his arms around her, holding her tightly just as he used to. He didn't let go, not for a long time, not until he knew she was feeling better. She always felt better after a cuddle from him. They eradicated all the bad in the world.

When Marcus finally let go, he was eager to show his mother what he'd found. On Marcus' second birthday Sarah and Richard had given him a stuffed animal shaped like a Dalmatian and Marcus carried it with him everywhere. At some point in the year, the Dalmatian they called Little

Marcus got lost. They looked everywhere but couldn't find him. Marcus never stopped asking for his stuffed friend, even when Sarah explained that she'd looked everywhere. But she was wrong, there was one place she hadn't looked. She never checked the windowless room with white walls, and as it turned out, Little Marcus had been waiting here the whole time. Marcus smiled widely as he proudly displayed his returned best friend to Sarah. His smile lit up her life. It was the last thing she saw before Richard grunted and she was brought crashing back to reality.

Richard pulled out of her roughly and collapsed onto the bed beside her, just as he usually did, but he didn't roll away. He stared at Sarah as if he were deep in thought, as if he'd had the idea of a lifetime. Sarah didn't like the look on his face. She didn't like it at all.

'I think we should move here.' Richard blurted out with absolute certainty.

'What?' Sarah asked, far too enraged to form anything more coherent than a one-word question.

'Well not here, necessarily. Just anywhere new. Somewhere nobody knows us. Somewhere we can have a fresh start.'

'A fresh start?' Sarah questioned, still not believing what she was hearing. 'How can we have a fresh start? Our son is buried in Wigan!'

'And he always will be. Nothing changes if we're not there.'

Sarah jumped out of the bed and wrapped herself in a dressing gown, keen to put as much distance between herself and this monster as possible.

'Here we go.' Richard exclaimed as he rose from the bed himself, heaving his boxers up. 'I mention him, and you lose your shit. What a surprise.'

'I'm losing my shit because I don't want to move away from my son!' Sarah exclaimed incredulously.

'There's nothing wrong with what I'm saying. We can't let him hold us back any longer.' Richard shouted.

Sarah felt as though she'd been punched in the stomach. 'Fuck you.' She spat with all the venom she could muster.

'Jesus Christ!' Roger yammered with his fists balled. 'I'm not looking for an argument, Sarah. I just… I think being here has been good for us. I don't think it's the worst idea to stay here a little longer.'

'You're not just asking us to stay here for a little longer though, are you? You're asking us to stay here forever! You're asking us to leave our boy forever!' Tears were streaming down Sarah's cheeks now.

'He's in the ground, Sarah. He's never coming back. It doesn't matter where we are, nothing can change that.'

Sarah began to pace the room, thinking maybe if she walked enough things would begin to make sense. 'How?' It seemed she had reverted to one-word questions yet again.

'How what?'

'How could we possibly afford to move here? Actually, come to think of it, how are we even affording this holiday?'

'Why does that matter?'

'Just answer the question!' Sarah demanded.

'We have enough money. Let's just leave it at that.' Richard said, turning away from the woman who never failed to spot a lie.

'No. I want to know.' Sarah stormed after Richard and turned him around. She wouldn't let him slink his way out of this one. Not again. 'Where did the money come from?'

Richard shook his head as if Sarah were asking a question

so ridiculous it didn't deserve an answer.

'What? Are you dealing or something?'

Richard laughed without a hint of joy. 'That's what you think of me?'

'What am I supposed to think? You won't tell me where the money came from!'

'Fine. I withdrew the money we put away for Marcus.'

Ice ran through Sarah's veins. Her head was pounding and her lungs collapsed. She wanted to fling herself at Richard. To scratch him and bite him and punch him and kick him. She wanted him to be afraid, because right now, for the first time in a long time, she wasn't afraid of him.

'I can't fucking believe you.' Sarah spat the words in the manner a child would spit out a bitter piece of fruit.

'Why do you think I didn't tell you?' Richard threw his hands up in defeat. 'I knew you'd react like this. Why does it matter that I've taken the money?'

Sarah said nothing. Tears continued to flow down her cheeks.

'It's not like he was ever going to spend it.' Richard continued; his voice cold.

'Fuck you.' Sarah didn't wait for a response, instead, she crossed the room quickly and left, slamming the door behind her.

Richard sat down on the bed in a heap. He wished he'd explained it better. He wished he'd told Sarah that he couldn't face returning to the place where they'd raised their son. Returning to a home in which they watched *101 Dalmatians* on repeat, a home in which they'd been happy. He couldn't return to the place Marcus had been alive. At least here,

Richard was only reminded of Marcus every time he closed his eyes. Back home he was reminded of him when his eyes were open too. He isn't strong enough to cope with that. He never will be.

Sarah arrived at the beach, relieved to find it deserted of tourists and stargazers. She collapsed onto a lounger and cried. Sitting there, alone beneath the stars, Sarah came to accept something she thought a part of her had known for months. She had to leave Richard. But with Richard's temper taken into consideration, it seemed the only scenario in which she would ever be separated from him was death. For months Sarah had accepted she would be the one to join Marcus in the great beyond. But her mind changed beneath the stars. She wouldn't allow Richard the satisfaction of his fresh start. Spending her life in a Spanish prison was a far more enticing option than spending the rest of her life with her abusive, alcoholic husband.

* * *

Roger returned to his penthouse later that night to find Nathan waiting for him. Thankfully, the room was spotless, maybe even cleaner now than it had been when he'd first checked in. The bed sheets had been changed, the floor had been scrubbed and most importantly, her body was gone. The room was no longer a crime scene, now it was just another hotel room in which hundreds of families will sleep over the coming years, blissfully unaware of the girl who took her final breath here.

'So, you went about your day as normal?' Nathan asked,

skipping the pleasantries of a hello.

'That's right.' Roger replied, struggling to meet Nathan's intense gaze.

'What did you do?' Nathan asked. He was sitting on the corner of the bed with a cigarette resting between his fingers. An ashtray rested on the bed beside him. From the contents of that ashtray, Roger guessed Nathan had been waiting for a while.

'Oi!' Nathan pressed, clearly he wasn't fond of being ignored.

'Sorry. What was the question?'

'What did you do today? Where did you go?'

'Um, the gym, the beach, I wandered into a couple of shops…'

Nathan raised a hand, gesturing for Roger to stop. With his other hand, he stubbed out his cigarette.

'I'm worried Roger.' Nathan spoke calmly but Roger could tell there was a fire within him, like a bomb with a minute left on its timer.

'Why?'

'Two reasons. Can you guess either of them?'

Roger remained silent.

'Well, the first thing worrying me is that you've been gone for almost ten hours and I don't think visiting the gym, the beach and then wandering into a couple of shops is enough to fill that time. So, I'm going to need you to tell me every single thing you've done today and exactly how long you did each thing for. Understood?'

'Like I said I started in the gym…'

Roger was once again cut off by Nathan's raised right hand. 'Not yet. I'm more worried about the other thing, so I'm gonna need to hear about that first.'

'What's the other thing?'

'Where'd you get the coke?'

Roger didn't know Nathan all that well, but he knew not to lie.

'Your friend.' Roger mumbled, staring down at his fingers which he rubbed together absently.

'Connor?'

'I don't know his name. I rang you and he answered.'

'Makes sense. I was busy so he took my calls for the day.'

Roger stifled a laugh. The man standing before him was a drug dealer in a small Spanish coastal town, and yet he thought it appropriate to use phrases such as: took my calls for the day. Somewhere in this situation, there was irony. Irony that the son of one of the world's most successful businessmen was now being lectured by a nobody drug dealer.

'Were you on my gear when you killed her?'

Roger flinched at the word 'killed'. Although he knew it was true, he still couldn't think of himself as a murderer. He nodded reluctantly.

'Right, then it's a problem. No more. Not until you're back in England at least.'

Roger's first reaction was one of rage, a rage-fuelled by addiction. The rage of a person who's just been told they can no longer have the one thing they need more than anything else. He wanted to punch Nathan. To march over to him, wrap his hands around his throat and wipe that smug grin from his face. But Roger knew he couldn't. Not now. Not ever. Not with what Nathan knew.

'You got any left from today?' Nathan asked, rolling a fresh cigarette between his fingers.

'A little.'

'Keep it. You don't get any more until I say so. And if I ever hear that you've bought from anybody other than me, I'll tell everyone your dirty little secret. In fact, no, I'll show them. Understand?'

Roger nodded. He understood perfectly.

'Good.' Nathan said, a smile etched upon his face. 'Now tell me about your day.'

Roger told Nathan about his day. He told him how he'd found a quiet corner of the beach to meet Connor and collect what he'd needed to get himself through the day. He told him how he'd watched the new Will Ferrell film at a cinema because in a dark room people couldn't stare at him. Finally, he'd headed to his favourite restaurant in town, Fernando's, where he'd eaten steak and washed it down with a couple of glasses of overpriced whiskey.

Nathan listened intently. At some point, he lit up another cigarette and he was still nursing it when Roger came to the end of his account. Nathan stayed silent for another few seconds and Roger became convinced he knew of his trip to the Scarlett Grove. He must have friends in all sorts of places. He probably already knew every step Roger had taken. The sun might have been on its decline but suddenly the heat felt unbearable.

'That was it?' Nathan asked casually. 'You came straight here after that?'

'Yeah.' Roger replied immediately. 'That's right.'

Nathan stubbed his cigarette into the pile of ash. 'OK. That's good then.'

Nathan didn't leave Roger's penthouse apartment for three-quarters of an hour. In that time they talked about a whole manner of things, the details of which aren't particularly important. After all, we've all seen enough crime shows to imagine the gist of it.

There is, however, one piece of information that sets the wheels of Tom's story in motion. A lie. A single lie will bring about devastation and suffering the likes of which this small coastal town has never seen. A lie told by Roger Wyatt at the conclusion of a long conversation. A lie told in response to a simple question.

'It was just me you called, wasn't it?' Nathan asked calmly.

When the moment came, something took over Roger. Something controlled his vocal cords and eased him through without a hiccup. He had a good idea what was helping him through. It was the very thing Nathan wanted to ban him from.

'Yeah.'

Nathan didn't doubt Roger's answer. After all, why would Roger lie?

* * *

Tom returned to his room expecting the worst. Joy wouldn't be waiting for him. She had her own life and her own room, and she surely had better things to do than wait around for him all day. He rounded a corner and stopped in his tracks. Joy was perched against the door of his room with a smile on her face and a bottle of wine in each hand. Tom smiled with his entire face.

'You didn't leave me a key.' Joy smiled as Tom arrived beside her.

'I seem to remember you didn't react quite so brilliantly when I tried to talk to you this morning.'

'Open the door.' Joy instructed with a grin.

Tom did as he was told.

Joy was wearing a white top, boasting her own art across the sleeves, and denim shorts. She poured a large glass of white wine for both herself and Tom, and then wandered back to Tom, who'd made himself comfortable on the couch, handed him his glass and sat beside him.

'I nearly left. I didn't think you were coming back.'

'Yeah, sorry about that. Busy day at the beach.' Tom was in no mood to recount his humiliating experience with Gabriella.

'A busy day at the beach?' Joy asked sceptically.

'There are busy days at the beach, you know.'

'Oh, I don't doubt it.' Joy's smile flashed wide and bright.

'Your tone makes me certain that you doubt it.' Tom laughed. It was crazy to him just how easily one conversation with Joy could transform a shitty day into one that's better than most.

'Well, I'm just not sure what exactly a busy day at the beach would entail. I assume you saved a life?'

'Just one life is an insult. I saved six lives. And they were all innocent little children.'

'You saved six innocent little children in one day?'

Tom nodded enthusiastically. 'I don't like to call myself a hero, but a lot of the people at the beach seemed to think it was appropriate.'

Tom was enjoying the conversation so much he didn't even

think of the significance of his first sip of wine. It went down easily as if he'd been waiting for it all day. That sip marked another day of continuous drinking, and now he was just two days away from breaking his three-day rule for the second time in a fortnight. Right then though, Tom could think of nothing he cared about less.

'I brought the wine though. I think that makes me the real hero.' Joy presented her glass to Tom as if it were an entirely new species she'd just discovered.

'That's hard to argue with.'

They ordered room service, a deluxe burger each, and spent the night playing *Mario Kart* and laughing at a terrible Adam Sandler film they found on *Netflix*. It was well past two in the morning when Tom nodded off with his head resting on Joy's shoulder and his arm wrapped around her.

Tom slept warmly. He dreamed of a magical smile and eyes that saw right through him.

Joy dreamed of nothing. She rarely did these days.

18

The Beach Hut

The next morning Joy eased herself out of bed without waking Tom and dressed silently. She felt surprisingly sprightly to say she and Tom had made their way through two bottles of wine last night. It didn't occur to her that maybe Tom had drank more than she had. Maybe he'd drank a lot more.

She scribbled a quick note explaining her absence, and slipped out of the room, edging the door closed behind her.

* * *

Sarah Tyler had a purpose for the first time in months. She needed a plan and she needed help. Not a lot of help, she didn't want anybody to catch wind of her intentions, nor did she want anybody to be considered an accomplice, but more than a few of the obstacles standing in her way would be easier to overcome with assistance. The smallest of these obstacles being that she doesn't speak a word of Spanish and the largest being the man she travelled to Spain with.

* * *

Tom awoke with a full bladder and a head that thudded with the echo of too much white wine. He checked the time and found that his alarm wasn't scheduled to ring for another thirty minutes. He rolled over, ready to enjoy his final moments of sleep with an arm around Joy but was drenched with disappointment. The bed beside him was empty but for a single scrap of paper. Scrawled in her surprisingly untidy handwriting, Joy had written:

I'll be back later, so long as you want me to, of course. If you don't, I'll probably come back anyway. If any kids look like they might drown today, let them. You deserve a break.

* * *

Richard was still snoring as Sarah, much like Joy had done just minutes earlier, slipped out of bed, pulled on some shorts and a purple vest, and glided gently out of the room. She also left a note on the bedside table, although hers wasn't as honest as Joy's. As she made her way through reception, passing the empty Lobby Bar, she allowed herself a wry smile. Today things would finally change.

* * *

Roger Wyatt hadn't slept at all. Instead, he'd lay in bed and watched as the black night sky had been invaded by a magnificent red uprising that slowly dissolved as the large ball of fire rose to its home in the centre of the sky. Throughout this unbelievable feat of nature, Roger's head pulsated with questions, all of which crashed into one another as they fought for his attention. One question was more aggressive than the others. One question scratched and kicked at the inner fabric of his brain until he could ignore it no longer.

Could he trust Gabriella Glover?

* * *

Gabriella woke with a start. Her sleep had been uncomfortable, plagued with nightmares and cold sweats. In her nightmare a man stood above her and, though he didn't say anything, Gabriella knew she was helpless. She knew she wouldn't make it through the night.

Much to Gabriella's disbelief, it seemed that her nightmare had followed her into the land of the living. The name displayed on her vibrating phone turned her blood to ice. She took a deep breath, attempted to compose herself, and then exchanged pleasantries with Roger Wyatt.

* * *

As Tom arrived at the beach, he was surprised to find that for the first time during his brief employment with the Scarlett Grove, somebody was out sunbathing before the beach officially opened. Tom wasn't entirely sure how to handle the situation. It seemed ludicrous to ask the guest to leave the beach for the twenty or so minutes until it officially opened, so Tom decided to leave her be. After all, the rogue sunbather was probably asleep, and Tom could think of better things to do than startle the life out of some poor sap sweetly dreaming beneath the Spanish sun.

Plus, he wanted to finish another chapter today, and Rose wasn't going to wind up in a Spanish jail cell if he didn't plant himself in front of his laptop sooner rather than later.

* * *

Richard's hangover wasn't his only concern when he woke. Thanks to a roughly scrawled note, he was informed that his wife had decided to spend her day on the beach. Richard rose to his feet with a groan. His stomach was far too precarious for breakfast, so he supposed the only option was to head to the beach and hope Sarah wasn't holding a grudge. He hadn't heard her return to the room last night, and for that at least, he was grateful. He was pulling a pair of shorts on when he spotted a half-empty bottle of beer that he'd opened yesterday. He quickly finished it. It seemed a shame to let it go to waste.

Suddenly Richard decided the beach could wait. First, he'd make a quick stop at the grocery store down the street. They always had great deals on English lagers, and he'd enjoy the beach more with a crate of beers resting beside him.

* * *

Roger didn't know why he called Gabriella, nor did he know why he was still so full of doubt. She'd said all the right things yesterday. Surely if she'd heard anything, she wouldn't have been so comfortable sharing a cramped office with him.

His mind was at war. Wasn't it believable that Gabriella really was just an ordinary hotel manager who, like most people in demanding jobs, enjoyed the occasional drink or two to alleviate the stress of her unbearable workload? Not to mention the fact that she was attracted to him, Roger was sure of that. Fine, she'd rebuffed his advances in the past, but things are different now she knows her job is safe. Maybe that little shred of reassurance has given her permission to give in to her deepest, darkest desires. After all, who doesn't want to fuck the man in charge?

At least by tonight, he would know the truth. He might even finally get what he's wanted all along.

* * *

Gabriella didn't know how or why she accepted Roger's invitation. It was probably because, try as she might, she'd been unable to think of a plausible excuse. And now, though she couldn't think of a worse way to spend her evening, she was destined to share a meal with Roger Wyatt at a little tapas place called Platos Y Bebidos. Gabriella barely disconnected the call before sprinting to the bathroom and vomiting violently into the toilet.

* * *

Sarah hadn't noticed Tom arrive at the beach hut. Truthfully, she'd gotten lost in the moment. Laying here, away from Richard, she felt free, just as she had on the secluded beach yesterday. It was no longer implausible that, without Richard, Sarah could find some semblance of happiness. She certainly hoped so at least.

* * *

Tom, meanwhile, was lost in Rose. She'd spent her last two days holed up in the hostel with Zach, who knew exactly how to solve their financial problems and leave their shitty jobs behind. It turned out the solution to their problems could be found in the back office of the nightclub Rose worked at. Zach's plan was simple. Rose was to distract the bouncer with friendly conversation, whilst Zach broke into the office and pointed his gun at whoever was in there. Zach didn't tell Rose how he'd come about this information, but he knew there would be at least thirty thousand pounds in there. Rose asked no further questions.

Rose wasn't entirely sure how to say no to Zach. Truthfully, she was terrified. Terrified because, should anything go wrong (and something was bound to go wrong), she'd been instructed to pull Zach's small handgun from her purse and point it at anybody who tries to intervene.

When the fateful night arrived, Rose talked to the bouncer, an intense middle-aged man named Diego, as instructed. All was going smoothly until she heard the gunshot. Suddenly

Rose had only two options. Pull the gun from her purse and risk wasting years of her life in a Spanish jail or flee before anyone can link her to the crime.

Rose was mere seconds away from making a decision that would have a colossal effect on the rest of her life, when Tom was interrupted by a nervous voice and an anxious smile.

'Hi.' Sarah whispered.

She may have spoken softly but that didn't prevent Tom from almost jumping out of his seat. He'd been so lost in Rose that he'd forgotten the real world even existed.

'Sorry, I didn't mean to scare you.' Sarah added, holding her hands up in apology.

'No, it's OK.' Tom took a deep breath to slow his racing heart. 'I'm sorry, what can I help you with?'

'Oh, I've been using one of the sun loungers and I haven't paid yet, so...' Sarah offered a ten euro note to Tom. He got the feeling there was more she wanted to say but decided not to press her, after all, he'd never even spoken to this woman.

'Yeah, of course.' Tom retrieved his wallet from beneath the table and collected the money from Sarah.

'It's OK, you can keep the change.' Sarah tried to sound upbeat, but Tom sensed something was weighing on her.

'Thank you very much.' Tom thought it was strange that the only two people to have given him a tip were the only two people to have caused him any trouble.

He handed Sarah her receipt with a smile, but she didn't leave. It seemed Tom was going to have to help her along if he wanted to hear why she was really here.

'Is there anything else I can help you with?' He asked delicately.

'No.' Sarah replied quickly and then paused, clearly fighting some internal battle. 'Well, I don't know really.'

Tom felt something in the atmosphere switch dramatically. Whatever Sarah was going to ask him, it was important to her. Really important.

'Go on.' He encouraged.

'Well, um, it's just that my hotel room faces out towards the front of the hotel, I can see the entrance and everything like that. The other day I saw you talking to somebody out there. I think he must have been a friend of yours.'

Tom was surprised, initially he'd assumed Sarah was talking about Joy. Then it dawned on him. She was talking about a man Tom certainly didn't consider his friend. A man with a thin beard and pockets full of cocaine.

'Do you mean…' Tom started but had no idea how to finish his question.

'Yeah. I just, I'd appreciate it if you could put me in touch with him.'

'Just to be sure we're talking about the same person.' Tom's head was spinning. Why on earth would she want to be put in touch with Nathan? 'You mean the man…'

'The man who arrived in a black car with tinted windows.' Sarah interrupted. 'You shook his hand.' Sarah raised her eyebrows as if to indicate she knew exactly what had been exchanged.

'He's not really my friend. I barely know the bloke.'

'Even still, you met him so you must know how to get in touch with him.' Sarah was not to be deterred. She came here for the number and she wasn't leaving until she got it.

'I don't. Genuinely. I was just collecting it for somebody else.' Tom felt like a child trying to explain why he didn't have his homework.

'Can you get it for me?' Sarah asked, her voice shaking with desperation. 'I'll pay you. I just, I need it.'

Tom had no desire to get caught up in any of this. He wanted to avoid anything that might force him back to Gabriella's office after the tongue-lashing he'd received yesterday. Still, he found himself saying: 'I don't want any money. I'll try though. I really will.'

A tear forced itself from Sarah's eye. She didn't wipe it away. It was a tear of joy, a tear of hope.

'Thank you.'

Tom, unsure of what to say, only nodded.

'I'll get here early tomorrow; will you be here?' Sarah's hands trembled, she hoped Tom didn't notice.

'I'll be here but I don't know if I'll have the number. I don't even know how to get in touch with the bloke who knows him.'

Sarah give Tom a hint of a smile and turned to the door.

'I saw what happened the other day.' Tom blurted out, surprising even himself.

Sarah turned to face him; her eyes burdened with tears. 'What do you mean?' She asked, her voice wavering.

'I saw what happened on the beach.'

Sarah looked down at the floor. Although a lot of people in her life seemed to know what Richard did to her, this was the first time somebody had spoken to her about it directly. Even after all this time, she still wasn't prepared.

'Whatever it was, and whatever you want this guy's number for, I just think you need to be careful.' Tom added tentatively.

Now Sarah had no trouble meeting Tom's gaze. She stared directly at him, gathered up the courage, and allowed a fraction of the frustration that had built up within her over the last few years to explode from within.

'Mind your own fucking business.'

Sarah left the beach hut without another word.

* * *

Richard had purchased a crate of twelve beers from the grocery store for the incredible price of thirteen euros. He arrived at the beach with his beers in a cooler and the sun on his back, only to find that his wife was nowhere to be seen.

He began to worry. Maybe she'd left the hotel. Maybe she'd left the country. Richard was covered in a cold sweat. He couldn't even begin to imagine what his life would be without Sarah. He looked down at the ice cooler with disgust, knowing its contents were to blame. He wanted to throw it into the ocean. He wanted to lock himself in his room until the cravings ceased. He wanted to, really he did, but he wasn't strong enough. A part of him knew he never would be.

Richard looked up from the cooler and saw something that made him crave a drink more than ever before. Sarah was leaving the beach hut and the mouthy little prick who worked there was following her out as if he knew her. Richard watched on as Tom shouted after his wife, but she didn't turn back.

Richard cracked open one of the cans and relaxed as the amber liquid warmed his throat. He wouldn't overreact but he wouldn't forget this either. Sarah couldn't be trusted.

Richard finished the can.

She couldn't be trusted at all.

* * *

Tom left the hut hours later. Rose had fled from the night club leaving a wounded Zach to face the consequences of his actions alone, and with that, his writing was done for the day. As he stepped into the sun he was surprised to see that Sarah had been joined by her husband. What was even more surprising though was the fact that, had Tom had not seen what happened between them almost a week ago, he would have thought they were just another couple madly in love. He wondered what had happened in their lives to make them this way. Whatever the case, he doubted life had been fair to either of them. Just as life hadn't been fair when it snatched his father away.

* * *

Roger was continuing his charade of acting normal, which meant spending his day trying to enjoy a relaxation retreat. It wasn't exactly a retreat, given it took place at the hotel in which he was staying. Nor was it a particularly relaxing experience, but that was understandable, given that Roger had slightly more pressing issues weighing on his mind.

After a hot stone massage that seemed to last an eternity, Roger was finally free to leave. Ready to prepare for the most important date of his life. A date that could change everything.

* * *

It had been almost a year since Gabriella had last been on a real date, and even then, it had only been a rebound that ended in rebound sex. Whilst she enjoyed the freedom of dating, she sensed there would be nothing freeing about tonight's experience.

She felt nothing but guilt as she slipped into a black dress and touched up her eyeshadow. She wasn't sure exactly what she hoped to achieve tonight, but at the very least she could set Roger's mind at ease. If only it were that easy.

* * *

Tom had no idea how he was going to get in contact with Nathan, but it seemed there were only two people he could turn to for help. The first was Joy, who he had no intention of asking, which left only Roger Wyatt. Tom wandered through the reception area, wondering how he could fabricate another meeting with Roger, when the man miraculously appeared before him, the pupils of his eyes two all-engulfing black holes.

'Excuse me mate. You don't know where Gabriella is, do you?' Roger asked as he strode towards Tom. 'I checked her office but she's not there.'

For a minute Tom was unable to speak, which infuriated Roger.

'Hello!' He added impatiently.

'Um, no. Sorry. If she's not in her office then she's probably in her room but I'm not sure which one's hers. If you ask at reception, I'm sure they'll tell you.'

Roger was clearly unsatisfied with Tom's response, but he

accepted it nonetheless. 'All right, cheers.' Roger turned and began pacing towards the reception desk.

Tom realised this would be his only chance, and he knew he couldn't afford to miss it. 'Um, excuse me, Roger.'

Roger turned back, infuriated that this unhelpful young man was going to waste more of his precious time.

'Can I ask you for a quick favour?' Tom added, praying Roger would say yes.

Roger said yes.

19

Small Plates and Big Drinks Part II

Gabriella hadn't intended to drink a lot. She planned to ease herself through a cocktail or two, never allowing herself to become drunk. She needed to stay sharp and alcohol was bound to get in the way of that. Ten minutes passed before she accepted drinking would be the only way to stop herself from crying.

It took Gabriella no longer than thirty minutes to work her way through the conversation starters she'd prepared beforehand. She and Roger made generic small talk about their upbringings (which were very different), about their business lives (which were very different) and even a brief overview of their romantic histories (which were very different). Throughout all this chatter, Gabriella threw back two strawberry daiquiris, which had been recommended to her by a plump waiter named Xabi. By the time the food arrived, she was good and tipsy.

They were rather conservative when it came to ordering, much to Xabi's relief, opting for just five dishes to share (patatas bravas, a chicken dish, a beef dish, meatballs and stuffed peppers). Gabriella hoped Roger wouldn't notice the way her hands shook as she picked at the food laid out before her. Her hands shook because, despite all his polite conversation, Gabriella never once doubted that the man sitting opposite her was a murderer. She saw Roger Wyatt as a man in disguise. The mask he wore was the polite, sophisticated and even humorous man sitting opposite her. It was what lay beneath the mask that scared her, and my God, was she scared.

Roger always suggested tapas restaurants for first dates. He did so because he found there was something quite intimate about sharing food, not to mention women became looser after a glass or two of sangria.

Gabriella didn't drink sangria. Instead, she helped herself through glass after glass of strawberry daiquiri, all without touching the food in front of her. Something about her behaviour felt odd to Roger. The image he'd built up of her, an image based on multiple meetings, didn't reflect the woman sitting opposite him tonight. Could this really be who she was away from the hotel? Or was this how she acted when she was trying to impress a man, like how some teenage girls pretend to be less intelligent to impress a boy. Or was it simply because she knew what Roger had done in his penthouse apartment during the dead of night?

'I take it it's been pretty stressful for you then, everything you've had to deal with over these last couple of weeks?' Roger asked as he shovelled patatas bravas into his mouth.

'It's not been a barrel of laughs.' Gabriella replied honestly. 'I think a lot of the staff were hoping you'd replace me.'

'What makes you say that?'

'Well, I don't know if you've picked up on it, but a lot of my staff think I'm selling out.'

'You mean because of us?' The news surprised Roger. It shouldn't have done. His briefing packet had made it explicitly clear that a lot of the locals were unhappy with the manner in which the Wyatt Foundation was purchasing such a significant chunk of the town's real estate. But Roger had not read the briefing packet or any other information he'd been given.

'Because of the Wyatt Foundation, yeah. It took the locals a while to warm up to us when we first opened. I think it helped that we hired a lot of people from the area. After a couple of years, the Scarlett Grove became one of their own. I think we were too.' Gabriella smiled at the memory. It seemed a lifetime ago now.

'So, you're saying I'm already doomed?' Roger asked with a chuckle.

'I think you'll survive.' Gabriella replied although she wished the opposite were true.

'As long as I have you by my side, I guess I'll be fine.' His canine grin returned. Gabriella suppressed the urge to vomit. 'You're not at all like I thought, you know.'

'How so?'

'Well, whenever we've had a meeting you've always been polite and proper, I just assumed that was who you are.'

'Am I not being polite or proper tonight?' Gabriella asked, beginning to worry she wasn't convincing Roger as she intended to, as she needed to.

'No, you are. You always are. But that's not all you are is what I'm trying to say.'

'Is this because you saw the mini-fridge I keep in my office?'

Gabriella asked with a smile, praying Roger had bought into the reckless version of herself she'd created just for him.

'It was certainly an eye-opener.'

'You know how it is with a high-stress job, sometimes you need something to take the edge off.'

'And you take the edge off with office beers?'

'Not always beers and not always in my office. I don't want you to get the wrong idea or anything. I don't drink every night and when I do, I rarely get into the state I was in that night. Again, if I said anything on that call, I truly am sorry. Nights where I get into a state like that are rare, honestly.'

Like a mist slowly evaporating at the end of a storm, so too did Roger's suspicions. He felt his entire body relax, meaning he was free to focus all his attention on Gabriella. She was a lot more fun than he'd expected, which meant she'd likely be even more fun once the lights were off.

'I don't want you to get the wrong idea either.' Roger said, his canine teeth on full display. 'I don't want you to think I make drunken calls to every person I do business with.'

'I must be special then.' Gabriella replied, cringing internally.

She hated herself for flirting with Roger. She hated herself for caring enough about her job to do this. She hated herself because, with a daiquiri or two in her system, she found herself enjoying moments with Roger Wyatt, a man she truly believed to be capable of murder.

'Are you getting the next round of drinks, or am I?' Gabriella asked with a flash of her eyelashes.

Roger felt certain this was going to be a very good night, one he would not soon forget.

Easing herself out of Roger's clutches hadn't been easy, especially because she'd had to do it without offending Roger or raising his suspicions. After two painful hours of forced flirting and awkward laughter, Gabriella first attempted to politely excuse herself. Roger hadn't accepted this, in fact, he seemed offended at the notion that Gabriella was willing to leave without him. He asked Gabriella if he'd done something wrong and she lied, insisting she was just tired. Roger said he thought they had been on the same page, and Gabriella did her best to remain calm, even though she and Roger hadn't once been on the same page.

'I wish I could.' She began with another flash of her wide eyes, eyes Roger clearly liked. 'But I don't want to get into anything until the deals finished. I think we've both come too far to risk ruining it all, especially when we can just wait and see it through.' Gabriella hoped her face hadn't shown that the thought of being intimate with Roger physically repulsed her.

'I've actually been meaning to talk to you about that, I asked the lawyers not to say anything so I could tell you in person, but in one week we're golden. Everything done. Finally.'

'Shit! Really?' Gabriella asked, hoping her devastation had disguised itself as excitement. 'I didn't know it was all so far along.'

'The signing of all the documents has been a formality for a while, hasn't it? Anyway, the exciting bit is the celebration. I'm planning something unforgettable. A spectacle.'

'A spectacle, huh?' Gabriella was surprised. Roger didn't seem the type of man to use a word with quite so many letters as the nine in spectacle.

'Trust me.' He replied confidently. 'Of course, you won't

have to do anything. I've already got most of it organised and I'll be sorting everything else tomorrow.'

'Wow, I'm impressed.' Gabriella lied. She was feeling many things right now, but awe wasn't one of them.

'I tell you what, I've changed my mind. I think I like this rule of yours.'

'Which rule?'

'Waiting till the takeover's gone through before... well, you know.' Roger flashed a smile that was supposed to be seductive. It wasn't. 'It just makes the party more exciting; I've got a better reason to celebrate.'

Gabriella felt her insides shrivel up and die.

'So, when is this spectacle?'

20

Dark Skies, Dark Moments

Sarah hadn't escaped Richard's sight since they left the beach together. Their dinner had been as unpleasant as ever. Sarah ate quietly whilst Richard picked at his food and eased his way through a bottle of red wine. When he finally decided they'd wasted enough time together, they headed back to the room. Sarah began to worry that Richard was planning on spending the rest of the night in there with her, and she simply couldn't face feeling his hands on her today. Thankfully, Richard had alternate plans for his evening. He was, he explained, going to spend an hour or two in The Clover, and though he didn't say it explicitly, it was clear Sarah wasn't invited.

Richard had been gone for less than half an hour when Sarah began to feel uncomfortable. She wasn't sure why, but some part of her night had been irregular. She'd been looking out of the window, watching a young boy try to tame a stray cat when all of a sudden, she became certain something was wrong. She replayed the day on a loop in her head, analysing everything Richard had said and done. For the life of her, she just couldn't understand what it was that had unsettled her.

Then, just as a key slots into a lock, Sarah knew why she felt so anxious. Richard had told her where he was going, and he only did that if he had good reason to lie about where he was actually headed.

Wherever Richard was, trouble would follow. Of that much Sarah was certain.

* * *

Without Joy for company, Tom had nothing to distract him from his writing. Nothing besides the hum of the mini-fridge, which acted as a constant reminder of the ice-cold bottles waiting in there. Bottles Tom wanted more than he could admit, bottles he wanted more than he could resist. Barely twenty minutes passed before Tom gave in and helped himself to a tiny bottle of gin and a slightly larger bottle of tonic. He promised himself this would be his only drink, that way he wouldn't have to count it in his weekly drinking rule, meaning he'd have one more day to drink (hopefully with Joy).

Exactly fifty-four minutes after Tom poured his gin and tonic, there was a knock at his door. He was instantly consumed with excitement. Joy had arrived and now his evening could really begin. He ran a hand through his hair, cursed himself for not showering, and headed to the door.

His heart dropped onto the floor as he opened the door and, instead of finding caramel eyes and hair that reminded him of autumn, he found the face of Richard Tyler. His eyes were glazed, and his teeth clenched. Tom's heart melted through the floor.

* * *

Admittedly, Richard hadn't considered all his options before banging against the door of the room belonging to Tom Jennings. His decision making was influenced solely by the alcohol flowing through his veins. Just seeing Tom's smug face made him crave another drink. He'd have one soon, once this was over.

Richard had left his room and headed to the Lobby bar, eager to catch up with a young scouse lad called Davey. Davey worked on a very irregular basis. His shifts were without pattern and a lot of the time he was drafted in as last-minute cover, meaning he could never tell Richard when to expect the pleasure of his company. Despite their limited time together, Richard and Davey had become close, or they'd become as close as a barman and a paying customer could possibly become. Davey was a good listener, and if there's one thing Richard excelled at after a couple of drinks, it was talking. Over the course of his holiday, he'd unloaded to Davey as if the young lad were his therapist. He didn't tell him everything though, he stayed clear of anything that could hurt his reputation with the lad.

Over the course of an hour, Richard told Davey everything, from waking alone to seeing his wife leaving the beach hut with Tom chasing after her. The whiskey made the memories hurt less.

At the mention of Tom Jennings, Davey raised his eyebrows and sighed. Thankfully, Richard had spent enough time with barmen to know how to ease a story from sealed lips. It usually took nothing more than a promise that the story wouldn't leave the bar and a generous tip when the next round was served.

Davey explained that each morning he runs down the beach in a desperate attempt to keep the paella and Spanish beer from ruining a body he'd become quite proud of. He runs through the town, down the coast and then back again. Davey said that about six or seven days ago he'd seen a young girl sneaking out of the beach hut. Richard asked what time he'd seen this at, and Davey said it couldn't have been any later than seven in the morning. Davey admitted he couldn't be sure what she'd been up to in there, but he very much doubted she'd spent the night alone.

As it turned out, Davey's story was the straw that broke the camel's back. Or more accurately, it was the piece of information that unhinged Richard Tyler. Davey, who was clearly enjoying how generous Richard was being with his tips tonight, happily shared that Tom was being put up in the hotel, the final room on the staff corridor.

Richard didn't even finish his whiskey. Instead, he rose to his feet, left a handful of coins on the bar and went in search of the staff corridor.

'Don't worry.' Davey shouted after him. 'He doesn't look the type to shag about.'

Richard didn't agree with Davey on that.

* * *

Tom just about had time to register the shock of seeing this vulgar man at his door before he felt the punch that knocked him to the ground. He didn't even have a chance to raise his hands in defence.

187

Richard had aimed for Tom's nose but instead caught him on the forehead, thanks to the whiskey, which meant the pain that rocketed through his knuckles was indescribable. For a moment he forgot all about Tom. Instead, he clutched his throbbing fist, urging the pain to subside.

Tom wanted to get up. He wanted to jump to his feet and fight back, unleashing all the anger he'd ever felt onto the vile man standing above him. But something inside him wouldn't allow it. He could only look up at Richard, who'd finished massaging his fist and was now reverting his attention back to the young lad crumpled beneath him.

Watching Tom fall had been good but seeing the look on the little bastard's face as he cowered up at him was better. The stamp felt better than both combined. Richard brought the heel of his foot up quickly and slammed it down onto Tom's nose, causing a spray of blood to explode from beneath it. He wanted to kick Tom again, just once more to make sure his message had been received, but he had enough sense to steer clear of anything that might enhance the situation. He had no intention of spending his night in a cell. Plus, from the look on Tom's bleeding and swollen face, it seemed his message had been received loud and clear.

'Don't ever speak to my wife again.'

Richard didn't expect to say anything else, but he added an extra seven words that surprised even himself.

'You don't know what we've been through.'

With that, Richard left Tom alone, bleeding on the floor.

* * *

Sarah couldn't remember feeling more awake in her entire life. She'd spent the last hour thinking of all the terrible places Richard could be and all the terrible things he could be doing. Each new idea seemed somehow worse than the last. She was contemplating leaving and going in search of her husband when she heard heavy footsteps echoing up the corridor. No doubt about it, Richard was back and he was swaying from side to side. Sarah filled with relief, maybe he really had just been to The Clover.

She jumped into bed and lay still, hoping Richard would leave her to sleep when he found her like this. She heard him open the door and freeze, just for a moment, as if something about the room shocked him. He then snapped out of whatever thought had frozen him and climbed into bed beside her, making no attempt to pull her from the sleep he thought she was enjoying. Richard was asleep within minutes but Sarah waited, just to be certain.

When she was finally sure that her husband wouldn't open his eyes until the sun rose, she turned around gently and observed him, looking for any indicator of how he had spent his night. The knuckles on his right hand were swollen and a purple hue was spreading between them. It seemed Richard hadn't been enjoying a quiet drink at The Clover after all.

Sarah just hoped that whoever had been on the receiving end of Richard's rage had deserved it, but some part of her knew that wouldn't be the case.

It never was.

* * *

Tom sat on the toilet holding tissue to his throbbing nose for twenty minutes. His vision was blurred and his eyes wouldn't stop leaking, but thankfully he didn't think anything was broken. He had no idea how he'd possibly explain his injuries to Gabriella but right now he couldn't think of anything besides the pounding pain at the centre of his face.

Once he'd stopped the bleeding, Tom poured himself another gin and tonic and drank the concoction with ferocity. He wanted the pain to stop and he guessed another drink would be the quickest solution. Tom finally collapsed into sleep sometime later, with his mini-fridge almost empty and his world looking considerably brighter than it had following Richard's assault.

He dreamed of nothing but Joy. Never once wondering why she hadn't come back as she'd said she would.

* * *

Roger Wyatt settled into bed without a care in the world. He didn't spare a thought for the woman who'd taken her final breath on the same bed in which he was now lying comfortably. She no longer mattered. It seemed Nathan really had fixed everything. Roger had nothing to worry about anymore. He was blessed with money and power and at the end of the day, that was all that really mattered. He'd never hurt anybody again. He'd never step out of line again. Because as long as he persisted, he would eventually get everything and anything he wanted.

The only thing he wanted now was Gabriella, and soon that wait would be over. He drifted off to sleep quickly, content in the knowledge that he didn't have long to wait.

* * *

Nine days. Gabriella only had nine days to ensure Roger saw justice, or at the very least saw some retribution for what he had done. Nine days. She needed to fix this and she would. At any cost.

Gabriella opened up her laptop and began to type, resigning herself to the fact that another night without sleep lay before her.

21

The Sunrise Building

Tom wasted no time in getting to the beach hut the next morning. He'd slept terribly, thanks to either the pounding in his head (alcohol-induced) or the throbbing in his nose (Richard induced) or a combination of both. The damage was bad, he looked like he'd been in a fight and there was no amount of concealer that could hide it. His right eye was an ugly mix of purple and black, his nose was almost comically swollen, and his eyes were bloodshot. To put it simply, Tom looked like hell.

Tom washed down three painkillers with a mouthful of warm water. He sat down to write but found that, with the ache in his head progressing steadily towards a migraine, Rose's world escaped him. Instead, he opened up a copy of *IT* that he'd left in the hut a couple of days earlier and tried to lose himself in the world of Derry and the sewers beneath it. With everything that had happened yesterday, Tom completely forgot that Sarah Tyler was supposed to be arriving any minute to collect Nathan's phone number, which meant he had no reason to worry when she didn't.

Hours passed and soon the beach was full of life. By all accounts, today was supposed to be the hottest day of the year and where better to celebrate such an occasion than by the sea? Tom read and napped and wasted the day completely. Not once did he think of Sarah Tyler or why she hadn't arrived at the beach. Not once did he worry about what might have happened to her.

After a day spent enduring the ferocious sun and a cataclysmic headache, Tom was finally free to retreat to the air-conditioned relief of his hotel room. On his way back he decided to text Joy (admittedly he would have text her earlier had Richard not knocked all the sense out of him yesterday). He thought a night with her might be the only way to overcome his migraine. He'd just about unlocked his phone when he was interrupted by a pair of high heels echoing against the marble floor.

'Tom, a word in my office.' Gabriella said sternly.

Tom's migraine worsened considerably.

The door to Gabriella's office had barely slammed closed before she began her assault.

'What happened to your face?' She asked as she took a seat behind her desk. She looked as though she hadn't slept in days, there were heavy bags beneath her bloodshot eyes.

Tom, who couldn't think of a believable lie, decided there was only one method of defence. 'I um, I'd rather not say to be honest.'

Gabriella gestured for Tom to sit down. He did as he was told.

'Look, I'm not gonna waste my time here Tom, I'm just gonna be honest with you. I don't give a fuck what happened to your face, but I'm the manager of this hotel and it's my job to ensure the safety of my staff and my guests. So I don't need to know the ins and outs of it all, I just need you to tell me that whatever happened didn't involve a member of my staff or a guest and that it didn't happen on the grounds of the hotel.'

'It didn't and it didn't.' Tom answered quickly. This wasn't the time for honesty, that much was clear.

'Good. I'm not going to take this any further but if the guests start to complain about the state of your face I won't have any choice, OK?'

Tom's migraine was so thunderous he began to worry he might lose consciousness and slump down in his chair. A part of him thought fainting would be preferable to soldiering on through the rest of this conversation.

'OK.' He whispered limply.

Gabriella loosened as if a tiny weight had been lifted. Her tone of voice became lighter, and Tom began to hope that maybe all was not lost.

'I um, I think I'm going to need your help with something.'

'What's that?' Tom asked.

'In eight days there's going to be some sort of party here. I don't know all the details yet but as far as I'm aware the dates set in stone.'

'Oh, OK.' Tom replied, struggling to understand what Gabriella was asking. 'Do you need me to be a waiter again?'

'I don't think you'll be a waiter this time, more than likely you'll be working at the front of house.'

'What's that?' Tom asked tentatively, feeling unsure about being asked to take on another role he had zero qualifications for.

194

'That doesn't matter now. There's something else I need to ask and it's more important than the work.' Gabriella's tone was no longer stern, more than anything it was desperate.

'What is it?' Tom asked, suddenly filled with dread.

'I was just hoping that if I ask you to do something on the night, even if it sounds a bit strange, you'll help me.'

Tom felt he was in no position to refuse Gabriella's ominous request, especially considering the state of his face and the fact that a guest of the hotel was indeed responsible for the bruises.

'Of course.' Tom began. 'Just let me know if anything comes up.'

'Good. I appreciate it, Tom. Thank you.'

And Tom knew she really did appreciate it. He could see it in her eyes. She needed a friend just as much as she needed a good night's sleep.

'It's OK.' Tom replied, and then more sincerely, he added, 'I am sorry about this.' He gestured to his face.

'It happens to the best of us.' Gabriella replied with a wry smile. 'Look I wanted to apologise about how I spoke to you the other day. It wasn't right and I um... Well, I appreciate you not bollocking me for it.'

'I nearly did.' Tom replied honestly. 'I guess I better get going then.'

Tom stood, turned and headed towards the door. As he walked he thought of Joy and how he'd like to surprise her tonight, hoping it would make the shock of his face more palatable. Maybe he could arrive at her room unexpectedly just as she had. With this thought in mind, he turned back to Gabriella.

'I'm sorry but could I ask for one more favour whilst I'm

195

here?'

Gabriella sighed. 'What do you want?'

Joy arrived at the door of Tom's hotel room exactly two hours after his impromptu meeting with Gabriella. It took Tom a minute or two to answer the door on account of the bottle of red wine he'd helped himself to. After his meeting with Gabriella, he'd certainly needed it.

Joy looked as vibrant as ever as Tom opened the door, but her vibrancy was suddenly replaced with concern. She rushed through the door for a closer inspection.

'Shit! What happened Tom?' There was genuine worry in her voice. For a second Tom forgot about everything. When he eventually remembered it hurt, especially knowing what was about to happen.

'Nothing, it um… It's a long story.' Tom said as he retreated into the room.

'Did someone hurt you?' Joy wasn't content with letting Tom dodge the question. She followed him into the room and closed the door behind her.

'It doesn't matter.' Tom poured himself another glass of wine without offering one to Joy. She either didn't notice or didn't care. The bruises on his face were still her most pressing concern.

'Of course, it matters.' Joy was growing frustrated at Tom's evasiveness. 'What happened Tom? Why won't you tell me?'

Had Tom left Gabriella's office without asking for a favour he would have told Joy the truth. He would have asked for her advice and listened to what she had to say because just that morning there had been nobody's advice he'd wanted more. But Tom now knew better than to tell Joy the truth, because she herself had never once told him the truth. And so, instead of answering Joy's question, Tom turned towards her and asked a question of his own.

'Who are you? Really?'

Joy, who was usually five steps ahead of Tom, fell momentarily silent. She stared at him innocently for a moment, Tom guessed she was weighing up her options.

'What do you mean?'

'I wanted to surprise you today. I went and spoke to my manager to ask what room you were staying in, at which point I realised you'd never even told me your last name which is ridiculous in itself, but she owed me a favour so she checked the system for anybody with your first name. And guess what, there's not a single person staying here called Joy.'

Tom wanted to be angry but he just didn't have it in him. His disappointment was too overbearing. He finished the glass of wine he'd poured just moments ago, thinking maybe it would help him feel better. It didn't.

'Look, Tom...' Joy began.

'No!' Tom was surprised at how violently the word echoed around the room, but he continued regardless. 'I want to know what you've lied to me about. You've either lied about staying here which is just bizarre or you've lied about your name which is, I don't even know what it is, insulting.'

'I haven't lied to you once!' She said firmly. 'My name is Joy. Joy Barren if my surnames that important to you. And I never told you I was staying here. Not once.' She stared at Tom resolutely, he doubted she'd lost many arguments.

'What, so that's just it?' Tom asked as he poured another glass of wine. He hesitated and then poured a second glass, leaving it on the counter to see if Joy would claim it. 'You're in the right because after knowing me for more than a week you've finally told me your last name? And I'm sure you told me you were staying here. You were doing your washing here! What else was I supposed to think.'

'You never asked me for my surname just like I never asked for yours. Why does it matter anyway? You've definitely never asked me where I'm staying, hence why I haven't told you.'

Joy collected the glass of wine waiting for her and took a large sip. It seemed she too thought a good Merlot might hold the secret to remaining calm.

'That's not just it though, Joy. We've spent hours talking to each other and I still feel like I barely know anything about you. It's all just fluff. I don't know anything real about you and this just proves it.'

Words escaped Joy. She could only shake her head.

'You wear the all-inclusive wristband for fucks sake! I don't think I'm crazy for assuming you were staying here.'

'We've known each other for less than two weeks.'

'Don't do that. Don't pretend this is less than it is.'

'What is it then?' Joy asked, the tone of her voice rising to match Toms.

'I like you. I don't know why you think that's such a bad thing.'

'I don't!'

'Then why are you lying to me?'

'Why does it matter?'

'Because I don't want to be treated like a prick!'

Joy said nothing. She turned and headed to the door.

'That's just it then, is it? Off you go?' Tom asked, praying

198

the answer would be no.

Joy turned back to Tom. Her chin wobbled and her eyes glistened with tears. She left before Tom could see her cry.

* * *

The knocking on Tom's door was faint but it woke him all the same. His eyes were heavy, and his mouth was painfully dry. He splashed his mouth out quickly, which restored some element of his awareness, and then glanced through the peephole to find that, for the second time that day, Joy was waiting outside his door.

Unlike before, Joy did not attempt to enter the room. Tom felt slightly unnerved by her lack of poise, this side of Joy was completely alien to him.

'Will you come for a walk with me?' She asked softly.

'A walk?' Tom asked sceptically.

Joy nodded.

'I dunno Joy. It's the middle of the night.'

'Please.' Now Joy did look up at Tom, and her eyes were brimming with desperation. He didn't think anybody in their right mind could say no to those eyes. He certainly couldn't.

'OK. Where are we going?'

They left the hotel and headed left down the coastal pathway. They walked quickly and silently. Tom had no idea what to say and Joy seemingly had no desire to say anything at all. The sky was beautiful at this time of night. Tom had never before seen so many stars up there and he was astounded by the way they captivated him.

They'd walked for a little over ten minutes when they arrived at a rather sorry looking block of apartments. A sign identified the building as the Sunrise Building, although Tom couldn't think of a building that more accurately represented rain. The walls were littered with graffiti and the slate roof was cracked and crumbling. Litter was scattered around the building and the light above the entrance flickered ominously.

Joy seemed to notice the way Tom stared at the building, his mouth slightly ajar and his eyes filled with shock, and decided to break the silence.

'It's not quite the Scarlett Grove.'

'I didn't say anything.' Tom replied with no real conviction, knowing his face had already told Joy everything.

'I know. It's this way.'

Joy led Tom up a flight of stairs and down a thin corridor towards apartment five. She unlocked the door and gestured for Tom to step inside.

Apartment five of the Sunrise Building was surprisingly bare. It consisted of a cramped kitchen, a living room that seemed too small for the two-seater couch within it, and a bedroom that was larger than both other rooms put together. The walls were bereft of any family photos or hints of personality. There was a huge collection of books piled against the far wall in the bedroom (Tom was pleased to see a couple of Stephen King titles), a small TV in the living room and a Macbook resting beside the kettle.

Joy stood silently as Tom took in his surroundings. He noticed lit candles had been scattered across the room and wondered if Joy had set them up when she decided to bring him here. He hoped so.

'What do you think?' Joy asked nervously.

'I think it's got more life than my room at the hotel.' He said with a smile, a smile Joy wasn't yet able to return.

Joy wandered into the kitchen. Tom followed her.

'I've got a bottle of wine if you want a glass?' She asked quietly.

'Yeah, sounds nice.' Tom noticed a dent in the wall that appeared to be the width and dimensions of a fist. 'Do you own this then?'

'Yeah, basically.'

'What do you mean?' Tom asked softly. He didn't want to rush Joy, but he knew tonight was his best chance to finally learn everything he'd been so desperate to know about her.

'It's my Dad's, but I doubt he'd be too pleased if he knew I was staying here.' Joy seemed to notice the way Tom was looking at her. 'We don't get on very well.'

She handed Tom his glass of wine and took a large sip from her own.

'Doesn't he know where you are?'

Joy shook her head and took another sip. Tom decided it might serve both him and Joy a little better if they momentarily changed the subject.

'When are you opening the library?' He gestured towards the tremendous wall of books.

'I thought you could have a VIP tour first.' She replied and Tom saw the first hint of the smile that he'd missed tremendously. 'Do you wanna sit down?'

Two minutes later Tom and Joy were sitting beside one another with their backs against the far wall of the living room, facing the couch. Tom had followed Joy's initiative in sitting here but couldn't stay silent about the ludicrousness of it all anymore.

'Why aren't we sitting on the couch?'

'The floor's more comfortable. Trust me.'

'So, the couch is purely decorative?'

'Essentially.' Joy replied with a laugh.

Tom finished the last of his wine, knowing he'd need extra courage if he were to ask everything he wanted to ask.

'If your Dad doesn't know you're here, does anyone?'

'Um, no. Well I mean you do and the people that have seen me here, but nobody from back home.'

'What about the rest of your family?'

'It's just me and my Dad.' Joy answered whilst awkwardly fiddling with the corner of her glass. 'Or it was I suppose.'

Tom noticed a single drawing on the strap of Joy's watch. It was a storm cloud, the ones that appear before a heavy onslaught of rain. He wondered if there was any significance to that.

'What about your Mum?' Tom asked lightly, not expecting the answer to be particularly pleasant.

'She died when I was two. Breast cancer. I don't really remember it, but my Dad told me it started and ended pretty quickly. Nothing anybody could do.'

'I'm sorry. That's awful.'

'It's shit. But so is life.' Joy replied with a resigned look on her face.

'What do you mean?'

Joy shrugged but Tom knew she was holding something back.

'What do you mean?' He asked again.

'Well, it's just how you view it all I suppose. People seem to think life is mainly happy with the sad moments being the rarities or whatever, you know, like happiness is common and unhappiness is uncommon. I just don't think that's right.'

'What do you think?'

'Look, there are definitely happy moments and I'm not saying I'm depressed or anything like that. I just think that unless you're super-rich or super lucky your life's likely to be mainly bad with fleeting moments of good.' She paused for a moment as if thinking back to the day she first thought this. 'That's just what I think anyway.'

Tom thought about what he'd just heard. He thought about everything he knew about Joy. He began to think that maybe the real Joy had been on display all along, in the drawings on her clothes and her views on the world and the distance she put between the two of them.

'I think I know what you mean.'

'Yeah?' Joy asked hopefully.

'I dunno if I agree with it necessarily but I definitely get it. My Dad died a couple of years back. There are definitely more sad moments than people like to let on. I suppose they just don't want it to be true.'

'Nobody does.' Joy replied flatly.

For a long while, they just sat there in silence. At one point Joy walked to the kitchen and returned with the half-empty bottle of wine. She and Tom passed it back and forth. Tom couldn't remember ever experiencing a more comfortable silence.

'I was going to bring you here, you know. At some point.' Joy said after finishing the last remnants of wine. 'This isn't just because we had a row.'

'Really?' Tom cringed at how desperate he sounded.

'You were right before. I know this isn't nothing.'

Tom smiled as if all the joy in the world was flowing through him. He couldn't find the words to say, not that they were needed anyway. Some things are beyond words.

'Can I ask you another question?' Tom asked when he'd enjoyed the moment an ample amount.

The clock had just passed ten to four. Somewhere outside birds were beginning to chirp.

'As long as it doesn't take long.'

Tom took a moment to prepare himself. 'What happened between you and your Dad?'

'Nothing in particular. He's a bitter old man who lost his wife and never found anything to replace her. It's just one of those things.'

'Those things?'

'Yeah, parents don't get to pick their kids and kids don't get to pick their parents. Everybody thinks you have to love them no matter what but, well that's just not realistic, is it?'

'That's a sad way to think.' Tom said, thinking of the way his relationship with his mother had grown distant since the death of his father.

'It probably is. Let's talk about something else.' Joy said. Tom was more than happy to oblige.

'How long have you been staying for?'

'My Dad bought it when the building began construction, which of course they never really finished. But that must have been at least five years ago now. Back before Roquetas De Mar really attracted any tourists, which is probably why they never finished the building.'

'It looks finished?'

'They finished the building but none of the amenities around it. There was supposed to be a pool and a gym and a restaurant and everything. Only one other apartment sold.'

Joy looked out of the window. Everything was silent apart from the chirping birds.

'I think it's time for bed. Come on.' Joy rose to her feet, took Tom by the hand and led him into the bedroom where they collapsed into sleep wrapped up in each other's arms.

Of all the nights Tom had spent with Joy, this was by far his favourite.

22

A Perfect Shift

The streets were quiet as Tom made his way back to the Scarlett Grove the next morning. Thankfully none of the beach dwellers seemed to notice or care that he was fifteen minutes late, although he guessed one or two might take issue with the fact that he hadn't yet showered.

Joy arrived as Tom was preparing to go in search of food. She was wearing a yellow dress, the only drawings on which were a sketch of Pac-man and a smiling face that, paired with the yellow background, looked an awful lot like an Emoji.

'What are you doing here?' Tom asked with unmistakable glee.

'I was hungry and wanted to see if you felt like sneaking into the Dining Hall again.'

'Obviously.'

* * *

Sarah's morning unfolded largely as expected. Richard

dictated that they would be spending the day by the pool (just as they had yesterday) and Sarah agreed whilst displaying the best fake smile she could muster (just as she had yesterday). They were by the pool before the clock struck ten and Richard had a drink in his hand not five minutes later.

Sarah spent her morning concocting a plan. She'd need half an hour to sneak down to the beach hut without raising Richard's suspicions. Difficult? Yes. Impossible? No. To see just how difficult it would be Sarah decided to test Richard's patience. She excused herself, politely of course, headed to the bathroom and waited in the stall for ten minutes, wondering all the while if Richard had even noticed her leave.

He noticed. Sarah found Richard waiting outside the bathroom like a bodyguard or, more accurately, a warden. A warden who no longer trusted his prisoner.

* * *

Tom and Joy walked hand in hand towards the hotel. Tom realised it was the first time he'd held Joy's hand since they'd fled from the tapas restaurant all those nights ago.

'Shit!' Joy blurted out, startling Tom. 'I completely forgot to ask. What actually happened to your face?'

'Oh, shit yeah. Well, it's quite a long story actually. There's a couple staying here at the hotel, a married couple, and on my first day at the beach I saw them hit each other.'

'Jesus! Really?'

Tom suddenly found himself thinking about what Joy had said about life being predominantly sad with rare moments of happiness thrown in. In the case of Sarah and Richard

Tyler, it seemed she was right.

'Yeah, it was bad. Anyway, the lady, she's called Sarah, came to see me the other day. She asked for my help with something and I guess her husband, Richard he's called, must have seen us together and assumed the worst. So, he showed up at my room later that night and hit me. He threw in a kick for good measure too.'

'Wow.' Joy took a moment to digest the avalanche of information she'd just been buried beneath. 'I have lots of follow up questions.'

'That makes sense.'

'Tell me over dinner.' Joy said as they entered the hotel and headed towards the Dining Hall.

* * *

Gabriella Glover had already ignored three calls from Roger and it was barely midday. She had good reason to ignore his calls, of course. She had only seven days to free herself from the almighty hole she'd fallen into, and she didn't plan on wasting any more time in the presence of that canine grin.

She spent her day buzzing around the hotel. She organised the things that needed to be organised and sorted the things that needed to be sorted. Most importantly though, she scheduled a meeting with her solicitor, a plump woman named Angelina, for the following morning. Angelina made no attempt to hide her confusion but accepted merrily, any excuse to send another bill Gabriella's way was good news to her.

Between her short conversation with Angelina and her

odd jobs around the hotel, Gabriella locked herself in her office and scrolled through local news sites. Still nothing. No breaking news. No shocking scandal. No corpse discovered on the beach or the woods or a derelict building.

Nothing. Absolutely nothing.

* * *

With plates piled high and wine glasses filled, Tom and Joy resumed their earlier conversation. Tom told her everything, from accidentally becoming a third-party member in a drug deal, as she already knew, to being sought out by a woman desperate for the number of that same drug dealer.

'So, what do you think?' Tom asked upon finally finishing his account.

'I'm not sure.' Joy replied, looking genuinely perplexed. 'What do you think she wants his number for?'

'I don't know. The obvious answer would be the same thing Roger wanted him for, but she doesn't seem the type. It seems more important than that.'

'To some people, there's nothing more important.'

'No, I know. She just doesn't seem the type.'

'You can't trust Nathan.' Joy spoke firmly, acknowledging the elephant in the room for the first time. Tom noticed Joy lower her hands beneath the table and wondered if they were shaking.

'What did he do to you?' He asked carefully.

'He's just not the type of person anybody should trust.' She saw the way Tom was looking at her and continued. 'I'm sorry but with everything we talked about last night and...'

209

Joy looked around anxiously as if Nathan might be sitting at the table behind her, sampling the pea soup and listening in. 'I'd rather not get into the specifics of it all right now. I will tell you at some point, I promise. Just for now, I trusted him and I shouldn't have done. I wish I hadn't.'

Tom let that hang for a while, thinking it over. He smiled at Joy to show her he understood, and she smiled back as if to thank him for it.

'You're going to give her the number, aren't you?'

'I think so.' Tom answered truthfully. 'I just don't know how I'm going to get it to her without getting another.' Tom didn't finish his sentence, instead he gestured to his face.

'I'll do it.' Joy replied calmly, and although Tom had a lot more questions, it seemed the matter was settled.

* * *

Roger hadn't exactly told Gabriella the truth about the spectacle he'd planned. He had, to his credit, organised the biggest firework display Roquetas De Mar had ever seen. The display was to take place on the private stretch of beach outside the Scarlett Grove and everybody staying at the hotel was invited to watch. So too were the forty people on the guestlist Roger had written up, all of whom were white-collar buddies of his. One noticeable absence from the guest list was Bill Wyatt. Roger decided this was the perfect way of telling his father to fuck off without having to waste any breath.

When Roger had tried to organise everything else though, including catering and waiters and music and all the other nonsense required for nights of celebration, he quickly realised he had neither the competence nor the patience to do so. Suddenly it became more important that he speak to Gabriella because now he needed to ask for her help. He just needed to convince her, and for that he would need his magic powder. But how would he get his hands on it?

After spending years surrounded by dealers, Roger had developed a keen eye for spotting them out in the wild. This particular dealer wore baggy jeans, a tight T-shirt and spoke in a thick Spanish accent. Roger overpaid for the gram but that didn't matter. He probably would have given his right arm for it.

He returned to his penthouse feeling refreshed, once again the man who could handle anything. With that in mind, he got straight back on the phone. He rang the catering people, the DJ, the band and everybody else he'd given up on earlier in the day. Nobody answered, because of course by now businesses were closed, but Roger was not deterred. He made six calls before he fell into a sea of blackness, all of which went unanswered.

* * *

Tom and Joy met outside the Dining Hall an hour after Tom's shift finished, allowing Joy time to fetch an outfit and Tom a long overdue shower. They ate large portions, shared a bottle of red wine and talked about everything and nothing before returning to Tom's room to try and decide who was the superior *Mario Kart* racer.

They drank and laughed and raced and at some point in the evening, Tom kissed Joy again. She kissed him back firmly

211

and passionately.

Tom slept sweetly and without dreams.

23

A Cosmic Fluke

As Tom finished his seventh new page of the day and Joy lounged by the pool, looking for somebody matching the description of Sarah Tyler, Gabriella left Angelina's office. She'd spent the last ninety minutes in a stuffy office on the fourth floor of a large building listening to Angelina explain that, with over ninety percent of the paperwork already submitted, there was simply no way the Wyatt Foundations acquisition of the Scarlett Grove could be derailed. Gabriella had asked all the right questions and exhausted all possible exit strategies, but none were plausible. She left the building consumed by a deep sadness that threatened to tear the sun straight out of the sky.

Gabriella took her time as she walked. She was in no rush to return to the hotel, especially given the mundane tasks that awaited her there. The job she had once adored had fast become tainted, so much so that it was now a chore. Her future had never seemed less clear.

She didn't make a conscious decision to walk past the Scarlett Grove, she just did. Somebody else could step up and steer the ship today. Not that it would make much difference. The waters were troubled, and a storm was on the horizon. A storm that would destroy the ship and kill the crew.

Gabriella checked into the Hilton Hotel, requesting a room with a sea view. She was no longer the captain of her ship but at least this way she could keep watch over it.

* * *

Sarah smiled when Richard suggested another day by the pool. This delighted Richard, who was blissfully unaware that his wife had an ulterior motive. They left early to ensure they reserved a pair of loungers just steps from the pool bar. Sarah smiled again as Richard ordered his first pint. For her plan to work she needed Richard relaxed and unsuspecting. The alcohol would certainly help with that.

Richard was pleasantly surprised when his wife, who was usually so opposed to his drinking (with good reason), asked if he'd like to join her in a mojito. He agreed enthusiastically and even watched Sarah walk to the bar, paying particular attention to the way her hips swayed as she went. Back when they'd first started dating, he never missed an opportunity to watch those hips move. He needed to start paying attention again, and he would. Especially if it kept her away from the beach and the prick working there. The thought of the beach hut set a cloud inside Richard's mind. He drank his mojito quickly and when he went to the bar to fetch himself another, he didn't offer to collect one for Sarah. Sarah didn't mind though. In fact, her plan was coming together rather perfectly.

Sarah wasn't sure how many mojito's Richard had helped himself to, but she was confident it would have been enough to sedate a small animal. Still, it didn't prevent him from asking Sarah to grab him another one. She thanked the barman who looked at her as if to ask why she was encouraging her husband to drink so excessively and headed back to find Richard dozing on his lounger. She set the drink down quietly and waited. After fifteen minutes spent watching Richard drunkenly snooze, Sarah became aware of a young woman staring at her from across the pool.

The girl smiled at Sarah, making it clear she was the focus of her attention, and then headed into the hotel. Sarah had absolutely no idea why, but she found herself following the girl. She knew she was probably sacrificing her only chance to fetch the number from Tom, but this seemed important. Call it intuition or call it dumb luck but Sarah knew the importance of the girl with doodles on her clothes and fire in her eyes.

* * *

Joy didn't have to look back to know Sarah was following her. She walked quickly and with purpose, striding through the reception area and into the lady's bathroom, which was thankfully empty. She wasn't sure exactly what would have happened if this hadn't been the case, but it certainly would have complicated matters.

Sarah entered the bathroom moments later. Joy acted quickly, moving the bin in front of the door to prevent any unwanted interruptions, least of all from the man Sarah Tyler shared a surname with.

'Do I know you?' Sarah asked, suddenly very aware of just how ludicrous it was to have followed a complete stranger into the bathroom.

'I'm friends with Tom. From the beach hut.' Joy added swiftly, unsure of how much Sarah actually knew about Tom.

'Oh, really?'

'Yeah. He told me about you and your husband.'

'Oh.' Sarah spoke even more quietly now. Her eyes diverted down to the tiled floor. 'What did he tell you?'

'He told me about what happened between you two on the beach.' Joy replied honestly. 'And he told me about what you asked him for the other day.'

'Did he get it?' Sarah's desperation almost exploded from within her.

Joy didn't like that she saw some of herself, the old her at least, reflected in Sarah. She shook the thought away almost as quickly as it arrived. 'He did. But before I give it to you, I want to make sure you know what you're doing.'

Sarah's entire body stiffened. The woman who, just seconds ago, had been withdrawn was now on high alert. 'I'm sorry, what?' She asked with disbelief. 'I don't know you and you don't know me. You have no right to look down at me. So, either give me the number or leave but stop pretending you care. You don't.'

Joy took some time to select her words. She knew one misstep could force Sarah back to the pool and back to her husband. 'You're right. I didn't mean it like that.'

'What did you mean then?' Sarah asked, her intensity unwavering.

'I know this man.' Joy said as she removed the hotel napkin

on which Roger had scrawled Nathan's number. 'He's not a good person. I can't stress that enough. Whatever you want from him, just be careful, OK? And if he offers you something for free don't accept it. You do not want to be in his debt. I promise you.'

'Thank you.' Sarah whispered as she took the napkin, her fight had disappeared now she had what she wanted. 'Don't leave right after me. Just in case he's awake.'

Sarah didn't need to explain who she was talking about. Joy already knew.

* * *

It was mid-afternoon when Roger awoke to the sound of a ringing phone. Normally he would have rejected the call and let sleep consume him once again, especially considering the sludge currently churning its way through his system, but nothing about the last couple of days had been normal. He answered the call and heard a familiar voice. Suddenly Roger felt soberer than ever before.

'You lied to me.' Nathan hissed.

Roger wished he'd prepared for this. He'd known it would happen but still, he'd emptied the baggie and now he was woefully unprepared for a conversation that would prove vital to his chances of survival.

'Oi!' Nathan pressed, enraged by the silence.

'What do you mean?' Roger asked, again cursing himself for his lack of preparation. He began searching desperately for any remaining white powder that would ensure this conversation ran smoothly. He couldn't find any. He cursed himself again, he'd promised to ration the bag.

'Who'd you buy it from?'

'I don't know.' Roger knew lying wasn't an option. This was Nathan's town and Roger was an impostor.

'Where did you find him?'

'What does that matter?' Roger asked rather defensively.

'You don't ask the questions, you answer mine.'

'Why does it even matter? It's just a gram. I needed it to feel better and now I do. That's all that matters.'

Nathan sighed. He took a second to think and then decided on an answer rather suddenly. 'I'll be there in twenty minutes.'

'What? Why?' Roger asked, hoping the panic in his voice wasn't as apparent as he thought it had been.

The line clicked dead. Roger swayed on his feet but didn't fall, maybe that was something to be proud of.

* * *

Joy explained what had happened in the bathroom, sparing no detail. Tom listened and when she'd told him everything they went for dinner. Not to the Dining Hall. Today they deserved something new and so they found a cafe where they ate omelette's and drank cocktails. Tom's three-day drinking rule was no longer in effect, but Joy had taught him that sometimes it's OK to break the rules.

* * *

Gabriella stayed in her room all day. Drowning her sorrows

218

with the contents of the mini-bar. She vowed to return to work tomorrow. She couldn't hide here forever but she could tonight and that was enough. Here she was safe. Here he couldn't find her.

* * *

Roger wasted no time. He packed enough clothes for a single night and left with his head pounding and his throat hoarse. When Nathan arrived at the penthouse apartment, Roger was halfway through the process of checking in to the Scarlett Grove Hotel and Spa.

Nathan hadn't expected Roger to be there. He wanted this to act as a warning rather than a punishment. Still, he needed Roger to know he was serious, which explained the stiletto heel he left on the bed. Roger would know exactly who it had belonged to.

Meanwhile, Roger was already missing the company of his powdery best friend. He had all the money in the world and yet he couldn't get the only thing he wanted; a little bag of white powder to help him through the night.

* * *

It may sound strange, or even difficult to believe, but Tom, Joy, Sarah, Richard, Gabriella and Roger all fell asleep at exactly the same time that night. Maybe it was some cosmic connection or an unexplainable fluke, but it really is true. One final act of camaraderie before the chaos begins.

219

24

The Magic Bistro and a Black Stiletto

Despite Tom's polite request for an extra hour's sleep, Joy insisted that he get dressed. She was excited. More excited than he had ever seen her. There was somewhere she wanted to show him, and she wouldn't say another word until they arrived there. She guaranteed it would be worth the wait and Tom knew without a doubt that she'd be right.

* * *

Sarah woke long before Richard, but she didn't move. Instead, she lay on her side with her eyes tightly closed, thinking of nothing but the napkin she'd hidden in a bundled-up pair of socks in her suitcase. She knew what would happen if she ever built up the courage to make the call. Getting the number had been one thing. Making the call was something entirely different and infinitely bigger.

Last night Sarah had been presented with the perfect opportunity to do it. Richard had slept so heavily she doubted even an earthquake would have woken him. But still, something had stopped her. Maybe it was how peaceful Richard looked as he slept. Maybe it was the fact that Richard was the only person who understood just how terrible a hand life had dealt them. Maybe it was just the uncertainty of who she would become without him.

At some point, Richard awoke, complained about how sore his head was and asked if Sarah wouldn't mind staying in the shade today. She didn't mind one bit. A room without distractions was the best place for her right now. At least it was until Richard started kissing her neck.

* * *

Gabriella turned her phone back on for the first time in over twelve hours to find eleven missed calls and twenty-three texts. The ship, it seemed, still needed its captain. Gabriella wasn't going to be the first to abandon ship. No matter how much she wanted to.

With her head still sore and her stomach no longer rumbling (thanks to a sensational full English breakfast), Gabriella headed back to the Scarlett Grove to see just how much damage had occurred in twenty-four hours without her supervision.

Thankfully there were no major issues for her to resolve. A member of the kitchen staff had called in sick (not for the first time) and Gabriella found somebody to cover the shift. Today's delivery from the suppliers had been short (also not for the first time), so she rang the suppliers and made it perfectly clear that she expected the missing bottles delivered within the hour. She spent the entire day working. Even the smallest tasks were now worthy of her attention. She'd do anything to take her mind off Roger Wyatt and his canine grin.

* * *

Joy didn't explain it, but Tom understood the significance of the day she'd planned for them. He knew that the deli they'd visited, where she'd insisted they both tried something called the farmyard omelette, meant more to her than she let on. It wasn't just the best breakfast in town (although there was a case to be made that it was), it was a place where Joy had memories, happy memories. And now she wanted more memories there, memories with Tom. He was a part of her life now and that meant giving him a glimpse of the life she'd once had.

Tom soaked up every moment. He lost himself in their walk across the beach. Time seemed to freeze as the sun reflected from the fire in Joy's eyes and Tom knew that no moment in his life had ever been so beautiful. They arrived at the end of the beach where they were faced with a small mass of jagged rocks obstructing their path. Tom knew what Joy was going to ask before she opened her mouth.

'You want us to climb this, don't you?' He asked, knowing he would do it without hesitation.

'It's not going to climb itself.' She replied playfully and began to shimmy up the wall without the slightest struggle.

Tom watched her climb for a moment and then began a significantly more awkward ascent of his own.

* * *

'I thought I'd made myself pretty clear.' Nathan said as Roger eased the door of his penthouse open. 'I suppose I should apologise because clearly, I did a bad job of it.'

Roger wasn't exactly taken aback to hear Nathan's leer. He'd known that finding the apartment empty yesterday would not extinguish Nathan's anger but instead ignite it. At some point in the night, just before he'd finally managed to fall asleep perhaps, Roger had accepted that running would get him nowhere. Like it or not he was now indebted to a lowly drug dealer with a thin beard and a condescending tone, and there's nothing he can ever do to change that.

Well, maybe there is one way.

'I'm sorry.' Roger replied calmly, holding his palms up as if to feign innocence.

'Look on the bed.' Nathan ordered.

Roger did as instructed and his heart sank. On the bed was a single black stiletto. On the bed was proof of what he'd done, proof of how much he needed Nathan.

'What's that doing here?' Roger asked, his voice trembling.

'I think you should consider yourself lucky that it's here.' Nathan was clearly thriving on Roger's fear. 'There's a lot of other places it could be. The front of the papers, for one.'

'You wouldn't do that though.' Roger replied, trying to launch an offensive. 'You'd go down too. You helped clean it up after all.'

Nathan smiled. 'Don't test me, Roger.'

'I'm not.' Roger fought the urge to look down, keeping his eyes firmly fixed on Nathan's.

'I gave you one rule, just one, and you've already broken

it. You shouldn't have bought it, and certainly not from a fucking bum on a street corner!' Nathan's frustrations boiled over. He took a deep breath to compose himself.

'Well, I can't exactly become a recluse, can I? I'm in the middle of a million-pound takeover!'

'You can't go out without it?'

Roger said nothing. Shame exploded within him. Finally, he shook his head, admitting a truth he'd long known but never before confessed.

'Putting that aside, I take it your little tapas date was business-related?'

'She's the manager of the hotel. I can't just cut contact with her all of a sudden! She had questions about the takeover and I have to be there to answer them. I can't even explain to you how important it is that this deal goes through without a hitch.'

'Oh, I know.' Nathan lit a cigarette and smoked as he spoke. 'I know just how important it is. I also know what would happen if any of this,' He gestured to the heel on the bed. 'got out. Which is why you need to start listening to me.'

'Fine. Fine, I will. Honestly.' Roger's hands began to shake 'But I need the coke. I need it.'

'I know you do.' Nathan threw a five-gram bag of cocaine onto the bed next to the heel. 'That should be enough for a couple of days at least.'

Roger wanted the coke more than anything, but he also knew when something was too good to be true. This was far, far too good to be true.

'Why?' He asked, hoping Nathan didn't notice the way his eyes lingered on the bag.

'I want something else from you now.'

224

Roger's heart sank. 'What do you want?'

'Truth is I used to spend a lot of time at your hotel. It served as a good way of selling large quantities of my product. I think the old owner knew, not that he ever said anything, but ever since his daughter took over things have been more difficult.'

'You used the Scarlett Grove to sell coke?'

'Not just coke. Guns. Passports. I provide for the people. Whatever they want.'

'How does this involve me?' Roger asked, his chest tightening.

'Well, it's simple really. You're going to turn a blind eye to my business just as the guy who croaked did. Oh, and I want a job. The assistant manager's job to be exact.'

Now Roger was just confused. 'What? You want to work at the Scarlett Grove?'

Nathan laughed, exhaling a large puff of smoke as he did so. 'Obviously fucking not. I'm not going to work there. I am going to be down on the books as an assistant manager though.'

'You're talking about laundering money?' Roger asked as the penny finally dropped.

'I see it as a win-win situation. I get my money into the banks and you get to see me once a week, that way you'll be able to make sure I'm always happy to keep our little secret.'

Roger's fear suddenly morphed into fury. 'You can't blackmail me, you prick! Plus I won't be there all the time to stop Gabriella from getting involved if she sees something she doesn't like.'

'Roger, there's a stiletto on the bed that tells me that isn't my problem. There are bloodstained bedsheets and pictures of this room that tell me I can use your hotel whenever I like.

225

And there's a body out there that tells me I can do whatever the fuck I want. In fact, you should be thanking me.'

'You bastard!' Roger screamed. If he didn't have a bump soon his head would explode.

Nathan placed his finger to his lips. Roger quietened as instructed. 'We don't need to make this a screaming match. Let's be honest, there's nothing for you to shout about. I'll be back first thing tomorrow to discuss the finer details of it all. I reckon you'll have calmed down by then, won't you mate?'

Nathan oozed power. He was everything Roger had spent his life training to be. Were he not currently being crushed by Nathan's power, Roger probably would have admired the man.

Nathan finished his cigarette and stubbed it into an ashtray. 'I'll see you tomorrow then mate.' Nathan smiled before he left, just to really rub salt into Roger's wounds.

It wasn't long before Roger made a significant dent in the bag of magic powder, just as it wasn't long before he collapsed onto his bed in a daze of bright colours and unending horrors.

* * *

Tom and Joy spent the afternoon relaxing on the very same stretch of secluded beach that Sarah Tyler had stumbled upon just days before. They didn't say a lot to each other. They didn't have to. Tom understood the significance of this moment and Joy trusted him not to ruin it with unnecessary words. They watched the sun settle at its peak in the sky and then slowly begin its descent back down to earth. It didn't matter to Tom that it was a day without writing or drinking, all that mattered was being here beneath the glaring sun on this secluded beach with Joy and her blazing eyes. He was beginning to think those eyes were all he would ever need.

'I've never brought anybody else here, you know.' Joy said softly, without looking at Tom. And with that, Tom's day became perfect.

* * *

When it finally seemed there was absolutely nothing left for her to lend a hand to, Gabriella decided to find out just what was included in Roger's spectacle. It took just four calls to uncover that, so far, the only thing Roger had planned was a firework display. Gabriella wanted to be frustrated. She wanted to be angry that Roger had once again shown his true colours, safe in the knowledge that both his reputation and his money would keep him safe from any repercussions.

But Gabriella wasn't angry. She actually felt a strange twinge of joy. She was no longer faced with a night of scouring through the Internet hoping to stumble across the discovery of a corpse (and what a terrible thing to hope for). Now she had calls to make, she had plans to finalise and she had an event to organise. She would make it a spectacle. Roger didn't deserve a reason to celebrate but she certainly did.

Gabriella picked up the phone and dialled, flicking back into her professional self without a second thought. Say what you will about Gabriella Glover, but she really is good at her job.

* * *

Tom and Joy didn't head back to the hotel when it became too windy to enjoy the beach. Instead, Joy led Tom down several side streets, twisting left and then taking a sharp right turn which brought them to a lively square. There were bars and restaurants and even, rather strangely, a bowling alley named after *Indiana Jones*. The square was overflowing with life. It could be found in the eyes of laughing children swinging foam swords at one another and in the smiles of couples sipping cocktails. Mariachi music filled the square. Tom never wanted to leave.

Joy pulled Tom towards a small restaurant consisting of a large patio dining area and an indoor section that offered nothing more than a kitchen and a bathroom. The name on the menu read 'The Magic Bistro' and Tom was inclined to agree. It really was magic.

Joy ordered for the pair of them, opting for the mixed platter for four and a pitcher of sangria. When the waiter, rather understandably, asked if two more people were joining Joy and Tom tonight, she politely shook her head and told the waiter they were eating like royalty.

'You're in for a treat.' Joy promised.

Tom didn't doubt it.

* * *

Sarah and Richard didn't leave their hotel room all day. Richard spent his day watching any English programme he could find on TV whilst Sarah read one of the utterly ridiculous and unrealistic romance novels she'd packed for the trip. Sarah wasn't entirely sure when Richard poured his first drink, but he moved on from the mini-fridge to room service at around four. Every so often Richard would attempt to strike up a conversation, raising insignificant topics such as his love of the bar staff and the weather. Sarah nodded at all the right moments, preoccupied with the phone number currently burning a hole in her brain. She was so preoccupied in fact, that she didn't pick up on the obvious trap being set by her husband.

'That lad from the beach hut seems alright too.'

'Who's that?'

'You know, the lad from the beach hut? He shows us to our loungers.'

'I can't say I've ever really noticed him.' Sarah lied.

'Huh, that's funny.' Richard replied without a hint of amusement.

Richard left the room five minutes later. Sarah barely noticed. She was far too lost in her own head to worry about the real world, but that was a mistake. She had every reason to be worried about the real world that night.

The night quickly became familiar for Richard. He drank in The Clover, enjoying whichever spirit was on offer that night. This wasn't the first time Sarah had lied to him. Richard knew that she lied to him almost as much as he lied to her, but this was different. This lie felt significant. This was no ordinary white lie; this was a betrayal. And whilst Richard should have been angry, furious in fact, he wasn't. He was crushed and the only way to feel better was to order another shot.

He drank until the night became a blur of images. A tall shot of Jack Daniels. A couple dancing on the sticky floor of The Clover as *Sex on Fire* bellowed through the speakers. Sarah sleeping soundly, looking undeniably beautiful, until she was harshly awoken by ice-cold water. Sarah gasping for air as a pair of hands settled around her throat. Sarah locking herself in the bathroom. A pillow wet with tears, tears that didn't belong to his wife, but to Richard himself.

Richard did not know it, but his midnight assault made Sarah's decision a simple one. Tomorrow she would make the call. And when the opportunity finally arises, she will take it. Of that, she has no doubt.

* * *

With their plates and glasses empty, Tom and Joy were finally presented with the bill. They were both counting out notes when suddenly Tom leaned towards Joy with a smile and a plan.

'What?' Joy asked enthusiastically, excited to hear the story behind the smile.

'Why don't we run?'

Joy's face suddenly became blank. Devoid of all emotion.

'We don't have to.' Tom corrected quickly.

Joy lay forty euros down on the plate. 'No. We don't have to.' She replied solemnly and set off quickly.

Tom lay his half of the bill on top of Joy's and set off after her, cursing himself for ruining such a perfect night.

He caught up with Joy a little outside of the square. She was sitting on a low brick wall and staring out at the ocean and the limitless possibilities that lay beyond the horizon.

'Joy, I'm really sorry.' Tom began as he arrived at her side. 'I didn't mean to…' He stopped dead when Joy turned around and he saw the tears in her eyes.

'You don't have to do that.'

'Do what?'

'Pretend that you're OK with the person I used to be! With the things I used to do.'

'Wait, I'm confused.' Tom said, suddenly frustrated. 'We ran from that tapas place like a week ago, and now I'm the bad guy for suggesting we do it again?'

'No, you're not the bad guy Tom.' Tears crept from her eyes. 'I grew up doing stuff like that and, I dunno, I suppose I've always liked it, and because of that, I think I'll always do it to some extent. Like at the airport when there was no real risk. But at the tapas place, that was different.'

'Why? Why was that different?'

'Because I didn't think you'd actually do it!'

Tom's head was spinning. He couldn't fathom what was happening and his temper was bubbling beneath the surface, threatening to erupt.

'Wait. What?'

'You did it!' Joy almost shouted.

'Because you asked me to?' Tom was almost lost for words.

'I know! But why? Why did you do it?'

'I wanted to. You asked me to do it and I went against you for a while but deep down I wanted to do it.'

'Who for? Me or you?' Joy asked, continuing to cry.

'What? Joy I don't understand…'

'Did you do it for yourself or did you do it for me?'

'A bit of both, I suppose.' Tom reached out to take Joy's

231

hands in his own, but she pulled away.

'I'm scared of this.'

'Why?' Tom once again stepped towards Joy, this time succeeding in placing a hand on her shoulder.

There was no answer to his question. Instead, Joy stepped towards him and kissed him firmly. Tom immediately forgot about the question he'd asked. They kissed with the horizon stretching out in front of them and when they were done Joy leaned forward and whispered into Tom's ear.

'Take me to your room.'

25

A Long, Long Day

Sarah awoke on the bathroom floor with her body stiff and her neck bruised. It hadn't lasted for long, but Richard had gripped her neck firmly and manically. The skin was tender to touch and any sharp movements brought on waves of pain so intense she had to bite her lip to prevent herself from crying. Any more sleep was out of the question, so Sarah set about finalising her plan. She no longer had any doubts. In fact, she was more determined than ever before.

* * *

Roger Wyatt arrived at the Scarlett Grove at the same time Tom sat down to write after an hour spent collecting money and showing customers to their loungers. He ignored the confused glances and startled expressions as people passed him, and headed towards Gabriella's office. He didn't knock or check to see if Gabriella was in, he simply opened the door and marched in.

Gabriella screamed. She'd been lost in a world all of her own, continuing to organise the finer details of a party she didn't want to host when the door opened and the figure of her nightmares stepped into her office. There was dried blood beneath Roger's nostrils and some more on his sleeve. It didn't take a genius to put the two together and arrive at four. His shirt was creased, and his pants were stained with what Gabriella hoped was toothpaste. Roger had never before looked so unkempt. It scared her.

'I'm sorry. I didn't mean to scare you.' Roger said, a little out of breath.

'It's OK.' Gabriella replied reassuringly. 'Is everything ok?'

'Um, well yes and no.' Roger sat down without being invited to do so. 'I'm fine. It's just that um, I've found myself with quite a bit of legal mumbo jumbo, you know? A lot of hoops to jump through and not a lot of time to do it in and I mean, it's all possible. Everything's going to go ahead as scheduled so you don't have to worry. I'm just going to struggle to organise some bits of the party, well I've actually called it a Grand Ball on the posters, but I don't suppose that matters right now. Anyway, I know it's a dick move but I was hoping that, so long as you're not too busy, you wouldn't mind lending a hand?'

Gabriella considered telling Roger that she knew he'd planned nothing besides a tacky firework display and that she was already well on her way to salvaging the evening, but decided against it. It was better to keep Roger on her side for the time being.

'That shouldn't be a problem.' She replied with a smile so fake it made her feel dirty. 'I'll get started on it this afternoon.'

'Great.' Roger said with a flash of those animal teeth.

'I don't mean to be blunt, but I think you've had a nosebleed.' Gabriella added with a hint of spite, determined to land at least a jab on Roger before he left.

'Oh shit.' Roger quickly wiped his nose, using the same sleeve that already boasted a crimson stain. Roger noticed the blood and looked back at Gabriella innocently. 'I get them all the time.' He laughed awkwardly.

Gabriella laughed along with him, enjoying watching him attempt to squirm his way out of the situation.

Roger carried the conversation on idly for a minute or two before finally excusing himself and leaving the office as quickly and abruptly as he'd first entered. Gabriella smiled. She'd won that round.

* * *

Richard started his day with one of his speciality insincere apologies that Sarah was so used to. Instead of acknowledging what he'd done and taking responsibility for his actions, which was all Sarah wanted, he crushed two paracetamol tablets, poured them into a glass of water and handed it to Sarah. Sarah had already taken four tablets of paracetamol, but she accepted the drink and drank it quickly. The second part of Richard's apology arrived twenty minutes later in the form of a question.

'What do you want to do today?'

'I was thinking maybe we could relax by the pool.' Sarah replied innocently, although her intentions were anything but.

* * *

Roger returned to his empty penthouse apartment feeling emptier than ever before. For the first time in as long as he could remember he doubted even his magic powder could help improve his mood. That didn't prevent him from snorting a line, it was better than nothing and right now he had nothing else. Maybe he'd never had anything else. Maybe the magic powder had been the only constant, or the only constantly good thing, in his life. Maybe he'd been bound to this fate since he first dipped his finger into a baggie and rubbed the contents against his gums. Not that it mattered now. His decisions had led him here and no amount of money or power could help him wriggle out of it. Roger was destined to spend the rest of his life worrying about the skeleton in the closet. A skeleton wearing stiletto heels and nothing else.

* * *

Nobody seemed to notice how strange it was that Sarah wore a thin cotton scarf around her neck even though the heat was sitting comfortably at twenty-seven degrees. Nor did anybody seem to think it was strange that during all of Sarah's trips to the bar, she ordered one mojito and one virgin mojito. The mojito was given to Richard, who was still making feeble attempts to make amends for his behaviour last night, and the virgin mojito she kept for herself.

Richard didn't notice that, unlike himself, Sarah wasn't feeling the loosening benefits of her cocktails. And by the time he was drunk, he barely noticed his wife at all.

* * *

Tom spent the day perfecting a chapter of his novel in which Rose befriends Isabella, a young street performer who plans to travel across Europe. Rose stumbles across Isabella accidentally, during her long walk to work one morning. She's so captivated by the music that she misses her shift and stays to watch Isabella's entire performance. When the police arrive to move Isabella on (they don't take kindly to busking in Barcelona), Rose helps her flee with her guitar and a hat full of coins. They spend the night drinking and talking and at the end of the night, Rose agrees to join Isabella on her tour. A decision that will have a profound impact on the rest of her life.

When his work was done, Tom returned to his room and squeezed in a quick shower before Joy arrived at his door. He suggested grabbing a quick bite but Joy insisted against it and dragged him to the bed so they could pick up from where they left off yesterday. Tom didn't object.

* * *

Sarah was no stranger to sneaking out of bed whilst her husband snored drunkenly beside her. After the worst of his outbursts, she would often sneak downstairs to patch herself up as best as possible. She had no prior medical experience but over time she'd actually become quite capable, even once closing a deep gash on her thigh with five stitches. Richard always noticed in the morning, when Sarah's cuts were suddenly bandaged and her swelling significantly reduced, but he never acknowledged it. Sarah hoped this was because by then Richard was sober and at least some part of him regretted what he'd done, at least Sarah hoped a part of him did.

Richard had managed to walk himself to their room, but he'd lost enough of his basic motor skills to require Sarah's assistance undressing. Unfortunately, he still had enough brain capacity left to recognise what he saw as a seduction attempt, and so he pulled Sarah towards him. Sarah resisted a little at first before accepting that the whole thing would be over quicker if she just let it happen. She wasn't willing to let him inside of her, not after last night, so instead she used her hand. It didn't take long and once he had finished Richard droned on about how he would return the favour tomorrow and then collapsed into sleep. Once he was still Sarah rushed to the toilet to wash her hands.

She waited for half an hour before finally beginning her plan, the first step of which was to sneak out of the room and make one of the most important calls of her life.

The room itself seemed to be against Sarah. The springs in the mattress screamed as she eased away from the bed. Outside the sea breeze rattled against the windows. Through it all Roger's breathing remained calm and steady.

Twelve steps to go.

Eleven steps to go.

Ten steps to go.

Her feet slapped against the tile floor.

Nine steps to go.

Eight steps to go.

Outside a dog barked. Sarah's heart stopped.

Seven steps to go.

Six steps to go.

Five steps to go.

Richard's leg thrashed against the duvet.

Four steps to go.

Three steps to go.

Two steps to go.

From the floor above, a baby began to cry.

One step to go.

The door was the final hurdle and it proved to be the most difficult too. The hinges groaned as the weight of the door pulled against the tiles. Nonetheless, Richard remained still and Sarah slipped outside, closing the door soundlessly behind her. Her heart was beating even faster now. The wheels were in motion and they couldn't be stopped.

* * *

Tom and Joy ordered room service, two large pizzas, and spent the night in bed. Tom noticed small scars on Joy's body, one on her lower stomach and two at the centre of her back. He wanted to ask about them but tonight wasn't the time. He and Joy both knew what tonight was for. They didn't leave the bedroom.

* * *

Sarah didn't take her phone from her pocket until she'd left the hotel and crept down a small passage that led towards the beach. A barman was finishing up the last of his cigarette and

Sarah tried her best to act inconspicuously until he stubbed it against the wall and returned to finish his shift. With one final glance to ensure she was alone, Sarah took the phone from her pocket and punched in the number from the crumpled-up napkin.

The call didn't last long. The man asked for five hundred euros, a price Sarah agreed to with no real understanding of the value of what she was purchasing. Not that money mattered to Sarah. Richard wouldn't check the accounts whilst they were on holiday, and even if he did, by tomorrow it wouldn't matter. The man agreed to meet Sarah at the beach at this time tomorrow night. With that, the conversation came to an end. The line clicked dead and Sarah returned to her room, slipping silently into bed beside Richard.

For the first night in years, Sarah dreamed sweetly.

26

Another Beer, Another Beer, Another Beer

Nothing particularly interesting happened to either Tom or Joy on Tuesday morning. They enjoyed some time together in bed before Tom left for the beach and Joy drifted back off to sleep. On his way to work, Tom made a swift detour to a grocery store where he bought a crate of Spanish beers. He knew the trouble this would land him in if Gabriella made a surprise visit to the beach, but that seemed unlikely. He hadn't seen her at all over the last couple of days, not to mention she'd seem scattered recently, as if the hotel was no longer her top priority.

Plus, Tom had a theory that the beer would only improve his writing. A theory that was quickly proven right.

* * *

Nothing particularly interesting happened to either Sarah or Richard on Tuesday morning. Sarah awoke before her husband and spent the time running over her plan for her impending meeting with Nathan. She will once again encourage Richard to drink himself into a state of incompetence and then, like the loving wife she is, tuck her husband into bed. After an hour or so to ensure he really is asleep, she will leave the room and meet the man that a strange woman in the bathroom warned her not to trust.

Richard groaned himself awake just after midday with no idea that his wife had spent the morning selecting which cash machine she would use to withdraw the money she intended to hand over to a drug dealer on an empty beach in the dead of night.

* * *

Nothing particularly interesting happened to Gabriella Glover on Tuesday morning. For one thing, the sleeping tablets she'd digested last night, after a long day of organising Roger's Grand Ball, meant she slept through the entirety of the morning. She dreamed of Callum and tried not to think of the significance of this when she awoke.

* * *

While it can be said that nothing particularly interesting happened to Tom Jennings or Joy Barren or Sarah Tyler or Richard Tyler or Gabriella Glover on Tuesday morning, the same cannot be said for Roger Wyatt. Roger awoke from his cocaine-induced sleep at four in the morning to find nothing but a thinning bag of magic powder on the pillow beside him and a stiletto heel hidden away in the wardrobe.

His head throbbed. At some point in the night, his nose had started to bleed, meaning the sheets around him were once again covered in blood and suddenly his hands were wrapped around that skinny throat. The throat of a girl whose name he couldn't even remember. He had stolen her life and he couldn't even remember her fucking name. There must be a special corner of hell reserved for people like him.

Roger needed somebody to tell him it was going to be OK. He needed reassurance and a friendly voice, and he needed it now more than ever. He thought about calling his father but there would be no reassurance there. His mother wasn't an option because she'd be sleeping next to the old bastard. Suddenly his phone was in his hand and he didn't know who he'd dialled but with each passing second, he became more desperate. He needed them to answer. If there was any semblance of decency left in the world, he was owed some relief after the relentless days of shit he had toiled through.

Roger didn't know how many times he tried to call Gabriella that morning, but she didn't answer once. Rage engulfed him. He'd done everything for her and she gave him nothing. It should have been her. It should have been her on the bed, helpless, gasping for air. The thought gave Roger a pleasant sensation, which he gave into without even removing his pants.

Roger was dozing on the edge of consciousness when he heard the knock at his door. He must have been asleep for a while because his underwear was no longer damp. Roger grunted to his feet and opened the door.

243

'Have you thought about it then?' Nathan asked as he strode into the room, biting into the bagel he'd brought with him.

Roger managed only a nod.

'And?'

'I'll do it.' Roger whispered.

'And if the manager tries to stop me?'

'She won't.'

'Excellent.' Nathan replied as if he'd ever had any doubt.

Nathan went on to explain the complexities of the arrangement. Sparing the more complicated details, Nathan planned to drop a certain amount of cash at Roger's apartment each Monday. When Roger reminded Nathan that he was under strict instructions to return to England at the first chance he got, Nathan explained that Roger will be responsible for finding a middle-man to take charge of the arrangement when he isn't here. The database at the Scarlett Grove will be programmed to show that Nathan works the same number of hours as both other assistant managers, which of course he will not. When Sunday arrives, Nathan's weekly wage will be transferred into his account, a wage that matches the exact amount of money given to Roger at the beginning of the week. Simple.

Roger tried to explain that the Scarlett Grove pays their employees monthly rather than weekly. To this, Nathan suggested that seeing as though the ownership of the hotel is changing, so too could some of their policies. Roger tried to explain that should his father ever find out about this, it would be the end of his life as he knew it. To this, Nathan suggested that should his father ever stumble across the truth of what happened in this apartment, it would be a whole lot worse.

Just like that, the conversation was finished. Nathan left with a smile, leaving Roger alone with the knowledge that he would spend the rest of his days trapped in a drug dealer's back pocket. That is unless he could find a way to shift the power dynamic back in his favour.

* * *

Joy left Tom's hotel room and headed back towards the Sunrise Building, walking with purpose, planning to quickly grab some clothes before heading back to the Scarlett Grove to enjoy more free food in the Dining Hall.

She tried not to think of the future as she walked. She'd never imagined she would stay here this long. The risks were growing every day, but she couldn't face leaving Tom, not yet at least. Soon though, she won't have a choice. Soon she will be forced to make a decision, and when that day arrives Tom will either understand or he won't.

Joy was so lost in her own head that she didn't notice the man staring at her from across the street. A man with long hair wrapped in a bun at the back of his head, a thin beard running the length of his jaw and an even thinner moustache. A man who had Roger Wyatt in the palm of his hand.

* * *

At first, Nathan had been sure it wasn't her. It must have been a trick of the light. She couldn't possibly be here. Although that became harder to believe when he spotted a crescent moon drawn lazily on the hem of her white cotton dress. Nathan doubted there was anybody else in Roquetas De Mar who drew on their own clothes.

Initially, he'd contemplated running after her, grabbing her and screaming in her face, demanding she explain why she'd lied to him. She'd told him she was only here for a night. She'd told him she'd need a month or two to make long-term arrangements for her father and then she'd come back and they could talk. Nathan was ready to explain everything, ready to show her the life he could provide for her here. Roquetas De Mar was his playground and his office. He worked hard and played hard and through it all she could be right here by his side.

He struggled to stay calm. His fists were clenched so tightly that his fingers felt as though they might snap. He could deal with the money she'd taken, what was five grand to a man like him? But he couldn't accept being lied to. She hadn't been home to help her father. Maybe the bitter old fuck had finally died. God knows it would be best for everybody if he did.

Nathan followed her, staying a good distance behind, all the way to the Sunrise Building. He couldn't believe it. She'd told him they'd sold this place months ago. Everything she had told him was a lie.

With one final look at the eyesore of a building she called home, Nathan left with nowhere to go, nowhere he needed to be until the middle of the night, but anywhere was better than here. He needed time to think. He'd show her who he'd become. He'd make her understand. And she certainly wouldn't lie to him again.

* * *

Tom enjoyed a very productive morning of writing in which Rose began her European tour with Isabella. The words came thick and fast and Tom felt certain that the six lukewarm beers were at least somewhat responsible for that.

He was so impressed with his work in fact, that he decided it was time to print out his manuscript and have a thorough review of everything he'd done thus far. And so, Tom slipped back inside the hotel and headed for Gabriella's office.

It could have been the six beers now in his bloodstream that gave him the confidence to let himself into Gabriella's unlocked and unoccupied office, or it could have been the excitement of nearly finishing his first novel. Either way, ten minutes and three hundred printed pages later, Tom crept out of Gabriella's office with his manuscript tucked safely beneath his arm.

* * *

Gabriella decided, once she finally got out of bed anyway, to work from her room today. She told her staff that she was coming down with the flu and didn't want to pass it on, but really she just wanted to avoid another unexpected visit from Roger. The reception staff were under strict instructions that, should Roger arrive, he be sent away as quickly and politely as possible.

She finished organising Roger's Grand Ball rather quickly and spent the rest of the afternoon and evening scouring local news sites once again. There was a story about a fire, a story about a burglary and a story about a fatal shooting. Gabriella knew it was unlikely to be connected to Roger, but she read on anyway. It seemed to be a gang-style execution; the victim had been shot in the head from point-blank range. Gabriella was shocked to learn that this had happened just a mile from the hotel, clearly Roger wasn't the only person in Roquetas De Mar capable of taking a life. Still, there was nothing that could be linked back to the youngest member of the Wyatt family. Not yet at least.

Gabriella decided to distract herself. She picked up her phone and dialled Callum. She was convinced he would answer. Those two years of marriage had to count towards something after all, but she was wrong. The phone clicked into silence.

Gabriella shook it off. She lit a cigarette, poured herself a large glass of wine and promised herself that no matter how low she felt she would never call Callum again. Instead, she downloaded *Tinder*, an app she hadn't used since the weeks immediately following her divorce. Her profile was saved, and she wasn't particularly selective as she swiped through the potential candidates. She just needed somebody to keep her from being alone tonight, and within an hour James Banks, a lawyer enjoying a week away, was in her room and in her bed.

As James slipped inside of her, Gabriella thought only of Callum. She wished he'd answered the phone.

* * *

Richard was pleasantly surprised to find Sarah was once

again willing to drink with him. Maybe this was how things would be from now on. Maybe he could drink without being transformed into a monster full of hate and rage. The monster who'd forced him to mistreat Sarah and neglect their son. The monster who had ruined Richard. The monster didn't deserve to be loved by anybody, let alone Sarah. She had stood by him through a year so dark that it had been impossible to imagine how light would ever return. But look where they are now, sharing a table by a pool filled with laughing children. Maybe this could be their life someday.

Richard was interrupted from these rare positive thoughts by a stark reminder of just how bad things had truly gotten. Sarah shifted in her seat and in doing so exposed the devastating purple stain across her neck. In a flash Richard was ripped away from the notion that he could once again be happy and left with nothing but the unavoidable reality that he would never again find happiness and, most importantly, he didn't deserve to.

It hurt to look at the bruise. A pain that burned Richard from the inside and the only way to extinguish the fire blazing within him was to drink. With enough drinks Richard can forget that deep down, in the pit of her stomach, Sarah hates him. She despises him and she has every right to. The only way to make the pain go away is to drink and continue drinking until he suddenly and inexplicably becomes seething with rage, because all he wants in the entire world is for Sarah to love him as he loves her, yet he knows that will never happen. And without Sarah's love, what's the point of anything?

Without Richard, Sarah and Marcus would have been happy.

Another beer.

Everybody would have been happier without him.

Another beer.

He's a cancer.

Another beer.

He's a tumour growing in their brains and maybe he killed Marcus.

Another beer.

Maybe God had spared their little boy from a life with his abusive, alcoholic, spiteful father.

Another beer.

Another beer.

Another beer.

The night became a blur for Richard once again. The last thing he remembered was the pain in his knuckles as they connected with Sarah's cheekbone. Then there was nothing.

* * *

Gabriella lay awkwardly next to James who, despite his undeniable good looks, had been an awkward, disappointing and ultimately selfish lover. Once it was done, he'd fallen asleep swiftly and was now snoring loudly. Gabriella wished it was Callum sharing her bed, but she knew she would never fall asleep with the man who had been her husband again and it broke her heart. Gabriella rolled onto her side so James wouldn't hear her cry.

* * *

The fires of hell are real. They're real and they're currently burning on Sarah's right cheekbone. The pain was sharp and unrelenting. Alone in the bathroom with tears rolling down her swollen cheek, Sarah sent a text asking Nathan to delay their meeting for twenty-four hours. She made sure to apologise, knowing men like him don't take kindly to hassle. With that, she turned her phone off and sobbed into her hands.

27

The Island of Palm Trees Part II

Tom didn't realise he'd forgotten his manuscript until he arrived at the beach, though the blow was softened by the large bottle of gin and two bottles of lemonade he'd bought from the shop. He poured his first glass before a single customer had arrived, trying all the while not to think about how long it had been since he'd gone twenty-four hours without a drink.

* * *

The pain in Richard's right hand woke him up, and the sight of the locked bathroom door sobered him up. He knew Sarah was in there and, though he couldn't remember exactly what he'd done, his swollen knuckles told him enough. Unable to stay here faced with the chilling truth of the pain he'd caused his wife yet again; he slipped a handful of paracetamol beneath the bathroom door and left the Scarlett Grove.

He stood outside the hotel for a long time, staring across

the street at the sordid building that offered Roquetas De Mar's cheapest alcohol and greasiest breakfast. Every inch of his being urged him not to go in. He knew he should walk away, away from the temptation, away from the monster he became.

For a moment Richard believed he could do it, he could walk away and maybe this time he'd be strong enough to finally fix things. To fix himself. Then he took a step forward and realised he was hopeless.

* * *

Gabriella woke up feeling happy. Not only had James left without waking her, which was undoubtedly the best way their sorry time together could end, but today was also her only day off this month. She showered quickly, ridding herself from the stench of last night, and dressed casually, in shorts and a thin navy jumper. She was careful not to make eye contact with any employees as she left, eager to avoid giving them a reason to ask for her help with anything, before embarking upon the fifteen-minute drive to the small cemetery outside St Mary's chapel. Her father's final resting place.

She stopped on the way to pick up two meatball sandwiches, one for herself and one for her father. It had become something of a tradition for her visits here. She talked and ate and left the other sandwich in front of his headstone. It made things feel normal, as if anything about talking to a slab of rock buried above her decaying father was normal.

She told her father about the hotel and the Wyatt Foundation takeover. She told him about Callum and how she'd been thinking of him more recently. She didn't tell him that Callum had ignored her call last night or that she'd settled for a lawyer with a beer belly and a thin penis instead.

She told her father about Roger and her overwhelming certainty that some poor girl had died at his hands. Her father would have known what to do. He would have made sure everything was fine. The thought brought a tear to Gabriella's eye which she quickly wiped away.

She ate her meatball sandwich in silence and hoped that, wherever her father was, he was enjoying a one too.

* * *

Joy's brief trip back to the Sunrise Building was not only to collect clothes, she also planned to grab her worn copy of *Forrest Gump* to prove to Tom that sometimes film adaptations really are better than the novels they're based on. With her bag packed and her hair washed, Joy left apartment five without noticing Nathan sitting at the bus stop on the opposite side of the street. Nor did she notice him rise from his seat and lurk behind her as she journeyed into the centre of town. She didn't even notice as he entered the grocery store thirty seconds after she did.

But Nathan noticed her. He watched her browse idly before collecting everything she needed to make mojitos and head to the till. Nathan smiled. Wow. She really has changed. Back when he'd known her, she would have taken everything she needed without paying. She wouldn't have felt any guilt about it either.

Nathan left the shop and waited outside, lost in his thoughts. The girl he'd known and loved had been a free spirit but maybe it was good that she'd changed. With him, she'd never have to steal again, and he'd make sure she didn't. He couldn't let her ruin the squeaky-clean reputation he'd created for himself. Especially not after last night. Especially not with a murder weapon resting in his backpack.

'You're not supposed to still be here.' Nathan said as Joy left the shop with a loaded carrier bag.

'Jesus Nathan!' Joy managed to reply after recovering from the initial shock of seeing him here. 'Are you following me?'

'What? You lie to me and straight away I'm the bad guy?'

'You will always be the bad guy!' Joy exploded.

'Things are different now. I'm different.'

'How? Explain to me how things are different?' She demanded.

'Well, first things first you're not in shitty old England anymore.' Nathan sounded like a salesman trying to convince a customer to spend more money.

'Why does that matter?' Joy asked as she began walking away at a remarkable speed. Nathan had to jog just to keep up with her.

'It's just us now. Nobody getting in the way. Your Dad can't bother us here.'

Joy turned around and shoved Nathan so hard that it took all his effort to keep from falling over.

'Don't you fucking dare mention my Dad!' She screamed before setting off walking again.

'I've got money now.' Nathan said as he caught up with her.

'You've always had money.'

'Not like this.'

'Alright then, how did you get it?'

'Why does that matter?' Nathan asked sheepishly.

'We both know how you got it and we both know why it matters.'

Nathan stopped following her, knowing what he was about to say would stop her in her tracks. 'You took him to the Magic Bistro? Even I didn't get to go there. He must be special.'

Joy turned and glared at Nathan, but she was far too shaken to form a coherent reply.

'Oh yeah, I saw you yesterday so I asked around, thought I'd find out how long you've been here for.' He continued. 'Turns out you've been spending a lot of time with him.'

'If you carry on following me, I swear to God I'll scream.' Joy's ability to speak thankfully returned.

Nathan only smiled at her. Joy hurried away without looking back.

'Aren't you going to tell me his name?' Nathan shouted after her. 'I'll still be here when you get bored of him.'

Joy's chin wobbled and her legs felt weak.

'Don't worry about the five grand. You need it more than I do.'

Joy didn't stop moving until she arrived at the Scarlett Grove.

* * *

Tom decided against retreating to his room to fetch his manuscript. He'd already enjoyed three strong helpings of gin and lemonade, and there seemed no better way to spend his afternoon than to copy the other beach dwellers and lie back on a lounger with a strong drink in his hand.

* * *

Joy let herself into Tom's room quickly, keen to escape the memory of her most recent unpleasant encounter with Nathan. Her hands wouldn't stop shaking and her legs had never felt less sturdy. Could she really subject Tom to the horrors she'd lived through? Suddenly everything was falling apart. She had mere days left here when just an hour ago she'd thought she had weeks. It was too soon to tell Tom the truth, but the only other option was leaving without him and that didn't bear thinking about either.

She was searching for an empty glass, and knowing Tom, she'd have to settle for a dirty one to pour a stiff drink into. She finally found one on the bedside table, resting beside something that caught her eye. Tom's as-yet-untitled manuscript. Without hesitation, she made herself comfortable and turned to page one.

Joy arrived at the end of the manuscript two and a half hours later. It was about her, that much was clear. Tom was talented too, even without having seen the final few chapters Joy knew he would make a success of himself. What's more, whether Tom knew it or not, he was closer to truly knowing her than anybody she'd met before. Joy didn't know how to feel about that. It certainly didn't make her decision about the future any easier.

She decided not to tell Tom she'd read his novel. Instead, she took a pen, crossed out the words 'untitled manuscript', and in its place wrote 'The Island of Palm Trees'. She then turned the manuscript upside down and left it there in the hope that when Tom eventually saw the new title, he'd like it.

She'd certainly liked what she'd read.

* * *

Tom didn't notice that his manuscript was upside down when he returned to his room, mostly he was just relieved to find that, with the help of three mints, Joy didn't notice the gin on his breath. They spent the night as they'd spent most of their nights together, laughing, drinking, kissing and smiling. Joy was Tom's morning and night. She was the words in his book and the reason for his smile. Suddenly not telling her how he felt was insane. They were lying in bed together, Joy's lips pressed against his own when he suddenly found himself pulling away.

'What's wrong? Joy asked with a startled expression.

'I think I love you.' Tom blurted out more violently than he'd intended.

For what seemed an eternity Joy said nothing. Instead, she studied Tom with those flaming eyes of hers, as if she were looking directly at his heart to see if he really meant the words he'd just said.

'You think or you know?' She finally asked.

'Well I um, I've never been in love before. I don't really know how to know for certain.'

'You don't know how to know?' Joy asked, with a giggle.

'I don't know.' Tom replied, suddenly feeling rather pathetic.

'That's kind of my point. I don't know if you can love somebody without knowing what love is. Especially if you don't know everything about that person.'

'Can you ever really know everything about anyone?'

'I don't know. Probably not.'

'So, by that logic, you don't believe that anybody can ever be in love. Is that what you're saying?'

'I don't think that's what I'm saying.' Joy replied honestly. 'Maybe I was wrong. Maybe you don't need to know everything about a person, but you definitely need to know a lot. And I think a lot of that comes with time. You know, see if you actually still like me when it's not new and exciting anymore.'

Tom got a sense that Joy was speaking from the heart. He wished he knew who'd hurt her. Somebody had taken her heart and laughed as they crushed it, and Tom had no idea how to put the pieces back together again.

'I take it you're freaked out by what I just said then?' Tom asked, deciding the only way to make this situation bearable was to hope they'd be able to laugh about it soon.

'No.' Joy placed a hand on Tom's thigh. He was surprised by how much it comforted him. 'I'm not freaked out. I just... Honestly, I haven't let myself get close to anybody in a long time.' Joy thought of her confrontation with Nathan earlier today. She shivered and lost her train of thought. 'It's like that night we spent in the beach hut. There's a reason I left.'

'Oh.' Tom did not attempt to hide his disappointment.

'No, it's not you.' Joy looked up to the roof, thinking she might find some inspiration up there. 'You scared me.'

'Why?'

'Because I liked you. I was scared because I woke up and I

259

didn't want to leave. I was scared because you ran with me.' She sighed. 'I don't know how to say it so it makes sense to you.'

'You could try.' Tom encouraged.

'I had a really weird childhood. We never had a lot of money and for as long as I can remember my Dad used me to fix that.' Joy noticed the concerned expression on Tom's face and rushed to correct herself. 'No. Nothing weird. It's just I was small and cute which meant nobody suspected me. In fact, even when I got older people didn't suspect me. Even now they don't.'

'Suspect you of what?' Tom asked with concern.

'Stealing things. Robbing people. A little bit of fraud and bribery.' Joy took a moment to gather her thoughts and attempt to organise them into a coherent sentence. 'The reason me and my Dad moved around so much was because sooner or later people caught onto us. We were scam artists Tom.'

Tom wasn't exactly surprised by this. In fact, he'd suspected it since their talk after visiting the Magic Bistro. 'What sort of scams?'

'Nothing bad. We weren't conning old women or swiping money from charity boxes. I did it because if I didn't, we didn't eat. My Dad was a bad bloke. He was a bastard and a wanker but he was still my Dad and he was all I had in the world. The truth is back then I probably would have done anything he asked. I needed him more than he needed me.'

Tears were brimming in Joy's eyes and Tom guessed he was the first person to hear this. He took a moment to plan his reply, careful not to misspeak and ruin everything.

'So, when we ran from the tapas place, what was that?

'I think I was testing you. I didn't think you'd do it. I thought it would give me an excuse to stop spending time with you.'

'Why did you want an excuse?'

'Because I was scared! Scared that if I told you all this you might understand and then where would we be? I left the beach with no intention of ever seeing you again and then all of a sudden you're there in the fucking laundry room and then we're on a date and then you actually steal the kids Switch and now you've been to my shitty apartment and I stay here all the time and I just... I didn't expect any of this.'

'But I don't understand why any of this is bad?'

'It isn't! That's the point.' Joy was staring at him with all the passion and intensity that existed in the world. 'We're here and it's good but I'm scared to be here. And I don't know if I love you but I definitely like you, and I might even love you and that scares me too. I want to see where this goes and, look I understand that this is an insane amount of information to be slapped across the face with, but... I dunno. At least you know now.'

Tom didn't reply. Instead, he kissed Joy more passionately than he'd kissed anybody before. They spent the rest of the night in the most wonderful blur of togetherness.

* * *

Sarah stayed in the bathroom all day, drifting in and out of consciousness until the clock on her phone told her it was almost time to meet Nathan. She unlocked the door slowly, feeling sharp jolts of pain with each movement, and found

261

the room to be empty. Now she just had to get to the beach without collapsing and she might finally have a way out of this wretched life she'd been left with.

Sarah had no idea how long she'd been waiting for Nathan. The pain in her cheek made it impossible to think straight. Her vision flicked in and out of focus and she couldn't hear anything over the sound of the waves. She must have been waiting for twenty minutes now. Maybe even thirty. She'd stuffed the cash she'd withdrawn (from the cash machine inside the hotel, she'd planned to take it from the machine at the petrol station in town, but she simply couldn't make the journey) into her bag which was currently resting beneath the desk. She hoped, once all this was done, that nobody would link her actions back here. Truthfully Sarah quite liked Tom, she certainly owed him a lot, and she didn't want to unintentionally implicate him into what was about to happen.

Sarah was interrupted from her thoughts and the blistering pain in her cheek by the sudden arrival of a casually dressed man with a large backpack and tribal tattoos on each arm. Sarah was speechless, she certainly hadn't expected a drug dealer to look so predictable.

'Sarah.' He asked.

She nodded. 'Are you…'

'Nathan. No, but I work for him.' He replied in answer to a question Sarah hadn't asked yet. 'Did you get the money?'

'Where's Nathan?' Sarah asked with a shaky voice. Why hadn't Nathan come himself? Why was she here? Was she really going to go through with this?

'You're lucky anybody came. Not many people fuck us around and still get given the time of day.'

Sarah said nothing. She stared down at the sand surrounding her bare feet.

'Where is it?' Connor asked as he took a moment to properly observe Sarah for the first time. Sarah felt his eyes linger on her swollen cheek. For a moment Connor seemed to forget why he was there.

'Jesus. Your face.'

Sarah said nothing. In fact, she couldn't even look up at the man who was so openly judging her. It's funny how even now, with Sarah somewhat resigned to the emotional and physical abuse, she'd never gotten used to the shame she felt as somebody looked down at her with eyes full of pity.

'It's nothing.' She finally mumbled.

Connor sensed the topic was not up for further discussion and retreated to his previous line of questioning. 'Where's the money?'

'In my bag.' Sarah replied gingerly, pointing to the small black bag under the desk. 'It's all there.' She added swiftly, feeling as though she had to prove herself to this man.

'I believe you. People tend to pay us what they owe us.'

Connor unzipped his backpack and removed a clear Ziplock bag containing seven pills of Percocet. He took one more look at the sad, defeated woman standing opposite him and felt himself loosen. She reminded him of someone, someone he'd long loved. Although that is a secret he'll take to the grave.

'You sure you know what you're doing with these?' Connor asked.

'Um, well no. Not really.'

'That depends I suppose. Are they for personal use or are they for whoever did that to you?' He gestured to the immense swelling around Sarah's right eye.

Sarah said nothing which was all the confirmation Connor needed. He'd seen situations like this before. In fact, he'd spent a lot of time uncomfortably close to a situation like this. 'Crush them to powder and put them in a drink. Booze usually works best. Four or five will probably be enough but if I were you, I'd use all seven.'

'Thank you.' Sarah said. She really meant it too.

Connor retrieved Sarah's bag. He didn't bother checking the contents, he knew it would all be there. People like her always paid in full. He looked up from the bag to find Sarah swaying on her feet, although he doubted she'd even noticed. He hated himself for what he had to do next, but his instructions had been clear and with the mood Nathan was in, the repercussions certainly didn't bear thinking about.

'There's something else too.' He added reluctantly.

'What's that?' Sarah asked, instantly afraid. Her hands shook violently.

Connor removed a Smith and Wesson 4500 pistol from his backpack. Sarah stared at it in silence for a long moment, mystified by its silent power. Suddenly, she realised what was about to happen. She retreated rapidly, moving until she collided with the rear wall, cracking her head against the roof in the process.

'Please. Please don't.' She begged.

'No. It's not like that.' Connor held the gun upside down, keeping his fingers well away from the trigger. 'I need you to take it. And from the sound of it, having another way to defend yourself against whoever did that to you will do you no harm.'

'What? I can't take a gun.'

Connor knew she was right. Putting a loaded gun into the

264

hands of this desperate woman – a desperate woman looking for a way out of her horrid life – could only result in disaster. But still, he had orders and a dirty gun was better in her hands than it was in his own.

'Listen to me.' He began calmly. 'I'm going to explain it to you and it will make sense. OK.'

Sarah listened. Connor showed her how the safety worked, and she listened despite the drumming pain that echoed through her head. He explained that he and Nathan use the hotel. Hiding illegal goods in the small air vents that were in every bathroom in the hotel. If Sarah had been able to think rationally she might have wondered if the staff at the hotel knew about this. She might even have worried for her own safety now she knew how Nathan conducted his business. But she wasn't thinking clearly which meant she listened silently as Connor guaranteed that the gun would fit in the vent. Finally, she found some semblance of common sense.

'What? So, I'm just supposed to leave a gun in my room forever?'

'What room are you in?' Connor asked patiently.

'Fifty-seven.' Sarah replied, her vision now so blurry that she could barely distinguish the features on Connor's face.

'I'll have one of my guys in that room when you leave. They'll take the gun when you check out.'

Sarah said nothing. She wanted to argue. Wanted to scream and shout, refusing to relent until Connor saw how absurd this whole situation was. But she couldn't. Her shame – shame at being here with this terrible man to rid herself of another terrible man – was unbearable.

'Here's what you're going to do. You're going to take the gun, you're never going to take the safety off it, and you're going to shut the fuck up complaining about it before I decide you're not worth the trouble.' Connor said with conviction. Sarah shut up immediately. So did her heart. With that Connor left Sarah alone with seven Percocet, a handgun and a crippling headache.

She bent down to retrieve Connor's backpack and was suddenly drenched by a colossal wave of nausea; a wave so big that it knocked her to the floor. The final thought Sarah Tyler had before she was consumed by the wave was how nice the cold sand felt against her burning cheek.

28

The Beach Hut Part II

Tom was lost in the memory of last night as he made his way towards the beach hut, replaying the events in a continuous, never-ending loop, now certain that coming to Spain was the best decision he'd ever made. He'd spent the morning intertwined with Joy beneath the sheets. So long, in fact, that he hadn't had time to shower. He was in such a rush that the manuscript waiting on his bedside table slipped his mind once again, meaning he still had no idea his novel now had a title. A name he would love, because this place really was an island of palm trees.

At least it was until he found Sarah Tyler unconscious on the sandy floor of the beach hut.

* * *

Sarah was lying in the double bed she shared with Richard at their home in Wigan. Downstairs she could hear Marcus laughing away. He was probably watching *SpongeBob* and

Patrick get up to all sorts of nonsense beneath the sea. Sarah had never quite understood that show (for one thing, why didn't the sponge float?), but nothing amused Marcus more than watching those underwater adventurers. The smell of bacon floated through the air. Crispy bacon, just how she liked it. Any minute now she would roll out of bed and follow Marcus' endearing laughter downstairs to begin another perfect day. She'd dress Marcus in his *Spider-Man* hat and scarf and they would head out to the tiny park at the end of the cul-de-sac. If the ice cream van makes an appearance Sarah will treat her little soldier to a bunny ears cone with sprinkles and sauce. She and Marcus side by side all day. She just has to open her eyes.

But for some reason, her eyes won't open. Marcus' laughter is growing maniacal and the bacon is burning. The smoke alarm begins to scream and still Sarah can't open her eyes. Now she hears Richard. He's in the room and he's berating her, thumping her with the vilest of insults. Sarah desperately tries to force her eyes open. To rise from the bed and defend herself. To tell Richard to shut his mouth before Marcus overhears him, but she can't move.

Now Richard's standing over her. She can feel his presence looming above her. His knuckles are coated in blood, her blood. He's gearing up to strike again and her cheek is on fire. Blood drips from Richard's knuckles and she still can't open her fucking eyes.

Sarah finally forced her eyes open to find, not Richard standing above her with a bloody fist raised, but Tom. And he looks absolutely terrified.

'Oh, thank fuck!' Tom breathed a sigh of relief as Sarah

opened her eyes. 'What happened?'

Sarah eased herself into a sitting position, trying to remember why she was waking up in such unfamiliar surroundings.

'I should ring an ambulance, shouldn't I?' Tom asked nobody in particular and began rooting through his pockets for his phone.

'No!' Sarah blurted out as she suddenly remembered the purpose of her visit to the beach hut. She looked around frantically for the backpack, the contents of which would surely be of interest to any arriving paramedics. 'No, I um, I'm fine. I think I just had too much to drink last night.'

'Too much to drink?' Tom asked furiously. 'Look at your face!'

'No. No. I mean…' Sarah tried to gather her thoughts but it was proving more difficult than usual thanks to the world-beating headache she was currently suffering through. 'You can't. You can't ring anyone!'

'Why not?'

'I know how this looks.'

'It looks like your husband kicked the shit out of you and left you here to die.'

'It's not like that.' Sarah protested. Inside her stomach was swimming. She hoped she'd make it out of Tom's sight before emptying what little was left in there.

'Stop lying!' Tom shouted.

A horrible realisation suddenly dawned upon Sarah. 'What time is it?'

'Why does that matter?'

'Just tell me the time!'

'It's just before eight. Why does it matter?'

'Oh fuck! I need to go.' Sarah climbed to her feet and lost

her balance. Tom reacted quickly and steadied her.

'You need to stay here and tell me what's going on.'

'I can't! I don't have time.' Sarah collected the backpack and pulled one of the straps over her shoulder. 'Look, Tom, I know we don't know each other but I need you to trust me.'

'Trust you to do what? Run back to him? Hope that next time he loses his temper he doesn't kill you?'

Sarah was touched by Tom's genuine concern for her safety. A part of her wanted to do what he asked, a large part in fact, and yet, she found herself saying 'I know what I'm doing. For the first time in years really I do.'

'Sarah you can't go back to him. What if he kills you?' Tom asked, begging Sarah to find sanity.

'I can guarantee you that's not where this is heading. Trust me. Please.'

Tom said nothing. He couldn't explain why but some part of him trusted the woman he'd just found lying face down in the sand. And so, even though he knew he shouldn't, he stood back and watched her leave. Ten minutes later he welcomed customers to the beach as if nothing had happened at all.

Sarah experienced no interference on her brief journey back to room fifty-seven. She attracted several concerned glances, but nobody offered a helping hand to the injured woman stumbling through reception.

She arrived outside her room, paused, placed her ear against the door and listened. Everything was quiet but that didn't mean he wasn't in there. Slowly, she unzipped the backpack, gripped the gun and after a moment of struggle, flicked what she assumed to be the safety off. She eased her finger onto the trigger and made a decision. If Richard was in there, if he steps towards her or tries to hurt her again, she'll kill him. She will shoot him dead and then wait for the police and confess to the crime.

Sarah eased the door open and burst into tears at the sight of the empty room. Her strength drained from her. She collapsed to her knees, crying freely. She'd been ready. She'd been prepared to do it and part of her was disappointed that she hadn't had the chance. She continued to cry as she hid the gun, the backpack and the Percocet inside the small air vent beneath the sink.

She risked a look at herself in the mirror, her cheek was an ugly bulge of purple and blue and her right eye was swollen shut. She thought about how she'd looked before she met Richard and cried some more.

Even Marcus wouldn't recognise her now.

* * *

That morning Joy finally made her decision. She was going to ask Tom to leave Spain with her. She had to. If she didn't, she'd regret it forever. At some point last night, Joy realised she thinks she loves Tom. She isn't sure yet but what if nobody's ever sure? What if the only way to know is to take the risk and hope that years from now you don't look back with regret? Maybe love isn't found in certainty but in the excitement of the unknown.

Her future is certainly unknown. But for the first time in months, Joy has reason to be excited. And for that, she is eternally grateful to the boy who swapped seats with her on the plane.

* * *

Richard arrived at room fifty-seven with trembling hands and tired eyes. He'd spent the entire night thinking, thinking about everything: life, Sarah, the son they lost. And through it all he'd resisted the urge to drink.

He'd nearly walked into The Clover yesterday. He'd made it all the way to the door before thinking of the locked bathroom door his wife was hiding behind. Suddenly the decision was easy. He chose his wife.

Richard took a deep breath. He was embarrassed, more embarrassed than ever before. He supposed that was the cruel irony of alcoholism, he drinks because of the shame he feels and the only way to escape it is to pour another drink. It's an endless cycle of suffering that sucks in all the colour in the world and spits it back out looking grey and empty.

Richard knocked on the door. He didn't want to use his key and risk seeing Sarah flush with panic at the sheer sight of him. He didn't want to see that ever again, though he knew the damage was already done. A part of him believed it could never be undone, but thoughts like that only served to push him back towards the bottle.

Richard heard her coming. He could think of nothing but how desperate he was to make things right and how badly he needed a shot of vodka to keep the shakes away. Maybe it really was too late after all.

* * *

Tom took his dinner break early. He needed something to

distract him from the unexpected horrors of the morning. He bought a cold turkey sandwich and bottles of both amaretto and coke. Back in the safety of the hut Tom discarded the sandwich and poured a large drink. Then he poured another.

And another.

And another.

* * *

Sarah didn't pay much attention to the words Richard said. It wasn't that she'd heard them before, although she had. It wasn't that she was still shaken from the nightmare she'd experienced back at the beach hut, although she was. No. The real reason Sarah didn't listen as Richard promised her that this time things would be different, was because the first thing Richard had done upon returning to the room was pour the entire contents of the mini-fridge down the toilet, insisting he needed to steer clear of distractions. And in doing so, he poured the seven crushed Percocet pills that Sarah had slipped into the bottle of red wine away too.

With Sarah's spirits at an all-time low and a loaded gun hidden in the bathroom, the Tyler's spent the next few hours talking through their problems. Richard promised he would get help. He promised to never touch a drop of booze again. He promised to start treating Sarah as she deserved to be treated. And though Sarah wanted these things to be true, wanted that more than anything, she knew better than to trust her husband. Because it's the hope that kills you. And where Richard Tyler is concerned, Sarah has learnt not to hope for anything, especially sobriety.

273

* * *

Gabriella finalised the itinerary for tomorrows Grand Ball just after midday. The festivities were to begin with a cocktail reception at four. Following this, the guests will sit down in the Suite Diamante for an early meal. After which they will briefly return to the Lobby Bar, allowing the Suite Diamante to be transformed from an elegant restaurant into an elegant ballroom. Once back in the Suite the guests will dance and drink and, if they're anything like Roger, poison their bodies with different pills and powders. Finally, the night will end with Roger's firework display that, according to the flyer's strewn around the hotel, promises to be the biggest display of loud bangs and bright colours ever to grace the skies of Roquetas De Mar. There was nothing officially scheduled to take place after that, but she knew what Roger expected to happen. The thought sent a shiver marching down her spine.

With a ball of dread resting in the pit of her stomach, Gabriella booted up her laptop and began prowling through the local news sites. Right now, she had only one method of escape. A method entirely dependent on the discovery of a murdered young woman whose only mistake was putting her trust in the wrong man.

Hours passed and there was nothing. Nothing to see. Nothing to save her from the man with the canine grin. With that chilling thought, Gabriella realised she needed a backup plan, and though it was mightily depressing, there was only one person she could turn to for help.

A person currently sleeping with a bottle of amaretto by his side.

274

* * *

Sarah and Richard spent the entire day in room fifty-seven. They talked for hours and when it seemed they'd finally exhausted all possible topics of conversation, they made their way to the balcony to enjoy the afternoon sun. Sarah read one of her books and Richard listened to a sports podcast. Things almost felt normal.

And they would have been normal if Richard had been listening to his podcast, but he wasn't. Instead, he was thinking about how much better the view would be if he had a whiskey to enjoy alongside it.

* * *

Tom didn't stir as Gabriella entered the beach hut. She took a moment to survey the scene, spotting the half-empty bottle of amaretto and understanding why Tom was sleeping on the job. On any other day, she would have sacked him on the spot. She wouldn't even have allowed the sleeping fool to spend another night at the hotel. He would have been out of the door just as soon as he'd packed his bags. But today was no ordinary day, and there was absolutely no chance Gabriella was going to sack Tom Jennings today.

'Tom!' She barked and nudged him with her foot.

Tom stirred, ready to politely tell whichever customer had woken him up to piss off, when he realised it was his boss standing over him and bolted to his feet.

'Gabriella, hi!' Tom saw the incriminating bottle resting at his side. 'Look, I can explain all of this.'

'It doesn't happen again, or you're gone. Is that under-stood?' She asked with complete authority.

'Yeah, of course, but I don't want you to get the wrong idea.' Tom spoke with care. He was a good distance beyond sober and knew better than to show it. 'This is the first time I've done anything like this.'

'I should think so too.' Gabriella replied with a firm tone and judgemental eyes. 'Luckily for you, that's not why I'm here.'

'OK.'

'I wanted to let you know that I've found somebody to cover your shift tomorrow.'

'Oh. OK, why?' Tom asked, suddenly feeling apprehensive.

'Tomorrow's the day of the ball I told you about. You said you'd help me.'

'Of course. What time do you need me to start at?'

'Get to my office for nine. And if I smell even the slightest hint of booze on your breath, I swear to God you'll be out of this hotel by ten. Do you understand?'

Tom understood perfectly.

29

The Sunrise Building Part II

The magic powder was helping. That was good. It was helping Roger think straight and right now he really needed to think straight. He'd woken in the middle of the night to a startling realisation, he couldn't agree to Nathan's demands.

Even if Gabriella somehow didn't notice an invisible assistant manager suddenly taking up space on the payroll (not to mention the burly men moving cocaine and God only knows what else in and out of her hotel), his father certainly would. The astute old bastard knew all of his investments inside and out. Most people in his position would be out enjoying what little time they had left, but instead, his father spends his spare time sitting by the fire and combing over every aspect of his business empire. And make no mistake about it, it is an empire.

Roger made the call early and, of course, the arrogant prick believed him. Nathan answered the phone with all the swagger of a man unaware that his imminent demise looms over him. Nathan said he was surprised it had taken Roger this long to work his way through the bag, adding that he would happily drop off more later. He even offered to take the stiletto with him now that he and Roger had come to an understanding.

It took all of Roger's willpower to thank Nathan for his generosity before hanging up. What Nathan doesn't realise is that Roger has been cornered his entire life. Cornered by his father and his reputation and the fake friends who only stayed with him when he flashed his cash. Cornered by a mother too afraid of her husband to defend her son. Cornered by a life he'd never wanted and money that he'd never been taught the value of.

Nathan doesn't realise that a man like Roger, a man who has spent his entire life trapped in a corner, will do just about anything to break free. Anything at all.

* * *

Nathan agreed to meet Roger at his apartment later that night without suspecting anything. He was far too preoccupied with his current task to worry about what awaited him later. His heart thumped against his chest as he approached the door, just as it had the first time he saw her. Not that she was here. She'd spent last night with the skinny little twat from the beach hut, but that didn't deter Nathan. Tom was a fling, a chance to experience something new (something worse). He certainly wasn't anything to worry about, but that didn't mean he wouldn't be dealt with should he continue to stand in his way. If he continued to be a burden, Nathan would kill him himself. He didn't like to get his hands dirty, not now he's capable of paying other men whose hands are already filthy. Still, exceptions can be made. Just as he'd made an exception for the street rat who'd sold coke to Wyatt. Nathan owned Wyatt now. He'd own her again soon too.

Now came the moment of truth. Nathan was about to discover if she was still the girl he loved. He pushed his key into the lock and his heart stopped. She hadn't changed the locks and Nathan knew why; it was because she knew he'd still have his key. Some part of her, either consciously or subconsciously, wanted him to drop by and surprise her. She was the same girl he'd once spent all his time with, and with those pleasant memories filling his head, Nathan let himself into apartment five just as he had so many times before.

The apartment had barely changed. There was no longer any trace of him or her father. Truthfully it was as if neither of them had ever been there. Nathan wasn't hurt though. He'd expected this. Plus his influence would be back in this filthy place soon enough. He'd make sure of that. He just had to wait for her to come back to him. It wouldn't take long. It never did.

* * *

After a trip to the butchers and another to a grocery store (Joy doubted Tom was the sort of man who could refuse a well-cooked steak), Joy headed back towards the Sunrise Building with her ingredients in tow. The sun was just beginning its retreat from the highest point in the sky, meaning she had plenty of time to prepare her feast. Asides from that she just needed to gather up the courage to ask Tom to abandon his life and run away with her.

Easy.

* * *

Nathan spent an hour in her apartment, searching through the entire property without finding anything interesting, without finding anything that could be traced back to the time they'd spent together. He wasn't disheartened. He'd always be in her heart. After what he'd done for her, how could she ever forget him?

With nothing else to do and no idea when she would be back, Nathan climbed into her bed and made himself comfortable. The sheets smelt familiar and he instantly became hard. He didn't act on it though. He was saving himself for her.

* * *

Joy arrived at the door of apartment five with no sense of the unwelcome visitor waiting inside. If she'd known, she would have turned and run, putting miles between them. Instead, she unlocked the door and let herself in, immediately locking eyes with the man who'd ruined her life.

For a long time, Joy said nothing. Her disbelief had trapped her feet in cement. She could only stare at him.

'This place hasn't changed a lot, has it?' Nathan asked lightly.

'How did you get in here?' Joy asked, clutching her shopping bags tightly as if they were her only means of defence.

'My key.' He replied as if it were the most obvious thing in the world. 'You know, from the first time you came out here.' Nathan's attention diverted to the shopping bags. 'That wine looks nice.'

Joy knew Nathan well. She knew that he would never change, and she knew that playing up to his ego was the smartest move. 'You're not having this one. There's a cheap bottle in the cupboard. I'm guessing you remember where the glasses are?'

Nathan did. He remembered everything.

It wasn't long before Nathan was sitting comfortably on the couch with a glass of six-euro red wine in his hand. Joy, also holding a glass of wine, leaned against the kitchen tops, wary of getting too close to Nathan.

'You know I think you actually converted me to cheap wine.' Nathan said, under the false impression that he was handing out a compliment. 'Whenever I drink the costly stuff now I dunno, it just doesn't taste the same.'

'Wine's wine. It does the same job no matter what it costs.'

'From what I remember it certainly did a job on you.' Nathan was testing the water, seeing how much leeway he would be given.

'From what I remember it did a different job on you.' She replied flatly, showing Nathan how carefully he needed to tread.

'I don't remember hearing too many complaints at the time.'

'I remember breaking your nose.'

Nathan's icy facade momentarily faltered but he recovered quickly. 'I think with the gift of hindsight we can both admit we made mistakes.'

'Some more than others.'

The conversation moved with the speed of two boxers dancing around the ring, exchanging blows with frightening accuracy.

'You know what, and I think this should highlight just how much I've changed, I agree with you. I'm ready to admit it, most of our problems were my fault.'

'They were all your fault.' Joy interjected, struggling to look at the leech sitting on her couch.

'Be that as it may, you're still the first person I ever really loved. In fact, you're the only person I've ever loved. And that's bound to drive anybody crazy.'

Joy said nothing. Her brain was operating at hyper speed, desperately trying to calculate an exit strategy.

'When you left I never thought I'd see you again. That's not to say I didn't think about you, quite the opposite actually. I even tried getting back in touch with you, but your number had changed and I guessed you were still moving around.'

Rage sparked the fire within Joy's eyes. 'No. We didn't carry on moving around.' Her fists clenched as she spoke. 'We couldn't. Not after what you did.'

'So yeah.' He continued, ignoring Joy's response 'I'd basically given up on ever seeing you again and then suddenly you were here. We talk just like old times and it's fucking perfect! But then you lie to me. And for the life of me, I can't work out why. Especially considering I'm the reason you came out here in the first place.'

Joy said nothing. She needed a minute to process every-thing. Nathan was deluded and egotistical and the more time she spent with him the more she feared him. He'd was unhinged and clearly his time in the sun had only served to fracture his mind even more.

Joy hadn't said much in the last thirty minutes. Instead, she'd listened to Nathan drone on, recounting the joys of the old days and, though it pained her to admit it, a lot of what he said was true.

From the moment they'd first met up until things imploded; they'd been everything to one another. Joy had welcomed Nathan into her way of life and even her father seemed impressed by the strapping young man she introduced him to. Things remained that way for some time. Easy and simple and important.

Then gradually everything changed. Joy began to see glimpses of the man Nathan was becoming and it was a far cry from the young man she'd fallen in love with. It wasn't just Joy who noticed these red flags either. Her father had a keen eye and a daughter to protect and he quickly made it clear that Nathan was no longer welcome.

After that things got better again. Nathan kept his distance and Joy's heart began to heal just as a broken bone does. Her life was better with Nathan firmly in the rear-view mirror. She was beginning to move on when Nathan suddenly returned to the foreground of her life and snatched away what little happiness she had left.

The memory chilled Joy. She suddenly decided she could take no more and interrupted their stroll down bad-memory lane. 'Why are you actually here? Because if it's just to reminisce you can fuck off now.'

'No. That's not why I'm here, though I was quite enjoying it. I'm here because I want to talk to you about what you asked me. Though it's a conversation I didn't expect to have for a while because you told me you wouldn't be back for weeks.'

Joy knew exactly what Nathan was talking about, but her circumstances had changed. Tom had changed everything and she loved him for it. She was relieved to no longer rely on money from the two men who'd ruined her past to support her future.

'What about it?' She asked.

'I'd like to propose a counteroffer, respectfully of course.'

'Actually, so would I.' Joy smiled as Nathan's eyes sparked with panic.

'Go on then.' He asked, trying to appear nonchalant.

'The money you owe me. Send it directly to my Dad.'

'What? Why can't you give it to him?'

Joy watched the cogs in Nathan's head begin to turn.

'No!' He suddenly grunted.

Joy said nothing. She stared down into her glass of wine, wondering how good it would feel to throw the contents of it into the face of the man currently glaring at her.

'You're running away? You're running away with him?' Nathan said as he clambered to his feet.

Joy said nothing. The situation was quickly spiralling out of control and if she didn't reclaim some power soon, she never would.

'Sorry, let me just check I've got my head around this.' Nathan began, wielding his empty wine glass as it were a sword. 'You want me to send money to your monster of a dad.'

'Don't you fucking dare.' Joy interrupted defiantly.

'All the while you're off living the dream with beach boy.' Nathan continued as if Joy had said nothing.

'No.' Joy replied, brushing off the fact that Nathan knew who Tom was and where he worked. 'I don't want your money. All the money you send to him stays with him, which it should do seeing as though you're the reason he can't make money of his own.'

'No, you're right. It's always a sad day when a thief can't steal anymore.' Nathan's voice was bitter and cold. 'I bet you're still taking his monthly deposits though. Funding your trip around the world on daddy's hush money.'

Joy said nothing. She focused on keeping a lid on her temper. It was threatening to boil over and ruin everything.

'You have no idea how lucky you'd be to stay here with me.' Nathan headed into the kitchen with his empty wine glass and refilled it.

'Oh yeah. The dealer's wife. It's what all the girls dream of.'

'You didn't seem that opposed to it when you were watching beach boy buy from me. Come to think of it you never seemed opposed to it. Then again, maybe that was just because it got you away from that twisted old fuck you call a father.'

'Don't talk about him!' Joy screamed.

'You know, I'll never understand why I've always been the bad guy in your eyes.'

'You know why!' Tears appeared in Joy's eyes and she fought hard to keep them from escaping.

'You wanted it. All of it. You wanted me. You wanted this life that's now beneath you. And you can try and convince yourself otherwise but we both know you're lying to yourself. The truth is I knew what you wanted better than you ever did.'

A tear forced itself free from the corner of Joy's eye. Nathan noticed and smiled; he had her exactly where he wanted her.

'Why are you here?' Joy asked timidly. 'What did you actually think this would accomplish?'

'Why didn't you leave?'

'You honestly want to know?' Joy needed to show her strength. She wouldn't let him win.

'Tell me.'

'Because I love Tom Jennings.'

For a moment, Nathan stood in stunned silence. Then he drained the contents of his glass and advanced towards Joy.

'Great. That's really great. And I assume he knows why you came out here in the first place?'

Joy said nothing.

'Does he? I mean if you love him you must have told him the truth.'

'I came here for my Dad's money. No other reason.'

'Don't lie to me.' The volume of Nathan's voice increased with every word. 'You could have called. You could have texted. You could have written a fucking letter. But you didn't and I know why.'

'You're wrong.' Joy's words were twisted with hatred.

'I think after you left you realised just how pathetic your life really was. I mean, it must have been easier than before given you no longer had any trouble staying out of daddy's clutches.'

'Stop!' Joy demanded.

'But even with that, you realised you couldn't carry on scraping by with that shit stain of a father.'

'Stop!' Tears trickled down her cheeks now.

'You came out here with no intention of ever going back.' Nathan was now so close that she could smell the wine of his breath. 'You can pretend you came here for your dad. I'm sure that's what you told yourself to justify it, but the truth is so much simpler. You missed me. You still want me.'

'That's not true.' Joy said, sinking away from Nathan's glare.

'It is. That's the reason you got in my car that day. Hell, it's the reason you kissed me.'

'Because you got me drunk! Were they really just ciders or did you bring your old party trick out of retirement and slip something in them?' Joy's fury had blinded her. She was no longer thinking strategically.

'Why's that matter? You always told me that people go after what they really want when they're drunk. It's true, isn't it? You hate yourself for it, but you want me more than anything.'

'Fuck you.' Joy spat.

Nathan stepped towards Joy, now there were just centimetres between them. 'It should be me you're running away with. But you got scared and settled for some scrawny little safe choice who'll never earn any money but that's fine. That's fine because he'll worship the ground you walk on and he'll do anything you ask, and he'll never turn into your father and that's what matters.'

'You need to leave.' Joy demanded, her hands shaking violently.

Without warning, Nathan lunged forward and gripped Joy by the throat, dragging her towards him. Joy planted her feet firmly and pushed him away with all the force she could muster. He stumbled but didn't fall.

'What the fuck are you doing?' Joy screamed. Now her voice did break and tears did flow. The memories were flooding back. Memories she'd spent years trying to suppress.

'I know what you need.' Nathan leered as he advanced towards her. 'You need somebody like your dad. daddy's little girl forever.'

Nathan reached for her again, but she shot backwards.

'I'll be just like him.' He continued. 'I'll drink and throw you around and tell you how to act and how to dress and who to fuck.'

Nathan's words stunned Joy. She was so consumed by the darkest of her memories that she didn't react when he lunged towards her. He wrapped one hand around her waist and the other locked around her neck like a vice.

Without thinking, Joy rocketed her knee into Nathan's groin. The hand on her neck loosened just enough for her to wriggle free. This was her chance. She planted her feet, leaned back, and used her hips to generate the power in a punch aimed squarely at Nathan's nose. A punch packed with all the devastation he'd caused her.

The punch was good. Nathan fell to the floor and for a minute Joy thought she'd done enough. She could run from this apartment and the memory of Nathan. She could run and she wouldn't stop until she was on a plane beside Tom and then maybe, just maybe, she could finally be happy. She was nearing the door. Everything was OK until suddenly it wasn't. Nathan's hand clamped onto her ankle and, as she tumbled to the floor, Joy knew she'd never be happy.

What a sad final thought.

30

Dark Skies, Dark Moments Part II

Tom didn't bother cleaning the beach when his shift ended. Tomorrow it would be somebody else's problem. Thinking of tomorrow, Tom dropped the bottle of amaretto into a bin behind the hotel, a night without drinking would do him good.

During the walk back to his room Tom thought about what Joy had said last night. Her thoughts on love and relationships and whether two people can ever truly know one another. He didn't know her completely, but he knew he loved her. He loved her with absolute certainty, and he couldn't wait to tell her.

His room was disappointingly empty, barring a note taped to the wall above the bed which read:

Come to mine. You're already late!

The note wasn't signed but Tom knew who'd written it. The Sunrise Building was only ten minutes away, maybe less if he jogged, and for that reason alone, Tom jogged the whole way.

* * *

Roger's plan was airtight. He was going to kill Nathan and return to his rightful position atop the food chain. Kill or be killed. Hunt or be hunted. He will laugh as he snatches the life from Nathan, just as a lion snatches the life from a gazelle. With the help of his magic powder, he is unstoppable. He's the man he'd always wanted to be. The alpha.

Roger snorted his first line just after midday and continued doing so at regular intervals throughout the afternoon. When Nathan hadn't arrived by the time the sun set, although no time had been agreed for their meeting, Roger decided to take matters into his own hands.

He made it halfway through the lobby before he collapsed. The ambulance arrived seven minutes later and rushed Roger to the nearest hospital. The attending paramedic reported the steak knife stashed away in Roger's jacket, but she didn't think anything of it. She assumed it was just the nonsensical behaviour of another junkie who's put white powder before everything else in life.

* * *

Tom only saw the blood. The door was ajar and thin splatters of crimson stained the cream carpet. He felt as though he was looking on from a great distance, safe from the horrors that lay within apartment five. For an age, he stood frozen in the doorway, unable to think of what had happened or when it had happened or why it had happened. He could only worry about who it had happened to, praying the answer wasn't Joy.

290

Summoning all the courage he could muster, Tom edged into the room, easing the door closed behind him. The blood splatters were thin in the living room which meant that whatever had happened must have occurred in the kitchen. He didn't look in there straight away. First, he took three deep breaths to prepare himself for what lay around the corner.

Tom felt an equal mix of relief and horror as he stepped into the kitchen. Relief because she was there, she was alive and under different circumstances he would have rushed to her and told her that he loved her. But he didn't, he couldn't. Not with the blood smeared across her face and matted in her hair. Not with her clothes and hands stained red.

He fought back the urge to vomit. Nathan was lying on the floor with his throat cut and his eyes closed. His blood was streaked across the walls and the kitchen tiles. An artery must have been severed because his blood was somehow also on the ceiling and now Tom did heave. Joy screamed. When she realised it was only Tom standing aghast at the edge of the room, she rose slowly to her feet and moved towards him. Nathan's blood dripped from her hands with each step she took.

'It wasn't my fault Tom. I promise you it wasn't.'

Joy continued to plead her innocence as Tom helped her away from the heinous scene in the kitchen. Thankfully some semblance of his sanity returned, and he began to understand the magnitude of the situation. He couldn't quite bring himself to sit next to Joy on the couch, so he stood above her, facing away from the drying blood and stiffening corpse in the kitchen.

He had no idea what to say. Nothing seemed right. This

was the sort of situation he'd written about a dozen times and now that he was here, experiencing the horrors first-hand, he realised just how wrong he'd been in his writing. Finally, he spoke without even realising he'd opened his mouth to do so.

'What happened?'

Joy was no longer crying but her hands shook viciously. 'He was here when I got back. He wouldn't leave.' She began to cry and Tom gave her a moment to compose herself, although he desperately wanted to shake her, demanding she tell him what she'd done.

'He grabbed me. I tried to get him off, but he wouldn't stop so I hit him… I tried to run but he caught me.' Joy was sobbing now, spitting her words out without thought or care. 'He pulled me down and then he was on top of me and he was hitting me.'

It was only as Joy said this that Tom noticed the fresh purple bruises swelling beneath the blood on her face. He felt himself soften. This wasn't her fault. It couldn't be.

'He wouldn't stop, and I kept screaming at him and trying to get him off but I, I just couldn't.' Again, Joy paused to compose herself. Tom sat beside her and wrapped an arm around her shoulder, cringing as the warm blood touched his skin.

'I started reaching out, hoping I'd be able to grab something to help. I found a wine bottle and I hit him with it. I hit him across the face and he started bleeding. The bottle I'd used had already smashed but I didn't know. I honestly didn't know Tom.'

Joy cried hysterically into Tom's shoulder and Tom hated himself because he could only think of how desperately he wanted to tear off his blood-stained shirt and burn it.

'Who was he?' Tom asked, desperate for the full story.

'We used to be a couple.' Joy shivered at the thought.

'Really?'

'I didn't tell you because,' Joy's lip trembled, and Tom saw how stubbornly she was holding back more tears. 'I don't know why. I was embarrassed, I suppose.'

'Right, OK.' Tom's mind was operating at such high speeds he was worried it might burn out and explode. 'Let's call the police. If we explain what happened, surely they'll have the forensic evidence or whatever to prove it was self-defence.'

'They won't.'

'How could you possibly know that?' Tom asked, his frustration bubbling over.

'Because I have a motive, Tom! I have a motive and a record.' Joy shouted. For the first time since he'd arrived at her apartment, she held his gaze. Her eyes were filled with something beyond fire, something new and frightening.

'What do you mean you have a motive? And wait, what? You have a record?' Tom's head was spinning.

'I told you how me and my Dad used to make money.'

'But how does that link to this? What was your motive?' Tom had never wanted a drink so badly in his life.

'Nathan was the reason I came out here.' Joy admitted shamefully.

Tom felt as though he was the one who'd had his throat slashed. The ability to think rationally escaped him.

'What? Why?' And then, with desperation, he added 'Do you love him?'

'No. Not at all. Last year something really bad happened. It was Nathan's fault. I came out here to tell him that he owed my Dad a hundred grand to make things right.'

'But even still, how would the police know that's why you came here?'

'People saw me with him. People knew what I wanted. His driver, Connor, I know him from back home too. He heard everything.'

Joy felt as if she were trapped in a bubble of shame. She wanted everything to end, including this conversation. Tom took a long moment to think but try as he might he just couldn't fit the pieces of this heart-wrenching puzzle together.

'What do we do then?' He asked desperately.

Joy said nothing.

'Joy!' Tom snapped. 'I need you to talk to me!'

Joy jumped to her feet and stepped towards Tom. Without thinking, he stepped back and raised his hand to shield himself. At that moment, Joy learned everything she needed to know about how Tom felt about her now he knew what she was capable of.

'Why? What do you need to know?'

Now it was Tom who was lost for words.

'Look over there.' Joy pointed towards Nathan's pale, blood-soaked body. 'That's there. That's forever. So, telling you the whole story isn't my biggest concern right now.'

Tom's emotions were no longer in conflict. Confusion had been slammed aside by a wave of hurt the likes of which he'd never experienced before.

'Are you being serious? I'm here! I've seen that mess in there and I'm still fucking here!'

'Exactly! Why?' Joy spat.

Tom took a moment to try and find some clarity in the

traffic jam of his mind. 'Do you love him?'

'What?'

'Do you love him? Is that why you came here, really?'

Joy said nothing. Tom nodded in acceptance. He turned and headed for the door.

'Tom.'

Tom turned back, willing her to ask him to stay.

'Don't tell anyone about this.' Joy said flatly, although deep down she wanted to say so much more.

'Never.' Tom said with absolute certainty.

Tom didn't know what to do or where to go. His room felt tainted. Everywhere he looked he saw Joy. Her scent was on the pillows and her laugh echoed against the walls. He couldn't stay in there. For a while, he walked around aimlessly. The summer holiday season was in full swing and it showed. More people were arriving each day and Tom found himself surrounded by people having the time of their lives. They were just as Tom had been an hour ago: young and vibrant with the priceless ability to look ahead into the wide expanse of their future. Tom hated them because he'd lost that ability and he'd never get it back.

Tom didn't think about the two bottles of wine he'd bought until he was back in the beach hut. He took a large sip from the bottle and was surprised to find the pain didn't stop, if anything it hurt more. It hurt how much he wanted another sip. It hurt how much he wanted to finish both bottles. It hurt that the only way to escape this horrid night was to lose himself in alcohol. Tom didn't want that. He didn't want to spend another night in a black hole.

He returned to his room to grab his laptop. He didn't

remember the manuscript. Not that it mattered. He needed a distraction. He needed something good to come of this utterly heinous night. He was going to finish his novel. He wouldn't sleep until he did.

Rose embarked upon her European adventure with Isabella and quickly found her one true love: travelling. They visited Barcelona and Madrid and Paris and Prague. Isabella performed and Rose explored. They never stayed in one place long enough for Rose to find work, which meant the entire trip was funded by Isabella. As a result, Isabella was in full control of where they went and who they met and how they spent their time. Rose quickly became frustrated with this arrangement, and her relationship with Isabella fractured. During their final night in Lisbon, their newfound friendship collapsed. Isabella made it clear Rose was no longer welcome on the tour. Rose was distraught. She had no money, no accommodation, and no job. She drank away what little money she had left and when the bars closed, she wandered back to the hostel she and Isabella were staying at.

There were six people in the dorm room when Rose arrived, all sleeping soundly. Isabella was on the bottom bunk at the far corner of the room. Rose crept through the dorm silently, not taking a breath until she arrived at her destination. She watched Isabella sleep and thought back to the good times. When they'd gotten drunk together by the sea in Barcelona. When they'd bribed a bouncer to sneak them into the 1975 concert in Dublin. Isabella had always been there for advice, just as Rose had always wanted. These thoughts were quickly replaced by what would happen if Isabella left without her. She'd have no choice but to return to her parents and apologise for what she'd done, before living out a miserable life controlled by parents who didn't love her.

Without another thought, Rose stretched out her hands and inched them towards Isabella's neck. The final page of the book has Rose sat alone on a train with Isabella's backpack on her shoulder and her whole life ahead of her. She smiles. She's finally happy.

With his novel finished, Tom watched the sunrise as his life had fallen apart - without warning.

* * *

Sarah wasn't proud to admit it, but she was surprised to find Richard sleeping soundly beside her. They'd been up late last night, talking until it felt as though there was nothing left to say. It was the best night they'd shared since Marcus passed, yet she could see how much he was struggling. She saw it in his forlorn glances towards the empty mini-fridge. She saw it in his disappointment after each sip of Sprite. But mostly she saw it in his trembling hands that he tried so desperately to hide from her.

She decided he deserved a lie in. She'd read somewhere that the first twenty-four hours are the most difficult in the fight to overcome addiction, and that gave her hope. Other articles suggested that each day was as difficult as the last, that it simply boiled down to the person's will to fight their disease. She hoped this wasn't true. She knew better than anyone just how weak Richard's will really was.

* * *

Gabriella had been raised to believe she could accomplish anything she set her mind to, and for a long while she'd believed that was true. It was only after returning from London with a broken marriage and a father to bury that she realised just how unfair life could really be. She was suddenly the manager of the hotel her family had built and there was no safety net to catch her if she fell.

Gabriella has had her fair share of setbacks, more than her fair share probably. But nothing has hurt more than preparing to leave the Scarlett Grove forever. Not giving up on her marriage, not giving up on life in London, not even giving up her pursuit to discover the truth about Roger Wyatt.

For Gabriella Glover, giving up has never hurt so much.

* * *

Tom arrived at Gabriella's office five minutes ahead of schedule to find that Gabriella herself wasn't there. His anxiety immediately doubled. He needed somebody to distract him from the image of Nathan's ruptured throat and he needed it now.

He spent five minutes pacing the tiny corridor outside Gabriella's office. She was never late and today seemed far too important an occasion for her to disrupt her usually impeccable timekeeping. Another ten minutes passed. His pacing became frantic and he had nothing to think about besides the ways Joy's hands had trembled as Nathan's blood had dried onto them.

With no sign of anyone, Tom went in search of Gabriella, assuming she was so busy that she hadn't yet had time to return to her office. He hoped desperately that he was right. If Gabriella was busy he would be busy, and if he was busy he wouldn't have time to think about how he'd left Joy alone with the body of a man she'd murdered in self-defence.

* * *

Gabriella was lost in thoughts of murder and coyotes and then, for a split second, she thought of Callum. Maybe when she left the hotel, she would reach out to him. Callum had his faults, but he'd been loyal and she couldn't say the same for herself. Their marriage hadn't been perfect but it had been functional, pleasant most of the time, and she'd singlehandedly destroyed it. She owed Callum an apology and she hoped that one day he'd be willing to listen to her, maybe even forgive her, although the latter seemed far less likely.

When Gabriella finally emerged from her daydream, she realised it was closing in on half-past nine. Not only did that mean Tom had been waiting at her office for half an hour (hopefully), but it also meant she'd lost out on thirty minutes of preparation time. She certainly couldn't lose any more. Without another thought, Gabriella rushed out of her room and towards reception.

She was heading towards the reception desk when she saw Tom scuttling into the hotel carrying a deceptively heavy box. He saw her and headed straight over.

'Hi. I um, I didn't really know what to do but the girl on reception said there was a big delivery of some wine Roger likes.' Gabriella noticed Tom's arms shaking under the weight of the box. He swiftly added 'I'm gonna put this down, if that's OK?'

'Yeah, of course.'

Tom set the box down and breathed a sigh of relief.

'Look, I'm sorry I wasn't there at nine.'

'It's OK. I guessed you'd just started earlier.' After yesterday, Tom was in no position to lecture Gabriella about her timekeeping.

'Yeah, I did.' Gabriella lied. 'Why don't you take that crate to the kitchen and while you're there see if you can get some of the kitchen staff to unload the rest of the deliveries? Then come to my office and we'll sort out everything we've got to do. Sound good?'

'Sounds good.' Tom replied honestly.

Anything to distract himself sounded good right now.

* * *

Richard had never wanted anything as badly as he wanted a drink. Their hotel room had become a prison, a prison he'd locked himself in. Originally, he'd decided the best way to stay sober was to remove himself from any lively or enjoyable situations but now he realised he'd gotten it all wrong. At least if he was surrounded by life, he'd have more to distract himself with. He'd have something to think about other than how desperately he needed something cold and bubbly in his hand and in his bloodstream.

Finally, when he could take the deafening silence of the solitary room no longer, he turned towards Sarah and took a chance.

'Have you seen the posters for the thing tonight?'

'What thing?' Sarah asked although she knew exactly what Richard was referring to.

'The ball that's happening.'

'Oh yeah, I have actually. What about it?' Sarah asked, praying Richard didn't want to go.

'Well, I dunno, I just thought it might be nice to get out of the room for a while. Maybe go and see what all the fuss is about.'

'Um, I'm not sure. Is that definitely a good idea?' Sarah asked tentatively, hoping Richard wouldn't take offence.

'No, of course, I understand what it sounds like but it's not that. It's just I'm going a bit stir crazy here and I think it would do me good to get out of the room, you know? To try and feel normal for an hour or so.'

'Richard, I'm really not sure.' Sarah insisted.

'Honestly, I'm not even thinking about drinking.' Richard lied. 'But I think if I stay cooped up in here, I will start to, you know. We can't stay in here forever.'

Sarah knew better than to trust Richard. He's lied to her before and he'll lie to her again and deep down, though she hated herself for knowing it, he'll drink again. But she couldn't argue with his logic. They did need to leave the room and maybe an hour of normality would be nice.

* * *

Roger felt numb as he listened to the elderly Dr Brenner explain the extent of his latest overdose. The doctor was kind and well-spoken, but he made it clear that if Roger didn't change his ways, he wouldn't live to see his thirtieth birthday. Roger had been low before, when he awoke to find a lifeless young woman sharing his bed a recent example, but this somehow felt worse. Maybe it was the pity in the doctor's eyes or the fact that his feeble attempt to retake the power Nathan had stolen from him had resulted in hospitalisation.

Roger was left with nothing but an abundance of time to ponder who he had become: a drug-addled murderer in the process of being blackmailed by a scumbag drug dealer. He also thought about why he'd ended up here. The answer was simple. It was all because of his cold and unloving father.

Right then Roger decided, should he make it through the week without being dumped in a cell, to kill his father. The thought made him smile. More than that, it made him hard.

* * *

Tom left Gabriella's office at four minutes past ten with a long list of tasks and precious little time to do them all in. He collected the table linens, encouraged the uncooperative kitchen staff to double-check they had enough finger food to satisfy Roger's guest list, and helped Gabriella organise the Suite Diamante, which mainly consisted of agreeing with her opinion on everything.

Then, with the sun at its peak and Gabriella feeling fairly confident that they were now on schedule to welcome their guests four hours later, Tom was given his most menial task of the day: to inflate the one hundred and fifty balloons that would be released into the Suite Diamante at the night's crescendo. It was mind-numbing work, but Tom didn't mind. If he was thinking of balloons he couldn't think of Joy and her shirt on which the doodle of a smiling face had been stained red forever.

Tom was so wrapped up in the balloons that he didn't spare a moment to look through the wall window of the Suite Diamante, meaning he didn't see the huge black cloud forming in the distance. A cloud billowing from the Sunrise Building, specifically apartment five.

31

The Suite Diamante Part II

The Scarlett Grove was braced to begin welcoming guests from three-thirty in the afternoon. Seeing as though, for tonight at least, Gabriella would quite literally be the face of the hotel, she had no choice but to look her best. She retreated to her room early, giving herself an hour to shower, apply her make up, dry her hair, step into her tight white dress and make her way downstairs to greet the people Roger Wyatt had deemed worthy of an invite to his Grand Ball.

It came as some comfort to Gabriella that she wouldn't be greeting her guests alone. Tom had been instructed to make himself presentable and meet her at reception. She'd even added a place for him at the meal (much to the dismay of the kitchen team), seating him on her left-hand side to ensure she always has a reason to turn away from Roger when she can stand his canine grin no longer.

* * *

Tom called Joy before he headed to reception. The temperature in his room tripled as he placed the phone to his ear. He waited patiently but her phone didn't even ring. Either it was off, or she'd blocked his number. The tennis ball of anxiety in Tom's stomach inflated to a beach ball. He was growing increasingly certain that he'd never see Joy again. The thought made him want to curl up into a ball and cry.

But crying wasn't an option and neither was disappointing Gabriella, so he pulled himself together and headed to reception.

Wondering all the while about Joy.

Wondering all the while if she was OK.

* * *

Richard, after a lot of hard work, managed to convince Sarah that they should eat in the Dining Hall rather than order room service again. Sarah had resisted at first, as politely as possible, but eventually, she'd seen no other option than to agree. She suddenly found herself hating her husband's sobriety. She found herself hoping that he'd pick up a drink soon because then she'd have a valid reason to buy more Percocet.

* * *

The first guests arrived at twenty to four, all of whom showed great interest in Gabriella and ignored Tom completely whilst sipping glasses of champagne. Tom was offered a glass but politely refused. Gabriella nodded approvingly as he did so, but her approval couldn't have been further from his thoughts. He wanted to be sober in case he heard from Joy. He distracted himself from his constant thoughts of her by engaging in conversation with an overtly sophisticated couple who sipped champagne as though it were water. They talked of the weather and their excitement for the night's events. Tom found himself staring at their glasses.

He tried not to think about what that meant.

* * *

Roger couldn't believe that his penthouse was empty when he returned from the hospital. It was almost five in the afternoon and he'd been certain that he would find Nathan waiting for him. He could picture Nathan's frustration when he arrived to find the penthouse empty last night. Roger imagined he became more enraged with each passing minute, safe in the knowledge that there would be a severe punishment for such an inconvenience.

Roger could have cried. The relief he felt was overwhelming. There was nobody to threaten him with the public release of his darkest secret. But why? Why wasn't Nathan here?

Suddenly Roger began to question his recollection of last night. What if he hadn't been on his way to see Nathan, but returning? What if he'd found the man he so despised and reminded him who's really in charge? What if he'd killed again?

* * *

At some point, Richard had fallen asleep. Sarah didn't know how long she watched him sleep, but it felt like hours. He looked just like Marcus when he slept. They both cuddled a pillow and slept with their mouths ever so slightly ajar. Sarah missed watching her little boy sleep.

She wondered what Marcus would think if he were still here. He certainly wouldn't be proud of her behaviour this week. And no matter how terribly his father behaved, he wouldn't want him to die. He'd want his father to sober up, and Richard would never be strong enough to do that without the support of his wife.

Sarah suddenly made a decision, a decision that even she couldn't quite understand. She decided to give Richard one final chance to be the man who had introduced her to the world's greatest pizza. It's what Marcus would have wanted. But the second he relapses she'll find the nearest divorce lawyer and put as much distance between herself and him as possible.

Marcus would have wanted that too.

* * *

With everything Roger had been through in the last few days, a part of him felt ready to surrender. It was the part of him that had always dreamed of being a success like his father. The part of him that had wanted to come to Spain and handle everything perfectly. The part of him that, despite everything, still wanted to make his father proud. Because at the end of

307

the day, if Bill Wyatt had smiled a little more, or taken the time to pat his son on the head, everything might have turned out differently. Gabriella might have liked the man Roger could have been.

A voice from deep inside Roger's subconscious told him it wasn't too late. That he could still make his father proud.

A much louder voice told Roger he was years too late.

The second voice was right.

* * *

When the clock struck five-thirty Gabriella's nerves were at breaking point. Many of the guests were already good and drunk, and all seemed well apart from the fact that the evening's host was nowhere to be seen. Gabriella had done most of the heavy lifting when it came to organising the ball, but it was Roger's night. Gabriella knew only six of the forty guests, the rest had introduced themselves as associates of Roger's in one form or another. A handful of the male guests made Gabriella wish she'd worn a different outfit. Her dress was in no way short but it was tight, and men, both old and young, stared at her for just a second too long. This was a problem. She'd intended to slip under the radar tonight.

* * *

Roger arrived at the Scarlett Grove ten minutes before the guests were due to take their seats in the Suite Diamante. He was greeted by a cheer from the flawlessly dressed crowd

308

gathered at the Lobby Bar. His magic powder was once again working its magic. Roger was beginning to forget that his life had suddenly become a playground bully pinning him to the ground. He was so consumed by the applause that he didn't notice the only two members of the crowd who didn't clap or cheer: Gabriella Glover and Tom Jennings.

* * *

Tom was beginning to sense that Gabriella had an ulterior motive for inviting him to the meal. She wanted to keep her distance from Roger, that much was clear, but her reason for doing so was much harder to decipher.

Roger rushed over to Gabriella as they entered the Suite Diamante and invited her to sit beside him. Tom clocked Gabriella's unease, it was hard not to, and took up the seat on the other side of her to find a small place setting with his name. Gabriella had planned for him to sit here. She must really need his help.

He just wished he knew why.

* * *

Richard awoke to an empty hotel room and his heart sank.

She's gone.

His heart sank even further into his stomach with the thought that followed.

Thank God.

Now he was free to drink without guilt or remorse. He

could run downstairs and have Davey pour him a drink so strong it would make his hair stand to attention. Then the sink in the bathroom began to run and Richard's heart sank lower than he'd ever thought possible.

Shit. She's still here.

He was irredeemable.

Sarah emerged from the bathroom moments later and Richard was awestruck for the first time in months. Her straightened hair sat just below her shoulders. Her white cotton dress wouldn't have looked out of place at any social event and her lips were as red as they'd been on the night they met. Richard was totally and utterly consumed by her, just as he had been all those years ago.

'What do you think?' Sarah asked nervously.

'You look lovely.' And she really did, but Richard's hands were starting to shake. She'd look even lovelier after a drink.

Sarah smiled. It had been a long time since she'd received a compliment. 'I thought I'd make an effort, you know?'

'I think it's a great idea. I'll jump in the shower now.'

Richard thought about kissing his wife but decided against it. There was no amount of make-up capable of concealing the bruise on her cheek. Every time Richard saw it his desire to drink became world consuming. He used all the strength he had to smile at his wife before disappearing into the bathroom.

* * *

The first course served in the Suite Diamante that evening

was a rather delightful French onion soup. Roger's guests were all very excited about the late arrival of the evenings guest of honour, meaning Roger was flooded with questions and compliments. This suited Gabriella perfectly. She spent her time sipping soup and making polite conversation with Tom. He stiffened when Gabriella asked about the girl he was seeing, and she decided not to press the matter any further. Gabriella had enough experience with complicated relationships to know that people in the midst of a complicated relationship never want to be asked about their complicated relationship.

The menu described the second course as a twist on a Caesar salad but to Tom, it was just another plate of underwhelming greenery. He and Gabriella had exhausted their topics of conversation and she'd now struck up a conversation with the elderly lady on Tom's far side. Tom didn't mind though; he saw it as an opportunity. The next time the champagne attendants lapped the table he helped himself to a glass. Gabriella either didn't notice or decided that, after Tom's hard work today, he'd earned himself a drink. Thankfully the bubbles made the salad more exciting. At least they did until he was interrupted by the one voice he'd been hoping not to hear tonight.

'Oi mate.'

Tom looked across Gabriella to find Roger Wyatt leaning towards him with his teeth bared.

'Hi.' Tom replied awkwardly.

'I just wanted to ask, um…' Roger glanced over to Gabriella to ensure she wasn't listening. 'Did you ever ring the guy? You know, Nathan?'

Tom, like Roger, was anxious that Gabriella might overhear them. 'No. I know it sounds like a lie, but it wasn't for me. It was for a friend of mine.'

'Whatever.' Roger fast became frustrated. 'Do you at least know if your friend got in touch with him or not?'

'Not for certain, but I'd assume so.'

'OK.' Roger nodded to himself, as if a weight had been lifted, and then retreated to his salad which, like Tom, he found severely underwhelming.

Nathan had been in business with other people. That was good. Maybe he'd finally realised it would be better for him to keep the son of one of the richest men in England on his side rather than in his pocket. But Roger still couldn't shake the feeling that maybe he'd found Nathan last night.

Had he?

The third course was a perfectly cooked beef wellington served with roast potatoes and steamed asparagus. It was the course Tom had been looking forward to most and yet, just as his plate was being set down in front of him some part of his brain subconsciously tuned in to the conversation taking place to his left. The elderly woman beside him had shifted her attention to an even older woman sitting opposite her. Their conversation was not particularly interesting, but Tom's ears pricked up at the mention of a fire. Something deep within him told him he needed to know more.

'I'm sorry.' Tom interrupted rather bluntly. 'What was that you were saying about a fire?'

The women were clearly not used to being interrupted but answered Tom's question nonetheless. 'There was a fire a little way down the beach.'

'Do you know where?'

'One of the old apartment buildings. It was never actually finished as far as I heard.'

Tom zoned out. His heart no longer beating.

'I heard the owner was drunk and dropped a cigarette on a rug.' The older woman added. She'd heard no such thing, but she always found rumours more enjoyable when she started them herself.

'What possesses some people?' The woman besides Tom retaliated, convinced the lie she'd been told was true.

Tom couldn't sit here any longer. He didn't excuse himself from the table. He didn't apologise to Gabriella or explain why he was leaving. Instead, he jumped to his feet and bolted out of the Suite Diamante without pausing to look back.

'You just can't get the staff nowadays.'

Gabriella was still in disbelief. The speed at which Tom had left made it clear that he would not be returning. At that moment Gabriella decided that the next time she saw the most eager man in all of Britain she would sack him on the spot, even if it meant she had to work in the beach hut herself. Now she just had to reply to the killer sitting beside her.

'Clearly not.' She muttered.

'Should we be worried? Did he have an important role tonight or anything?'

He was supposed to keep you away from me.

'No. Not really.' Gabriella lied.

'That's a relief. The way I understand it you've organised quite the spectacle.'

Gabriella took a good look at Roger for the first time and felt a sudden sense of dread. His pupils were dilated, and his skin was a ghostly shade of white with dark circles engulfing his eyes. He seemed to be forcing the smile that usually came so naturally to him. There was something wrong with him, something worse than usual.

'Most people here think you've organised quite the spectacle.'

'I wanted to apologise about that. I've had um, well there's no other way of putting it, a really shitty week. In fact, a lot of what kept me going was knowing that tonight I'd get to come here and see you. I really value my time with you, Gabriella.'

Gabriella had two options. She could answer honestly and tell Roger there was nothing she dreaded more than having to spend time with him, or she could lie and tell Roger that she felt the same way.

'I feel the same way.'

Roger couldn't hide his delight. 'I was hoping we could have a chat after the fireworks. I feel like there's a lot I've wanted to say to you throughout this whole ordeal and unless I'm mad, I think there are probably some things you'd like to say to me too.'

Gabriella couldn't decide whether to laugh or cry. She did neither.

'So, do you fancy it? Sneaking off after the fireworks?'

Gabriella was spared from lying once again by Roger's ringing phone. He apologised for the interruption and checked who was calling. Gabriella didn't see the name on the phone, but it certainly wasn't good news for Roger, whose face flushed so white Gabriella thought she could almost see his skull.

Roger recovered just enough to excuse himself before rushing out of the Suite Diamante to accept a call from the man he hated most in this world.

* * *

As Roger was leaving the Suite Diamante, Tom was sprinting down the beach as fast as his legs could carry him. The billowing cloud of smoke in the sky brought tears to his eyes. There were dozens of apartments on the beach. It couldn't be her. He was going to arrive at a random building where a confused pensioner had fallen asleep with a lit cigarette in her hand and burned down the building just as the old woman had explained.

But Tom didn't believe that, not really. If he did, he wouldn't be running as though his life depended on it. His lungs burned and his legs begged for mercy, but it was nothing compared to the wrenching ache of his heart.

It took Tom less than six minutes to arrive at Joy's apartment.

What was left of it at least.

32

The Clover

Deputy Inspector Blanco was an experienced police officer. She'd spent over twenty-five years working for the Roquetas De Mar police force and during those years she'd seen the worst of people. She'd seen heinous crimes that had shaken her to her core and changed the very fabric of who she is as a person. Just as avid cinema fans become desensitized to on-screen violence and avid porn fans become desensitized to naked bodies in real life, Deputy Inspector Blanco soon became desensitized to tragedy. She'd seen more heartbreak than most, more than most could handle.

Her years spent upholding the law had turned Blanco cold and emotionless, which meant that a measly little fire at a dilapidated apartment building on the bad side of town did not affect her. Especially considering it was reported that the fire had only claimed two lives. The reports were sketchy but allegedly somebody had spotted the fire and banged on doors to warn people, although only two of the apartments were occupied anyway. The reliability of the incident report was questionable considering the only eyewitness was Emma

Whitworth, a confused English pensioner who'd been unable to identify even the gender of her saviour. Still, Emma had no reason to lie and if Blanco's time on the force had taught her anything, it was that people with no reason to lie - don't.

There are tips, rules and practices that every police officer learns at some point in their career. These things include how to spot a lie during an interrogation, the way a person carrying a weapon holds themselves, and most importantly, a person acting suspiciously at a crime scene is almost always involved in the crime.

For the last hour or so there had been no such suspicious behaviour. Onlookers came and went showing nothing more than vague interest. Blanco was counting the minutes until she was relieved of her duty when suddenly, as if he'd appeared simply out of thin air, she was gifted a prime suspect.

The sound of shoes slapping against the sand rang heavy on the air. He was young, no older than twenty-five. He was English, that much was obvious, and he had loved whoever lived in the building. He cried as only those with a broken heart can. Blanco watched as the young man collapsed to the floor. She decided to give him some time to compose himself before she approached.

* * *

Bill Wyatt wasn't surprised when he heard the news, he was only surprised it had taken so long. Roger had never been the son he'd wanted. Bill had realised this when his son scraped through high school by the skin of his teeth. He felt betrayed by his genetics. He'd wanted a son who would share his ambition and cunning and tenacity. A son with whom he could sit and share a bottle of whiskey whilst talking of their plans for the future. Most importantly, he'd wanted a son to be proud of. Instead he'd been stuck with a son he simply disliked. A son he hated.

Some of Bill's friends, those in charge of overseeing the businesses he'd already acquired in Roquetas De Mar, had been tasked with keeping a watchful eye on the actions of Bill's only son. For the most part the reports that made their way back to Bill had been better than expected. Roger had become a popular figure in clubs and bars, but he appeared to be taking his work seriously. Bill was beginning to think maybe he'd been wrong after all. Then a brief phone call confirmed what he had known all along.

* * *

Roger's hands shook as he answered the call. His bottom lip trembled and for a terrible second he thought he might cry.

'Are you still in the hospital?' Bill didn't bother with formalities. He never did when it came to his son.

'What? No! I'm at the hotel. We're celebrating the takeover.' Roger hoped this would make his father proud. As usual it did not.

'Well, that's something at least. Tomorrow I'll be there to oversee it all.'

Roger felt his blood boil and his skin melt. How dare the old man try and steal this accomplishment from him?

'No! This is my deal.' He replied defiantly.

'Oh, you think this is your deal, do you? Let me tell you something son, it isn't. It's pity. It was your final chance to make something of yourself, and it's a chance you've royally fucked.'

'How exactly? Because as far as I can tell the deals gone through and everybody on my end seems more than happy.' Roger's fists were clenched and his jaw was tight. It took a lot of restraint not to take his anger out on the wall beside him.

'Oh yeah, of course. You're right. And I suppose they'll continue to be delighted when they find out about the overdose that could have killed you last night?' From the silence that followed, Bill knew his punch had landed.

'How do you know about that?' Roger mumbled.

'I have lots of friends in Spain, Roger.'

Now Roger really lost control. His vision began to blur. His fists were clenched so tightly that his nails drew blood as they ripped into his palms.

'You've had them watching me?' He shouted.

'I don't know if those are the words I'd use. I asked some people to notify me if you ended up in hospital or prison.'

At the mention of prison, Roger dug his nails even further into his palms. Blood dribbled down his wrists.

'It's a shame because your mother really thought you'd kicked it. It's going to kill her this. I hope you know that.'

'Fuck you.' Roger spat down the phone.

Bill laughed; it was a sound Roger hadn't heard in years. 'The second this call ends I'll be getting the accountant on the phone. By the time I arrive in Spain tomorrow you'll have a million pounds in your account. It's enough for you to move anywhere and do anything you like. Just so long as

your mother doesn't have to watch you kill yourself anymore.'
Bill was astonishingly calm, speaking as though Roger was a
colleague.

'What? You're banishing me?' Roger was beginning to
attract concerned glances from the guests that passed him.

'It's simple. You either move away with a million pounds
or you come home with nothing.'

'Don't you dare come here tomorrow!'

'Or what?' Even through the phone, Roger knew his father
was grinning.

'Or I'll fucking kill you!' Roger screamed.

Bill laughed once more and ended the call. The three guests
who'd been unfortunate enough to overhear Roger's threat
quickly scurried away. Roger didn't notice. He was only
aware of the white-hot rage that had overcome him. He felt
no pain the first time he punched the wall, despite the skin
around all four of his knuckles splitting open and leaving a
bloody stain on the once pristine wall, but he certainly felt it
when the second punch fractured two of his knuckles.

* * *

The Dining Hall was bustling with happy people and even
happier chatter. Among all this pleasantness sat Sarah and
Richard Tyler, a couple who, try as they might, would never
be happy again.

Richard quickly took to picking at his fingernails in a feeble
effort to distract himself from his burning desire to uncork a
bottle and drink the whole thing just as quickly as he could.
Three of his fingers were bleeding. Not huge amounts of

blood, barely any more than one might bleed from a paper cut. It was the sort of injury that nobody would notice unless they were actively looking for it.

Sarah noticed Richard's bleeding fingers immediately, and the blood was not all she noticed either. She noticed Richard's eyes follow anybody with a beer or a cocktail. His longing was almost cannibalistic, she could see how much he needed it. It might not happen today and it might not happen tomorrow, but at some point her husband will give into his disease and retreat back to the cowardly, monster of a man she'd come to know. She just knew it.

* * *

Tom hadn't noticed Deputy Inspector Blanco standing outside the Sunrise Building. He hadn't noticed anybody for that matter. All he could see was the plume of grey smoke rising into the sky. It took minutes to calm his breathing, to finally bring himself to a state of mind in which he could think rationally. Suddenly he became aware of somebody standing over him. His heart leapt to the top of his chest, beating thrice a second. It must have been Joy! She was here and she was waiting for him and most importantly, she was alive!

Tom leapt to his feet and his heart shrank back down to the pit of his stomach where it would remain forever. It wasn't Joy. It was a middle-aged police officer with short black hair and a grave expression.

'English?' She asked with such certainty Tom wasn't sure if it was a question. 'You know who lived here?' Blanco's

English was fluent thanks to multiple run-ins with drunk and disorderly British tourists.

Tom suddenly felt anxious. There was at least one dead body in the wreckage of the Sunrise Building. He didn't know if fingerprints could survive a fire, but if they could he was in big trouble.

'What's your name?' Blanco demanded.

Tom had read many novels in which characters experience the strange sensation of fight or flight. In these novels it always seemed as though the characters experiencing the phenomenon were aware of the experience, and that by the time they acted it had almost become a conscious decision. Tom didn't have that same experience. He wasn't aware that he was experiencing the phenomenon until he took two quick steps away from Blanco, turned and sprinted down the beach. He didn't hear Blanco demand that he stop running just as he didn't hear her take chase after him. He flew down the beach with the same ferocity with which he'd sprinted up it just minutes before.

Blanco took chase though she knew there wasn't much point. She was a fifty-seven-year-old woman with a knee that would soon be replaced and a back that creaked when she bent down. Still, she had a feeling about this young man, and she chased her suspect until her lungs emptied. She watched him flee up a thin alley and disappear.

After taking an embarrassingly long time to catch her breath, Blanco returned to the scene of the crime and sent out a description of her suspect. She didn't expect the search to wield any results, there must be close to a thousand Brits currently in Roquetas De Mar, but maybe she'd get lucky.

* * *

Gabriella was beginning to feel a faint glimmer of hope that her problem had resolved itself. Clearly Roger's call had been so distressing that he'd had no choice but to leave the hotel. As dessert was served Gabriella began to think she might even enjoy the ball after all. She relished in the sweetness of profiteroles and cream for just one bite. For as she returned to her plate for a second taste, the doors of the Suite Diamante swung open and Roger Wyatt strutted back into her life.

To say that Roger looked dishevelled would be putting it lightly. A towel was wrapped around his right hand as some sort of makeshift bandage. Gabriella couldn't see what had happened for Roger to require such an accessory, but the sight of it filled her with dread. A black storm cloud had just rolled into the Suite Diamante and now everything seemed dark.

Gabriella intended to only sneak a glance at Roger's injury but the crimson stain resting above his knuckles distracted her. She stared for so long that Roger noticed the focus of her gaze, as did several others seated around the table.

'Did I miss anything good?' Roger asked, desperately trying to recapture some of his familiar charm.

Gabriella was taken aback by just how dilated Roger's pupils were. Staring into his eyes was like staring into the dark vacuum of space. She looked away quickly.

'The wellington was excellent.'

'Well, at least I got back in time for dessert.' Roger thrashed his spoon into his bowl and consumed an entire profiterole.

Gabriella knew she had to ask about Roger's injury. It was unavoidable given he'd caught her staring at it.

'Is everything OK with your hand?' She asked delicately.

Roger looked down at his hand before he spoke, implying that the wound was so insignificant he'd forgotten it was there.

'Oh yeah. I banged it against the bathroom door and opened up an old cut. It's nothing serious.'

'That's a relief.' Gabriella lied.

'You weren't worried about me, were you?' Roger asked, flashing Gabriella his gleaming coyote teeth.

'Not even a little bit.' Gabriella replied honestly.

'Either way, it takes more than a little cut to keep me away from a good time.'

'So I've heard.'

'You've not been reading up on me, have you?'

'Should I have?' Gabriella asked innocently. Her neck stiffened. He couldn't know. Not now.

'No. You just seem to know a lot about me. It made me think that maybe you'd done your homework.' Roger's magic powder was working a treat. His life might have been imploding around him but he slotted back into the skin of his aggressively charming former self without a hiccup.

'It's my job. I have to do my homework.'

'So, it's just homework then? You never take a quick look out of personal interest?'

'What would I be looking for?' Gabriella's mind was consumed with the hours she'd spent scrolling through local news sites, searching desperately for proof of Roger's crime.

'I dunno. Anything that takes your fancy I suppose.'

'Well there's been nothing yet, but I'll be sure to keep you updated if anything comes up.'

Shivers thudded down Gabriella's spine. When she found

her proof, she'd make sure to keep him updated. Along with the police, journalists, bloggers and anybody else who would listen.

* * *

Tom hadn't looked back once. The sound of Blanco's boots slapping against the sand had quickly fallen away and by the time he reached the main road he knew he was alone. Just as he would be for the rest of his days.

He walked aimlessly with nothing to do but think. He thought of everything, the immense weight of his mistakes, his guilt, the thought of never seeing Joy again. The pain would never stop. The guilt would never fade. He was consumed by emptiness. He had nothing.

He couldn't go back to the hotel. Not tonight and probably never again. He needed to find somewhere though, somewhere to escape from himself. At that exact moment, music began to blare from The Clover as if God himself was personally directing Tom. He knew the sort of people he would find in there and right now he couldn't think of a better place to be.

* * *

Sarah's anxieties only heightened when Richard suggested they play cards at the Lobby Bar until the Grand Ball began. She didn't want Richard to spend the next forty-five minutes surrounded by an abundance of people enjoying the liberating effects of colourful drinks in tall glasses, but they needed somewhere to pass the time and nowhere would be free of temptation.

Richard found a table near the window looking out towards the pool and Sarah headed to the bar. She decided the best way to keep her nerves straight was to ensure that she herself fetched all their drinks back to the table. She might not be able to tell Richard of her doubts, but she certainly wouldn't turn a blind eye.

Sarah ordered two diet cokes.

Over at the table, four of Richard's fingers were now bleeding.

* * *

After the plates were collected, the guests were asked to retreat to the Lobby bar so the Suite Diamante could be transformed into the elegant ballroom that was so popular within the local community. Gabriella intended to linger with the group for a minute or two before slinking away to her office to double-check that everything was prepared for her night in hiding. The only problem was she hadn't anticipated the number of hands she'd have to shake or the abundance of compliments she had to receive. It seemed that, based on the hotel's general aesthetic and incredible dinner service, Roger's esteemed guests had decided she was doing a splendid job managing the Scarlett Grove Hotel and Spa. No matter where she turned, she found somebody waiting to catch her attention. Male guests were approaching her with the pretence of complimenting the hotel when really they just wanted the pleasure of unzipping her dress later that evening. Gabriella spent so long awkwardly talking to strangers that the opportunity for her planned side door dart escaped her. She had no choice but to smile as Roger climbed onto a chair to make a joyous announcement.

Roger, who's pupils were somehow still expanding, tapped a spoon against the side of his glass and proudly announced that the Grand Ball was ready to begin. Applause filled the room. Roger concluded his announcement by asking if the wonderful lady responsible for the night's festivities would join him for the first dance.

With all eyes fixed firmly on Gabriella, she had no choice but to take Roger's clammy hand and allow herself to be led into the Suite Diamante. Roger instructed the band to play something slow, something perfect for a slow dance.

* * *

The Clover was everything Tom expected it to be. The walls were dark, the staff were unfriendly, and to honour the establishment's Irish roots there were a smattering of Guinness posters displayed proudly behind the bar. When Tom finally adjusted to the dim lighting and heavy smoke, he made his way to the large bar at the back of the room.

He knew the only way to escape his overbearing thoughts was to drown them in drink, and that's exactly what he did. He drank quickly and without hesitation, never once even taking a second to turn and observe his surroundings. If he had, he would have seen a familiar face.

* * *

As the music played and Gabriella swayed with Roger, she began to feel as though she would never escape. Roger must have somehow learnt of her plan and he was now doing everything in his power to prevent her from leaving.

As Roger slid his hand from her shoulder down to the lowest crease of her back, she had to fiercely resist the urge to lash out. Nothing was going to plan. Her heart was racing, and Roger found that all the more encouraging. He sniffed her hair and Gabriella felt tears welling behind her eyes.

She was alone in a crowd of unfamiliar faces. Alone and hopeless. Which is strange, because at that very moment a young couple out walking their dogs made a truly startling discovery on the outskirts of town.

* * *

The Suite Diamante opened to lowly guests like the Tylers' ten minutes earlier than expected, which meant that whilst Richard headed into the party, Sarah was sat on a closed toilet willing herself not to cry. Sitting with Richard had been unbearable. His fingers were shredded and dripping with blood and he gazed towards the bar with an almost inhuman desperation. The sight of him broke her heart. Then again that was nothing new. Richard had been breaking her heart for years.

When Sarah eventually composed herself, having finally accepted Richard genuinely was trying his best, she returned to the Lobby Bar to find their table bereft of playing cards and, more importantly, her husband. Music blared from the Suite Diamante and Sarah's heart stopped. Richard was alone and he was drinking. She just knew it.

* * *

Richard soaked in every last detail of the Suite Diamante. He immediately spotted the resemblance between this room and the handsome room in which he and Sarah had tied the knot. It was uncanny, from the navy-blue ribbons wrapped delicately around the white chair covers to the identical chandelier glistening proudly. What surprised Richard the most though, was the fact that this room seemed to have the same subtle charm of the Country Home in Wales. The stage in the Suite Diamante was portable and looked as though it had been constructed just minutes ago, just as the stage he and Sarah had danced on for the first time as husband and wife had been.

This was the sign Richard needed. He'd asked the universe for help and it had responded enthusiastically. He'd never wanted to drink less. He only wanted to be with Sarah, just as he had all those years ago in Wales. He wanted to be the man he'd promised to be as he and Sarah had stood hand in hand at the end of the aisle.

Sarah didn't have the time to appreciate the beauty of the Suite Diamante, nor did she have the time to observe the striking resemblance between this room and the ballroom of the Kinmel Country Home in Wales.

She only saw Richard standing at the bar, grinning widely.

* * *

Gabriella spent her entire dance with Roger desperately racking her brains for an escape plan. When the music finally died, she and Roger accepted the generous applause that followed, with Roger's hand still wrapped around her own like a vice. She was about to excuse herself with some terribly concocted story about checking on the safety of a guest, but Roger beat her to the punch. He politely informed Gabriella that, although he was already beginning to slur his words, he needed another drink to keep himself going.

'Strawberry daiquiri? I remember how much you like them.' Roger said excitedly, trying to elicit an emotional reaction from Gabriella as he cast her mind back to their terrible date at Platos Y Bebidos.

'You know me.' Gabriella replied with an abundance of false cheer.

With a flash of his canine teeth, Roger headed for the bar. Gabriella waited, waved at Roger when he turned back to smile at her, and then disappeared into the crowd without looking back.

* * *

Sarah arrived at Richard's side approximately four minutes before Roger turned and waved at Gabriella. She knew that rushing towards the bar wouldn't end well. She should have walked over casually and nonchalantly asked Richard what he'd ordered for the two of them, but her body simply wouldn't allow it. She knew better. She knew what alcohol transformed him into. She'd been berated by him. Abused by him. Beaten by him. And no matter how many promises he made; she will never forget what he's put her through. She will never forget that for months she'd contemplated taking her own life just to escape him.

'Everything OK?' Sarah asked.

'Yeah. I got you a gin and tonic. I feel like one of us should take advantage of the open bar.' Richard replied with a smile as if his dazzling teeth were the best way of regaining Sarah's trust.

'Oh, OK. Thank you.'

Richard handed Sarah her drink and collected one from the bar for himself. It appeared to be a pint of coke, but Sarah knew how easily spirits could be concealed in that dark liquid.

'Do you want to go and find a table?' Richard asked.

Sarah said nothing as she weighed up her options.

'I think that one's free.' Richard gestured to an empty table in the far corner of the room.

'What's in your drink?' Sarah asked more suddenly than she'd intended.

'What do you mean?'

'What's in your drink? What did you get from the bar?'

'It's a coke. What do you think it is?' Richard asked defensively.

Sarah said nothing. She and Richard spent a long moment staring at one another in silence. Anybody who happened to look towards them right now would have struggled to decide if they were sharing a look of love or hatred.

'Really? You leave for two minutes and automatically assume the worst?' Richard said. His disbelief rivalled only by the hurt he felt.

'Yeah. You know what, that's exactly what happened. And it's a completely justified reaction, by the way.'

'You know it's not like that this time.'

'Do you know how much I want to believe that? Do you have any idea how much I want you to be who you were when we first met?' Sarah didn't notice the tears forming in her eyes.

'Jesus Sarah! You think I don't want that? Do you think I like who I am?'

Sarah said nothing. The words rattling around her head were too cruel.

'Taste it!' Richard thrust his drink towards Sarah.

'That's not the point.'

'Taste it!' Richard yelled. Thankfully, the audience was now applauding the end of a dance which meant only those closest to the bar heard his outburst.

Sarah tasted the drink. It was coke. No vodka. No rum. No gin. Just coke.

'Do you believe me now?' Richard asked with venom. 'Have I passed your test?'

'It's not a test. And it's not as simple as me just believing you.'

'What's it about then?'

'It's about Marcus' Hot tears rained down Sarah's cheeks. She made no effort to wipe them away. 'It's about the way you make me feel. It's about the swelling on my cheek and the bruises on my neck.'

Neither Sarah nor Richard noticed the well-dressed man with the hugely diluted pupils arrive at the bar beside them.

'It's not a choice! Why can't you understand that? I don't want to drink!' Richard's defence fell and tears began to litter his cheeks.

'But you do. And you always will.'

Richard said nothing. His anger had evaporated. He replayed the three words his wife had just said on a loop.

You always will.

Richard pushed past Sarah and rushed out of the Suite Diamante. Sarah contemplated chasing him. She contemplated apologising for what she'd said. She knew that therapists and everybody involved with AA would lament her behaviour, but she did nothing.

Truthfully, she was relieved.

* * *

Roger didn't pay any attention to the couple arguing beside him. He was too busy thinking about Gabriella, about something he'd seen in her eyes as she'd waved at him just now. He'd seen a pair of eyes that didn't trust him. A pair of eyes that he himself did not trust. A part of his brain was screaming at him, screaming that Gabriella remembered everything he'd told her the night he'd stolen the life from the girl wearing the black stilettos.

Roger needed to find out what Gabriella really knew. He had no idea how to do it, but he was sure his magic powder would help. He could only think clearly with that delicious white powder clogging up his system.

By the end of the night, there would be an awful lot of white powder clogging up Roger's system.

* * *

Tom drank to forget. He wasn't particularly fussy about what he drank either. He began with gin and tonics, finishing two in quick succession. This didn't escape the attention of the bartender, who took it upon himself to suggest Tom move onto a nice glass of whiskey. Tom agreed even though he'd never liked the taste of whiskey. He knew the bartender was only looking to make a bigger profit and cared far too little to object.

It was impossible not to obsess over all the things he should have done. He should have stayed. Even when she asked him to leave he should have stayed. He should have stayed and helped and then they would have been together. No matter what happened they would have been together and that was all that mattered.

Tom ordered another shot of whiskey, his third in total, and as the barman set about pouring it, Tom overheard somebody shout the name of the man he hated more than anything.

'I know that! But I don't know where he is now, do I? And I can't remember Nathan ever taking this long to get in touch. Not after a meeting with that fucking Wyatt fella anyway.'

It couldn't be a coincidence. Sure, there were probably a lot of Nathan's in Roquetas De Mar, but he doubted any others had reason to meet with Roger Wyatt. Tom turned to find the man who had driven Nathan to the Scarlett Grove over a week ago. The man who had collected Joy from the Lobby Bar on his first night in Spain. He turned to see Connor, who looked incredibly concerned about the whereabouts of his boss.

* * *

Gabriella barely made it out of the Suite Diamante before she was stopped by a member of staff, a young girl named Maria with jet black curly hair and a tan most women would kill for. Maria explained that Bill Wyatt was on the phone, insisting that he speak with Gabriella as a matter of urgency. Gabriella thanked Maria, although she wasn't at all grateful, and asked her to transfer the call to her office.

Gabriella quickly ran the numbers. Bill hardly ever contacted her and certainly never as a matter of urgency. No doubt the old man just wanted to let her know that the paperwork had been finalised and the hotel was now officially a part of the bulging Wyatt Empire, which also meant Gabriella was now a very rich woman. The thought made her feel dirty. She'd sold her soul. She'd sold her family's greatest treasure to a tycoon and his canine son.

* * *

Five minutes passed before Sarah finally decided to do something. No matter what he'd done in the past, and though their marriage had no future, Richard had spent the last two days trying to make himself better.

Truthfully, Sarah had no idea what he was going through. She didn't know what it felt like to depend on something just to feel like herself again. And though she would never forgive Richard for the things he'd done; she couldn't turn her back on him now. He needed her help. She owed him that much.

* * *

The number of obnoxious customers in The Clover seemed to be increasing by the minute, making it impossible for Tom to eavesdrop on the conversation taking place at Connor's table. Tom had never before seen the slim man sitting opposite Connor, but he knew his type. A tattoo sleeve on each arm sporting tribal designs he knew nothing about. A hairstyle modelled on a character from a popular TV show (*Peaky Blinder's* in this case) and eyes that wandered from woman to woman. He was the type of man to pride himself on his aggression and bravery despite never having been in a fight before.

Tom stopped drinking the second he saw Connor. He was well beyond sober, but he needed to keep his head as clear as possible if he were to have any success deciphering what the two were saying. Not that it mattered. He couldn't piece a single sentence together. Tom began contemplating abandoning this futile task and returning to his whiskey when he heard a single word, clear as day. That word changed everything. Just a single word spoken at a table in The Clover changed Tom's life forever.

That word was joy.

* * *

You always will.

That was what she'd said to him. Richard now knew he would always be the villain in her eyes. He'd spent the last two days putting his body through hell, denying his diseased insides the medicine they desperately needed, and this was how she thanked him. He hated her. He knew it now. A part of him had always known it.

Richard's drinking started in the wake of his redundancy. He was ashamed of his failure; ashamed of what he'd become: a newly married man who could no longer support his wife. He drank to escape the shame, and for a while it worked.

That is until he began waking up not only with a pounding head but also with terrible memories. Memories of fists and blood and tears. Memories of Sarah begging him to stop. Richard couldn't live with these memories and so he started drinking to forget. He got drunk and hurt his wife again but this time it was the alcohol's fault. Not his. He was the victim. A victim who needed to escape from himself and there was only one way to do that. Even now, there was still only one way to do that.

Richard slipped Davey a fifty euro note, and the young lad handed him a bottle of whiskey in return. Richard left without answering any of Davey's questions, tonight he needed to drink alone. There was nothing to be said. He is an alcoholic and his wife hates him for it. She always will.

The first sip was everything he'd needed. So too were the second and the third. Sarah would be here soon. She'd love to find him like this. Love just how quickly he'd proved her right. She'd savour every minute of it just as she always did. But not this time.

Richard won't be her broken man anymore. When she gets here, he'll make everything right. Sarah is the reason he drinks. That much is clear now. He just needs Sarah to know it too.

It was her fault. It was all her fault.

* * *

Bill didn't waste any time with the usual pleasantries, instead he got straight to the point. He explained, in no uncertain terms, that Roger was no longer involved with the Wyatt Foundation. Gabriella couldn't believe it. Her luck had finally changed. She'd been drowning and Bill Wyatt had tossed her a life jacket.

Still, she couldn't help but wonder why. Did Bill know what Roger had done? Had the body been found? Had she been proved right after the longest, hardest week of her life?

No. No, she had not.

Bill answered Gabriella's subtle questions with startling honesty, explaining that Roger had always struggled with substance abuse problems and he now desperately needed help. It was what Bill said next though, that chilled Gabriella to her very core.

'Anyway, I'll be there first thing tomorrow morning. I can't let it go on any longer. Without help, there's no knowing how much he could hurt himself.' Bill paused for a moment. 'Or somebody else, for that matter.'

She's dead anyway.

Gabriella knew she should tell Bill about her suspicions, and she would, just not tonight. Tonight, she needed to put as much distance between herself and Roger Wyatt as possible. She thanked Bill for informing her of the news. Truthfully, he seemed embarrassed. Gabriella wondered how he'd feel when he found out that his only son was a murderer.

She's dead anyway.

The line clicked dead. Gabriella rushed to collect the bag she'd stashed under her desk. She opened it, grabbed her laptop by the screen, and was about to pack it away when it flashed to life. The laptop displayed the last site she'd visited, which happened to be a local news website. A site with breaking news.

Body Discovered in burned-out car.

* * *

By the time Sarah arrived at room fifty-seven, Richard had made his way through a third of the bottle of whiskey. He was sitting on the bed, waiting for her to arrive. As the door opened he leapt to his feet, fists clenched and jaw locked.

Sarah wasn't surprised to find him with a drink in his hand. She would have been more surprised to find him sober. She was still disappointed though. She should have known better, but seeing her husband overcome by his demons hurt Sarah every time.

'You must be loving this.' Richard leered.

'Why? Why would I want this?'

'Because you were right! You said I'll always drink and here I am, good and drunk. You couldn't be happier.'

'You're deluded. You're actually insane!' The contempt in Sarah's voice was impossible to miss.

'You know what I think?' Richard slowly advanced towards Sarah. 'You're not happy unless you're the victim. Think about it. It makes so much sense! You used to like me when I was drunk. You said I was fun to be around.'

'You didn't use to fucking hit me!' Sarah spat back, unable to believe what Richard was saying. Unable to believe how much she hated her husband.

'You encouraged me to drink and when I did you started argument after argument. We argued about nothing constantly. Genuinely, can you remember one argument that actually meant anything? That had any substance to it?'

Sarah said nothing. Tears were once again taking up refuge on her cheeks.

'You pushed me and you pushed me and you knew what would happen. I'd either fold or I'd snap and I know which one you wanted. You wanted me to snap and I did, and you fucking loved it. Finally, you were the victim. It made you special and important because all of a sudden you weren't like every other boring wife. All of a sudden you had a story. People would listen to you and take pity on you. You were interesting and that was the only thing that mattered.' Richard was crying too now. His fists still clenched.

Sarah said nothing. She couldn't speak. Richard had touched upon something she'd hidden away deep within herself. He'd unlocked the chest in which she hid the truest form of herself. Maybe he was right.

'You could have left. You could have gone to the police. I have no friends. No family. There was nobody to support me. They would have locked me up, but you didn't want that. You had your story and that was enough. And then things got even better for you.'

Sarah's world stopped. She knew what Richard was about to say and she'd kill him before she let him utter those words.

'Don't you dare!' Sarah demanded, advancing towards Richard.

'Marcus got sick.'

'Don't you fucking dare!' Sarah slapped Richard hard across the face.

Richard continued, undeterred to Sarah's frantic punches and slaps. 'He got sick and then he died. There's nothing more interesting than that.'

Sarah was blind with rage. She'd never experienced anything like it before. She pushed Richard as hard as she could, using the weight of her entire body to force him away from her. He went stumbling backwards over the bed.

'Don't ever speak about Marcus again!' Sarah screamed.

Had it not been for the noise from downstairs somebody would have checked on the commotion. But the music was too loud and the fireworks would begin soon. Nobody will interrupt the Tyler's tonight.

Richard didn't reply. He, like Sarah, saw red and sprinted towards her, gripping her by her hair and throwing her across the bed. Sarah hit the floor hard and before she could climb to her feet Richard was on her again. He gripped her by the neck of her dress and lifted her so their eyes were level. Sarah spat in his face, enjoying the look of disgust that followed.

Richard screamed and catapulted Sarah into the bathroom. She crashed into the mirror which shattered into pieces. Sarah thudded to the floor, surrounded by shards of glass. She was in such terrible pain that she didn't notice Richard's distracted stare.

Richard was looking past his wife, towards a small air vent that had creaked open in the commotion. He stepped towards it as Sarah winced and cried on the floor. Something metal glinted inside the vent. Richard reached in and retrieved the gun his wife had stashed away. Sarah tried to grab Richard's leg and he kicked her in the stomach, hard. She writhed in pain. For a long moment, Richard just stared at the gun in his hands, utterly speechless.

341

Finally, he whispered a single word.
'Wow.'

* * *

Tom couldn't think clearly. He finished his whiskey, left forty euros on the bar and marched to Connor's table. He didn't hesitate and he didn't leave Connor with any time to react. He simply pulled his fist back and launched it into his nose.

The punch was merciless, powered by the heartache and devastation coursing through Tom's veins. Connor, who was caught completely off-guard, tumbled from his chair and down onto the beer-soaked floor.

For the moment that followed, everybody, including Tom, seemed trapped in a state of shock. Connor's friend couldn't believe what he'd seen. He stared up at Tom, utterly dumbfounded, without removing either of his hands from his pint glass. Everything happened in slow motion. Connor rolled on the floor in a heap. Tom doubted he'd be getting back to his feet any time soon. Everybody else in The Clover seemed content to ignore the ugly scene unfolding beside them. Those playing darts continued to play darts, those telling stories continue to tell stories.

Tom's fist screamed in pain. He hadn't thrown a punch before and he'd surprised himself with the venom that powered it. After the longest second of his life, Connor's tattooed friend jumped to his feet. Tom was wrong. This man had been in a fight before.

* * *

The news was unclear, but even with the precious few details available, Gabriella felt certain this was the proof she'd been looking for.

The victim was confirmed as a young woman who the police estimated had been dead for several days. Gabriella's mind was racing. Everything lined up with what she knew. She had to inform the police, that much was clear, but she couldn't risk it here. She'd get in touch with them the second she arrived at the Hilton. With any luck, Roger would be behind bars before the sun rose. And with the Wyatt Foundation's acquisition of the hotel already confirmed, there would be no reason for her not to remain in her position as manager under the watchful eye of Bill Wyatt.

Gabriella almost had a spring in her step as she pulled her bag over her shoulder and checked the time, the fireworks were due to begin in two minutes. If she rushed, she might even get a chance to watch the final colourful explosions from the balcony of her hotel room. If the view lined up perfectly, she might even be able to watch the police arrive. If so, she'd drink a glass of wine and toast to better days, all whilst Roger is forcefully shoved into the back of a police car.

'Everything OK?'

Gabriella froze. The coyote had found her in her den and with a flash of his teeth she knew she was in trouble.

Gabriella nodded, hoping the terror behind her eyes didn't show.

'Where'd you go? Roger asked, grinning relentlessly. 'You left me carrying two drinks.'

'Yeah, I'm sorry about that.' Gabriella was relieved to finally

343

rediscover the ability to speak. 'I just had to um…'

'You had to take a call, didn't you?' Roger interrupted.

Gabriella said nothing. She could hear her heart smashing against her ribcage. Roger studied her every move, his diluted pupils not missing a thing.

'Was it important?' He pressed.

'No. It wasn't anything that mattered. Not really.' Gabriella's voice quivered and her hands began to shake. She hadn't even convinced herself of the lie she'd told, never mind Roger.

'Really?'

Gabriella nodded, worried her voice might betray her again.

'Because I spoke to the girl at reception when I couldn't find you, she said you were taking a call from my Dad. He didn't have anything important to say, did he?'

'He just um.' Gabriella looked around for anything that would serve as a viable excuse to leave the room. She found nothing. 'He just called to congratulate me on the paperwork being finalised.'

'That was it? He didn't say anything else?'

'No. Should he have?' Gabriella asked innocently.

Roger studied her intently. Gabriella feared he knew exactly what she was thinking. He bared his canine teeth and advanced further into the room.

'Me and the old man had a bit of a row. I thought he might have mentioned it.'

Gabriella decided lying would only increase Roger's suspicions. 'He did mention that actually. He told me he's planning to fly out here tomorrow.'

'Typical, isn't it?' Roger replied rather jovially. 'I do all the hard work and he swoops in for the glory.' He laughed without joy. 'Is that all he said then?'

'Yeah. That was it.' Gabriella lied.

'OK good. I suppose you'll be wanting to come to watch the fireworks then?'

A large bang broke the silence. Gabriella jumped and checked her watch; a firework had exploded a minute early.

'Sounds like we're missing it. We better get going.'

'Definitely.' Gabriella agreed with a smile that felt unnatural on her face.

Gabriella felt sick. She'd missed her chance to escape. There was nothing she could do. She was stuck here and now Roger would be even more reluctant to let her out of his sight.

'Come on then.' Roger held the door for her. His smile wide and his eyes inviting.

Gabriella knew better than to trust Roger. He'd seen the bag on her shoulder and hadn't asked about it once. He knew she'd been planning to leave. With no other options, Gabriella set the bag down and walked towards Roger, praying her legs wouldn't crumble beneath her.

She moved past Roger and into the hallway, waiting to feel his hand on her shoulder or the small of her back, but she didn't feel anything. Roger had stayed where he was, standing in the doorway, continuing to smile at her. Something was wrong. Something was very wrong.

'Is everything OK?' She asked.

Outside the fireworks began. The walls of Gabriella's office were illuminated with spectacular shades of blue and red and purple.

'You forgot your bag.' Roger replied calmly. 'It's OK. I'll

grab it for you.'

Gabriella wanted to cry. Her feet were blocks of concrete and no matter how much she wanted to run and scream and beg for help, she just couldn't. She could do nothing but watch on helplessly as Roger strode into her office and retrieved her bag. Roger placed the bag onto the desk and began rooting through it, something quickly drew his eye.

'Come in here a second.' Roger ordered, the smile vanished from his face.

'What about the fireworks?' Gabriella asked, trying and failing to sound cheery.

'Come in here.' Roger demanded.

Gabriella did as she was told. Her legs finally worked, taking her exactly where she didn't want to go.

'What's wrong?' Gabriella asked timidly as she stood on the unfamiliar side of her desk.

Roger picked up Gabriella's laptop and showed her the screen.

Body discovered in burned-out car.

'Anything you want to tell me?' Roger asked.

His smile had returned now.

Wider than ever.

* * *

Aaron, the man sharing a table with Connor, had lost the ability to think. Connor was out for the count and now the guy who'd hit him didn't seem to know what to do, which made him an easy target. Aaron jumped to his feet and swung his pint glass towards Tom's face.

Tom saw the glass speeding towards him and made a desperate attempt to lunge away but he was too late. His evasive action prevented the glass from smashing into his nose at least. Instead, it exploded against his jaw.

At first, Tom felt nothing at all. Then he became aware of pain worse than anything he'd experienced. His jaw, which had somehow not broken, was now home to a wide gash from which blood gushed as if it had been desperate to escape his body for years. His white shirt was quickly stained an ugly shade of maroon, a stain that would never be washed off. His jaw wasn't his only source of agony though. A jagged piece of glass had wedged itself into his left shoulder like a piece of shrapnel from a heavy artillery weapon. The pain was excruciating but arriving at the smoking wreckage of Joy's apartment had hurt more.

Aaron was taken aback by the extent of Tom's injuries. He stepped back, weighing up the need for another attack. He decided quickly that Tom deserved more punishment and geared up for another attack, this time without a weapon, but he was too late. His moment of hesitation saved Tom's life.

Tom knew there was only one way to win this fight, he acted quickly and without thought, launching his right foot forward with everything he had. As his foot connected with Aaron's groin Tom felt certain he heard something pop. Aaron screamed as if he'd been shot and dropped to the floor, clutching his groin and dry heaving violently.

The crowd in The Clover were hushed now. All eyes seemed to be flicking between the young man with blood dripping from his jaw and the bartender, wondering who would blink first. Tom didn't wait to see what would happen if the bartender blinked first. He rushed out of The Clover

347

as quickly as he could, praying all the while that he wouldn't pass out.

As Tom pushed through the doors of The Clover and ran out towards the sea breeze, his legs buckled. He fell to the ground and a fresh grenade of pain exploded from his shoulder. He looked up, desperately fighting the blackness that threatened to overcome him. Suddenly Tom began to fear he was already unconscious, either that or he was hallucinating. He must be. Because over there, just across the street, he saw a familiar face rushing through the doors of the Scarlett Grove Hotel and Spa.

It was her.

Joy.

33

Black Smoke

Emma Whitworth had lived in Roquetas De Mar for the last four years. She'd spent the first sixty years of her life in Euston, working and living in the beating heart of England's busiest city. Her husband passed away on her sixtieth birthday and without him, it seemed there were very few reasons to stay in London. Emma was growing old and life hadn't always been kind to her. She deserved to spend her twilight years surrounded by sun and laughter and happiness. Her husband had left her a small amount of money and she used every last penny to purchase a small apartment in what she'd been promised would become a charming little building on the beach of Roquetas De Mar.

Emma had been told the other units would sell in the blink of an eye but four years down the line she had only one neighbour, a young girl. In the first year of Emma's Spanish adventure, the girl had shared the apartment with a middle-aged man whom she assumed to be the girls' father. Whilst Emma did not like the father, she became awfully fond of the girl.

At some point, a young man began staying with the father and daughter occasionally. Emma had taken an instant, unexplainable dislike to the young man which was strange because he was polite and welcoming. Still, Emma thought something inside him might be broken. Emma hadn't been surprised when the unpleasantness broke out in apartment five, nor did she feel any guilt about being the one to call the police. She'd been awfully sad when the girl left though, especially after learning what the young man had done to her father. The thought sent a shiver down Emma's crooked spine.

Despite two years spent living in apartments just six feet apart, Emma had never caught the girls' name. She liked her bright eyes and the fact that she always wore unique, eye-catching clothes, but there was little else she knew about the girl. Still, she'd missed her after she left. Then again, maybe she just missed the company.

Emma had been overjoyed when the girl had returned. She made her a coffee, all the while trying to remember her name (she still couldn't), and they chatted like old friends. Emma never asked about the girl's father, she knew the answer wouldn't be pleasant.

Emma had never been one to pry but she'd noticed a new fella leaving the girls apartment recently. She guessed maybe he was the reason the girl smiled more now. She just hoped he was better than the last one.

She hadn't seen the girl or her new fella in a day or two when she smelt the smoke drifting across from apartment five. She moved as quickly as she could, which at her age wasn't very quickly at all, leaving her room and struggling across the hall.

She banged on the door and asked if everything was alright. No response. From within the apartment, Emma heard a crackling noise. Oh God, how could she help? She shouted again and again there was no answer. The door was becoming hot to the touch.

Emma was still pounding on the door when she heard somebody darting up the stairs. They wore a black sweatshirt and leggings. Not that Emma paid this stranger any attention. All she knew was that this person was younger than herself and therefore much more likely to be of assistance in this terrible situation.

'Please help.' Emma gasped. 'I think somebody's in there.'

'I'll get them.' The person in black ordered.

Emma wanted to stay but she wasn't ready to die just yet and her lungs wouldn't put up much of a fight against the smoke. She hobbled down the stairs and out onto the beach where she told a man with an ice cream cone to ring the fire department. Then she said a prayer for the girl in apartment five.

Emma watched her home burn until the skies turned dark. Nobody else left the building. Not the girl who lived opposite her or the person dressed in black who'd only been trying to help.

Little did Emma know that those two people were one and the same.

* * *

After Tom left her apartment yesterday, Joy had slipped into what could only be described as a blackout. It was as if the

351

contents of her brain had been erased with the ease of deleting a picture from a phone. When she finally came around, she was sitting on the beach with the sun rising slowly in front of her. She took a long moment to compose herself, to try and make sense of the jumbled collection of bad memories thrashing around her head.

She had no idea that, at that very moment on the opposite side of the beach, Tom was watching the sunrise whilst trying to do exactly the same thing. If Joy had known that she would have felt better. She might even have asked him for help. But she didn't know. She only knew how much danger she was in.

Joy's plan had been so full of holes she'd been certain it wouldn't work. As Tom had written the final word of Rose's story, Joy came to the end of a five-mile hike. She'd walked quickly and with purpose, passing white stone municipal buildings before heading down a long stretch of motorway. Walking was considerably more difficult in the Spanish heat and she felt as though she'd travelled fifteen miles when she finally got a glimpse of her intended destination - a petrol station.

Joy didn't experience any difficulty at the petrol station. She hadn't anticipated any, but there was always a chance of arousing suspicion when asking to purchase a container full of petrol without a car to put that petrol in. Thankfully, being a female in this sexist and unforgiving world does offer the occasional perk. They're massively outweighed by the cons, of course, such as the gender pay gap and slut-shaming and the constant judgement based on the clothes you wear and the things you say. But some perks exist all the same.

This particular perk being a middle-aged man who believed everything he was told by a young girl providing she batted her eyelashes, smiled widely and spoke in a suggestive tone of voice. If a man had told the cashier he needed the petrol canister filling up because his car had sputtered to a stop a short while away, or if the story had been told by an elderly woman, the cashier wouldn't have been interested. He certainly wouldn't have offered them a lift back to their car. An offer Joy politely refused.

One uncomfortable conversation later, Joy began her five-mile hike back to the Sunrise building, which was significantly more difficult now she was lugging a five-litre container filled to the brim with petrol.

Joy got straight to work when she arrived back at the Sunrise Building. She scattered the contents of the container across the far side of the room, then spread pieces of paper around the other side, covering Nathan's body entirely. The sea breeze was strong today and that was important, she opened the windows wide.

Joy lit the three pieces of paper closest to the door and watched the fire slowly spread from one piece to the next. When she was convinced her plan would work, she left the room, locking the door behind her. She was going to miss the Sunrise Building. It was the only place she'd ever felt at home.

Joy rushed downstairs; grateful Mrs Whitworth hadn't seen her leave. When she reached the bottom of the stairs she slipped on a black sweatshirt, pulled the hood tight, and headed back. Mrs Whitworth had no chance of recognising her, the lenses in her glasses seemed to be getting thicker with each passing day.

The fire spread faster than she'd anticipated. Mrs Whitworth was already at her door, anxious and afraid. There were tears in the old woman's eyes and Joy felt an overbearing sense of shame. She was burning down this sweet woman's home in a desperate effort to protect her own interests. It wasn't fair. It never would be. But Joy couldn't think about that right now. She'd think about it once she was on a plane looking down at this unholy place, and not a second earlier.

Joy waited until the white hair of Mrs Whitworth disappeared from view before easing the window at the end of the hallway open. She didn't bother looking down. She knew it would only discourage her and she had no time to waste. She counted to three, steadied her breathing, and jumped.

She landed hard, crashing down onto her side. Her elbow was grazed and bleeding. Her knee jarred awkwardly but nothing was broken and that was as good an outcome as she could have hoped for. She limped down the beach, acting as inconspicuously as a person wearing a thick black sweatshirt beneath the blazing Spanish sun possibly can.

She didn't stop at the Scarlett Grove. She didn't even check to see if Tom was in the beach hut. There was somewhere else she needed to be, and time was of the essence. Now she just had to hope the biggest risk she planned to take today paid off.

The biggest risk, a risk she would have considered insane under any other circumstance, was asking Connor for help not twenty-four hours after murdering his best friend.

Nathan and Connor had always been simple men, men who liked things to be easy and saw no reason to make anything difficult for themselves. They never changed their runners (not unless they had a good or unpleasant reason to do so), and they never once tried to expand their territory. They never looked for more because they didn't want to lose what they had.

Joy was the only thing Nathan had ever lost and she'd been the only thing he'd ever tried to get back. In Nathan's mind, even relationships were simple. If he loved her, she had to love him back. That was just how things worked. Joy just hoped Nathan hadn't ever sold the villa that operated as his headquarters. She was owed that much luck at least.

The villa looked as if it had been snatched from a music video. There was an infinity pool looking out towards the ocean, complete with palm trees and a fully stocked pool bar. When they hosted parties (which they often did), Nathan and Connor hired a team of bartenders to serve the guests. There would no party today though, not with the man in charge of their operation currently missing. In fact, this villa may never host a party again.

Joy couldn't describe what the inside of the villa looked like because she'd never been invited inside. Nathan insisted his work existed in a separate world to her, a world he'd never allow her to become a part of, not even to show his girlfriend the inside of his home. Back when they'd been together Nathan had talked about getting a place that could be just their own but, as with a lot of things Nathan said, it proved to be just words.

When she'd met Nathan two weeks ago, which in her mind was only ever a business transaction, Nathan hadn't mentioned the villa. Instead, he insisted they meet in a swanky bar he'd hired out for the three of them.

She should have known then that nothing good could come from reaching back out to the man who'd ruined her life. She should have known the reason he'd hired out the bar was to prevent anybody spotting the various substances he slipped into her drinks. She should have known that men like him never change, but she'd been desperate. Things back home had been almost impossible recently and it only seemed right that Nathan's money be used to straighten things out. But his money wasn't worth what she'd been through in the last twenty-four hours. No amount of money was.

The villa's garden opened out onto the beach and Joy was relieved to find Connor sitting on a lounger. He didn't look towards her. He wasn't looking at anything. His head hung low and he massaged his temples delicately.

Joy paused before she spoke. This was the moment of truth. If Nathan had told Connor of his plan to visit her yesterday, she'd never leave this villa.

'Hi.' She said tentatively.

Connor jumped. Clearly in his line of work, there's usually a less pleasant outcome when somebody sneaks up on you.

'Haven't seen you in a while.' Connor said with no real interest or enthusiasm, though he did briefly lose the ability to think straight when he saw it was her. 'In fact, last time I saw you, you told us you wouldn't be back for six months.'

Joy took a deep breath. The rest of her life depended on how Connor answered her next question.

'Is Nathan here?'

Connor studied Joy intently for a long moment before finally arriving at a decision. Seeing her had brought back the memory of Sarah Tyler's shaking legs as he'd left her with a gun she didn't want.

356

Joy forced herself to breathe normally, she couldn't give anything away.

'Fancy getting me a beer since you're already up? I assume you remember where they are.'

'Yeah, I remember.' Joy made her way behind the bar and pulled a beer from the humming mini-fridge.

'I suppose Nathan doesn't know you're still here then?'

'Not yet.' Joy replied, praying her confidence seemed genuine.

She reached out to hand Connor the beer, willing her hands to stay sturdy, knowing that if he was planning to attack her this was his best opportunity.

Connor accepted the beer without a word of thanks. He opened the can and took a large gulp. Joy stood awkwardly beside him, wanting to sit down but keen not to seem overly familiar.

'Nathan isn't here.' Connor said flatly.

'Shit!' Joy whispered, ensuring it was loud enough for Connor to hear.

'What do you want with him?' He asked without wanting to hear the answer. He'd spent enough time listening to Joy talk about Nathan to last a lifetime.

'I need some help. I thought he'd be able to give me what I need.'

'How'd you know we still lived here?' Connor was no longer disinterested, now he was suspicious.

'I didn't. I just hoped you did.'

'Good for you.'

'Do you know when he's going to be back?' Joy asked without emotion. She had fooled a lot of people in her life, but she'd never needed to succeed quite so desperately.

Connor's face was a blank canvas. 'No. No idea.'

Joy began to worry Connor wasn't going to bite. He was going to finish his beer and leave her here, alone and out of ideas.

'What is it that you need anyway?' He asked, finally taking the bait.

'Passports.' Joy said, ensuring her eyes held firm contact with Connor's.

'What's wrong with the last one I made you?'

'I need a new one.'

'Oh shit. You're in trouble, aren't you?'

'Can you do them?' Joy asked, firmly steering the conversation away from any mention of her troubles.

She had a story prepared as to why she needed new passports, but she wanted to avoid telling it at all if possible. Hopefully, Connor would stop worrying about her reasoning when he heard how much she was willing to pay for his services.

'It depends.' Connor took another swig of his beer. 'Will you sit down? You're freaking me out standing above me.'

Joy did as instructed and sat on the sun beside him. 'What's it depend on?'

'Who the other passports are for?'

'I only need one other one.'

'Exactly. Who for?' Connor asked. This was the longest conversation he and Joy had ever had without Nathan sitting between them. He probably would have enjoyed it she wasn't only here out of desperation.

'Why does that matter?'

'Because I doubt Nathan will be too chuffed if I made a passport for you and another bloke. And you know, just between me and you, I don't think he ever got over you.' Connor was enjoying himself now, waiting for her to stumble into his trap. If she was here to use him, he'd make sure he used her too.

'He's just a friend. Besides, I've got more than enough to pay for them.'

'It's not that skinny guy I saw you with at the bar, is it?'

Joy said nothing. Connor laughed.

'Wow. Your tastes have changed.'

Joy chose to ignore this, knowing nothing good could come from bringing Tom any further into the conversation. 'Like I said, I've got the money.'

And there it was. She'd stepped into Connor's trap. He had her right where he wanted her.

'It's been a while. Prices have gone up. You know how it is, inflation and all that.'

'That's not a problem.' Joy said, holding her eyes steady and her breathing calm.

'Somebody's confident.' Connor smirked as he finished his beer. 'Five grand a piece.'

'Transfer or cash?'

'Cash. Fifteen if you wanna transfer.'

'Transfer it is. And I need them done by tonight.'

'No chance.' Connor hid it well, but he was delighted. He held all the cards and they both knew it. If he was going to help Joy walk out of his life once again, he was going to make damn sure he got what he deserved for it.

'Twenty grand if you get them done today.' Joy wasn't making an offer. She was telling Connor how much she was going to pay.

Connor wondered if she'd really stay away this time. If

she did, how long would it take him to forget her? Would he ever?

'When do you want them for?'

'I wanna be on a plane by midnight.'

'Oh yeah? You off anywhere nice?' Connor asked sarcastically.

'Wherever the plane takes me.'

'You really are in trouble, aren't you?'

Joy said nothing, knowing whoever spoke first would lose.

'You remember how this works? Everything I need?'

'Yes.' Joy answered with absolute certainty.

'OK then.' Connor got to his feet and idly tossed his empty can in the direction of the bar. 'Wait here, I'll get the account details. Once you've sent the money I'll get started.'

With that Connor disappeared inside the villa that Joy had never been invited inside of.

There are several immensely difficult obstacles to overcome when creating a new identity for yourself. The first is finding somebody willing to help you do it and the second is ensuring that person is competent enough to create something that not only looks real but also has all the required technical mumbo jumbo to get you onto planes without setting off alarm bells. Joy had found this person in Connor. He was a talented forger. She'd been using one of his passports for the last three years and never once had she encountered a problem.

Another obstacle to overcome is finding the funds to pay the forger. For Joy, this hadn't been a concern. She'd turned to an untouched bank account; an account she'd sworn she'd never use. An account funded by a man she hated almost as much as Nathan. She didn't want to give her father the satisfaction of knowing she'd needed his help once more, which he would when he checked the account and found it had been emptied, but spending another night in this Godforsaken town simply wasn't an option.

Once these obstacles have been overcome the rest is fairly simple. You need a passport photo of yourself, for obvious reasons, which is easy enough. Before the fire, Joy had hung a white bedsheet across one of the walls and used a self-timer app to take a picture of her face, expressionless as required. When it came to a picture of her travelling partner though, her options were limited. Mainly because her travelling partner did not yet know he was going to be her travelling partner.

Joy was beginning to regret not involving Tom earlier when she remembered the answer to her problem could be found online. On the Scarlett Grove's website to be precise. The picture Gabriella had taken of Tom for their 'Meet the Team' page was perfect. The background was neutral, and Tom hadn't smiled because he'd been given a stern talking to just minutes earlier. Joy didn't believe in fate, but this softened her disbelief.

Finally, all she needed was a new name for both herself and her travelling partner. Names that she and Tom would (hopefully) hold for the rest of their lives. Surprisingly, this was easy too. She used a pair of names she'd stumbled across in an unfinished manuscript. Names that felt as if they'd been created for this very moment.

Joy spent the rest of the day waiting. As expected, she wasn't invited into the villa. Truthfully, she was relieved. She could only imagine what lay in there, but she knew it wouldn't be pretty. After today she'll never return to this place. Nor will she ever return to Roquetas De Mar. She will leave Connor and the Sunrise Building just as she left Nathan, firmly in the past.

Time ticked on and Joy began to worry the passports wouldn't be finished in time. She'd worked out that they needed to be completed by eight if she was to have time to find Tom, inform him of her plan and somehow convince him to agree to it. So long as they were at the airport by ten, they would have time to buy their tickets, providing their new passports worked, and fly to somewhere they could enjoy the rest of their lives.

Tom Jennings and Joy Barren had died in the fire at the Sunrise Building. She wouldn't miss Joy Barren, but she would miss Tom Jennings. She'd miss him a lot.

Joy didn't know how long she'd been waiting when she overheard Connor on the phone discussing Nathan and why it had been so long since he'd gotten in touch. She heard mention of Roger Wyatt and wondered if (and how) the son of one of the richest men in the world was now the prime suspect in Nathan's disappearance. Not that it mattered. She wouldn't lose any sleep if Roger Wyatt hung for a crime she'd committed.

Joy had lost all track of time when Connor finally returned holding two new passports. He handed them over without a word. Joy rifled through both of them, as far as she could tell they were perfect. The real test would come when they arrived at the airport later, a test they couldn't afford to fail. Logically she knew far too much about Nathan and Connor's drug operation for Connor to risk anything like that. The passports would work. She was sure of it.

Joy turned to leave, assuming her transaction with Connor was completed when he surprised her by opening his mouth.

'You haven't seen Nathan, have you?' Connor asked, never once even considering that Joy had anything to do with his disappearance. She couldn't have. Deep down he knew.

It wasn't the question that surprised Joy but the way it had been asked. She'd expected the topic to arise at some point, especially given the coincidence of her randomly arriving at their home a day after her ex-boyfriend went missing, but she hadn't expected Connor to ask with such genuine concern and anguish.

'Not since we all saw each other.'

These next words hurt Connor, but they needed to be said all the same. 'You two stayed out later than me though. You didn't argue or anything after I left?'

'No. No argument. We talked about what I've been doing, what he's been doing. And then he told me that he still loved me.' It pained Joy to recall this next part, so much so that she wanted to throw up, but she knew she needed to tell the truth. 'I told him that I'd missed him and then we kissed.'

Connor cringed and hoped Joy hadn't noticed. If she had, she'd hidden it well. 'It was more than just a kiss the way I heard it.'

'And you believed him?' Joy asked with a hint of real disappointment in her voice.

Connor said nothing.

'You haven't changed, have you?' Joy asked, not expecting a reply but knowing the answer all the same.

'You haven't seen him since then?'

'No.' Joy lied. 'And to be honest I'm glad.' That part was the

363

truth.

Joy turned to leave once again and once again Connor called her back.

'Have you ever met Roger Wyatt?'

'Not personally. I know somebody who knows him though. Why?'

'What do they say about him?' Connor chose to ignore Joy's question, instead forging ahead with his own.

'Nothing good.'

With that, Connor made a decision. A decision that would drive him to The Clover, where he would come face to face with the very man he'd spent the day making a passport for.

'Yeah, that's what I heard too.' Connor said flatly. 'He's not going to be happy about this, you know.'

'Who?'

'Nathan. When he asks who gave you the passports, you tell him it was somebody else. Just like last time.'

'He won't find me.'

'Make sure he doesn't.' Connor warned. As far as declarations of love go, Connor's was about as subtle as they came.

Joy arrived at the Scarlett Grove five minutes before the fireworks were scheduled to begin. She rushed into the hotel to find the man she planned to escape with later that night, armed with nothing but honesty and two passports. One belonging to Miss Rose Evans and another belonging to Mr Zach King.

34

An Every Colour Sky

There were less than five minutes until the firework display was scheduled to begin when Richard Tyler discovered the gun his wife had hidden in the air vent.

He held it relaxed in his palm, his finger nowhere near the trigger, but Sarah had never been more afraid. The pain in her ribs was excruciating, each breath burned as it left her lungs. Her head had become heavy. More than anything she wanted to give in to the blackness, allowing herself to fade into nothingness so she didn't have to watch this horrific situation unfold.

'When did you get this?' Richard asked, still staring at the gun.

Sarah said nothing. There was no way to diffuse the situation. There was no way out. Richard was holding a gun and she knew that sooner or later he would turn it towards her. That it would be the last thing she ever saw and maybe all this was her fault. She'd had every chance to leave him. Every chance to fight for herself. Yet she'd taken none of them. She was a coward, and she would die a coward. Alone and afraid.

Richard didn't take well to being ignored. He lashed out with a brutal kick that caught Sarah in her stomach, breaking two of her ribs. She wanted to scream but the air had abandoned her lungs like troops retreating from a battlefield when all hope is lost. She gasped for breath frantically, desperate to answer Richard's question before he launched another attack.

'A couple of days ago.' Sarah finally managed.

'Why?' Richard asked, unable to see through the thick cloud of disbelief that had encompassed him.

Sarah said nothing. She braced herself for another blow, but nothing came. She looked up to find Richard deflated, still staring at the gun. His anger had dissipated, it had been replaced by something new. Sadness.

'You were gonna kill me?' Richard wasn't looking at the gun or even at Sarah now, instead, he looked down at his own feet.

'I don't know.' Sarah replied honestly.

'What the fuck else were you going to do with it?' Richard snapped.

Again, Sarah said nothing. Richard slouched onto the chest of drawers beside him. Sarah pulled herself, slowly and painfully, into a sitting position. The pressure on her lungs lifted slightly.

'Where'd you even get it?'

'That doesn't matter.' Sarah replied, keen to avoid mentioning any other names. She couldn't give Richard other targets.

'Suppose not.' He replied, clearly deep in thought, internally assessing his options.

'I wasn't going to use it.' Sarah whispered. Confident she was speaking a truth she'd known all along but never allowed herself to admit.

Richard said nothing. His mind was elsewhere.

'Will you put the gun down please?' Sarah asked quietly, careful not to upset the fragile new equilibrium.

'There's a big part of me that wants to kill you, you know.'

'Are you going to?'

Richard shrugged. He hadn't looked at Sarah since he'd taken his perch atop the chest of drawers.

'It's almost been a year, you know.' Sarah said quietly.

Richard said nothing.

'Almost a year. Can you believe that?'

Again, Richard said nothing.

'Richard!' Sarah shouted, growing frustrated. 'We lost our son and you've never once had anything to say about it. Do you even care?'

'Of course, I care!' Richard leapt to his feet; his anger had returned with a vengeance. The gun was now pointed directly at Sarah and that was good because she'd be back with her boy soon enough. 'You have no right to think you care any more than I do!'

Richard began to cry. Sarah was too startled to speak. For the first time in years, she felt as though the man who'd introduced her to the worlds best pizza had returned.

'He was my son.' Richard continued through heavy tears. 'He was my son and he loved me. He loved me almost as much as I loved him and there isn't a single fucking second that I don't think about him.'

Again, Sarah said nothing.

'We were a family, and we were happy.' Richard looked

down at Sarah through tear-filled eyes. 'Even you loved me back then. You did, didn't you?'

Richard looked down at the face of the only woman he'd ever loved and saw nothing but fear.

'I did.' Sarah answered honestly. She was crying too, not just because of her broken ribs.

'And now?'

'I don't want to love you anymore.' Sarah looked up at her husband. At that moment she only remembered the good times. She remembered the best pizza in Wigan and their wedding in a Welsh Country Home. She remembered the kisses and the laughter and not wanting to sleep so her days with him didn't have to end. She remembered raising a son they had both loved more than they'd ever thought was possible. She remembered everything and realised she didn't want her final words to be a lie.

'I don't want to love you, but I still do.'

'Good.' Richard said, nodding his head as if he'd finally settled on a decision. 'I needed to hear that.'

Without hesitation, Richard placed the gun against his temple and pulled the trigger.

Sarah screamed uncontrollably but nobody heard her. In the fleeting moments before Sarah lost consciousness she thought only of Marcus and Richard and the cherished moments the three of them had shared.

* * *

Gabriella didn't even reach the door of her office before Roger yanked her back inside. His hand clamped onto her shoulder and threw her backwards with impressive force. Gabriella crashed into her desk and collapsed to the floor. Her laptop landed next to her, still displaying the article about the abandoned car and the body discovered within it.

Her brain was paralyzed with fear, incapable of forming a single coherent thought. She couldn't think of a way out. She couldn't urge her body to fight back. She didn't even notice that the spire atop the Diamond Hotel Award for Excellence had slashed through the palm of her right hand. Blood was seeping onto the tiled floor, the glass award now stained red.

'You lied to me.' Roger shouted, the veins in his neck threatening to explode.

Gabriella said nothing as Roger moved towards her, looming over her with venom in his eyes and his canine teeth bared. Her body seemed to activate a deeply embedded self-defence system, and before she knew it, she took action.

She planted her palms firmly onto the floor and catapulted her right leg forward into Roger's groin. The tip of her high heel made contact first and Roger let out an almost inhuman scream. On any normal day, the sound of such a scream would have attracted the attention of everybody in the reception area. But today was no normal day. The firework display was in full swing, creating an every colour sky, and the sound of Roger's scream was lost like a flame in a snowstorm.

Gabriella didn't waste time or energy trying to stand, instead she crawled towards the door as quickly as she could. Her knees screamed as they dragged across the tiles, but it didn't slow her down. She was almost at the door, her hands just inches from the corridor where she could stand and run and scream and put everybody she found between herself and Roger, when it all went wrong.

A blade of ice ripped across Gabriella's spine as she felt his hand clamp onto her foot, the very same foot she'd rammed into his groin. Gabriella kicked with all her might, chopping her leg up and down, frantically trying to shake off the predator that had latched onto her. Her fingernails were embedded into the floor beneath her, but she could do nothing to prevent Roger from hauling her back into her office.

Roger slammed the door closed as Gabriella scrambled backwards, hoping to reach the phone and call for help before it was too late. She didn't come close.

'Do you want to know what I was thinking about when I killed her?' Roger snarled. Outside a firework exploded and Roger was coated in a wall of red light. 'I wished it was you.'

He grabbed Gabriella by the neck of her dress and lifted her. Gabriella kicked and fought but to no avail. Roger dropped her down onto the desk with a thud. Gabriella never saw the slap that followed coming, but she certainly felt it. Roger swung his hand around with blinding speed and connected firmly with Gabriella's cheek, snapping her neck to the side in a painful jerk.

Gabriella wanted to cry but she wouldn't give Roger the satisfaction. She held firm and stared up at him with defiance, defiance that infuriated Roger. He wanted her to fear him. He wanted her to know he was in control. He wanted her to know she was helpless.

He slapped her again, on the other cheek this time. An angry clap echoed throughout the office. Gabriella yelped; she simply couldn't help it. With that, she gave Roger exactly what he wanted, and now that he'd had a taste he could not wait for more.

Gabriella was in a daze. She had no time to react as Roger once again gripped the neck of her dress. He didn't lift her this time. Instead, he tore the dress, ripping the strap on the right-hand side and exposing the bra that lay beneath. He paused for a moment, finally enjoying the sight he'd been desperate to see for weeks.

His pause gave Gabriella just enough time to react. She leapt forward and clawed at Roger's face, feeling his skin rip beneath her nails. Roger wailed and stumbled backwards, clutching his bleeding face. Gabriella didn't pause. She had one chance to escape and she was going to take it. She reached down beneath the desk, desperately searching for the only item in her office that could be used as a weapon.

Roger finally recovered and advanced towards Gabriella with blood dribbling from the three large scratches on his face. He was just a step away from her when Gabriella finally found what she was looking for. She grabbed the Diamond Hotel Award and swung it around just as fast as she could. Roger, partially blinded by the blood in his eyes, never saw it coming.

The award exploded against his temple, smashing into what seemed like a million pieces and opening up a huge gash on Roger's forehead. Blood spurted from the wound and Gabriella felt sure Roger would crumble to the ground. She watched with wrenching hope as Roger swayed, his legs threatening to abandon him.

From somewhere, maybe it was his magic powder or the knowledge that after tonight he would have nothing, Roger found the strength to continue standing. Despite the blood pouring from his forehead, he advanced towards Gabriella again. This time he would make damn sure she couldn't fight back. He grabbed her by the neck and tightened his grip. Gabriella clawed frantically at Roger's hand, but his grip was unbreakable. With his free hand, he tore away the other strap from her dress. Gabriella wanted to scream but the precious little air in her lungs needed to be preserved.

Outside another firework exploded and the crowd cheered.

* * *

Joy didn't know where to find Tom. She'd been hoping to find him at the Lobby Bar with a drink and a smile, both for her. But when she rushed through the doors of the Scarlett Grove, she was left disappointed. The reception area was deserted. It seemed that everybody had gathered outside to applaud fireworks. She doubted Tom would be there. After yesterday, after everything he had seen, she doubted he'd want to be anywhere near smiling people.

Joy banished thoughts of yesterday from her mind. She was racked with guilt for exposing Tom to a world he should never have been a part of. Tom was normal. He was from a normal town; he'd had a normal childhood and he'd been destined for a normal life.

All that changed when he met her. She'd liked Tom from that very first day, but nothing scared her more than the thought of depending on somebody again. Even still, she'd eventually given herself to Tom. She'd given herself to him completely and at some point, she'd allowed herself to believe he could give her the normal life she'd always wanted.

She was wrong. Instead of Tom pulling her into his

colourful world, she'd pulled him into her dark and twisted one. The only world she'd ever known.

The young girl working behind the reception desk was timid and lazy and appeared to have taken the empty hotel as an excuse to catch up on one of her favourite shows. Regardless, this girl was currently Joy's best chance of finding Tom. She sprinted over to the desk and approached the same woman who not fifteen minutes earlier had informed Gabriella that Bill Wyatt was waiting to speak to her.

'Hi. You don't know where Tom Jennings is, do you?'

Maria removed her earphones with more than a hint of frustration. She hadn't bothered learning the names of her colleagues unless they had the power to fire her, so her reply was no help to Joy at all.

'Who?' She asked in a voice far less courteous than the one she'd used with Gabriella.

'He works in the beach hut.'

'Oh, he's been working with Gabriella all day. I don't know where he is but she's in her office. Go down that corridor and to the right, it's the door at the end. Knock first though. I think she's on a call.' Maria smiled falsely as she did with every customer.

Joy didn't stop to thank Maria. Instead, she rushed off in the direction she'd been pointed.

Maria thought it was odd, seeing somebody in such a rush to see the strange young man that worked in the beach hut. She didn't think about it for long though, because three minutes later something much stranger happened.

The young lad from the beach hut pushed through the hotels' doors as if he'd overheard her conversation. Maria couldn't take her eyes away from the blood he was covered

373

in. It poured from his jaw, and his shirt that had once been white was now a dark shade of red.

Maria didn't hesitate. She picked up the phone and dialled the police. She told them there was going to be serious trouble at the Scarlett Grove Hotel and Spa tonight.

* * *

Gabriella continued desperately attempting to claw her way out of Roger's clutches but with his hand wrapped around her neck, escape was beginning to seem impossible. Roger was releasing his grip just often enough to ensure she didn't slip out of consciousness, whilst using his free hand to unbuckle his belt. When he finally got it undone, he moved his slimy fingers to Gabriella's stomach, continuing downwards until they arrived at her underwear. He pulled at them roughly, expecting to tear them off but the strength of the material surprised him.

Gabriella took advantage of Roger's surprise and kicked out fiercely, catching Roger on his left kneecap which twisted sharply. Roger's hand left her underwear and bolted down on her lower leg, holding it still.

'Stay still!' He commanded. Gabriella wriggled more than ever.

Roger used his knees to pin Gabriella's legs down and now she really was trapped. Her hands were pinned beneath her back and her legs were locked into position. Sweat dribbled down Roger's face. It mixed with the blood on his cheek and Gabriella thought she might be sick. Maybe if she was sick he'd stop. Maybe he'd be so disgusted that he wouldn't be able to go through with it. Unfortunately, it's impossible to be sick when your windpipes are closed.

Gabriella slowly lost all hope. She wanted to cry but she would never let Roger see the vulnerability he was clearly so desperate for. If her dignity was the only thing she had, she was going to hold onto it until the end.

Roger's hand retreated to his own pants. He unzipped them and began pulling them down when the door of the office flew open. Roger turned to find a girl with a bruised face and electric eyes staring right back at him.

For a long time, Joy felt as though she'd stepped through a door that led to the past, her past. She didn't see Gabriella, instead, she saw herself. She saw herself cowering, helpless and afraid. She didn't see Roger, instead, she saw Nathan. She saw the time he'd spiked her drink after an argument, ensuring she became more agreeable for the rest of the night. She saw the time he'd strangled her as they were having sex, remembering the panic she felt when she became certain he wouldn't stop. Worst of all she saw him standing over her father, his fists bloodied and her father screaming. She saw the chair in which her father would be forced to live out the rest of his days. Then suddenly she didn't see Nathan at all.

Now she saw herself cowering beneath her father's stern glare. She saw the first time he'd demanded she stole food from the corner shop. She saw the time he'd broken her nose after she'd refused to steal from the sweet old woman in apartment six of the Sunrise Building. She saw him crouching outside her bedroom door and taking a picture of her in her underwear. She saw the lie he told her when she questioned him about it. She saw him selling the photo to other men in the caravan park.

She saw it all and she was unable to move. There was nothing she could do. She stood in the doorway of Gabriella's office reliving the worst moments of her life.

Roger froze when the door flew open. Beyond anything, he was in disbelief, disbelief at how close he'd come to finally getting what he wanted, only for it to be snatched away at the last moment. He'd already dampened his underwear but he would have been more than ready when the moment finally arrived.

He wasn't going to let it end like this. He wasn't going to be stopped. He was ready to show his father and Gabriella and every other person who'd ever doubted him just what he was capable of. He was done with being told what he could and couldn't do. Finally, he snapped back to life. He was about to begin his attack on this new girl when he realised his hand was no longer wrapped around Gabriella's throat and his knees were no longer restraining her legs. He panicked and span back around to find he was too late.

Gabriella was on her feet, lunging towards him with all the hatred she'd stored inside of herself. Hatred for the Wyatt Foundation. Hatred for Roger. Hatred for herself and the choices she'd made. Life wasn't fair. Especially not when you find yourself pinned to a table by a psychopathic drug addict who's torn away your clothes. Especially when he gropes your breasts, and you can feel just how excited he is by the thought of raping you.

Gabriella flew into Roger's stomach and the pair tumbled to the floor. Roger smashed into the bookcase. The expensive books Gabriella had never read toppled onto the floor beside him.

Joy watched it happen in slow motion. The woman, who she assumed to be Gabriella, launched herself into Roger, knocking both of them to the ground. Finally, something in Joy clicked. She no longer saw herself. She was looking at another woman, a woman who needed her help and Joy was going to help her. No matter the cost.

Roger scrambled towards Gabriella, his head throbbing and blood still pouring from the deep gash in his temple. He couldn't let her escape. He had to show her the type of man he was. He had to show somebody that he was more than just Bill Wyatt's spoiled brat. Even if that meant being worse than people expected, at least he would be his own man. He couldn't fight who he really was anymore.

He grabbed Gabriella's thigh and pulled her towards him. Suddenly he felt a blistering pain in his back. Joy had lifted the heel of her foot and slammed it down onto the arch of his spine. For what seemed an eternity Roger couldn't catch his breath. He writhed around on the floor desperately searching for any remaining air hidden at the bottom of his lungs. It seemed there was none.

Joy was preparing to slam her heel down once more when Roger finally found the air he'd been searching so frantically for. He raised an arm in self-defence, more out of desperation than anything, yet somehow it worked. His outstretched arm flew into the bottom of Joy's heel and knocked her off balance. She careered backwards, hitting the floor hard. Before she had time to open her eyes Roger was on top of her.

He was operating purely on his survival instincts now. He

was outnumbered. Somehow he needed to even the odds. While he had hit Gabriella with the palms of his hands, he used his fists on Joy.

He was going to kill her. Nothing else mattered. He had to kill them both. First, he would kill the girl who'd ruined everything and then he would kill the woman who'd been asking for it all this time. A jolt of lightning scorched up his wrist as he hit her, he'd broken another knuckle for sure.

The girl was unconscious though, and that was all that mattered.

The first punch Gabriella threw had embarrassingly little effect. She'd tried desperately to muster up enough strength to prevent Roger from unleashing another blow on the girl. Unfortunately, she just didn't have the strength. Her fist bounced off Roger's skull. Her whole body was shaking now and as Roger turned to face her, she knew there was nothing more she could do. She'd given everything she had, and she could be proud of that at least. In a final act of defiance, she spat at Roger's face. For a brief second, before he hit her again, she felt nothing but satisfaction. Maybe that was enough.

Roger's punch sent Gabriella stumbling into the bookcase and down onto the floor. Blood streamed from her broken nose and a cut above her eye. Roger reached out to snatch what remained of her dress away when the door flew open once again. Roger almost didn't recognise the weedy bloke who'd collected his drugs, after all the lad looked as though he'd lost a fight with a brick wall.

Roger opened his mouth, ready to tell the kid to fuck off, but never got the words out. Tom moved with lightning speed and used a hand already coated in dried blood to break

Roger's nose.

Blood exploded from Roger's face almost identically to the fireworks exploding above the beach. Tom hadn't even thought about the punch. He'd seen Joy lying on the floor, bruised and bloodied, and acted on instinct alone. Roger wobbled and before he could regain his balance, Tom threw another punch, equally as vicious as the first, practically destroying Roger's already broken nose.

Roger let out a long, low scream and fell to the floor, clutching his devastated nose. Tom's vision was blurred and blood streamed from his gaping wounds, but it didn't stop him.

He jumped on top of Roger, pinning him to the floor and punching him repeatedly. A wide-cut opened on Roger's cheek and his eyes became glazed. Still, Tom didn't stop. He punched him again and the cut widened. Blood was now smeared across the whole of Roger's face.

From a distance that seemed miles away, Tom heard Gabriella beg him to stop. He ignored her and punched Roger again.

Gabriella watched on in horror. Tom was relentless. It was clear Roger was no longer a threat but still, he continued. Gabriella hated Roger more than anyone in the world, but she wasn't about to sit here and watch the man be beaten to death.

'Stop Tom!' She shouted over the roar of the firework's grand finale.

Tom didn't answer. He unleashed another blow. Roger's face was now swollen beyond all recognition.

'Tom, you're going to kill him!' She screamed desperately.

Tom threw another punch. Roger's eyes closed.

Gabriella pulled herself to her feet and placed a hand on Tom's shoulder, trying to ease him out of the trance he was in.

Tom panicked when he felt the hand rest on his shoulder. He didn't think, he just reacted. He turned and launched whoever the hand belonged to away from him. Gabriella crashed against the wall, with the back of her head taking the brunt of the force, and collapsed to the floor in a heap.

For a moment Tom relented. He saw what he had done to Gabriella and began to worry he was the same as Roger. He'd hurt Gabriella just as Roger had, and he'd abandoned Joy just as Nathan had. Maybe the truth is he's just the same as those foul men. Just another bully who'd ruin the life of anybody unfortunate enough to take a chance on him.

But no. This wasn't his fault.

This was Roger's fault.

This was Nathan's fault.

Tom had to fight for what he wanted and the only thing he wanted was lying unconscious on the floor. He couldn't bear to look at Joy. He couldn't handle seeing her hurt, especially not when it was his fault. If he'd stayed with her yesterday, when she'd needed him, none of this would have happened.

Tom punched Roger again. Unaware that the girl he loved was watching on in horror.

Joy had seen it all. Her mind had eased back to consciousness just as Tom knocked Roger to the ground. She watched on, dazed and desperately trying to make sense of the horrific images playing out before her, as Tom continued without remorse or regret.

When Tom threw Gabriella against the wall, Joy knew it was too late for them. She had introduced Tom to her world and now he was trapped in it, consumed by it. She'd wanted to become more like him, and it broke her heart to see that he'd become more like her. He now embodied all of her worst traits and she barely recognised him. She watched him punch Roger again and knew he wouldn't stop. Not until Roger was dead. She couldn't let him do it.

She was the murderer. Not Tom.

Tom pulled back to punch Roger once more when Joy thrust something sharp and thin into Roger's neck. Blood exploded from the wound just as water explodes from a hose. Tom pulled away as the warm liquid splattered across his face. He looked around, desperately trying to understand what had happened.

Joy was crying. The spire from the Diamond Hotel Award was lodged deep into Roger's neck, and even now blood was gushing from the wound. Tom fell back from Roger's body and crawled away until his back hit the wall.

Joy approached him slowly. Her face covered in Roger's blood, but her tears cut through it all the same.

'Why did you do that?' Tom asked, his voice shaking.

'You're not a killer.' Joy replied gently.

'Neither are you.'

Joy was crying loudly now. Outside the fireworks finally came to an end, followed by rapturous applause. The sky was black. Tom doubted it would ever change.

'I am.' Joy rested a blood-stained hand on Tom's cheek. 'I don't want to be but I am.'

'This wasn't your fault. None of it. It can all be OK.' Tom pleaded desperately, trying to convince himself as much as he was trying to convince Joy.

Joy shook her head.

'We can be OK.' Tom was crying now too.

'You can. And I need you to listen to me.'

Tom shook his head. He couldn't think clearly. His head was pounding, and he needed everything to be fine, although deep down he knew things would never be fine again.

'When the police arrive, you need to tell them the truth.' Joy explained delicately.

'No. No, they'll arrest you.' Tom shook his head frantically.

'I won't be here.'

'We could just explain…'

'No.' Joy interrupted. 'You can explain. You saw what was happening in here and you helped. Then I killed him. You don't know me. She won't argue.' She gestured to Gabriella who was slumped against the wall. 'She didn't see it. She'll agree with you.'

'Don't go.' Tom pleaded with everything he had.

'I'm sorry.' Joy kissed Tom delicately. Neither of them wanted the moment to end but it had to. Joy had to leave and Tom had to stay.

'I love you. I really do.' Tom whispered, the pain in his head beginning to overpower him. Black spots danced in front of his eyes and he could no longer feel Joy's hand resting against his cheek.

'I know.' Joy couldn't bring herself to say those three words back. Saying those three words would make all this real. It would make her feelings real. It would make this hurt so much more.

Joy took one final look at Tom, allowing him to lose himself in her magnetic eyes for the final time.

Tom watched her open the window, knowing he'd be unconscious in seconds. The pain was unlike anything he'd ever experienced and a part of him began to worry these were his final moments.

'I won't ever tell them your name.' He said with some difficulty.

'You don't know it.' Joy replied with regret.

Tom lost consciousness almost immediately.

35

Questions, Questions, Interrogation

The night of the firework display at the Scarlett Grove Hotel and Spa will live forever in the memory of the good citizens of Roquetas De Mar. Early police reports gave only vague details of the incident. Two men had been killed in the Scarlett Grove on Friday the nineteenth of June and three people were currently in hospital being treated for wounds relating to the incident. These three people were all considered suspects and would receive formal questioning as soon as their health allowed it.

An official report wasn't released for another two days, during which time the streets were ripe with gossip. The most common theories seemed to involve the two English suspects masterminding the entire incident. Some thought they were drug dealers looking to inherit the territory. Others thought they were having an affair and finally killed those who stood in their way. Some even thought they were simply unhinged psychopaths who used the new scenery as an excuse to satisfy their bloodlust.

They were all wrong, of course. But they were not the

only people struggling to make sense of the incident. In the hours that followed the arrival of the police, nobody could make heads or tails of what had occurred in both the manager's office and room fifty-seven. It didn't help that the only suspects were all rushed to the hospital with injuries ranging from mild to severe. It was uncertain whether the male suspect would even make it through the night.

The attending officers interviewed everybody they could find. A woman named Maria made things even more confusing when she explained that one of the suspects, Mr Tom Jennings, arrived at the hotel already covered in blood. This was of particular interest to Deputy Inspector Blanco, given she'd had a run-in with the very same young man at another crime scene just hours before two people were murdered at his place of work. That was when Tom Jennings became her main suspect.

Sarah Tyler was the first to wake. She had three cracked ribs and a mild concussion. She didn't seem to notice as Deputy Inspector Blanco entered the private room she was being treated in. Blanco pulled a seat to Sarah's side and made herself comfortable. She wanted Sarah to speak first but from the blank expression on the woman's pale face, she doubted she'd say anything without encouragement.

'Hi, Sarah. I'm Deputy Inspector Blanco. Do you feel OK to answer some questions?'

Sarah nodded.

'Can you tell me what happened tonight?'

'He killed himself.' Sarah replied coldly, without looking at Blanco. 'He shot himself. He killed himself.' Sarah began to cry. Still, she stared at the roof as if the answers to ending her misery were printed up there.

'I'm very sorry for your loss.' Blanco said softly. 'When the staff were treating you, they noticed your right cheekbone is broken. They suspect it's been broken for a couple of days now. Can you tell me anything about that?'

'He killed himself.'

Blanco pushed her frustrations aside. She needed answers and she needed them now, but she doubted a firm tone was the way to entice them from this broken woman.

'Sarah, I know you're hurting. You've been through something terrible. I can't even begin to imagine how you're feeling. But what's important now is getting the answers that you deserve. Can you help me with that?'

'He killed himself.'

'The gun. Do you know where your husband got that? Or who gave it to him maybe?'

Sarah suddenly sat bolt upright in bed. Blanco was relieved. Clearly, the mention of the gun had brought Sarah back to the real world.

'Marcus. Where's Marcus?' Sarah asked frantically.

Blanco was taken aback. She had no idea who Marcus was or how he was involved in the incident that had taken place at the Scarlett Grove.

'Who's Marcus?' She asked tenderly.

'Marcus! My son! Where is my son?' Sarah screamed, demanding an answer.

Blanco tried to calm Sarah, but it was no use. She asked about Marcus hysterically until the doctors had no choice but to give her something to help her sleep. In the thirteen hours before Sarah regained consciousness, Blanco learnt of Marcus and the disease that eventually took his life, at which point she disregarded any question of Sarah Tyler's guilt.

There were small holes in her story. The question of why Sarah's fingerprints were on the gun for example, but the coroner and the forensic team both agreed that Richard's death came by his own hand. It didn't take long for Blanco to put the rest of the pieces together. The bar staff made it clear Richard liked a drink and the people in the surrounding rooms weren't shy about spreading stories of the arguments they'd heard echo from the walls of room fifty-seven. Blanco hated these people. People who'd made no effort to intervene but were more than happy to tell their story once it was too late. If somebody had been brave enough to speak out, maybe Richard Tyler would still be alive.

Blanco decided to clarify the details with Sarah once she'd fully recovered, but it was clear now that the incident in room fifty-seven was unrelated to the horrors in the manager's office.

By the time the sun rose, Sarah Tyler was the least of Blanco's problems. Bill Wyatt was due to arrive within the hour and he certainly wouldn't rest until he had answers. Blanco issued strict instructions to keep Bill in the waiting room.

He shouted and screamed and threatened to sue every single member of the Roquetas De Mar police force, but strangely he didn't seem sad at all. Not once did he ask to see the body of his son or to say a final goodbye. He was angry, furious in fact, but never once did he appear sad. His lack of emotion startled even Blanco, a woman who'd spent over twenty-five years surrounded by grief and mourning.

Another two hours passed before Gabriella Glover awoke.

Her nose was broken, her body was badly bruised, and her concussion was severe. Physically she would heal, mentally she would not. Years of therapy will never plaster over the cracks her psyche sustained that night.

Blanco entered the room slowly and introduced herself calmly. She explained the situation they found themselves in and, overwhelmed by sympathy for the scared lady lying before her in a hospital bed, offered to question her at a later time. Gabriella denied this offer vehemently. Blanco respected her for that.

'What would you like to start with?' Blanco asked gently.

'What do you mean?'

'We can start wherever you'd like. Whatever you feel most comfortable with.'

'Oh. Sorry, I just thought you would have had a list of questions or something, that's how it usually happens in films.'

'If this was a film the detective interviewing you would be much better looking.' Blanco joked, knowing witnesses tend to be more forthcoming if they feel comfortable with the detective.

Gabriella smiled. That was important. She began her recollection by explaining the phone call she'd received from Roger in the dead of night and her constant scouring of the local news in the days that followed. Blanco listened silently until Gabriella was finished.

'Why didn't you call us earlier?'

'Because I didn't want the acquisition of the hotel to fall through.' Gabriella answered truthfully, hating herself for being so selfish. 'The hotels all I've ever had. I've spent all the best days of my life there and I just, I couldn't be the person to fail it.'

'OK.' Blanco replied without expression or judgement, although she lost a lot of respect for the manager of the Scarlett Grove.

Blanco asked Gabriella to explain what had happened at the Grand Ball and Gabriella did so in perfect detail. She told Blanco that Roger had arrived well over an hour late. Blanco asked how Roger had looked when he arrived and Gabriella answered honestly, stating that Roger had looked like a man who knew his days were numbered. Gabriella told Blanco of Roger's disappearance from the Suite Diamante to answer a mystery phone call, after which he returned with blood on his knuckles, although Gabriella guessed that wound was self-inflicted. Blanco interrupted Gabriella at this point to ask about the behaviour of Tom Jennings during the meal.

'Um, well for the first couple of courses he was normal. We talked a little bit but not about anything important.'

'What happened after the first few courses?' Blanco prompted.

'He left.'

'He left?' Blanco was not surprised. She already knew that Tom had left without a word of warning. She'd spent the last few hours listening to thirty-seven tales of what had happened during the five-course meal in the Suite Diamante. She just needed to know if Gabriella was telling the truth. People seemed to think Gabriella and Tom were close, and it would make uncovering the mystery of the evening considerably more difficult should one of her three suspects lie to her.

Gabriella nodded.

'Did he say where he was going?'

'He didn't say anything.' Gabriella replied coldly.

'How did that make you feel?'

'He doesn't still have a job at the hotel if that's what you're asking.'

Blanco nodded. It had been exactly what she was asking.

Gabriella continued explaining the evening. She talked, regretfully, of her dance with Roger. She explained how she had tried to sneak away, planning to stay at the Hilton Hotel for fear of Roger's intentions. Blanco listened intently as Gabriella recalled the call she'd received from Bill Wyatt, a man who, unbeknownst to Gabriella, was currently downstairs demanding that his son's body be flown back to England, informing her of Roger's dismissal from the Wyatt Foundation.

Gabriella cried as she explained what happened in her office, telling nothing but the truth until it came to the moment she lost consciousness. At this point in her story Gabriella lied, telling Blanco that Roger momentarily overpowered Tom and, when she tried to help her friend, Roger threw her against the wall. After that, she didn't remember anything.

Gabriella will never be able to explain why she lied to protect Tom Jennings. Maybe she was blinded by her hatred for the man who'd tried to tear her underwear away from her, or maybe it was some strange feeling of pity for the most eager man in all of Britain. Most likely it was because, before the night of the fireworks, Gabriella had considered Tom a friend. And as pathetic as it may sound, Gabriella had never before had the pleasure of a true friend.

After almost two hours of questioning, Blanco wished Gabriella a speedy recovery and left her in peace. One thing was clear to Blanco, Gabriella Glover was a victim. Her list of suspects dropped to one.

Sixteen hours passed before Tom Jennings returned to consciousness. Blanco used the time to her advantage. She gathered evidence, a good amount of evidence, from a variety of places across Roquetas De Mar. Given the extent of Tom's injuries, he was allowed another day of recovery before facing Blanco's questions, by which time the English press had arrived and made Blanco's job all the more difficult.

The gash on Tom's jaw had required sixteen stitches and the wound on his shoulder had needed seven. His concussion was severe and the amount of blood he'd lost was frightening. Several doctors were surprised he'd survived. Still, twenty-four hours passed, and Blanco was finally allowed into the private hospital room in which Tom Jennings waited. Blanco took a deep breath before she entered. This wasn't questioning. This was an interrogation.

'Hi, Tom. I'm Deputy Inspector Blanco, do you remember me?'

Tom said nothing.

'Nothing to say at all?' Blanco asked calmly. She'd been in this situation countless times over the years. She was going to enjoy coaxing a confession from this young man.

Again, Tom said nothing.

'OK. It actually suits me that you don't want to talk because I can show you all the things I've found.' Blanco opened the briefcase she'd brought with her and removed a photo taken from the Scarlett Grove's CCTV. It showed Joy entering the Scarlett Grove on the night of the fireworks.

'Do you know who she is?'

Tom shook his head.

'It's funny you should say that because here's a picture of you two together.' Blanco presented another photo. This one taken from the CCTV at Platos Y Bebidos. It showed Joy sipping a strawberry daiquiri and Tom laughing like a fool beside her.

'I suppose you still don't know who she is?'

Again, Tom shook his head.

'Well, the couple in this picture actually left without paying their bill. More than two hundred euros worth of food and drink went unpaid for. Still, nothing to say?'

'Nope. Nothing.'

'Well at least you're talking now, that's a start.' Blanco replied, her tone now overtly condescending. 'So just to clarify, you don't know the girl in this picture?'

'I don't know her.'

'Good. She doesn't seem like the type of girl you'd want to know in all honesty. Shall I explain why?'

Tom said nothing.

'We have good evidence that the girl in this photo has been living in apartment five of the Sunrise Building for the last few weeks. The building which burned down the other day, just before we first met. Anyway, we now know the fire originated in apartment five, did you know that?'

'No.'

'I suppose you didn't know that the apartment actually belongs to a Mr Kyle Thurman?' Blanco asked, studying Tom intently for any sign of emotion.

Tom shook his head. His expression flickered slightly, and Blanco knew why. The name had shocked him and that was good. Slowly she would show him that there was no reason to stay loyal to a girl who'd abandoned him.

'OK. Let's move onto something else, do you know this man?' Blanco presented Tom with a photo of Nathan that had been taken from one of his social media accounts. Nathan was standing in the garden of his villa with a smile on his face and a beer in his hand.

Tom studied the photo for a long while before returning with the answer Blanco expected. An answer she knew to be a lie.

'Never seen him.'

'Hmm, that's strange.' Blanco replied smugly as she handed over another photo taken from the Scarlett Grove's CCTV. This photo showed Tom shaking hands with Nathan. Blanco enjoyed watching the cogs whir inside Tom's head as he tried to think of an excuse.

'I don't know what this is.' He replied flatly.

'OK. Well seeing as though you don't know anything, I suppose I'll have to explain this whole thing to you. We know you didn't kill Roger Wyatt. From the bruises on your hands, we know you knocked him around a bit, but your fingerprints weren't on the murder weapon.'

'Why am I being questioned then?' Tom asked, finally showing the edge that Blanco had expected.

'Well just because you're not a murderer, doesn't mean your innocent.' Blanco paused, waiting to see if Tom would interject. He did not. Blanco had rarely seen a suspect act so defiantly in the face of such overwhelming evidence.

'So, in the wreckage of the Sunrise Building, we found a body. A couple of hours ago that body was identified as Nathan Piner, which means we now have reason to believe the girl in these photographs is a murderer.'

Blanco waited for any hint of reaction. Nothing came. She

continued undeterred.

'We've checked the murder weapon against yours and Gabriella's fingerprints. As I said before, yours aren't a match. Gabriella's were but she's explained the story to me, and I believe she was unconscious at the time of the murder. Can you confirm that?'

Tom nodded.

Blanco smiled. 'Good. So anyway, Gabriella told us that a girl she'd never seen before arrived at her office and attempted to help her. We believed the girl that arrived was the girl from the photographs and Gabriella has since confirmed that. We also believe she was the person to take Roger Wyatt's life, which means this girl took two lives in the space of thirty-six hours. And say what you like, we know you know her.'

Again, Tom said nothing. His face was icy and cold.

'Seeing as though you're still not speaking, I'm just going to be honest with you. Somebody needs to serve time for this. There hasn't been a murder here for two years and since you arrived there's been three and a suicide. The town needs somebody to blame. You might not think so, but having somebody to blame, having closure, it's the only way people heal. Now I know you didn't directly have a hand in any of these murders, but I know who did and I have a problem with all of them. A man took his own life, we can't blame him. Nathan killed a rival drug dealer, we can't prosecute a dead man. A woman died at the hands of Roger Wyatt who himself is also dead. And as I said we can't throw a dead man in jail. That leaves me with you and her.'

Blanco once again held up the photo of Tom and Joy.

'Now I know she's responsible for the death of Roger and

Nathan. I know it, my team knows it, Gabriella knows it, and deep down you know it too. So, in an ideal world, she'll serve the time she deserves. But you're causing me a problem. You're not telling me anything and if we can't find this girl, the blame shifts to you.'

'What? Why me?' Tom asked angrily. Blanco tried to hide her smile. Anger was good, anger meant she was getting somewhere.

'You're facing one charge of theft, one count of aiding and abetting and another of withholding information. You're looking at a good few years in a cell. Unless you help me.'

Tom said nothing, he was trying to absorb the bucketload of information that had just been thrown at him.

'Do you recognise this?' Blanco asked as she heaved a manuscript out of her briefcase. She felt sure this was the key to breaking his defence.

Tom stared at the manuscript dumbfounded. He recognised the handwriting immediately. Joy had scribbled out the words 'Untitled Manuscript' and written 'The Island of Palm Trees' in her terribly untidy handwriting. Despite the awful, irredeemable situation Tom was in, he found himself smiling. The title was perfect.

Blanco noticed the smile and pounced immediately. 'Something funny?'

'No.' Tom replied, wiping the smile from his face.

'You wrote this, didn't you?' Blanco asked gently, hoping maybe Tom's passion would inspire a change of heart.

'Yeah.' Tom nodded. His expression was softer now.

'I flicked through some of the pages. You're talented.'

Tom said nothing.

'Do you want to do this for a living? Write, I mean?'

Tom nodded.

'Think about it. Do you really think that's going to be an option for you if you serve time? People don't take kindly to convicted criminals. Trust me, I've worked here for long enough to know that.' Blanco was speaking softly now, willing Tom to give her the information she needed so desperately. 'Supporting her means abandoning this. And think about it, really think I mean. Your future's here. You have something to be proud of. Something to build a life around. There's no future with her Tom.'

Tom said nothing. He suddenly looked sullen, as if he'd finally realised how bleak his future looked.

'I don't think I'm the only fan of your work either.'

'What do you mean?' Tom asked.

Blanco handed Tom one final photograph. It was taken from the CCTV footage at Almeria airport. It showed Joy boarding a flight.

'She left that same night, flew to Marseille. The police there are looking for her but, well let's just say I'm not getting my hopes up.'

Tom said nothing. He was buried beneath the colossal weight of the decision he needed to make.

'Would you like to know the name she's using now?' Blanco asked, excited about finally playing her trump card.

Tom said nothing.

'Rose Evans.'

Tom smiled widely. Blanco shifted uncomfortably in her seat, she'd expected to see frustration or anger. Wasn't this a betrayal of trust? Wasn't it her way of dragging Tom and his work into the gutter alongside her?

The smile on Tom's face ignited a burning rage within

Blanco. 'Something funny?'

'Yeah. Yeah, it is.' Tom replied, still smiling.

'Look Tom. I need your help. At this point, it's either you or her. Tell me something and I can help you. Tell me where she's planning on going. We know she's not going to stay in Marseille. Where's she going?' Blanco was begging now. She needed this confession desperately. The town was growing impatient with the lack of progress and so too were her superiors.

'I don't know.' Tom answered truthfully.

'You have to give me something Tom! She left you! You're only hurting yourself by keeping quiet!'

Tom said nothing. He was on the brink of making the biggest decision of his life and he had no idea if he was throwing away his best chance of happiness or setting himself up for the exciting writer's life he'd always wanted.

'I'm getting sick of waiting here, Tom. I need you to tell me something!' Blanco demanded.

Again, Tom said nothing.

Blanco took a deep breath. She collected the photos and the manuscript and placed them back into her briefcase. She slowly got to her feet and returned the chair on which she'd been sitting to its original place at the foot of the bed. As Blanco reached the door, she turned back and gave Tom one more chance to make a sensible decision.

'Final chance Tom. Who is she, really?'

'You already know.'

'What does that mean?' Blanco asked, certain she'd finally broken through to him.

'She's Rose Evans.' Tom replied with a smile.

About the Author

Michael Walsh-Rose is an author and screenwriter living in Rochdale, Manchester.